HUNGER POINT

HUNGER POINT

A NOVEL

JILLIAN MEDOFF

ReganBooks

An Imprint of HarperCollins*Publishers*

HarperCollins books may be purchased for educational, business, or sales promotional use. For information please write: Special Markets Department, HarperCollins Publishers, Inc., 10 East 53rd Street, New York, NY 10022.

FIRST EDITION

Designed by Ruth Lee

Library of Congress Cataloging-in-Publication Data

Medoff, Jillian.
 Hunger point : a novel / Jillian Medoff.
  p. cm.
 ISBN 0-06-039189-8
 I. Title.
 PS3563.E26H86 1997
 813' .54—dc20   96-29468

97 98 99 00 01 ❖/RRD 10 9 8 7 6 5 4 3 2 1

For my parents,
Lewis and Naomi Medoff
and
my sisters, Kimberly and Mara
and
in memoriam
my beloved Mary Sacks Boyar
(1914–1991)

I say unto you:
one must still have chaos in oneself
to be able to give birth to a dancing star.
I say unto you:
you still have chaos in yourselves.

FRIEDRICH NIETZSCHE,
Thus Spake Zarathustra

ACKNOWLEDGMENTS

With heartfelt thanks to the brilliant and fearless *Judith Regan* and her remarkably talented editors, Jennifer Gates Hayes and Kristin Kiser, and for the invaluable advice and generous support of the following individuals: Carolyn Fireside, Bill Contardi, Mike Lubin, Caron K., Mary Morris, Mona Simpson, Jonathan Dee, A. Elizabeth Mikesell, Dr. Nan Jones, Frances Jalet-Miller, Sheri Holman, Kitty Stewart, Andrea Amadio, Dina Siciliano, Steve Reynolds, Abbe Bates, Brock Pennington, Ben Schrank, Dawn McAvoy, and Lisa Sewell.

Finally, with love and gratitude to the Blue Mountain Center, and to my gifted and gracious agent, Alice Fried Martell, a woman who is as wise as she is kind.

L ook at these breasts! They're huge!"

I grew up jealous of my mother's love affair with food. Other families gathered around the dinner table to discuss report cards and whose turn it was to walk the dog. When I was a kid, the meal itself took center stage, and food was treated like a favored child.

"Can you believe how big they are? They're absolutely to die for!"

The meal continued with my mother's running commentary on every aspect of those breasts: how my father should have marinated them in barbecue sauce, not soy, because they taste too salty, no? and Frannie! Don't eat the skin. You won't lose weight if you eat the skin.

"We're eating, Mom," she'd say to my grandmother, who had the uncanny ability to call just as we sat down. "Chicken. Absolutely delicious. Marinated in some soy thing. Yes, the girls are here, but some of us are on diets"—she glanced at me, a narrow eyebrow raised—"so no skin." She nestled the phone in her neck to tell us that Grandma didn't want us to worry about our weight, we're skinny enough as it is.

She got up, waving her fork in the air like a baton. "No, I *am* listening. I heard every word." She lifted the breast from her plate and walked through the kitchen. Wrapped in the phone cord, she picked off the meat with her long red nails. She gnawed on the bone, sucking off what she could, then threw it out and hung up, the receiver streaked with a faint oval of grease.

"Grandma says hi. God, this chicken is so good, it's like a sickness with me." She canvassed the table as we ate. "Frannie!" she yelped. "What are you doing?!" I froze in my seat. And slowly, so slowly, I loosened my grip on the forbidden skin and slid it palm-down onto my sister Shelly's plate. "Dear," she said with annoyance. "I love the skin more than you, but do you see me eating it? It's *fattening*."

When we were very young the amount of food we could consume was an endless source of amusement. "A whole half a steak!" my grandmother exclaimed as Shelly fisted a piece of sirloin. "A whole half a steak! Where does she put it?" She shook her head in fascination and delight. "Shelly's got your appetite, Marsha!" she said proudly. "Now stand back, let the child eat."

By elementary school, my ability to consume seven Twinkies in one sitting was no longer cute. "Frannie, you're getting fat," my mom said solemnly. "You're too pretty to be heavy. You want boys to like you, don't you?" The word *fat* assumed a meaning as deadly as cancer. Getting *fat* was worse than losing your job, worse than being jilted at the altar, worse than living in a trailer park and growing up without shoes. "You need to start watching yourself," my mother instructed, "before it's too late."

I went to my first Weight Watchers meeting when I was ten. Shelly, who was eight with soft creamy skin, blond angel hair, blue eyes the color of a cloudless sky, and "legs like a gazelle," stayed home. "We're a team, Frannie," my mother said, lining up in front of the scale. "The first one to lose ten pounds gets a new bathing suit."

I wasn't an ugly kid, nor, looking back, was I particularly fat. I have long, curly brown hair that kinks like moss when it rains, green eyes, and a lot of "those could become melanoma" freckles across my nose and chest. Not your All-American beauty, but certainly not Medusa. Rather than bicker with my mother, I carried the Weight Watchers passbook where they recorded my weight, I listened attentively to the lecture, I even raised my hand once to ask where all the fat went when you lost it. All the chubby women hunched in their folding chairs laughed at my precociousness, but I was genuinely curious. I wanted to know if there was a redistribution between the skinny and the fat; if I had a chance to look like the ladies behind the Clinique counter whose advice my mother sought, or if fat was predetermined like blue eyes and strong bones, and would eventually find its way back.

My father was on the road a lot selling women's sportswear, so my mother served us TV dinners. "Don't eat the potatoes, Frannie. Potatoes are starch. Starch makes you fat." Shelly rarely spoke during meals. She fixated on her aluminum tray as if afraid someone would snatch it away. "Why can't I be on a diet?" she asked. "I need to be on a diet, too." Defiantly, she laid down her fork. My mother reached over. "You don't need anything of the sort. Here"—she scraped the gravy off Shelly's Salisbury steak—"you're dieting. Now eat."

At eleven, I was more interested in calories than in going to the Girl Scout Jamboree and sleeping in a tent. I cut out pictures from *Seventeen* of girls with perfect thighs, I counted bread servings, I made frothy shakes from powdered skim milk, water, and fifteen cubes of ice. I did leg lifts and donkey kicks on my bedroom floor. In the cafeteria at school, I sat with a turkey sandwich while everyone else ate fish sticks and macaroni and cheese, golden, gloopy, mouth-watering macaroni browned on top with crushed bread crumbs. I was good, so good, I was invincible until Friday nights when I would reward my week with rocky road ice milk, the whole carton, in front of the TV.

When Shelly entered junior high, she was put in a special program for gifted children. She kept to herself, wrote impressive book reports, and started doing weird things with food. She wasn't "shoveling it in," but she did eat large quantities of only one thing. At first, it was turkey or chef salads or giant bowls of Rice-a-Roni. But then it progressed to spaghetti with margarine and hot honey sandwiches. My mother got worried, especially when my sister fell in love with peanut butter milk shakes and, despite her magic legs, put on weight. I was still gaining and losing the same ten pounds, so my mother took control and helped us plan our meals. The three of us sat at the kitchen table; my mom used a calculator to tally our calories, and as she dictated, I wrote down our breakfast, lunch, and dinners neatly on a yellow legal pad:

Breakfast

1/2 cup raisin bran, 1 piece of dry whole wheat toast, 1/2 cup skim milk, 1/2 banana

Lunch

2 pieces of toast, 4 ounces of water-based tuna, 1 large lettuce leaf, tomato and cucumber slices, 8 carrot sticks, 1 tbsp. vinegar, 1 apple

Dinner

1/2 dry baked potato, 4 ounces of chicken breast (no skin), string beans without butter, small salad with oil and vinegar, 1 chocolate Alba shake

With boy-girl parties and Seven Minutes in Heaven to deal with, I tried hard to stay on my diet. But sometimes I didn't and always vowed in my diary to get back on track.

November 11—BAD day. Debi Parker got her period in gym. You could see the blood right through her gym suit.

Breakfast

1 piece of toast—no butter, 5 handfuls of dry cereal, 21 M&M's

Lunch

Skipped lunch (ate all those M&M's)

Dinner

3 chicken breasts with no skin; 3 pieces of sourdough bread; 12 string beans; lettuce, carrots, and celery with mustard; 1 chocolate Alba shake; 3 bites of pound cake and 3 spoons of ice cream; 12 diet candies; 2 bologna sandwiches with ketchup (eaten in bed)

Dear Frannie, You are a FAT pig. You are TOO FAT. Tomorrow you CAN'T eat ANYTHING. I hate you, you PIG. Signed, Frannie.

My mother was so proud when I lost weight, she called my father in Des Moines, in Scranton, or in Newark while I stood on the scale. "Two pounds this week," she sang into the phone, giddy with success. Shelly cheated all the time and never lost weight. "I thought you *wanted* to diet, Shelly," my mother moaned. "I'm trying to *help* you. I have the same problem," she added. "It's genetic."

The best times I had as a kid were during the holidays. My mother got caught up in the spirit of the season and allowed Shelly and me to eat whatever we wanted from Turkey Day all the way to New Year's Eve. My mother is Jewish and my father is Protestant, so we didn't celebrate Christmas or Hanukkah like most people. We didn't go to church, decorate trees, light candles, or spin dreidels. Our family celebrated by eating. We had honey-baked ham, eggnog, and reindeer cookies coated with green and red sprinkles, as well as latkes, matzo ball soup, roasted chicken with crispy, greasy, unbelievably delicious skin. We thanked God for my mother's indulgence and ended the bacchanalia with ceremonial food hangovers and New Year's dieting resolutions. Having no religion never bothered me because I, unlike most children, was exposed to so many culinary possibilities. Even now when people ask about my religion, I just say that in my family we worship the man who invented SnackWell's.

When Shelly and I entered high school, my mother went to work full-time as a real estate agent. She still watched our weight, and we still heard "I wouldn't eat that if I were you," but despite my mother's eagle-eye, Shelly, once tall and gangly at 130, ballooned to 175 pounds. At first there was pleading; promises of new clothes; weeks on Pritikin and Scarsdale; trips to Nutri-systems, Overeaters Anonymous, and the always forgiving Weight Watchers. She even sent my sister to Camp Galaxy, a diet camp in the Poconos. At Camp Galaxy, Shelly had weekly weigh-ins and aerobics. Shelly wrote that she and another camper set up a black market with the candy bars counselors brought back from town. A candy bar without nuts could bring in $7, with nuts or caramel, $9. At the end of the summer, Shelly came home from Camp Galaxy five pounds heavier than when she left.

Horrified, my mother wouldn't take her to the Forgotten Woman, the store for big-lady clothes. "Shelly," she said, "you're smart enough to realize that if we buy those clothes now, you won't have anything to wear when you lose the weight." Shelly shrugged. "And you're retarded enough to think I'll lose weight just because you said that."

I drove Shelly to the mall myself and bought her size eighteen jeans. She lived in those jeans and wouldn't even try to diet. Furious at Shelly's attitude; tired, I'm sure, of being called retarded; and disgusted by my sister's lack of will, my mother retaliated by speaking about Shelly in the third person. "She can be any way she wants," she told me. "I'll just stay out of it."

Freed, Shelly ate Snickers and put the wrappers in my mom's purse. At dinner, she wolfed pizza while my mother sat in indignant silence. I developed a respect for my sister's stoicism that has haunted me since, especially when she got a scholarship to Cornell, came home for winter break a stunning 135, and went immediately to Loehmann's, where my mother joyfully outfitted her in new mini skirts. They buddied up after that, and Shelly was treated differently, with admiration, and perhaps a little fear.

I didn't see much of Shelly during college. She hung out with girls who wore black turtlenecks, quoted Proust, and talked about setting up grassroots women's coalitions. I, on the other hand, went to Syracuse, learned how to use a beer bong, prided myself on my ability to drink seven Kamikazes without throwing up, and had a lot of sex. Not a lot of good sex, but I made up in quantity what I lacked in quality. Needless to say, my sister and I didn't have much in common. Except our weight.

One summer when we were both home, we spent the day at the pool. Having gained a few pounds like everyone else in college, I was very self-conscious, and wore a long shirt over my bathing suit. Shelly told me to take the shirt off, that I wasn't fat.

"I'm a cow," I told her. "And you can say that because you're skinny."

"I work at it." She stood up and shook out her towel. "It's not as hard as you think."

A few days later, I walked into the kitchen and found Shelly standing at the freezer, gobbling my mother's secret stash of frozen Girl Scout cookies.

"Jesus, Shelly." Startled, she looked up, then sauntered into the bathroom. Through the closed door, I heard her gagging, then the sound of the toilet flushing. When she walked out, I accused her of making herself throw up. She laughed. "Who doesn't?" she said. "I *told* you: I work at staying thin. It just takes *discipline.*"

A few days later, I was alone in the kitchen. I'd been skipping meals, trying to stay on a turbo-charged Weight Watchers diet. I felt lightheaded and dizzy, but loved the ache in my belly, the low rumblings of hunger, the sour nausea that rose within me. I ate lettuce with mustard, gnawed a few carrots. When I put the lettuce away, I spied some diet pudding. I took a few spoonfuls, just for taste. Then I ate a piece of cheese and two slices of turkey and a spoonful of peanut butter and a big glob of Cool Whip. Perspiring, I shut the refrigerator, opened it, shut it again. I peered in the freezer, and saw the Girl Scout cookies.

I left the freezer open. Mist rose from the ice, cooling my face. I imagined the cookies melting in my mouth, the sweet taste as they slid down my throat, the salty nut rolling on my tongue. What was one? I thought. I closed the freezer door. NO, I told myself. NO. I opened the freezer again. Then I reached into a box and nibbled on a cookie. My mouth filled with the chocolate taste, and what's one more? I'll just have one more. As I bit into another, relief flowed through me, warming me, seducing me. Released, I ate the cookie in two bites. Then seized with sudden panic, I ripped the box open, using my teeth to tear the cardboard. I gnawed on the frozen cookies until they were mushy and I could gulp them without chewing, then I tore into two more boxes and gobbled them all, one after the other, desperate to fill myself. I didn't taste the chocolate, I didn't taste the nuts, I just watched my fingers working, not attached to my hands, not attached to my body, not really attached to me at all. I gulped milk, and the cookies expanded in my stomach, the nuts grew big as acorns. I felt everything rising so I rushed into the bathroom and lay on the floor. I thought of Shelly hovered over the toilet, the curlicue of her ponytail as she dipped her head. I imagined her body in a bathing suit; two long tapered legs; a tight, flat stomach; the slender curve of her waist. I could feel myself sweating the oily chocolate, could feel it seeping out of my pores and coagulating into lumps of dimpled fat. I stuck my finger in my mouth, tentatively at first, then harder, so hard, I jabbed the back of my throat. I gagged until I spewed milky brown water and I kept gagging, heaving chunks of unchewed cookie. A few times I missed the toilet, and spots of chocolate sprayed the clean white tiles like droplets of blood. Exhausted, I rocked on my haunches, promising myself that I would never, ever do this again. I lay on the floor and didn't move until I heard my mother calling, "GIRLS! Who ate all these cookies?"

For me, the worst is over. I still feel sometimes that my mother loves food more than she loves me, but I realize that it's not eating or even being thin that's so enticing to her. For my mom, it's the ritual: the fervent devotion to weight-loss success stories; the self-righteous exchange of a gooey brownie for its sugar-free substitute; the sweet surrender of eating off plates after guests leave; and the unfailing reverence for Monday mornings, the beginning of a new week of dieting. Despite her Jewish upbringing, *this* is my mother's religion. And because she needs it so much, I let her have it.

I'm all grown up now. I'm careful about what I eat, and I do worry about calories and fat grams, but I don't obsess about trying to fit a size ten body into size six jeans. At this point, I have more important things on my plate, so to speak. I don't know why I, unlike Shelly, was able to escape the torment of my body, because neither of us seemed able to rid ourselves of the torment of our mother. Maybe I just outgrew all that nonsense about cellulite and trailer parks and boys who won't call girls whose legs are too fat. But that's me. Unfortunately, my little sister Shelly wasn't so lucky.

PART ONE

CHAOS

1

My mother, Marsha, claims she takes tranquilizers only as a last resort. "I don't *need* them," she tells me. "They just take the edge off. It's a choice," she adds. "A conscious choice."

She's downstairs with my father, David, drinking decaf from her *Life's a Beach* mug. Lying in bed, I start to rise, but slump back, knowing what awaits me. My mother will be on the phone with her sister Lillian, ranting about the stupid house painter she hired who used magenta on the shutters instead of the dusty rose she picked out. Hunched over the table, my father will read the *New York Times* from cover to cover, then he'll agonize over the Word Jumble in the *Daily News*. He'll go to the refrigerator, but when he tries to get back to his seat, he'll be blocked by the phone cord that stretches across the kitchen like barbed wire. He'll ask my mother in a voice as tight as the cord to kindly move into the den if she wants to use the phone. Rolling her eyes, she'll pull the cord up and over his body so he can pass.

I know I have to get out of bed; however, I'm smart enough at twenty-six to recognize that though their behavior hasn't changed, my presence at the breakfast table is absurd. They may love me, but I also know they view me as a houseguest who is turning a weekend stay into an all-expense-paid lifelong residency, and who (to their horror) constantly forgets to flush the toilet and shut off the lights.

My phone rings. "Frannie? It's eight-thirty. You asked me to wake you at eight-thirty." My mother is calling from the downstairs line. When I moved home two weeks ago, she reinstalled my old line, which I thought was a nice gesture on her part. "And don't forget to shut your curlers off," she continues. "I found them on the other day. You could have burned the whole house down."

"I won't," I tell her, wondering when I left my curlers on. We're alike in that respect, always worrying about the house burning down. The truth is, I rarely use curlers in my hair since I have nowhere to go except to Rascals, a restaurant in the mall where I work three nights a week.

My mother took the day off from work, and we are spending it together. Sharing what she calls a Day at the Spa. We are getting our hair cut, our nails done, and then we'll sit in the sauna and pretend not to look at each other's bodies. She is treating us to Spa Day to balance the afternoon, which will be spent with my sister, Shelly, who checked herself into St. Mary's Hospital last week, and is now allowed visitors. It's not that I don't want to see my sister; I'm just not ready to see her in her present living situation. Although, if pressed, I'm sure she'd say the same thing about me.

Recently laid off from my secretarial job at Revlon, I first posed the question of moving back home when my mother was bedridden after a facelift. I whipped up fat-free smoothies, agreed when she said Oprah was putting on weight, rubbed vitamin E on her stitches, and caught her up on *General Hospital.* Because she was groggy, it didn't dawn on her until I was well into how Luke and Laura met that I should have been at work. "Frannie," she asked me, "why do you know so much about this show?"

"We watch it in the conference room. I called in sick today to be with you. We could have fun all the time if I lived here again. What do you think?"

"What do I think about what?"

I rested my head on her shoulder. Her head was swaddled in bandages so I tried to be careful. "We could be roomies again. My lease is up, but we both know I can't afford that apartment. If I move back, I can save money *and* keep you company. You seem so lonely."

"I'll be back at work in a week," she said, pulling away. "I'm hardly lonely. What about moving in with Abby?" Abby, who I've known since elementary school, is my best friend and has her own shoebox-sized apartment on Madison Avenue.

"You've seen Abby's place. She can barely fit her own stuff in there. Come on, Mom. You can teach me all about real estate." I'll waitress while I look for a day job, I decided. Then at least she'll think I'm trying.

"You're serious about this?"

I nodded. She peered at me suspiciously through the gauze. "Since when do you want to be in real estate?"

"You don't think I'd be good at real estate?"

"I didn't say that. I said—"

"Mom," I interrupted, "this could be good for us. You're moving into your Golden Years. We won't ever have this time together again."

She didn't answer me at first. Then she said, "You're always welcome here, Frannie. But Daddy and I are used to our own way of doing things."

"So you don't want me to move home." I felt a pang of panic, wanting her to beg me.

"I didn't say that. You can move home, but it can only be temporary. We're too old to live side by side."

"It will be temporary, I promise." I grinned. "Think about it, Mom, it'll be like old times. We'll have a ball."

"Yippee," my mother muttered, adjusting her bandages. "Like old times." What we didn't say was that she let me move home because she was freaked about Shelly, nor did we mention that I was asking to do it because I didn't have anywhere else to go, being broke, without health insurance, and adamantly opposed to living without cable.

I roll over. My feet get cold from the sudden draft, and I curl up under the sheet. My twin bed is old, and the springs are so worn that if I put my hand on the floor, I can actually do a push-up, the mattress rising with my body as if it is a person moving beneath me. It's rough sleeping alone after having boys to roll around with. And it's pathetic, I know, to fantasize about having sex with a strapping young man with my parents next door, but I obsess all the time. I imagine him running his fingers across my lips, caressing my thighs, cupping my breasts, whispering to me in a voice soft as rainfall ...

"FRANNIE! We have a big day." She's closing in on me, tapping her nails on the banister.

"Stick a Pop-Tart in the toaster, Mom!" I yell. "I'll be right down." I groan as I tug on the nightgown I found balled in my closet. What was once a beautiful silk nightdress is now hooker attire. The empire waist pushes my breasts up so high, they peek out the arms. The thin material clings, and strings from the unraveled hem hang like fringe. But it's soft and smells faintly of Gee, Your Hair Smells Terrific shampoo, so I sleep in it. Bracing myself, I put on a robe and head downstairs to greet the family and partake of the breakfast hour.

"Daddy forgot to buy you Pop-Tarts." My mother picks up the phone. "Do you realize how much fat is in one Pop-Tart? Have toast. Daddy bought sugar-free jelly."

"Toast is fine," I tell her, looking at my father, who is engrossed in the paper. He does all the grocery shopping for the household. Obsessed with cooking, he spends hours poring over recipes. A number of times, I've walked in on him watching Julia Child. He hunches forward boyishly on the couch, his mouth hanging open, staring at the television screen as if catatonic.

I rummage through the pantry, wondering if my mother hid my Pop-Tarts. I can't understand why it is so hard for my father to remember the most simple things about me. I am happy to buy my own, believe me, but he makes such a big goddamn deal about it. "I'll do the food shopping," he says firmly, spreading coupons around the table like it's his own little kingdom. Then he doesn't even listen when I ask him for something. For a second I consider that my parents have conferred about this, but I know that's impossible since they rarely speak to each other.

"Put something on your feet," my father says as I walk to the table. "The floor is freezing."

"I'm fine, really." I slide a piece of the paper away from him. He cuts his toast into four perfect squares and scrapes each one with guava jelly. The sound grates on me like a rusty wheel. My father, though thin and unimposing, is the world's loudest eater, and can be ten times more annoying with a piece of toast and a cup of coffee than if he crouched on the table and brayed like a donkey.

One thing about my parents that is simultaneously fascinating and horrifying is how obsessively they take care of themselves. My father sits on the driveway for hours with an aluminum sunboard, and looks like a tanner, taller version of Buddy Holly. My mother, through a vigilant combination of Weight Watchers, the Zone, recipes from Oprah's kitchen, and the StairMaster, has maintained a shapely, middle-aged figure. And they both sport full heads of hair that they attend to with the painstaking devotion of botanical gardeners.

Shelly was blessed with my father's long legs and Nordic coloring but I inherited my mother's predisposition to the pear-shaped hips of Russian immigrants. People often remark that from far away, the four of us could be siblings. But appearances can be deceiving. If you look closely, you can see dark pouches around my father's eyes and the way lipstick bleeds into tiny wrinkles around my mother's mouth. And now that she's had a facelift, her skin is tight around her eyes and her small mouth gapes open like a clam when she speaks.

"Spa Day starts at nine-thirty, Frannie. Hair at ten, nails at eleven. In fact," my mother says slyly, "I've made appointments for us to have massages." She waits a beat, expecting me to be thrilled.

"I don't think I can go today, Mom," I say nervously. The decision wasn't easy to make since I have a few problems with the power of choice. I know I should go, if only to be nice and satisfy her sudden urges for mother-daughter outings. Shoe-shopping and bed and bath boutiques are fine, but it drives me mad to watch her flit around the beauty parlor, reminding everyone that Shelly is applying to Harvard Law in the fall. "I'm sorry, Mom, but I don't think I have time to get my hair done today." I look to my father for support. He slurps his coffee so hard, it sounds as if he has a piece of balloon stuck in his throat and can't catch his breath. Bent so far over his mug, he looks like he is using the hot coffee to open his pores.

"Hi, Lillian," my mother says into the phone. "I know it's early in Tempe, but who told you to move to Arizona? If you still lived on Long Island, you'd be on my time. Hold on." She covers the receiver. "What do you mean you don't want to go? Do you realize how hard it is to get two appointments with Collette in the same morning?"

"I thought I'd call a few places about jobs," I say slowly. "I do have to find a job, you know."

"Frannie, you can look for a job any day of the week. Today we made plans!" I want to tell her that I am sorry, that I know I'm being childish. Instead, I sip my coffee and count the headlines on the front page of the *Times*. "I did this for you. It will be *fun*, dammit!"

I clench a fist to hide my raggy nails. My mother always says—Jesus, I sound like Forrest Gump—that you can tell a lot about a woman by the way she takes care of her fingers and toes. She has her nails done once a week at the Nail Lady in Lindsey Point, then she drives all the way to Manhasset to see Collette, who does her hair. Collette is my mother's guru. I met her only once, but she made me very tense. She's painfully thin with frizzy hair the color of patent leather and black eyes ringed so heavily with eye liner they look bruised.

"We'll strip it and rinse with henna," Collette had said, cradling my mother's head. "Then we'll tease it—big—to give it some life, some personality. Lately it's been looking sallow and under the weather." They talked about my mother's hair like it was a person to be muscled into shape. Being around Collette makes me feel like a bloated, dopey girl with trailer-park nails and a dead animal on my head.

"Daddy." I kick him lightly with my bare foot. "Do you think I should go today?"

"Your mother made you an appointment," he says, still working the Jumble. He squints at the blank spaces.

I glance over and study it. "The word's ACCRUE, Dad." He raises his eyebrows in wonder and pencils it in.

My mother hangs up and digs a spoon into a jar of sugar-free jelly. She alternates her mornings with sugar-free jelly and guava. When she's in a good mood, she treats herself to the highly caloric guava jelly, but when she's mad or anxious, she makes herself eat the sugar-free kind. She waves the spoon with a blob of jelly on it as she speaks. "Aunt Lillian thinks you should go. She thinks it's great that we have the opportunity to be together. Your cousin Beth won't even call her. And I'm paying for the whole thing."

"Oh, please. Beth is a coke whore who'd sell Aunt Lillian's jewelry to pay for drugs. Aunt Lillian should consider herself lucky. You said so yourself."

"That's not the point. And that's a disgusting way to talk about your cousin. She's still a person."

"Whatever," I say. "I want to make some calls and get some things together for Shelly. I don't have enough time to do everything. I'll go with you next week."

"There is no 'next week.' Collette's going to Europe." She crams a piece of toast in her mouth, throws the jelly spoon into the sink, and walks out. "Just forget it, Frannie. Don't go. But this is the last time I do something nice for you."

"What's the big deal?" I ask my dad. "I'm saving her fifty bucks."

He chews on his pencil. "Your mother's upset about Shelly. She wants to spend the morning with you. She thinks it will make her feel better."

"Oh," I say quietly, knowing this of course, but wishing he hadn't said it out loud. Suddenly feeling ungrateful and selfish, I walk to the stairs and call out that I've changed my mind.

"Too late!" my mother calls back. "I canceled for you. I think it's best if I just go by myself."

After my mother leaves, I grab a Hefty bag to fill with things for Shelly. My father is still sitting at the kitchen table. "Aren't you going to work?" I ask tentatively. My dad was often unemployed as I was growing up. Territories shrunk, business was bad, the recession hit. There were a lot of reasons why. But like most salesmen, he's resilient, so he was always able to pick up a line somewhere— clothing, eyeglasses, paper products, you name it. This year, he's peddling novelty giftware: sweatshirts, mugs, and greeting cards, but I'll never forget him sitting in this same spot, scouring the want ads, eating guava jelly sandwiches. I think that was when he fell in love with the Jumble.

My dad looks up at me. "I have a meeting in the city."

"If you'll be in Manhattan anyway, why don't you come with us to see Shelly?"

"I thought it best if you girls went first. I'll go when she feels more settled in."

"You mean when she's cured."

"Don't put words in my mouth, Frannie," he says as he walks out of the kitchen.

I can't figure out how he feels about me being here. When I moved in, he carried all the boxes out of my apartment in Great Neck, wheezing, red-faced, up and down the stairs, but all he said was, "I'm sure you'll find a job soon and then I'll have to do this all over again." He must think I'm pathetic when he sees me sitting on my bed, dwarfing the furniture he bought at Sears fifteen years ago. But maybe, maybe I make him feel younger, and when he sees me, he just assumes I've been here all this time. Sometimes he hovers outside my room, about to say something, but then he just moves the door back and forth, as if checking the hinges. I pretend that he's about to ask me if I need a ride to the mall, or if I finished my college applications, none of which he asked when I lived here the first time, the real time.

I take the bag up to Shelly's room, where I light a cigarette. My father's allergic, so we don't smoke in the house, but he's downstairs so I doubt he can smell it.

Random family pictures are scattered on top of Shelly's dresser. We both have the same furniture, white with gold inlay, all the edges carved into fat curls. I pick up a photograph of Shelly, my mother, and me that my father took in Florida last year. It is a great shot of the three of us on the beach wearing sunglasses. Shelly's in the middle, wearing an oversized windbreaker that hangs to her knees. My mother and I are in short-sleeved shirts and we have our arms around her. Shelly's face is drawn, but it looks like she's laughing. I think about taking the picture to the hospital, but then I remember that we were in Florida for my grandmother's funeral. Staring at it carefully, I also remember how sunburned I was when the picture was taken, and how much it hurt to have Shelly pressed against the tender skin of my shoulder. Shelly wasn't laughing at all. She'd just passed out, and my mom and I were holding her up because she was too weak to stand on her own. Her head is tilted, and the shadow from a lock of hair just makes it look like she's smiling. My father put the photograph in a novelty frame. Apparently he also forgot that Shelly was practically comatose from hunger and fatigue, and crying right before the shot was taken.

I throw some of my sister's old bras into the bag. I hear my dad in the hall and quickly stub out my cigarette on top of the dresser. Then I spray rancid perfume, and wave my hand in the mist to spread it around.

"Frannie?" My father knocks lightly and tells me he's leaving.

"Okay." I speak to him through the crack. "See ya." I try to push the door closed, but he blocks it with his foot. "Why are you being so secretive?" he asks.

"I'm not being secretive, Daddy." I tug on my robe. "I don't have any clothes on."

He quickly pulls back. "I left something for Shelly on the table. Please take it to her. I hope you and your mother have a nice visit."

"Yeah, should be a regular riot."

"You don't have to be snotty." I roll my eyes as he ambles downstairs. Hit with a pang of guilt, I wait a beat, then race down and catch him in the garage. "Maybe we can have dinner on Friday night?" I say breathlessly. "You can cook something for us."

"Maybe." He gets into the leased Mercedes he can't afford to buy. "We'll see." As he backs out of the driveway, he rolls down the window. "Hey, Fran?" I lean forward, hoping to hear him say how much he likes having me home, how he can't wait to have dinner with me on Friday. "Don't smoke in the house, huh? It makes the whole place stink."

Back in Shelly's room, I pick up the picture again and study it. I don't think any of us believed that Shelly would get so sick. In fact, I though she decided to stop making herself throw up. She never regained the weight she lost in college, but I guess we figured her preoccupation with her body was something she'd get tired of, like hot honey sandwiches. She was always on some sort of kick, but nothing lasted longer than a few months. In high school, she wanted to join the Peace Corps, then the Libertarian Party, then a kibbutz. When she got to Cornell, she became a raging feminist and stopped shaving, then she wanted to teach English, then she was going to be an anchorwoman. But she finally settled on law school, and when she graduated two years ago, Abby's father, Lonny, hired her as a paralegal. "I'll work for Lonny through law school," Shelly told me. "Then the D.A.'s office. I want to be the youngest judge appointed to the bench."

I shrugged. "Sounds good to me," I said, jealous she had her whole life lined up and I couldn't even decide whether to have tuna or turkey for lunch.

It wasn't until last June that she started to disappear. When she passed out on the beach, I knew she was in a bad way, but I attributed it to a combination of the anxiety that comes with being out of school for a year and our grandmother dying. But as the months went by, Shelly continued to lose weight. My mother and I tried to talk to her, but she told us that she had things on her mind, that she had started seeing a therapist, and we should mind our own business. So we did. In our defense, she was always bulked up in clothes, so we never actually saw her body. And she didn't do anything weird with her food, she didn't exercise obsessively, she didn't drone on about how fat she was. She simply stopped eating, and over the year, she got thinner. And thinner. And thinner. Since there was no drama, I never felt comfortable confronting her. Neither did my mother, but that didn't stop her from talking to *me* about it. "Frannie," she'd whine, "she's *wasting* away. Who the hell is this therapist she's been seeing? Why isn't she *doing* something?! Do you think I should call her?"

"No way, Mom. Shelly would *kill* you. Stop being so melodramatic." I hated when my mother talked about my sister's weight. It made me feel fat and ungainly, in a sick sort of way. But then one afternoon, I looked at my sister, I mean, I really *saw* her. Her heart-shaped face had shrunk and I could almost make out the outline of her skull under her thin blond hair. Her blue eyes bulged in their sockets and her cheekbones jutted out beneath them, carved into her face as if cast in stone. I couldn't stop seeing my grandmother's face, shriveled from old age. For a second, I couldn't catch my breath. Jesus, I thought. Je-sus. Who *is* this girl?

"Why are you sleeping?" At first my mother's voice is far away, but when she repeats herself, I realize she is hovering over me.

Quickly, I sit up, my heart pounding. I talk loud and fast, trying to convince her that I wasn't sleeping, I was only resting, but my voice comes out high-pitched and tinny.

"Frannie, please." I look up. She is dressed in her day-off attire: a fuchsia jogging suit, $19 sneakers that look like real Nikes, and socks with little pom-poms on the heel. She holds her newly painted nails away from her body, her fingers spread open like a Japanese fan. I smile at her, but I know there's no way it's going to be a guava day. "Get up. Get dressed. Let's go. We're late." She shakes her head at me before leaving.

I really was going to make some job calls, but hit with a wave of exhaustion, I climbed into bed. I can't break the habit of going back to bed after breakfast. Sometimes I sleep until mid-afternoon, getting up just as people are leaving their offices. It hasn't helped my job search, but I'm just so tired all the time.

I finger my black interview suit. We bought the suit during my senior year at Syracuse, back when my mother seemed to have faith in me. Now she seems convinced that I don't want to work, which isn't true. I just don't know what I want to be and it seems pointless to commit to one thing until I figure it out. If I wasn't so stupid about my life, I would have gone to law school or gotten an MBA. Then I'd *be* something already, or at least on my way.

I don't know why, when you're born, they just don't assign you an occupation. Right from the start, you'd know what to do, and there would be no need for aptitude tests, career counselors, or stupid questionnaires in *Cosmo* like "Is Your Career Right for *YOU?*," the one I filled out at the pool. The results said I should work independently, which annoyed me, so I went back and kept changing my responses until I fell into the "works well with other people" range.

"FRANNIE! Come down!"

I jump up, put on my Keds, and race downstairs. My mother has the phone in her hand, and with the chopstick she is using to dial, she indicates that I should sit. I look at the Jumble and notice that one of the words my father filled in is TROOM. I'm not sure if TROOM is a real word, so I scratch it out and fill in the squares with MOTOR. Then I cross out MOTOR too, figuring TROOM is a salesman's term only he knows.

I watch my mother get tangled in the phone cord, wearing *my* favorite earrings, and I can't believe this is my life. I am a freak: I'm a grown woman, four years away from my thirtieth birthday, and I'm sitting at my parents' kitchen table on a Wednesday morning. I have a job where I wear orthopedic shoes, an apron embroidered with a yellow duck on the bib, and a name tag with *Wanda* typed in because I don't want anyone to know my real name. I'm giving this plan one month. One month to find a job, land a man, and get my life in order. A month isn't that long. I smile, having told Shelly the same thing about St. Mary's. "It's just a month, Shelly. Do your time and get out. How bad could it be?"

My mother hangs up. "Let's go. Grab my keys, please?" She holds out her hand so I'll notice her freshly manicured nails and be reminded, once again, how I failed her. She also points to the present lying on the table. When I see it, I get a pang of jealousy. It's not because my father bought Shelly something special—I mean, she *is* in the hospital—but I feel like he doesn't even realize I'm alive. All he had to buy me was one stupid box of Pop-Tarts. I guess he feels I'm lucky enough to be living at home. Or maybe he just loves her more.

In the car, my mother puts a pair of my dad's boxer shorts on her head so her hair can "breathe" without the hot sun ruining her color. My dad has his boxers starched with his shirts, and the legs stand at attention. It's funny that my mother, who won't leave the house without perfect nails, will sit in her car with boxers on her head, but she tells me the car is her private sanctuary. "It's not like I'm *really* outside," she says when I point out that people stare at her. In fact, she had a phone and a CD player installed. If she could convince Collette to do her hair in the front seat, all she'd need is a hot plate and she wouldn't have to get out of the car for anything except to go to the bathroom.

When we pull out of the driveway, I play with my mom's vial of Valium. At this moment, I'd give a body part to swallow a handful of her pills and soothe my fluttering stomach. But they give me a foggy head and I have to save the ones I steal from her for the nights I work at Rascals. Besides, taking her pills in daylight makes me feel like I've become my mother, even before I've been myself, whatever self it is that I'm supposed to be. Then I want to crawl into my little twin bed. And that's the last thing I need, to be in my bed in the middle of the day. If a bed is any indication of how small a life has become, then I, Frannie Hunter, am queen of a fucking anthill.

"*hy is there so much traffic?*" *my mother whines as we line up at* the Triboro Bridge. I shrug. She always asks me questions I'm not sure I should answer. I know she's mad that I didn't go see Collette, but I also know she took a Valium and a half (the extra half, she said, was for Shelly's good luck), so she's probably sedated.

Sunlight streams in, and I flip down the visor. My mother wears large, black wraparound shades to shield her skin from the sun. I want to tell her that there's an obvious Quick Tan line where her neck meets the curve of her face, but she's in such a bad mood, I don't say anything. I even pretend not to notice when she crosses three lanes of traffic without signaling.

I rest my head against the window, feeling the faint stir of anxiety. As I watch the cars whip by, I concentrate on counting them until my heart stops racing. I often find myself palpitating in fits of panic for no real reason, my senses so heightened, I can actually feel myself feeling, so I count in my head to calm myself. But I refuse to end up taking Valium like breath mints. A "conscious choice," my ass.

"I wish Daddy had come," I say to my mother, who points to her CD case.

"He doesn't understand these things, Frannie." She points again, this time with urgency. I sigh heavily to remind her that I am not her slave, and pull the case into my lap. Soon, Johnny Mathis booms through the car. "Daddy had a meeting with a client," she says dreamily. "Rather than expecting him to sit in a hospital, don't you think we should thank God he has somewhere to go all day?"

As we inch through traffic, my mother hums to herself. I watch as she cranes her neck forward, focusing on something in the distance. Suddenly she jams on the brake. "Sorry," she mutters. "So, do you think this place will help Shelly? They say it's one of the best hospitals …" She trails off as she makes her way onto the FDR Drive.

"For what?" *Say it, Mom, just say what it is.* I feel my rage toward her building, but keep silent and swallow hard.

"Dear," she says in the tired voice usually reserved for my grandfather. "Don't start."

"You should just say what it is. It's anorexia, Mom. An eating disorder. It's like being addicted to alcohol or heroin or, I don't know …" I pause. "Valium. Maybe if you were able to say what it is, she wouldn't be in that hospital."

"It doesn't help to blame me, Frannie. I know Shelly has *anorexia.* There, I said it. Happy? I just don't know if committing herself to a hospital is the best answer. It seems to me like it's an escape. What's going to happen when she gets out?"

"Mom, let it go. Even Chubby said Shelly needed to go to St. Mary's. You were at that session. You heard her reasons."

Marilyn Rucker is Shelly's psychiatrist, whom she secretly calls Chubby. A month ago, before Shelly admitted herself to St. Mary's, the entire family met Marilyn at her office for a family powwow. Chubby is sweet-faced and rotund, and I felt like she really wanted to help Shelly. My mother, on the other hand, says she can't understand how someone with such an obvious lack of self-control with food can possibly help Shelly deal with her own weight problem.

We waited in the reception area. Shelly was swaddled in a quilted yellow jacket that she refused to take off even though it was eighty-five degrees out. I stood in front of the door that closed off Chubby's office. "Isn't it nice to be together?" I said. "Just a *normal* family from Long Island visiting the big city."

At that moment, Marilyn appeared in the doorway. I stared at her huge body filling the door frame and felt a flush of embarrassment. Smoothing away a loose strand of hair, she invited us in. I felt her staring at me like I was retarded. I wondered what Shelly told her about me. It couldn't be all bad, I reasoned. I'm basically well-adjusted, considering.

Shelly immediately sat in the chair closest to the door. My father sat in a chair next to her. My mother opted for the couch. I was still standing, unable to pick a spot, worried that Chubby was assessing our relationships by where we chose to sit. Finally, I parked myself next to my mother, but not too close.

As I sank into the leather couch, I debated whether I should go into the mental health field. Chubby must be doing pretty well, I thought. I definitely want a job where I can have my own office and decorate it tastefully. *Tasteful.* What a great word. It's a food word, like *succulent.* My mother was listening intently to Chubby. I cocked my head as if to say, Look at me, Chubby, I'm a young professional helping my sister get rehabilitated. I would have worn a suit, but no one told me your office was so *tasteful.*

"Shelly, do you want to start?" Chubby asked. Shelly looked at her hands and murmured something about Chubby going ahead. Chubby leaned forward. "I asked that you come today to help you understand why Shelly decided to go into St. Mary's. As a family therapist, I believe it's important to involve everyone in Shelly's treatment."

"We want to help Shelly in any way we can, Marilyn," my mother said. She rolled the name Marilyn off her tongue slowly, as if she could thin her out by stretching her name into long, elaborate syllables. "But I don't know if hospitalizing her is the best idea."

"That's not your decision, Marsha," Chubby said pointedly. She looked at my sister as if asking permission to continue. Shelly shrugged. "Shelly is severely depressed," Chubby continued. "In order for us to deal with the depression, we must first stabilize her weight."

"I realize this, Marilyn, but I don't know what can be done for her in the hospital that we can't do out here. Frankly"—my mother looked up at Chubby's diplomas—"if Shelly is *that* depressed, I don't know if she's in a position to determine what is best for herself." I followed her gaze. Chubby got her medical degree from SUNY Albany. "In fact," my mother said dryly, "I don't know *who* is in the best position to help her." If only you were thinner, Chubby, I thought sympathetically, then my mother would take your advice more seriously. She wouldn't even care where you went to school.

"Well, who should we listen to?" I jumped in. "The person who got her here or the person trying to help her?"

"Frannie." My father shifted in his seat. "Don't talk about your mother like that."

"How do you know I was talking about Mommy and not about you?" No one said anything for a second, and the words hung in the air like a cartoon bubble. I took a deep breath. "Shelly's not an idiot. If she feels she needs to check into a hospital, then she should. End of story."

My mother rolled her eyes. "Please, Frannie, Shelly should be with people that love her. A hospital just feels so anonymous to me."

"And forcing your daughter to go on a diet is loving her?"

"I never forced you girls to do anything. I was just afraid that if you didn't watch yourselves, you'd end up heavy and miserable."

"Bullshit! If we ended up heavy, *you'd* be miserable." I turned to Chubby. "We had to be perfect. For my mother that meant being thin."

"That's not true, Frannie." Like me, my mother looked at Chubby. Her voice was even and controlled. "I was very overweight as a teenager and very self-conscious about my body. My mother, in fact, fed me *too* much because for her, feeding me was showing she loved me. I made the conscious decision to teach the girls that food is not a replacement for love, that eating right and accepting your body is much more important." She leaned back. "I did what I thought was best. Given the opportunity, I might do things differently, but my intentions were good, and I won't apologize for them."

We sat in an excruciating silence. Having gotten up late, I didn't have time to shower and I knew I stank. I turned my head slightly, trying to smell myself. The digital clock flipped a number once then twice as we waited. Chubby wrote something down. It pissed me off that she wasn't saying anything, especially at $150 an hour. She was totally wasting my sister's money. No wonder Shelly was severely depressed.

Finally, Chubby spoke. "It's obvious that we all care about Shelly and we want her to make the best decision about her treatment. For any patient, our first challenge is to arrest the symptoms of her disorder. We try not to dwell too much on the past, not at this point." I knew that was directed to me. Oh fuck you, Chubby. "I think most families have good intentions, but there comes a point when good intentions aren't enough, and a patient needs care that her family isn't capable of providing." That, I know, was for my mother.

"So you're saying I can't take care of my daughter?"

"No. I'm saying that Shelly needs inpatient professional care. This isn't a new disorder, Marsha. St. Mary's is staffed with some of the best clinicians in the Northeast."

"What are our other options? What if Shelly moved home? David, don't you think ..." She trailed off.

Everyone shifted to look at him. "I don't know," he said quietly. "Shelly should decide." Oh shut up, I thought. Until you get a backbone, you should just shut up.

Shelly sat, her lips pursed. She wore baggy jeans, her long legs crossed, and she bounced her foot so hard, I could hear the fabric rub. Look at me, Shelly, I commanded in my head, let me see you smile. Instead, she looked at Chubby. "I just want them to understand that I didn't mean for this to happen. That if anything, I'd rather not do it at all."

"We know that, Shelly!" my mother blurted. "Which is why if you just came home with us rather than going to the hospital, we can spend some time together and figure this out."

"That's not what I meant." Shelly shook her head as fast and as hard as she bounced her foot.

Marilyn motioned to my sister as if waving a wand. "Right now, we want to stop Shelly's weight loss," she said firmly. "Then she can decide her next step."

From the corner of my eye, I saw my mother watch Marilyn

trying to maneuver her girth in the soft seat. She wasn't going to be undone by this fat lady, not my mother. "She's my daughter. She should be with me." Hunched in her seat, still wearing her yellow jacket, my sister buried her head in her hands. She looked like a quilted bumblebee awaiting capture.

"If you really want to help Shelly," Marilyn said calmly, "you will support her decision." Softly, Shelly cried. I wanted to run to her, but I was paralyzed.

"She is my child," my mother said, her voice breaking. "I want her home." She stuck out a finger. "Shelly will go into a mental hospital over my dead body."

From somewhere in the coat, I heard my sister's voice. It was muffled through yards of down and a thick coating of tears. "Bang bang," Shelly whispered. "You're dead."

"I feel like Shelly hates me," my mother says, licking her lips as she clutches the wheel. Her eyes are glazed. "Ever since she started seeing Marilyn, she acts like she hates me. Nothing I say is ever right."

"Mom, you missed the exit." For five minutes, I've watched her nudge the car over as if to change lanes, but never quite making it. "Pay attention! We're in a CAR!" I yelp.

"Jesus, Frannie. Lighten up." She hunches over as we finally exit the FDR Drive. Sunlight hits her hands and they suddenly look like old lady hands, wrinkled and spotted with large freckles. I look at my own hands, and wonder when they will betray me. I shouldn't have blown off Spa Day. Not today. I tell her so and she shrugs. But then she turns to me. "When were you going to let me know, Frannie?" she asks.

"Let you know what?"

"That you were fired from Revlon."

"I didn't get fired, I was laid off. And that was like a month and a half ago."

"Shelly told me you got fired."

"Well she's wrong. And I've asked you not to talk to her about me." I reach into her fake Gucci bag for a sugarless caramel which I unwrap and stick in my mouth. "Would you please use your blinker?"

My mother turns to look at me. As she does, she knocks the wheel and we swerve into the next lane. I hear a squeal as the car next to us also swerves. The car honks wildly. My mother jams on the brakes and we both lurch forward. I suck in my breath so hard, I almost swallow the caramel, but it gets caught in my throat. I panic with the feeling of being unable to breathe. "Jesus, Mom!" I sputter as the candy dislodges and slides down. "Watch what you're doing. Mom? Mom, you okay?"

Trembling, she takes a deep breath. "I would appreciate it if you let me do the driving. All your futzing around is very distracting. I'm the mother here. I can drive."

Eventually, we turn onto 75th Street. We circle the block a few times until someone pulls out. "I didn't realize how nice it is," I say as my mother parks.

"What is?"

"The hospital, Mom."

I turn to look at her. The boxer shorts have slipped over one eye. One leg droops, like a doggie ear. She looks like a pirate. I snicker. Yo ho ho. I snicker again, trying to stop myself. Then I start to laugh. My laugh gets looser and more resonant and soon, it's the hollow laugh that unravels inside your stomach, that's so deep, you can't get to its end. I try to stop, but the laughter takes on a life of its own and disconnects from my throat as if it is outside me. My eyes fill with tears.

"Frannie, are you all right?" I snort through my nose once, then twice, which only makes me laugh harder, but it isn't laughter any-more. I am dry-heaving spasms. "I hardly see what's so funny." Indignantly, she pulls the boxers off her head.

I hiccup and feel my throat closing. My brain feels like it's all broken up. The car seems small, abnormally small, too small for my head. I stick my face out and squint into the sun, which ripples like fabric. A cab whips by. I imagine it accelerating out of control, swerving wildly, and smacking into us. I gasp, unable to swallow, feeling as though the candy's still caught. I can't breathe, and I'm suddenly petrified I'm going to pass out. I bend over and slowly, slowly, the moment passes. My heartbeat slows and I can hear myself panting. Through my tears, the hospital comes into focus.

My mother reaches out. "Frannie? Say something!"

I stare at her. I want to speak, but can't.

I lean forward and suck in air. A wave of heat flushes me once, then twice. I blink. Blink again, and the waves subside. It's just anxiety, I soothe myself, nothing you can't handle. I cough, clear my throat. "Mom," I choke out, tapping the window. "We're here." I swallow. "We've arrived."

3

t. Mary's is a psychiatric hospital nestled in a strip of brownstones on the Upper East Side of Manhattan. The front of the hospital is brick and there is an ambulance entrance, but it is disguised by a wooden electronic door. There is a glass double door that serves as an entrance for patients and visitors. The door is usually papered with neon-colored leaflets that look like concert advertisements, but are really notices of 12-Step meetings. It doesn't look like a hospital; it looks more like a private museum.

"Are you okay? What happened?" my mother asks.

I nod, but my head throbs. "Nothing. I got nervous, I guess. I had an anxiety attack." That one hit me hard. Usually, they're not so potent.

"You want one?" She holds out a Valium. "It might take the edge off."

I shake my head. My mother's pocketbook hangs from her arm, the clasp open.

"Your bag's open," I hiss at her.

"So's yours." She points to the Hefty bag. There's a hole in the bottom of the bag and I am dragging Shelly's bras along the dirty hospital floor. I sigh, pull the bras out of the bag, and stuff them into my backpack.

As we walk through the lobby, I keep glancing at my mother, hoping she doesn't notice how institutional the hospital looks on the inside, how gritty the walls are, and how part of the floor sags where the linoleum is worn away. It is one of those moments when I feel the need to hide things from her; the underbelly of life, things that don't particularly bother me. I've been to college. I've stood in a frat house, tongue-kissing some guy who chugged grain alcohol punch from his sneaker. I am hardly fazed by dirty tiling.

A tall woman walks over. "I'm Diana," she says. "I'm the admitting nurse for the Eating Disorders program."

My mother shakes her hand. "I'm Marsha Hunter, Shelly's mother." Diana turns to me. "You must be Frannie. I can tell you're sisters. You both have the same smile." She motions to a small waiting room that has twenty or so plastic seats and a television chained to the floor. "Visiting hours don't start for another fifteen minutes, but you can wait here."

"Jesus," my mother whispers, glancing at the chairs. "For the money this place costs, you'd think they'd have a classier-looking waiting room."

"Mom!" I look apologetically at Diana, but she turned away. I sit in a plastic seat, the Hefty bag at my feet. Next to me, my mother taps her nails on the armrest. "I have to go to the ladies' room," she says.

"Do you want me to ask Diana where it is?"

"I'm afraid to go in this place."

"So don't sit down. Mom, this is a hospital. I'm sure they clean the toilets. Insane people hate germs, too, you know."

"Frannie, please." She lowers her voice. "Shelly is not *insane*. She's bright and she's sensitive, but she's not *insane*. Your lack of compassion is really unbecoming, don't you think?"

Silently, I kick the Hefty bag. Right now, I'd give anything to be back at that frat party, drinking Hunch Punch and making out with some guy I didn't know.

I can feel my mother shaking as we ride in the elevator. Shelly told me that each floor houses different afflictions. It seems to me that the more fucked up you are, the higher you go. The floors range from mild depression all the way to schizophrenia, which is at the very top floor in the penthouse suite of mental aberrations. Shelly is parked smack in the middle on Floor 3, Ward 17, Eating Disorders and Related Addictions. The elevator dings and the doors open.

"I am not ready for this," my mother mutters. She has a look on her face that pains me; her eyes are wide and glassy and her lips twitch as if she's fighting back tears. "Do you think I left the stove on? Maybe I should call your father just to be sure."

We trudge down a long hallway with two other couples. Outside the locked ward, we wait for someone to let us in. "Isn't this ridiculous?" my mother mutters, loud enough for everyone to hear. "This is supposed to be a hospital, not a prison."

I shrug and inch away from her. "It's not that bad," I say, more to myself than her.

It takes a long time for a nurse to show up. I watch my mother clench a fist. No longer hazy, our near-accident jolting her back, I suppose, she fidgets like a child. I, on the other hand, hold myself still as a stone, although I am aware I am tight with the feeling of expectation.

My mother turns to the woman closest to her. "Well here we go," she says, trying to appear flip. "It won't be that bad." As we hear the jingle of keys, she squeezes my hand, pinching my fingers between her rings. "I mean it can't be much worse in there than it is out here, now can it?"

Inside, I look for Shelly. I see a cluster of girls, many who look like teenagers, sitting in a big well-lit room, curled on couches, watching TV or reading. No one talks to anyone else. I can't tell if the room is filled with tension or it is my own anxiety that makes me edgy, but I want to scream at everyone to just CALM DOWN. There's constant movement and clatter and an occasional bang that makes me jump. I notice a girl on the phone. She's about my size, not too fat, not too skinny, and the sight of her comforts me. As she waves her hands dramatically, her voice booms through the room. As I look around, my eyes keep returning to her.

In the back, there's a Ping-Pong table, a handful of chairs, and shelves overflowing with magazines, coloring books, paperbacks, and board games. Beyond what looks like a dining area, there's a circle of chairs for group therapy, I guess. It's eerie to see the chairs set up with no one in them. It's like walking into a torture chamber and seeing the equipment empty and idle, but knowing it's used for unspeakable things.

The girl on the phone laughs as if she just heard the funniest joke in the world. At first, I laugh, too, but after a while, the sound grates on me and I try to shut it out. Two more girls rush by wearing sweat pants and thick socks. At one glance, they seem really regular. But when I look closely, I can see that their clothes hang loosely and they have the underdeveloped bodies of twelve-year-olds; no breasts, no hips, just angles of long knobby bones. The girls are also extremely pale, as though they haven't been in the sun for months.

I walk over to the windows. On the wall, there's a row of paper flowers. Some are pretty, the strokes of the crayon even and inside the lines, some are weird, with small faces drawn on the petals. There is one at the end that's especially crude with black petals and an orange stem. At the bottom, I see the name Shelly scrawled in purple crayon.

Diana touches my shoulder. "It's an interesting flower. Shelly made it in art therapy."

"Is it supposed to mean something?"

"No, not really. Not always."

My eyes rest on a girl who stares at me. I glance away, but I can feel she's focused intently, which seems odd because I feel like the visitors should have the privilege of staring at the patients, not the other way around. Her hand rests on a tall intravenous feeder, a skinny pole that has sacs attached filled with murky liquid. The pole is on wheels and the girl pushes it as she walks toward me. Long, transparent tubes hang from the pole to the girl's face where they are lodged in her nostrils. A piece of white tape holds the tubes in place. The tension of the tubes jammed into her nose throws off the symmetry of her face, pinching her top lip into a sneer.

"My name is Cynthia," she says, openmouthed, sucking air in abrupt breaths. Her voice is nasal. "My parents couldn't come today, primarily because my mother's dead." She pushes the feeder closer, and I can see the liquid moving through the tubes. I feel pity for this girl Cynthia who can't be any older than fifteen. She stares at me arrogantly, as if daring me to look away.

"I'm Frannie, Shelly's sister." I hold out my hand, which she cradles then drops.

Cynthia licks her lips. "Shelly's the new girl. She didn't want you to come today."

"She didn't?" Last night, Shelly said she couldn't wait to see me.

"She said in group that your mother just had a facelift. And that you were fired."

I was *laid off*, you psycho. "Why didn't she want *me* to come?" It dawns on me that Cynthia said Shelly is *new*. Shelly's been here a whole week.

"She doesn't want you to think she looks stupid. She'll get used to it. I wish I had a sister. I don't have anyone. My mother's dead, you know."

"How long have you been here?" I ask slowly.

"Three months and six days. This time. I was supposed to get out yesterday. I have an apartment, you should see it, it's really grand, but they gave me the tubes. I told Shelly about the apartment. Maybe she'll live there when we get out. I have to gain six pounds before they take away my tubes." She stops short. Holds my gaze. Her voice is chilling. "But we'll see about that."

"You will," I say gently, afraid to look at her dead-on. Vacant and glazed, her eyes are like ice-blue marbles. The air is suddenly light around my head. I hear a whirring and my heartbeat quickens. I take a deep breath and motion to my mother. "Mom, this is Cynthia."

"Hello, dear." My mother stares at the tubes. "Do you know where Shelly is?"

Abruptly, Cynthia turns away. "This is the day room. You stay here." And she shuffles off with her feeder, the wheels clattering on the linoleum as she moves off the rug.

"Oh my God." My mother watches Cynthia. "I hope Shelly doesn't …" She trails off, then turns to face the wall. She touches Shelly's flower. "Shelly's very bright, but she never was that good in art, was she?"

*   *   *

"How long is Shelly supposed to stay in this place? Marilyn said thirty days. Do you think she'll have to stay that long?" My mother smooths her hair three times, staring at everyone who passes. "Why do they get this way? Not *all* these girls have terrible mothers."

"Mom, stop." I feel like an outcast. Everyone else has buddied up, and Shelly has yet to appear.

"Why? Everyone blames me. Especially you. You're the one who keeps saying that I forced Shelly to diet, that I made her obsessive, that I didn't confront her. As far as you're concerned, it's all my fault."

"Mom, please." I play with my T-shirt. "Sometimes I just say things."

"Mommy?" I hear a slight whisper like the rustling of paper. I turn around and see my sister, who stands, arms crossed, waiting. I draw in my breath. For the first time in a year, Shelly's wearing running shorts and short sleeves. Her bare arms and legs are so thin, I could wrap two fingers around them. They don't even look like real limbs, more like pegs. It amazes me that she has the strength to stand on her own. Trying to appear casual, I look around for a chair that I could lower her into in case there's an emergency.

"Shelly?" my mother asks.

"You were expecting someone else?"

"You just look so different ..."

"Different how?"

I lean forward to hug her. "Don't touch me," she snaps, stiffening. I smile stupidly.

"Frannie—I mean Shelly—Frannie's just happy to see you." My mother puts her arm around my sister, but Shelly jerks back. "Fine," my mother says. "No touching."

"I *am* happy to see you," I tell her. She chews on her lower lip. Her blue eyes are watery and dart around the room, as though she's frantically searching for someone. A week ago, she looked drawn, but she didn't look sick. Now she looks deathly. Under the fluorescent light, her skin is gray, her hair is stringy, and her lips are chalky. I have that same, sudden feeling of unfamiliarity I had when I first noticed how skinny she'd gotten. But this time, I can't stand looking at her. I wish this girl would go away and bring my sister back.

"I was working on something. I lost track of time and didn't shower." She reaches up and touches her hair. Almost instinctively, I reach up and touch my own.

"Shelly, you look great." My mother leans in to run her hand across my sister's hair, but Shelly recoils. For a second, the hand is caught in mid-air. "What were you working on?"

"Just something for Lonny." She gnaws at a cuticle. "It occupies my mind. Otherwise all I think about is being in here."

My mother tries to soothe her. "You just got here. It takes time to get adjusted."

"Please don't say 'I told you so,' Mom," Shelly says.

"I'd never say that, Shelly. Look, you made a decision. If Marilyn was wrong, and this place doesn't work out, well, we'll just cross that bridge."

Shelly mimics her in a high-pitched voice. "'We'll just cross that bridge ...'"

My mother looks at me, her lips parted. She has the same look she had years ago when, during a winter break from Cornell sometime around her feminist days, Shelly announced she and her friends were moving into a group home. "It'll be like a real commune," she said defiantly. "We're pooling all our money ..." she paused ... "we may even have a baby." My mother didn't say anything but, like today, she had glanced at me behind Shelly's back. Make this go away, Frannie, I felt her saying, make this stop.

I look at my mother and sister who are waiting for me to say something. Not knowing what else to do, I close my eyes and make a wish.

Shelly leads us through a corridor. It's much nicer than I expected. The walls in the ward are painted in pretty pastel colors and there are a lot of windows, so the place is filled with sunlight. It's a hell of a lot nicer than the reception area, or my parents' house, come to think of it. We have shabby furniture bought when they first got married. It's also really dark all the time so we live in shadows like we're rodents.

"We're encouraged to express our creativity," Shelly sneers as we pass an oil painting of a farm. "To get in touch with our feelings. Frannie, isn't this place the biggest joke?"

"I guess," I say carefully. I touch the frame. "This is nice."

Shelly shrugs. "Cynthia did this. The girl on hyperalimentation."

"She's a very talented young girl," my mother offers. "Is she an artist?"

"She's thirty-two, Mom. And she was with the ballet until she fried her brain. It was so sad when they tubed her. For weeks, she gulped water in the shower before weigh-in. No one noticed until she hyperventilated and passed out. It was amazing, everyone screaming and Cynthia lying on the floor, peeing all over herself. Now they make us wait until after weigh-in to take showers."

"How'd she fry her brain?" I ask nervously, peering into the bathroom.

"Starved herself. No oxygen. She should've gotten tubed a long time ago, but someone fucked up. They don't like when we talk about it."

"She starved herself in here? I thought they were supposed to monitor you." Wide-eyed, my mother glances at me. Someone fucked up.

"This place isn't as well-supervised as they like to think. Everyone sneaks laxatives, water pills, speed. Girls throw up in towels, send them down the laundry chute, whatever." As Shelly speaks, I notice a twinge of pride in her voice. "Some girl drank ipecac. She vomited blood, but lost a pound so I guess she felt it was worth it."

"Would you?" my mother asks quietly. "Shelly, would you feel it was worth it?"

"Why do you always ask questions that you think are so probing, but that are really just retarded?" My mother tries to light a cigarette. "Mom!" Shelly exclaims. "You can't smoke in here! This is a hospital." She rolls her eyes as we walk into her room.

"This is Bernadette." We turn to look at a girl lying on a bed. Bernadette is much more filled out than Shelly. Her face is bloated and a little lopsided. She nods, but doesn't open her eyes.

"Bernadette's bulimic," Shelly says, loud enough for Bernadette to hear. "There's a lot of animosity between the anorexics and the bulimics. The bulimics don't think they get enough attention."

Silently, Bernadette flips Shelly the finger, but smiles mysteriously as Shelly laughs.

Shelly rips open the present from my father. Inside is a white sweatshirt with the words JUST DO IT silk-screened in big block letters.

"It's from Daddy," I tell her. "He thought it would be inspirational."

"He's so weird. He called me the other day to ask what *habeas corpus* means."

"He probably wanted to talk, but didn't know what to say," I tell her wisely. "What did you tell him?"

"I told him what it meant and he thanked me. Then he hung up." She snickers. "Like, hello Daddy, I'm not in my office right now." She busies herself putting on her sneakers. "He said he was going to be here today." She sounds upset and won't look at me.

"He had some meeting."

"Bullshit. He didn't want to visit a loon hotel. He only wishes this was my office."

She's right, actually. My parents can't wait for Shelly to be a real attorney. They constantly ask her their idea of lawyerly things, like if my mother can sue the cleaner's for losing a blouse. It's obvious they think more highly of her, which kills me because I'm the older sister: the one who's supposed to have better clothes, make more money, and get married first. Until she landed here, she had me beat in almost every category. Now I guess we're tied.

Bernadette finally rises from her bed and tells Shelly she's going to watch TV. "You want anything?"

Shelly shakes her head. "Only to check out of here."

Bernadette smiles. Her teeth are gray. "Me first," she calls over her shoulder.

"Nice dental work," I note.

Shelly sighs. "Frannie, she has no enamel. It's a symptom of bulimia. Perhaps you've heard the word?" My face burning, I mumble that I'm sorry, but I'm getting pissed. It's extremely difficult to keep up with my sister when she's in one of her moods.

My mother walks toward a small closet. "So how's your therapy going?" Inside, she rearranges the clothes. "Marilyn said you'd have another therapist in here. What's he like?" She peers out. "Or is it a she?"

"Her name is Katie." Shelly turns to me. "So how's life at home?"

"How do you think? I'm giving myself a month. Just like you. Actually, this place isn't so bad, Shelly. Personally, I wouldn't mind a few days here just to chill out."

"Don't talk like an idiot, Frannie. I know what this place looks like." Her eyes water, and she pulls me up from the bed, takes off all the sheets, and starts to remake it.

When we brought Shelly here, she didn't seem overtly anxious. She sublet her apartment to another paralegal in Lonny's office, and she'd already brought her things back home, so she parked her Subaru in my parents' driveway and got into the backseat of my mother's car with a suitcase and some books. "You can always call me," I said over the headrest. "I mean, I know we haven't spent much time together lately, but I'm still your sister. I'll come every day. That is, if you want me to." She didn't say anything, so I added, "Shelly, everyone has problems."

"Frannie." She sighed. "Please stop acting like you feel sorry for me."

Chubby met us in the lobby. Shelly started to walk away but my mother grabbed her. "You'll call me, right? And don't worry, okay?" Shelly tried to shake her off, but she clutched harder and turned to Chubby. "Call me about anything," she said as Chubby hooked her arm through Shelly's and inched her away from my mother. Right before she was led into the elevator, Shelly sadly held my gaze. I started to say something, but she turned before I could get the words out. I hated myself for not saying something when I had the chance; not goodbye, not I'll call you, not even good luck.

"So do you think Katie is helping you?" my mother says from the closet. "I hope you're not focusing on the past, Shelly. This is the time to focus on your future. Applications aren't due until February, right?"

"Yeah, my big future," Shelly says, but my mother is already back in the closet.

"Why did you tell her I was fired?" I whisper.

"I didn't. I told her you were laid off."

"She told me you told her I was fired. So did Cynthia," I add.

"Frannie," Shelly says, exasperated. When she swallows, I can see her entire jaw. "I don't care if you were fired. Hasn't it occurred to you that I have other things on my mind?"

"Why would you say something like that? I realize that." Annoyed, I change the subject. "We almost had an accident on the way here. Mommy was completely toasted."

"She told me she was easing up." Shelly looks at my mother, who is busy unfolding the things in Bernadette's closet. "MOM! That stuff's not mine!"

"I know, dear." She sticks her head out. "I just want to help out. It makes me feel better. You know, this place isn't so bad. The people seem very competent."

"Then you move in." Shelly's voice cuts through me like a sword. "You and Bernadette can trade war stories." She laughs, but her laugh is hollow and fake, and she sounds like she's about to cry.

"Mom," I cut in. "Why don't you take a walk? Let me and Shelly talk."

"Fine, you girls talk and I'll find a place to smoke." My mother runs her hand along the door frame before walking out. "Really, this place isn't at all what I thought it would be." She turns to us and smiles. "Thank God."

"I can't stand this," Shelly says when we're alone. "She makes me crazy."

"She doesn't know what to do, Shelly." I want to tell my sister that she's being an asshole, that for once, our mother is trying, but I'm afraid of her reaction.

"Cynthia told me you didn't want her to come." I pause. "*Me* to come."

"That's not true. I just said that I didn't want you to see me *in here*." Her voice breaks. "It's *embarrassing*, Frannie. Anyway, Cynthia is a fucking lunatic. Why are you listening to her?" She turns away. I wonder what her back looks like, tempted to lift her shirt. "I had everything in place," Shelly continues. "I was going to work, getting my applications ready. I feel like I just gave up. Don't you understand? I ruined my life—it was *in place*." She wipes away a tear. "Do you realize how long it will take me to undo this?"

"This is a beginning, Shelly. This isn't the end. And whose life is perfect? Look at me? I'm back at home with Morticia and Gomez."

She doesn't answer. "They want me to gain seventeen pounds before I can leave," she says suddenly. "They won't let me see the numbers, though. We get weighed backwards. How will I know when I get there? It makes me crazy not to know. Jesus, I can't imagine what I'll look like if I gain that much weight. I haven't been that big in a long fucking time."

"You've gotten very thin, Shelly," I say slowly. She doesn't know? She can't see?

She shrugs. "I just don't like when they watch me eat. It makes me feel all needy when they watch. It makes me feel like I'm crippled and completely helpless." She puts her hands on her hips. "I shouldn't have come here. I'm not like the other girls. They talk about food all day. They're grotesque. I'm not like that. I have a job. Lonny counts on me. Maybe Mommy was right. Maybe I should stop before I get in too deep. Do you think *I'm* grotesque? You're my sister, Frannie. You have to tell me the truth." She starts to cry.

I shake my head. "No, Shelly," I say softly, feeling a rush of love for her. "Of course not. You're so pretty. I just want you to get better."

"Don't SAY that!! I'm NOT like them." She takes a step and accidentally trips over her own feet. Her T-shirt flies up, and I can see her stomach and chest. Not only is her skin stretched so tight I can see the outlines of her ribs, but her body is covered with a soft down like that of a baby chick.

Startled, I blink rapidly. Do not move. Do not let her know that you know. I fold my hands in my lap. I clear my throat. "I understand that, Shelly. You aren't like them."

"You are so lucky, Frannie, not having law school to worry about. You are so free; you can be anything." She lies back on the bed. "I hate this place. They just want to fatten me up and process me out. God, I'm so fucking tired. It seems so much easier to take a razor and slide it across your wrists." She looks at her hands and then up at me. "They say you can't even feel it."

My mother walks in. "I want a cigarette, but they told me I have to go to the roof. What's this?" She pulls a cord sticking out of the wall. Suddenly, a bell goes off.

"Mom!" Shelly sits up. "That's the emergency alarm!"

"I'm sorry." She backs away. "I didn't know."

A nurse rushes in. "Is everything all right?"

"I pulled the cord," my mother says, her voice breaking. "I didn't mean to."

"It's okay," the nurse says sweetly. "I had to get Shelly anyway." She looks at her. "It's time for meds."

"I keep forgetting this is a hospital," my mother says, watching Shelly leave. "Everything's normal, but skewed at the same time." She shakes her head. "She looks horrible, doesn't she? I want to take her out of here."

"And bring her to your house? She's where she belongs, Mom. And frankly, I don't think it's so terrible." I don't. It seems so peaceful. And it's not like she has to get up at six A.M. and traipse through New York in high heels for jobs she won't get. I don't understand why she called *me* free. *She* has a plan. What could be more free than that?

I hear a piano being played. I think Shelly should take advantage of this place. It might be nice to sit around and talk all day. If you think about it, there isn't much of a difference between Shelly's situation and my own. In fact, she's got the better package. Neither of us can smoke in our rooms, neither of us can have men sleep over, and neither of us can eat what we want without someone commenting. But *she* doesn't have to live with my mother.

"I hate hospitals," my mother says. "It makes me depressed just to be here."

"*You're* depressed? How do you think Shelly feels?"

"Who knows? She seems so mixed up. I just don't know how she got so bad so fast. We talked every day, I thought I knew what was going on. Once she found Marilyn, she told me to butt out. It wasn't like I didn't try, you know."

"Maybe you didn't try the right way."

"Maybe there is no right way. Maybe this is the best it's going to get. Maybe you girls should appreciate what you have. I'm not perfect, but I'm here, aren't I?"

"*Here* is a relative term, Mom."

"Why are you talking about me?" Startled, I look up. Shelly's standing in the doorway. "At least close the FUCKING door!" She walks over to a sink. She leans forward, and before my mother and I can stop her, she smacks her head against the mirror. "I asked (Bang!) you both (Bang! Bang!) not to talk about me behind my back! (Bang!) Don't talk about me like I don't exist because I DO (Bang! Bang!)!"

I jump up to pull her away and realize that she's hitting a sheet of plastic; there's no glass in this place. "We didn't mean anything by it, Shelly. Really, truly we didn't." I try to put my arms around her, but she pulls away.

"We didn't, Shelly." My mother tries to light a cigarette, but her hand trembles.

"You are lying!!" Shelly whirls around. "AND YOU CAN'T FUCKING SMOKE IN HERE!!"

"Shelly," my mother stutters, "please calm down. Don't you think you're overreacting?"

"I am NOT overreacting!" Shelly screams. She leans over the sink again, staring into the fake mirror as if daring herself to make contact. "Why don't you both go home to your lives and leave me alone? Just leave me alone."

"Shelly," I start to say, but my mother cuts me off. "Well, fine then. Okay, we'll go," and stands up.

I lurch forward. "MOM! Wait!"

"You heard her. She doesn't want us here. We can come back another time."

"That's fine with me," Shelly says. "If you want to go, go." Tears stream down her face. "Just leave me here, I don't care. I don't need you."

"We don't want to leave you, Shelly," I say. "It's just hard to see you so unhappy."

"I'm not unhappy." Shelly starts crying out loud. Her sobs are deep and guttural and I feel myself wanting to cry with her. "I'm just sick of everyone talking about me like I'm a case study. I AM a PERSON!"

"Okay already. We're sorry." My mother holds up her cigarette. "Let's take a break from all this, go up to the roof or wherever, and have a smoke." She reaches for my sister's hand. "Come, come with me. Listen, Johnny's nephew went to Harvard. Johnny said he'd call him. Maybe he'll write a recommendation. It's good, isn't it, to have recommendations from alumni? And he's a big mucky-muck at IBM."

"Mom." Shelly sighs. "*Mucky-muck* is not a word."

"Fine. Strike it from the record, Counselor." Shelly giggles as they walk, holding hands, toward the door. My mother tells me that they'll be right back.

I start to say something, but a slow shiver of anxiety runs through my body, like lightning that hits the roots of a tree and travels up through its limbs. I lie down on Shelly's bed. I've got to get a job. And a life. If I don't, I'll end up here, too. Starting tomorrow, I'll call advertising agencies. I haven't hit advertising yet. I roll over. The thought of getting on the phone and calling people I don't know makes me very, very tired.

Sunlight filters through the window, casting shadows of the bars across the blankets and against the walls. I hear the sound of a siren scream and then fade. As I feel myself drifting, I think about my mother and Shelly together on the roof. I have a sudden craving to go up there and let them watch me as I walk to the edge of the roof, dangle a leg over, show off a little, *Look, Ma—no hands*, and take a step forward. Just one small step so I can free-fall along the side of the hospital, belly-down, arms spread like wings.

I stroke my stomach, squeeze a roll of flesh. Just two minutes, I tell myself, burrowing my nose in Shelly's pillow, imagining myself floating from the sky and sleeping peacefully forever. And I close my eyes and breathe deeply and silently wonder what my mother and my sister are saying about me.

So why do you want to be in advertising?" From behind the desk,
the man smiles. I uncross my fingers and point to my résumé.
"I majored in communications." He holds the résumé close to his
face. He's well-dressed in a pin-striped suit and a red silk tie. He
doesn't look that old, maybe late forties. He's actually kind of
handsome.

"I'm really good with people. I think advertising is all about
people. I'm a real people-person." Oh Jesus, Frannie, shut up. I'm
sweating in my suit, which isn't surprising since it's almost July and
I'm wearing wool.

"We have an entry-level spot open," Mr. Richards—or is it
Richman?—says. "We're looking for one, maybe two years of experience."

"That's me." I proceed to tell him my job history, and soon I
notice his eyes slowly roll back until I can see the whites. Then they
close. I stare intently, afraid he's dozed off.

He snaps up. "You went to Syracuse." He smiles. "My daughter is
at Ithaca. Gets mighty cold up there." Mr. Richley is droning on.
"The job is in trafficking. You'll report to the vice presideennnnn ..."
he trails off and his eyes roll. And very, very slowly, they close. Soft
grunting noises come from his half-open mouth until it, too, closes.

47

Then he snaps awake. "… president of marketing." He talks with his eyes shut.

I eye him carefully. He must have some kind of disorder. I start to talk about working as a trafficking assistant, so I understand the job when his eyes open. "That's why we called you," he says, and I'm listening, but not really because I'm waiting for him to nod off. He starts to tell me about the firm, then he nods very slowly and his eyes flutter and he's mumbling something annnnnnd theeeenn they close. I breathe deeply, afraid I'm going to start laughing. "So." He blinks. "Oh, wait, I lost my thought." He starts talking again, but I can't hear him because I'm focused on his eyes, waiting for him to trail off … "Well?"

"Well what?" I ask politely, my head cocked. I clutch my suit in my sweaty hand.

"What do you know about telecommunicaa …" Mumbling, he loses himself. His eyes flutter as he grunts.

"*Communications*," I cut him off. Dreamy, he nods, his eyes closed. "I worked at a PR firm for a while," I say. "I learned a lot about telecommunications. I did a lot of things. With communications … and … uh … telecommunications." I cannot believe I just said that.

"We're involved in all areas … so …"—I try hard to pay attention—"… the work is very technical. Ideally, we want som … momom momo …"—he dozes off—"and … mmom … momo …"

His mumbling becomes hypnotic and I sway as I watch him. I am listening so intently, I begin to drift off, and as he mumbles "mmom … momo …" I actually hear myself mumbling "mmom … momo …" right along with him—out loud.

"What?" he asks sharply, snapping up.

"What?" I say, startled.

"What did you just say?"

"I don't know," I blurt out. Oh God, please let this be over. "I lost my thought."

"Oh." He shuffles some papers, his mouth set. "We're seeing a number of people." He sticks my résumé in a folder. "Why don't you leave a number?"

I can't believe this! I wasn't making fun of you; I got caught up in the moment! "It's on my résumé," I say, trying to be cheerful. This isn't my fault, Mr. Richter. "My address is in there, too." I point to the folder.

He doesn't even look down. He nods, looks me straight in the eye. For the first time in the past hour, he's fully awake. "We'll call you," he says.

"Sounds like sleep apnea," my mother suggests when I tell her about the interview. "You don't want to deal with that every day."

"But I mumbled out loud! Right along with him! Right to his face!"

"Frannie, it wasn't meant to be." Then she tells me that Carol, her assistant, is leaving for her honeymoon. "Why don't you fill in for a few days?" she asks. "I don't mind if you look for a job as long as you don't tie up the phones."

"But I wanted *that* job, Mom. I want a *real* job."

"You'll find a real job. And in the meantime, you can work for me. It's only for a few weeks. Besides, if you're serious about finding a *real* job, you have to get up before two." She smiles slyly. "You can get up when I get up—at seven-thirty."

I groan.

Two days later, I'm wearing Carol's maroon On-Target jacket, looking at a receipt from Dr. Wallace B. Frank, a marriage counselor. I found the receipt tucked away in a file marked *Personal.* Apparently, my mother and father went to see this guy four times last month. I know it's not a big deal, it just bothers me they didn't tell me. I want to lean forward to study it, but Carol's jacket is two sizes too small and every time I move, I'm afraid I'll split it down the back.

When I said I'd fill in for Carol, my mother said I'd have to wear a maroon jacket like everyone else in the office. I found it amusing the way she hovered over me, barking orders like a drill sergeant. It reminded me of how she planned family trips; low-calorie salad dressing bottles lined up on the kitchen counter, fat-free muffins cut up in plastic Baggies, sugar-free sucking candies stuffed into her purse. "Yes, ma'am," I saluted. The phones lit up and I stuttered, "Good morning, On-Target Realty," and accidentally disconnected someone. I looked at her sheepishly, but she wasn't amused. "I'm not joking, Frannie," she warned, "this is business."

I crumple the receipt into the pocket of my jacket. Business or not, you sure can stumble on a lot of secrets in a four-person office, especially when one of those persons is your mom.

On-Target Realty is located in Great Neck. Years ago, the owners, Mr. and Mrs. Bennet, hired my mother to be an agent/office manager. She hired Carol, a woman she met at the gym, to be a secretary, but from the looks of it, Carol also takes care of her personal life.

I really don't know how my mother makes money for the company because she never shows houses. Usually, she's on the phone with her sister and her father. But she does get paid to do something, I suppose. Two years ago she hired her hairstylist Collette to help design a company logo. Then she ordered business cards and memo pads, and had the great idea of making everyone wear maroon jackets like the gold jackets worn at Century 21. "If you look like a Fortune 500 company, you'll get paid like one," she said after she returned from a marketing seminar. Mr. Bennet finally got her to stop agreeing with everything he said by saying "Roger, J.B." and referring to the four-man company as The Firm, but the maroon jackets stayed.

"Abigail Friedman, please." I disguise my voice since I've already called Abby three times this morning. She's an associate with an entertainment law firm in New York that represents major sports figures and celebrities. When she took the job, we had visions of her hooking up with the Jets or jamming with the Stones, but so far the only famous person she's seen is the back of Dom DeLuise's head when he was sitting in a conference room.

"May I ask who's calling?" her secretary says.

"Nancy Drew."

A minute later Abby gets on the line. "Very funny," she says, laughing. "Our secretaries read, you know. And I told you not to call me until this afternoon. I'm filing a complaint which is due at noon."

"What kind of complaint? Ann Taylor sold out of the blouse

you want? Abbeee, I am *sooo* bored. Let's meet for lunch. I'll come into the city." Like my mother, I've done nothing all morning but talk on the phone. In between my personal calls, I'm making cold calls, asking people if they are thinking of selling their homes. I never should have said I'd do this.

"Right. I'll just tell Woody Allen's assistant I can't meet with him because I have to meet *you* for a turkey burger. Did I tell you that I'm finally getting my own client?"

"Who? The Beastie Boys?" She doesn't answer. "Who then?"

"I'm not telling you now."

"Fine, be a baby. At least go with me tonight to see Shelly. Abby, she keeps asking for you. She's been there a month and you've only been twice."

"I thought she was supposed to get out already. My dad keeps telling me how much he needs her. I'm sick of hearing what a great little worker she is."

I look around the office. You and me both. "She's getting used to it. I guess that means she's getting better. Look, she needs us." Twisting, I take off the jacket.

"I can't go tonight. Maybe Monday." Then for the third time today, she tries to get me to go out with one of the lawyers in her office. "Frannie, Baldwin's a nice guy."

"I refuse to go out with anyone who has a last name for a first name." I say this with hesitation because I've never turned down a date in my life. But there must be something wrong with him because even though she has a guy, Abby would never set me up with someone she'd want for herself.

"Oh please. It's his mother's maiden name. He's from Boston and his family is really rich. They were Pilgrims or on the *Mayflower* or something. What's the big deal, anyway? It's just a name. Remember when you made everyone call you Veronica?" I went through a period when I hated the name Frannie. I especially hated Francine. Veronica sounded more sexy, more intense. Sometimes, I even had my friends call me Ronnie like I was a rocker-chick in a heavy metal band.

"I have another call." I put her on hold. "On-Target, may I help you?"

"Is Marsha Hunter in?" It's a man's voice. Very deep, very sincere. "This is Daniel Reynolds returning her call."

"Well, then you must be important." I look behind me. My mother is on her knees, peering underneath the Xerox machine. "Mrs. Hunter is very busy, but I'll see if I can put you through."

"I appreciate that. And let me tell you, you're doing a fine job. Every salesman knows that the only way to the boss is to flatter her assistant. How am I doing so far?"

"Fine. But where'd you hear that? *Swimming With the Sharks?*"

"*How to Get a Job in Five Easy Steps.* This is step two."

"What's step three?"

"I don't know. I haven't read that far."

I laugh, but not as hard as he does. I imagine that he's big and burly with a sexy smile and a lock of hair curling in his eyes. I want to whisper something lascivious. *Step three is a warm bath at your place.* I settle back. The phone is the greatest invention. You can have complete relationships without worrying about the size of your thighs. "Step three is not appearing too eager," I say firmly. "Hold on." I turn in my chair. "MOM! PHONE!"

"Frannie, really. This is an office." As she sits down, she points to my jacket.

"Sorry." She's trained Carol to say "Please hold for Mizz Hunter" in a high-pitched, Girl Friday voice, but when I see her standing on a chair in the kitchenette, it's difficult for me to take our professional relationship seriously. I realize Abby is on hold. When I try to get her back, her secretary is waiting. "Ms. Friedman had another call. She'll be right with you." As I wait, I realize everyone in the world has someone to answer their phone. Except me.

Abby gets back on, rushed and important. "I gotta go. I haven't done anything all day but talk to you. I'll call you tonight. Oh, one more thing." Her voice sweetens. "Baldwin says Friday night is fine. Ciao, Veronica."

In my mother's office, Mr. Bennet is laughing at something I can't hear. It's almost time for lunch, and I want to ask them to watch the phones so I can go out for my tuna on rye, but I feel funny interrupting. I stand in the doorway and rustle some papers, but they either can't hear me or have chosen to ignore me.

My mother has several pictures on her credenza. There's one of Shelly, me, and Abby in my parents' kitchen; one of my grandparents at a wedding; one of my mom and Aunt Lillian on a cruise ship; and one of my father that I brought from home. "Where did this come from?" my mother asked when she noticed it.

"The den."

"I know where it came from. I meant, why is it here?"

"I didn't see one, so I brought it in."

"I have one of Daddy, but the frame broke." She eyed me suspiciously. I wondered if she was worried that I noticed Mr. Bennet flirting with her, his big belly poking out from his maroon jacket. He always strolls into her office and stands over her. Sometimes he doesn't say a thing; he just watches her. He chuckles at her jokes in long, drawn-out wheezes that last beats longer than any normal laugh I've ever heard. Maybe when I saw Johnny hovering over her, his belly practically lying on her desk as if it dropped from his body, it bothered me a little, especially the time he was touching the lapels of her jacket and she shifted slightly, but didn't move. He didn't know I was watching. He touched her like she wasn't wearing a jacket at all.

Mr. Bennet stands behind my mother's chair, looking over her shoulder at a spreadsheet. "Look." She gestures. "If we cut back, we can bring Daniel in. We need another agent. Meg and I can't handle it all ourselves anymore."

"I know, Marsha," he tells her, "but do we have to discuss this now? I'm hungry. Let's eat and then we'll talk about it."

"He keeps calling, and it's not fair to put him off. Just make a decision already."

"I've made a decision. We need another agent, I agree. But I don't know if it should be Daniel. Why do you like this guy so much, anyway?"

"Because he's smart and dynamic. He's a *real* salesman. We need him."

"Oh," Mr. Bennet says, sounding hurt. "A real salesman."

I clear my throat, and they both look up. "It's twelve." I point to my watch. "Tuna time."

"Frannie, will you cover the phones?" Mr. Bennet asks. "Your mother and I have a lunch meeting."

"Fine. I'll starve." My mother gives me a mean look. "I'm just kidding," I tell her. "Go meet."

I return to my desk and they spend more time in her office. I can't see what they're doing, but it takes a long time before they're ready to leave. I imagine Mr. Bennet pushing her up against the wall, rubbing his belly against her, the flap of his maroon jacket riding up, while my mother makes squeaky noises, struggling to get away. I lean back, but don't hear any signs of a problem, so I work on my résumé, debating how to change the employment history around so it doesn't appear like I can't hold down a job.

When they finally leave, Mr. Bennet keeps his hands to himself, but I can see through the glass windows that the minute he's out the door, he propels my mother to his car with his hand resting against the small of her back. They look goofy in their twin maroon jackets, and he keeps smiling up at her as she maneuvers herself into the car. She waves to me from the front seat.

I print out a copy of my résumé and study it. God, I'm such a loser. And a liar. But if I told anyone my *real* job history, there's no way anyone would hire me. I have nothing to do until my mother and Fat Boy return, so I start listing all the guys I've slept with. Not only do I have a difficult time remembering their names (not that I knew all their names to begin with), but I become panicked that I've never been tested for AIDS or herpes or hepatitis or genital warts, or any of the other diseases that make sex in the nineties such a daredevil sport. So, just for kicks, I open a new document and rewrite my résumé, describing my job history the way it *really* happened.

Francine Vanessa Hunter
739 St. James Drive   Lindsey Point, NY 11223   (516) 555–3433

Objective

Position in creative field that requires a real people-person. Job should not require individual to wear a headset.

Education

B.A., Syracuse University

Major: Getting stoned, having sex, sliding down snowy hills on cafeteria trays.
Minor: Communications

Financed 100 percent of education. Thanks to my parents' inability to save money and the Student Loan Service, I will be in debt for the rest of my fucking life.

Experience

Present   **Rascals Steakhouse, a Division of Cuisine America,** *Food Server, Lindsey Point Mall*
You don't have to be a brain surgeon to figure out what I do.

One Whole Year!   **Revlon Incorporated,** *Administrative Assistant AKA Secretary, NY, NY*
Reported to the VP of sales who traveled all the time so no one was around to monitor my phone usage. Got free makeup, tote bags, umbrellas, and T-shirts. Laid off, which sucked since the makeup made great gifts and the cafeteria lunches were killer.

Eleven Days   **Something Painful I've Blocked Out**

Four Months   **Jamaica Time Shares,** *Sales Assistant, NY, NY*
Sold time shares in St. Thomas, Jamaica, and Bermuda. Took job thinking I'd get one free. Fired for insubordination and excessive personal phone calls.

Two Months   **Tom and Susie's Pet-O-Rama,** *Sales Assistant, Lindsey Point Mall*
Thought it might be fun. Liked it for about an hour. Forgot to lock the cages and the animals escaped. Let out an expensive parakeet, which was found stuck in an air conditioning vent. Bloody pieces of bird pulp got caught in the ridges of the vent, feathers were everywhere. "Your heart's not in it," Susie said when she gave me my last paycheck. "Think of it this way, Frannie. Most of us are on AM. You, my dear, are on FM." I took my check and thanked her. "Who needs therapy?" I told her, using the check to wave goodbye. "I'll just readjust my frequency."

One Excruciating Year   **Nine West Shoe Stores,** *Sales Assistant, Lindsey Point Mall*
Nothing more need be said.

Seven Months   **WPGN Radio,** *Sales Assistant, Brooklyn, NY*
Sold radio time for a small station. Commute sucked. I quit, thinking I had experience and would find something better. I was wrong (see above).

Six months   **Wayne & Malice Public Relations,** *Trafficking Assistant, NY, NY*
Responsible for trafficking ads through art and marketing departments. Sounded like a much better job in the paper. Worked on an American Express campaign that involved pictures of real people using their AMEX card in restaurants all over the world. Accidentally added the client's only set of negatives to another client's courier package which was sent to a remote island in Japan. I was "let go."

"Abigail Friedman, please. It's Sandra Day O'Connor."

As I wait for Abby to pick up, a man strolls into the office. He's tan and handsome, in the silver-templed, older-man way I'm beginning to like. I smile and hold up a finger.

"I'm here to see Marsha Hunter." He rests his hands on my desk and leans forward. "I'm Daniel Reynolds and you must be Marsha's assistant." He smiles when I nod. "You're as pretty as your voice."

Maybe it's the suit, but there's something sexy about this guy. He's the kind of guy—man I guess—whom I wouldn't normally notice since my taste leans toward twenty-six-years-olds wearing baseball caps high-fiving each other around a keg. But look at me now, all flushed and moon-faced at the sight of his double-breasted navy suit and perfectly polished loafers.

Abby's suddenly blathering in my ear. "*Stop* calling me. I'm a lawyer for Christ's sake. Just because you don't have a goddamn thing to do …"

"Gotta go, Abigail. Destiny's calling. I'll get back to you." I hang up and look at Daniel.

"Step four," he says. "Never show up empty-handed." He opens his briefcase and takes out a sunflower. Red-faced, I feel girlish and silly and can't stop smiling. I wish I could run my finger through his layered hair, which, though thinning, curls boyishly at his collar.

"Thanks," I say. "I'll put this in something." I smooth my skirt, which suddenly feels tight in the behind, stick the flower in a can of Diet Coke, and put it on my desk. "Ms. Hunter is out. But you can wait in her office." I try to sound professional because I know my mother would kill me if I flirted with the man she's trying to hire. It's the least I can do for her. If this Daniel is hired, it might keep Mr. Bennet off her back.

"I think I'll just sit here and enjoy the sunlight." He glances at me. "And the view."

I fumble for a witty retort, but I'm stumped. I stare at my computer. The silence between us is so intimate, it's impossible to move. When I look up, Daniel is rummaging through his briefcase. "They sure have you slaving away," he says.

"Not really. It's not that busy. I mean, we're always busy, but today just seems to be slow. Probably because it's so beautiful out."

The perfect day to have a picnic in the park—just you, me, and my pretty voice. "Why don't you wait in Marsha's office?"

"Sure." He waves. "Put me any place you'd like." Daniel walks into my mother's office and looks around. I admire the lightness of his step. It's particularly appealing when I compare his walk to Mr. Bennet's waddle. "Can I get you anything?" I ask, standing in the doorway.

He shakes his head, looking not at me, but at the picture of my father. "Nice-looking man." He pushes the frame with his pointer finger. I suddenly notice his wedding ring. I guess I didn't see it before, or maybe I wasn't looking for it. But seeing it startles me. From the way he acts, you'd think he'd have the foresight to hide it. As he bends to look at the picture of my dad, I notice a donut of scalp where hair should be. Forget you, Mr. Flirtatious Married Man. I'd rather have a single twenty-six-year-old, blinded by tequila shots, dancing in his wet socks, over you anytime.

He's still pointing at my father. "Mr. Hunter?" he asks. As I nod, he glances at the picture of my mother and aunt. "You know, I always forget just how good-looking Marsha is." He sits in my mother's chair and plays with a paperweight.

I don't like Daniel Reynolds's pretty face anymore, or his trim body, or his wedding-banded finger, which sticks out like an erection. And I certainly don't like the way he touches my mother's things. "She's very pretty," I tell him. "And happily married."

"Almost as pretty as you." He points to the picture of me. "That's you?"

"Uh huh. I'm Veronica." I shake my hair. "But everyone calls me Frannie."

"Oh." Daniel pales slightly beneath his tan. He also loses his toothy smile, but it quickly reappears, as if he merely blinked. "I thought you were Carol. I never met her in person."

"Who brought the flower?" I hear my mother's voice as she walks through the office. Mr. Bennet shuffles behind her, holding his maroon jacket.

"Hi, Mom. I'm in here with Daniel Reynolds."

"I brought you tuna, Frannie. With low-fat mayonnaise." She smiles at Daniel.

"Thanks, but I'm not hungry."

"An hour ago you were starving." I take the sandwich and try to leave the office, but Mr. Bennet is blocking the doorway and I can't get through.

"I brought the flowers for Frannie thinking she was Carol. I didn't realize she left already for her honeymoon." Daniel gets up from my mother's chair and shakes her hand.

"So you've met?" my mother says. She glances at me, narrowing her eyes. I bet she's worried that I told Daniel about how Mr. Bennet flirts with her. Don't worry, Mom, I say telepathically. I won't give away your secrets. Besides—I watch Daniel pump Mr. Bennet's hand—I think we have bigger fish to fry. "Yes," I tell her. "Daniel was admiring your family album."

"I was just remarking on how good-looking your daughters are. And you, of course," Daniel says, not looking at my mother, but at the picture of my father who is still staring into the room, eagle-eyed and trusting, his smile unwavering.

"Thank you." My mother stares at Daniel, her cheeks flushed. "I have a great plastic surgeon." My mother never focuses on any-one when she talks to them, so to see her gazing at him, her eyes filmy and soft, is really unsettling. I want to knock her with my elbow so she'll blink. For a second, I wonder if she's zonked, but she never takes Valium during business hours. She keeps smiling, and when Daniel says that she can't be serious, she laughs. Actually, it's not a laugh, it's a giggle, in a voice that's high-pitched and whiny. I know the giggle, but it's not my mother's. It's the giggle of a high school girl who is talking to a boy she likes, her voice strained and artificial like a guitar string being pulled too tight.

Suddenly uncomfortable, I take the deli bag and edge past Mr. Bennet, who, like Daniel, is staring at the picture of my father. Suddenly my mother is all business. She shoos Mr. Bennet out, claiming she has a million things to discuss with Daniel and closes the door.

Mr. Bennet and I stand outside her office and he shuffles his feet, looking lost and forlorn. For a second, I worry he's going to start scratching at the door. He puts on his jacket, and sucks in his stomach to close the gold buttons. Through the closed door, I can hear Daniel and my mother laughing. "Well, back to business," I say. I hold up the bag. "Tuna, Mr. Bennet?"

I don't want to say anything to anyone about Daniel until I know for sure. The last thing Shelly needs to deal with is the possibility of our mother's mid-life crush. So the next time we visit her, I try to keep everything light. My sister doesn't look much better, but her mood is improved. We sit on the roof in plastic folding chairs, staring at the view of New York, and marveling at the sunset. We even have a few laughs about Mr. Bennet's flirting when my mother goes to the bathroom. "No way," Shelly says, smoking. "And Mommy flirts back?"

I shake my head. "No, I think she's aware of how pitiful he is."

"What about this new guy?"

"What new guy?" I busy myself by lighting a cigarette.

"Abby said you told her Mommy hired a really handsome guy."

"When did you speak to Abby?"

"She stopped by yesterday afternoon. What? Why are you looking at me so funny?"

I can't stop staring at Shelly. Every time I see her, it freaks me out that this is my sister. It's not just that she's skinny. Everything about her is shrunken. Her lips are shriveled as though she's aged ten years, and her skin, which was so creamy and clear, now has the texture of parchment paper. "I'm not looking at you, Shelly," I say. "Stop being so paranoid."

Shelly fidgets in her seat, holding her hands in her lap and cracking her knuckles until the sound gets to me and I ask her to stop. Around us, mothers and daughters sit together, talking quietly. There's a girl crying and a nurse is hovering over her, holding a tissue. I want to tell Shelly my fears about Daniel, how he *is* handsome, but in a sleazy way, and how, when Mommy looks at him, she gets all girlish and stupid in a way she never is with Daddy, and it scares the hell out of me. But when I see my sister hunched over, her bony shoulders sagging like she doesn't have the strength to hold herself up, I can't bring myself to say anything. Besides, for all I know, the tension between my mother and Daniel is something I made up to enhance my own loveless life.

"Hey, Shelly, did you know that Mommy and Daddy went to a marriage counselor?"

"Uh huh. They've been going for about a year. I helped them do their taxes and saw all the receipts."

A year? An entire fucking year? "Huh. How 'bout that? I didn't know you did their taxes. Do they make a lot of money?"

She shakes her head. "Don't tell Mommy I told you, but they have a lot of debt. The last time Daddy lost his job, they went through their savings. They're doing okay now, but they're still paying off their credit cards and they spend everything they make. I hate thinking about it."

"No one tells me anything!" I say just as my mother joins us. I grind out my cigarette with my toe, then lean forward to check that it's out.

"That's because you can't keep a secret," my mother says, smiling. "It's beautiful out tonight, isn't it?" She turns to Shelly. "Is it supposed to rain tomorrow?"

"How the hell is she supposed to know?" I cut in.

Shelly shrugs. "Mom, have you asked Johnny about calling his nephew for the Harvard recommendation?" She glances at me, but I'm looking at my mother.

I can't keep a secret. Is that so? Who found the picture of Daddy facedown in your desk drawer and didn't say a word? Who? Around me, the sound of the anorexic girl's crying fills the air like fog.

"This is delicious." In the supermarket an hour later, my mother chews a sample of honey-roasted turkey breast. The teenage boy behind the counter is wearing a white butcher's coat covered with multicolored buttons. "Don't you think, Frannie?"

I lean forward, trying to read the guy's buttons. One is hand-made and half-hidden under his lapel. I read it and burst out laughing. WE CHALLENGE YOU TO BEAT OUR MEAT is scrawled in Magic Marker.

"What's so funny?" My mother squints. "Tell me, I could use a laugh."

"Nothing." I turn away. "You wouldn't get it."

"Fine." She looks at the boy. "Can I have another sample please? For my daughter?" The boy slices another piece of turkey. When I look up, he winks at me. "Frannie, here, he cut you some turkey." She nudges me with the cart.

"Mom, I don't want any turkey." I try to move away, but she shoves her hand under my nose. "Come on, Frannie. You love turkey." I start to laugh again. "Frannie, tell me. What's so funny? Are you making fun of me?" She peers over her huge sunglasses, which keep slipping off her nose, and lightly touches her face. Ever since the facelift, she's gotten into the habit of pushing her cheeks up, and holding them as if her face is made of clay and she can mold it with her fingertips. "I told your father we'd pick up some things for dinner. Tonight, it's chicken marsala." She rolls her eyes, but smiles. "Daddy's a strange bird, isn't he?"

"I think he's sweet." My mother shrugs and turns to the boy. "Mom, come on. The last thing you need is another piece of turkey."

She waves. "Okay, take me away. That turkey just *sings* to me." She looks at me, but I'm smiling at the butcher boy. "You're flirting, aren't you? Is that what it is?" I shake my head. "Daddy said we needed some basil. Where's the basil in this place?"

"Am I wearing a name tag?"

"I'm just asking. You don't have to get all huffy, especially after making fun of me."

"I wasn't making fun of you and I wasn't flirting. Certainly not the way Mr. Bennet flirts with you. And," I add slyly, "the way you flirt with Daniel."

"What is that supposed to mean? I'd hardly call my relationship with Daniel flirtatious." She tugs on her zipper. "Damn this thing." Then she insists that Daniel is a professional, just a friendly guy who's teaching her the art of selling. Besides, she says, he's ten years younger. And married.

"Whatever, Mom. What Ever. I just don't trust him. I think he likes you." I smile, adding, "And I don't mean *professionally*." She laughs slightly, but I can tell she's getting annoyed. That slight little laugh always comes right before an outburst of anger, so I try to lighten the conversation. "Trust me, Mom. I know men. Just remember that you're a very attractive woman for your age. I see the way guys look at you."

"Frannie, please. Your father and I have been married for thirty years. Can we change the subject now?"

"But you've been seeing a marriage counselor, right?"

She stares at me. "How do you know about that?"

"I found the receipts and Shelly confirmed it. Why didn't you tell me?"

"It's not something I felt you needed to know."

"You told Shelly."

"You know, Frannie, there are some things that people like to keep private. Besides, it came up in the context of another conversation. Sometimes you are just like my sister. You have to know *everything*. Aunt Lillian would drive Grandma crazy with all her questions." She eyes a Zucchini Lasagna Lean Cuisine. "I wish your father wasn't so caught up in this cooking thing." She examines the calorie content. "I like TV dinners."

I hold up a carton of fudge ripple ice cream. I almost throw it in the cart but catch myself, thinking of my sister's legs. I feel my own thigh, imagining cellulite packed on like cottage cheese, then exchange the ice cream for yogurt. "If Grandma was alive, would you tell her about Shelly?"

My mother shrugs. "I would probably want to, but I don't think she would understand. She hated it when I dieted. She always said that I was starving myself." She sighs. "She should only know from starving." She smooths my hair away from my face. "I wish you pulled your hair back. It hides your pretty face." She laughs self-consciously. "Grandma always said the same thing to me."

"You do have a pretty face." I smile. "You're also in great shape and smart and have two men after you. Three if you count Daddy." She tells me to stop. "But it's true. Admit it. Daniel flirts with you. And it's obvious you find him attractive, too. There's nothing wrong with finding another man handsome. It's not like you're leaving Daddy or anything, right?"

She whirls around. "Frannie, SHUT UP! I DON'T have to defend myself to you! JESUS H. CHRIST!"

Neither of us moves for a long time. Finally I tell her I'm sorry. "I am, Mom," I say sincerely. But she won't talk to me. "Come on, Mom. I was an asshole. I'll tell you what I was laughing at before."

"When you were flirting with the boy?"

"I wasn't flirting! I was laughing. The kid behind the counter is wearing a button that says WE CHALLENGE YOU TO BEAT OUR MEAT." She looks at me blankly. "I told you you wouldn't get it. Anyway, Mom, you *must* lighten up. Here." I reach into the freezer and pull out the ice cream. "This will make you feel better."

She laughs. "It's going to take more than food to make me feel better these days. More then men, too," she adds. But she tosses the carton into the cart. "What the hell, Frannie. We have the rest of our lives to worry about our weight."

"And you're married, I'm the one who's desperate." I pull out another carton. "We should eat both of these. Fuck all the men in the world." I laugh. "I mean, who cares about men? Grandma was right—we should eat what we want and *be happy*."

My mother looks pained. "What's wrong?" I ask. "Are you thinking about Grandma?"

She shakes her head sadly. "No." She rolls forward. "I'm thinking about Shelly."

I huddle against the pay phone. "You die," I say the second Abby picks up.

"What's wrong? Where's Baldwin?"

"He's at the table. How could you do this? You're supposed to be my best friend."

"What are you talking about?"

"This guy's an asshole. He showed up stinking DRUNK without any CASH. I'm paying for drinks and probably dinner. You're supposed to bring money when you take a girl out. Don't they teach you anything in law school?"

"Baldwin wouldn't do that. He has pictures of his parents on his desk. You have to believe me. I would never set you up with a loser."

"What about Michael Previs?"

"Frannie, that was in the tenth grade." She tells me to go back to the table, that she'll pay for dinner. I don't say anything. "Okay," she says. "And a new outfit. Just go back and be nice. Make believe nothing's wrong."

The story of my life, I think, steeling myself. I will act like a lady. Maybe I came on too strong. I'll calm down, I'll act normal. But as I approach the table, I see that it doesn't matter how I act. My date, who comes from such a cultured family as to be endowed with a last name for a first name, has passed out, facedown, in his salad.

When I get home, I expect to see my father on the couch, but the den is dark. I grab an apple, and I'm about to pick up the phone to yell at Abby again, when I hear someone in my dad's office. Quietly, I stand in the doorway.

"She knows." I hear my mother's breathy whisper. "Frannie knows. You have to stop." Through the crack, I see her sitting in a short nightgown, cross-legged on the floor with the phone nestled in her shoulder. Her head is bent and her hair hangs like a curtain. She looks up. I jerk back. My heart jumps, positive she saw my shadow. But then there's a drawn-out "Yes" and I relax.

"I know," I hear her say. "Me, too." Then she laughs in that whiny giggle that makes me hate her. "But Frannie's here ... until she finds a job, I guess. Then I don't know." I lean forward again. "I feel the same way. I told you that."

Her face glows in the moonlight as she fingers a lock of hair. For a second, she looks like a teenager. "No," she says. "No, that's not possible." She sounds so happy. This is so unfair. How can she do this to me? "I was with Shelly. I tried to call you from the hospital—twice—but you didn't pick up. I felt funny leaving a message."

My mind races. Does Shelly know? She'd never talk to Shelly about this, would she? She murmurs, so I move as close as I dare.

"In an ideal world, that could happen. But what am I supposed to do about Frannie? Throw her out on the street? I don't think she is capable of taking care of herself. She's ..."

DON'T SAY THAT! I can so. I've only been here two months. I practically just *moved in*. I open my mouth as wide as I can and bite into the apple. I chew loudly and belligerently, smacking my lips like a cow.

"Who's there?" she hisses. Then I hear a whisper and the sound of the phone being gently hung up.

*   *   *

In the kitchen, I hike myself on the counter. Covering her breasts with her arm, my mother walks quickly to the refrigerator. She stands with her back to me, gulps juice from the carton, and swallows a Valium. Peeking out from her nightgown, her underwear hangs like a diaper.

I reach into the cabinet. "Glass?"

She shakes her head and I want to smack her. I can't imagine what any man could see in her. Her legs are soft and rippled with cellulite, her stomach is distended behind her sheer gown, and her breasts sag like cones. I hop off the counter and arch my back, making sure she can see the entirety of my body through my gauzy dress; the muscles in my legs, the way my breasts stand out like small, perky headlights. She glances at me and stiffens.

"Who was that on the phone?" I ask.

"Grandpa. He can't sleep. Just lonely, I guess." She takes another drink of juice. "How was your date?"

I shrug. "He's really rich. His family was on the *Mayflower.* He wants to marry me, but I don't know. It seems a little soon." My head pounds. I take a deep breath and count the tiles above the stove. My mother studies me in the warm kitchen light. As she watches me, I feel powerful. "I hope ..." I say slowly. Her brown eyes dart around the room, flirting, it seems, with telling me. "... that Grandpa feels better. Maybe we should plan a trip to Florida."

She nods, relieved. "That's a good idea. We should go on a trip. You can invite your new boyfriend." She walks out of the kitchen and snaps off the light, leaving me alone in the dark.

"I'm moving out, Mom. As soon as I find a job."

"It's okay, Frannie," she says from the next room. "Having you around makes me feel young." She giggles and utters a self-conscious "Oh," covering her mouth as if she burped. She hides a smile behind her hand, which infuriates me. She's not supposed to be this way! She's supposed to be guilty and nervous and begging me not to tell anyone!

"Hey, Mom!" I call sharply. "Next time you get the urge to talk on the phone in the middle of the night, especially when I'm here, don't, okay?"

"This is *my* house." She inches up the stairs. "I'll speak to whomever I want. Maybe you shouldn't be sneaking around, listening to my calls."

Maybe, Mom, but I live here too, and it will take a crane to get me out now. You, as they say, have just made your bed.

5

My *father has a novelty sign Velcroed to the dashboard of his* precious Mercedes. The sign has a picture of a frog flat on its back. Kermit's head is hidden in a puff of smoke and the words *I'll croak if you smoke* are across the top. Every time I flick my ash, my hand knocks the sign. By the time I finish my cigarette, the sign is on the floor.

I look at my watch. Even though I'm late, I drive slowly and smoke another cigarette. I hate maneuvering this big boat, but I needed cash when I moved home so I sold my Honda Civic. Shelly's car is available, but it doesn't have air conditioning and it's so humid outside, it feels like we live in Vietnam.

By the time I reach Rascals, I'm all agitated. Every time I get here, I feel like a Waffle House woman, white-haired and road-hard with leathery skin and grapefruit calves. It is my destiny, I'm afraid, after four years of high school and four more of college, to work the graveyard shift, wear thick-ribbed support hose, and flirt with the fry chef.

"You're late," Paulie says as I rush past him.

"I know. I'm sorry. My sister's in the hospital. She just had a baby." I smile sheepishly at him. Even though he's good-looking, tall, with black hair and olive skin, I can't take him seriously because he believes all my lies and always lets me slide. I wonder if that's why he never made it in the real world. Maybe no one else takes him seriously either.

"Frannie, you don't even have your uniform on."

"I just got it from the cleaner's." I rush into the ladies' room and pull my crumpled uniform from my gym bag. I put on black pants and a white shirt and my duck apron with its strings that hang behind me like a tail. They should tell you in college that even if you get A's, even if you take classes like "Deconstructing Mass Communications: Survival on the Information Highway," you're still going to ask "You want fries with that?" when you get out.

I pull my knotted tie over my head, throw some pens in my apron, and console myself that I don't have to work at Limited Express, or worse, dishing out frozen yogurt, places often frequented by people I know. When I see people from high school eating dinner off the Happy Hour buffet, I always steer clear of the area. The last thing I need is to witness a Lindsey High reunion while I'm trotting by with a tray of nachos.

The dinner shift is in full swing by the time I make it to my first table. I breeze past Paulie and pick up a handful of checks from the hostess stand. "Frannie," the hostess says, looking at my name tag. "I mean Wanda. The people at table two have been waiting for a while."

I grab four menus. "Why didn't someone else pick them up?"

"They look like big tippers. We saved them for you."

"Thanks. I appreciate it." I whip through the dining room, side-stepping a busboy carrying a tray of soup bowls. I take the order and walk into the waitress station. As I key in my server number, I feel someone brush his cheek against my hair.

"You're late," Artie says, nuzzling my neck. "I missed you at line-up. Paulie said if you were late one more time, he'd fire you. Did you see Shelly today?"

I nod. Bile rises in my throat as I feel his warm breath on my ear. I met Artie when I started working at Rascals. Like me, he's looking for a real job and waiting tables at night to pay his bills. He had a really good job once in real estate, but was fired when he made a pass at a client's wife. He claims she wanted him to, but I'm

not so sure. He's always rubbing against me, tickling my back, trying to give me neck massages. I can't stand it when he touches me.
He's got spindly arms, skinny chicken legs, and bloodshot eyes
because he's allergic to contact lens solution but too vain to wear
glasses.

I nudge him away. "Shelly's fine. I'll tell you about it later." He
lifts my hair with his hand and traces my ear with his finger. I feel
my skin itch, but I'm paralyzed. He is so sleazy and I am so stupid.
I never should have slept with him.

"Frannie," someone calls. "The hostess just double-seated you. Do
you want me to pick up one of your tables?"

"No, thanks." I grab a tray. "I'll get both. I need the money." I
walk quickly through the restaurant. As I approach the table, I smile
and introduce myself.

"I'll have the Captain's Salad with vinaigrette dressing on the
side," the woman tells me, pointing at the menu. She speaks loud
and slowly, as if I'm a foreigner. "Is your chicken fresh?"

I nod. "Yes," I lie.

"Okay, I'll have that, but I don't want any water chestnuts.
Actually, forget that. I'll just have the dinner salad." She looks up.
"Can you throw some chicken in that?"

"It'll be $1.50 extra."

"I don't care. Whatever it is."

The man orders the fish. "Can you broil it with no butter? I
can't have any oil. I'm on a low-cholesterol diet." I'm your waitress,
I tell him silently, *not* your nutritionist. "And can I have rice instead
of potatoes?"

Shit, another special order. "We're out of fish." I smile. "How
about roast chicken?"

He looks up. "Chicken's okay. Can you skin it?" Can I do *what*?
I snarl at him.

"Oh, that sounds good," the woman says. "I need another
minute."

"Marlene, I'm hungry. Just eat the damn salad." He's right,
Marlene. I don't have time for this. Eat the fucking salad.

Marlene smiles. "I guess I'll have the dinner salad. But please throw some chicken in. You haven't forgotten the chicken, have you?"

Yes, I forgot the chicken you mentioned two seconds ago. I'm actually retarded, lady. They hired me only because of affirmative action. I look at her and blink. "What chicken?"

I've *got* to get a real job. At least tonight I can look forward to meeting Abby for a drink. She's staying at her parents' house and we're getting up early to see Shelly. I haven't told Abby about my mother's affair. Not that Abby's in any position to judge. She's been sleeping with a married man for three months, although she's also a compulsive liar, so I'm not sure exactly when it started.

Someone tugs on my apron. I smell Artie's aftershave and whirl around. "Can you take these waters to table six?" he asks, spewing saliva. His face is flushed and he's sweating like a beast. "I'm in the weeds, Frannie," he begs. "Please?"

I grab the waters and watch him rush away. He is so pathetic. The time I fucked him, I woke up with a vicious hangover. My tongue felt like it was covered in a sock. That was one margarita too many. Not to mention the Valium I had as an appetizer. Miserable, I was really quiet, and he kept asking what was wrong. I didn't think fast enough and told him about Shelly. Now he asks about her all the time, like he's a member of my friends and family calling circle.

What I really want is a guy who puts on a suit, not a name tag and an apron when he dresses for work. Is that so much to ask? Artie wouldn't be so bad, but he whines all the time, and smacks his lips really loud when he eats. He should meet my dad. They could form a band.

When I walk into the dining room, I stop short. One of my tables is filled with girls I knew in high school. "Frannie!" Melanie, the fattest one, screams my name, the way she'd yell "Go, Lindsey!" during football games, her ass, not so fat then, in a red and white cheerleader's skirt. "How *are* you?" Her eyes glisten from too many martinis. Melanie is a short girl with frizzy hair that hangs around her face like a weeping willow. In high school, Abby and I called her The Troll. "What are you *doing* here?" I look at her stuffed into a bright red suit, a fat ripe tomato on toothpicks, and wish I could throw a glass of wine in her lap.

I look around. "I'm starting law school in the fall. I was gonna go to Israel and Egypt this summer, but you know, it's not the best time to travel." I smile. "And you?" *Still on probation at Weight Watchers?*

Melanie sips her wine, her little finger crooked like a small, pink worm. "I'm working for MTV. In publicity. I love it." She squints. "Who's Wanda?"

"I'm just filling in for someone."

Melanie turns to her friends. "Frannie and I went to high school together. She and her best friend almost got thrown out for getting stoned in the bathroom. How is Abby, by the way?"

"She just made partner at her law firm. And she's dating the drummer from R.E.M. You should know him, right? Since you work for MTV? Everyone's great." I start to walk away, but Melanie asks me to have a drink with her when I'm done.

"Sounds grand." I adjust my apron, and try to wipe a smudge of ketchup off the duck's beak. "Well, good to see you." I turn away. "Call me if you need any legal advice."

Back in the kitchen, I stand over the garbage can and with my fingers eat leftover Caesar salad from a customer's plate. *I work for MTV. I love it.* Stupid, fucking cheerleader.

One of the waiters calls into the kitchen. "There's a table out here that's really pissed off. The lady says she's been looking for her waitress for ten minutes."

Paulie looks up. "Which waitress?"

"Wanda."

I hear them talking, but I don't look up. I gulp Diet Coke from the soda fountain. When I turn around, Paulie's standing right next to me. Startled, I almost drop my glass. "Wanda? You're Wanda tonight, aren't you? We'd all like to sit around and drink sodas, but YOU HAVE TABLES WAITING!"

"I'm coming, Paulie. Give me a minute here." I smile. "Don't get all crazy, Paulie. Stress is really bad for your heart."

"Frannie, don't do this to me. You have customers waiting for their food." Paulie points to the pass-out bar where plates of food sit, congealing under the heat lamps that don't work. "Get this shit out of here."

"I'm coming. Why are you so anxious? You remind me of my mother." I grab the plates and flinch as I burn my hand. "Shit, shit, shit. Since when do these work?" I reach for a napkin, stack the plates on my arm, and rush out of the kitchen.

"Hey, Artie," I yell, "there's a girl on table seven who says she wants to meet you. I went to high school with her. She's wearing a red suit. Sort of Rubenesque. She's been eyeing you all night. Go say something to her, but don't tell her I told you."

The first thing Abby tells me at O'Reilly's is that she doesn't want to stay out late because she's having breakfast with her boyfriend Everett at her apartment in the city.

"You were supposed to drive me to see Shelly. I don't have a car."

"I'm sorry, Frannie. I want to see Shelly, too, but I made a commitment."

"Abby, I can't believe you. Sometimes you are so fucking selfish." I stare at her in the bar light. Even though I've known her forever, I'm always amazed by how pretty she is. She has chocolate-brown eyes, thick auburn hair, flawless skin, and a shelf of round, firm breasts that she accentuates with tight blouses. She also has very white teeth that make her look like a girl-next-door Playboy Bunny, and she's perfected this smile where she bites on her bottom lip as if to say "Oh? You want to fuck me, too?"

"Look, I'll have breakfast with Everett then come get you out here. I won't be late. I promise." She signals for the bartender. Although she hikes herself up to make sure he gets a gander at her chest, she'll huff in indignation if he says anything. "Guys have no idea how heavy these are," she whines in mock disgust, cradling her breasts delicately as if they are eggs. I look down at my underdeveloped chest. "You've certainly been dealt a hard deck, Abby."

I've known Abby since the third grade, before she had any breasts to speak of. In the sixth grade, when a Slam Book went around and someone wrote, "Steals, lies, and talks behind everyone's back" about her, I scratched it out and wrote, "Plans to be the first woman president. Best place to sleep over." Then in the seventh grade, I got my period in P.E. and accidentally left a stained wad of toilet paper on a bench. When I got back from my shower, a bunch of girls were pointing at it and laughing. Abby picked it up and said it was hers. We've been best friends ever since.

She hands me a margarita and sips her own, looking around at what's available. Lindsey Point doesn't have much of a singles' scene, since most people out here are married. But this is where Abby met Everett so she considers it a good-luck place.

"Do these pants make my ass look fat?" she asks, whirling around.

"No," I say dryly. "Your ass looks fat without the pants."

"Thanks for the ringing endorsement," she says, laughing. Abby knows she has a powerhouse body. She works out every day. She's even left work at four-thirty to ensure herself a spot in aerobics, God forbid she should miss an hour of grapevining and step-kicking. "I'm serious. Do I look fat? I couldn't find anything to wear. All I have are suits."

I roll my eyes. She always manages to remind me that she's a lawyer, and I'm a nothing. "Abby, please. Stop fishing."

A guy swivels around on his bar stool and makes believe he's looking at the door, but I can feel him trying to look at us. I stare at him, then turn away, and in that three-second interval, I can tell he's not our type. It's a skill I perfected in college. Some people learn to speak Mandarin Chinese, I developed a radar for men. Who's to say what's more important?

The guy bends over like he's dropped something. When he sits up, he's facing us. "You girls sound like sisters."

Not knowing who he's after, Abby and I ignore him. I ask her if she wants another drink, but she shakes her head. "I'll buy," the guy chimes in. "I'm Pat, by the way."

Abby looks up. "Okay, Pat by the way. Two margaritas and a round of shots." She smirks at me. "Tequila, Señorita Frannita?" I shrug.

"Two margaritas and two shots coming up," Pat says. "Hey," he asks Abby, "has anyone ever told you that you look like Demi Moore?"

"I *am* Demi Moore," she says and lights a cigarette as Pat turns to pay for the drinks. Sometimes I get jealous when guys crawl all over her. But I admit that I get attention, too. Especially when I'm in a dark bar at one-thirty in the morning. The argument exists that at one-thirty in the morning, any girl, even a 350-pound transvestite, is attractive to men, but I have to go with what works for me.

We suck down our shots, thank Pat, and move farther down the bar.

"Pat by the way is annoyed," Abby whispers.

"I know." I sip my drink and stare at him over the top of the glass.

"He's just so cheesy." Abby rolls her eyes. "Demi Moore. Right. I mean, I hardly look like Demi Moore. Although we do have the same coloring. Do you think I look like her? I mean, just in the face." She glances at me. "Frannie, I'm talking to you."

"I feel sorry for him. He doesn't look so bad. I mean, he's kinda cute."

"Oh please. He's a Rat Boy." She pushes me slightly. "But go … go talk to him."

"He is not!" Rat Boy was a guy I slept with in college who treated me like shit. At first, we used the term *Rat Boy* to describe any guy who blew us off, but over the years, it morphed into a reference to a guy who's so undesirable, we wouldn't even consider talking to him. "Besides," I add, "he said *you* looked like Demi Moore, not me."

"Do you think he cares who he gets? It's two in the morning."

"Forget it, okay?" I rest my foot on the ledge of the bar so my leg will look as thin as possible. Abby leaves me to go to the ladies' room—translation: to check out the talent in the rear—and I shake my hair, lick the rim of my glass, and gather my confidence by counting my blessings.

Blessing 1: I don't have to pay rent, electric, or phone bills.
Counter-argument: I am a grown woman living with my parents and I spend so much money on drinks and going-out clothes, I couldn't pay rent even if I wanted to.
Blessing 2: I sleep as late as I want and I don't have to wear pantyhose every day.
Counter-argument: I walk around my "office" wearing an apron with an embroidered duck on the bib. My biggest mental challenge is making change out of $50 for a $17.89 bill, and my biggest ethi-

cal debate is whether to give the old woman on table eleven caffeinated coffee when there's no decaf at the waitress station.

Blessing 3: I talk to my sister every day. We're really getting to know each other.

Counter-argument: Shelly lives in an insane asylum.

Blessing 4: I have a best friend who would never ever leave me.

Counter-argument: Abby is prettier, richer, and has always had more boyfriends than me. But (sub-blessing) she always pays for things. Unfortunately, she only does this because she's afraid of losing me. She never got over the terrible time she had in the tenth grade when I was the only person who liked her. But I digress.

Blessing 5: Even if I met a guy, I don't have to worry about rushing into anything sexual, ultimately dooming the relationship, because I don't have a bed big enough to have sex in.

Counter-argument: I can't meet a guy to save my life. I am going to end up a shriveled spinster who brews tea and lives with cats. I will die alone in a pool of my own urine.

"Oh my God!" Abby clutches me. "It's Melanie Henderson. The Troll lives. Look at her. She's huge!"

"She was at Rascals tonight. We've already caught up. Where were you?"

"I met some guy in front of the bathroom. He told me some bullshit story about being a record producer. He asked me to audition for his next video."

"I forgot. You're Demi Moore." I wonder: (a) if the guy said that, (b) if he was great-looking, (c) if there was a guy, and (d) if she went to the bathroom. I spot a pay phone. No guy. No video. She was checking her machine to see if Everett called.

"Shit, here comes Melanie. Hide me!" The time in the tenth grade when no one liked Abby was because Melanie caught her in a lie. Melanie was dating some guy Abby liked, so Abby told everyone Melanie had crabs, but I don't think she expected the entire cheerleading squad to turn against her. For weeks they made phonies and egged her house. And of course, I stood by her.

"Abby, you're twenty-six. Don't you think Melanie may have gotten over the crab thing?"

We watch Melanie shuffle to the bathroom, dangling her shoes in her fingers. Her blouse hangs over her skirt and her red jacket is tied around her waist like a sweatshirt. "Go, Lindsey!" Abby yells and Melanie turns briefly, but resumes her loping gait, one hand clutching her shoes, the other her stomach.

"What were you saying about crabs?" Abby asks.

"You told me that you lied about Melanie having crabs. In the tenth grade."

"I didn't say crabs. I said gonorrhea. Hey, I decided to sleep at my parents' tonight. We can get up and go right to Shelly. So stop calling me selfish."

"What about Everett?"

"I fucked up. Breakfast was Sunday ... Hey, Barguy! Two margaritas, please."

I enjoy a brief moment of satisfaction, knowing she did call her machine. "Listen," I tell her, "next time you see The Troll, make sure you say I'm going to law school. Tell her I'm going to Harvard. Oh yeah, you just made partner."

"You *told* her that?"

I shrug. "She put me on the spot. She was with Angela Whitehead."

"Her name's Blackhead, although now it's Avery. Did she look pregnant? I heard she's pregnant."

"Is she going to keep it?"

"Frannie, she's married. She can even tell her parents." Someone says something and Abby whips around, prepared to assess and conquer.

"Everyone else's lives are so much better than mine," I mutter. I'm slurring, but not too badly; not enough so I won't drive. I don't mind being drunk and driving, but I do mind being drunk and depressed, which is where I'm headed.

Abby hands me another drink. A tall guy wearing a suit lifts his glass in greeting. Abby raises her own drink and grins. "That guy is hot."

"So go over there." I have caught the eye of a guy who isn't wearing a suit, but who is really big, like a football player. "It's not like Everett would care," I continue. "God, that guy is cute."

"Of course he'd care, Frannie. Everett loves me." She giggles. Abby is pretty drunk, too, although unlike me, she's a happy drunk. I watch as my frat boy gets up and leaves. Feeling rejected, I suddenly wish I were home in my bed. Suit guy keeps staring at Abby. Occasionally she looks up and bites her lip.

"You're on my fucking foot, Abby!" I blurt out.

"Sorry." She giggles again. "I'm sorry. Can you drive?" she slurs, her elbow slipping off the bar. "Or should I?" She points at me. "Friends don't let friends drive drunk."

"I can drive fine." I look at her face, but it blurs. "I just want to go home." A tear slips out of my eye.

"Come on, Frannie. Just stay." She drapes an arm across my shoulder. "You're my best friend in the whole world and I have to tell you that that guy is so handsome, I'd fuck him on the pool table right now, balls and all." She laughs hysterically.

I see Melanie swaying next to the jukebox, although the music has stopped. "So go." I push her. "Go get him. Or else The Troll will." I take out my keys. "I'm leaving."

She squints at Melanie. "I'm just kidding, Frannie. I would never cheat on Everett."

Hit with a wave of nausea, I feel the room spin. No more bars. No more no more. Why can't I meet someone who loves me? In movies, girls always have two guys to choose between. I can't even find a drunk guy to throw myself at. I hate my life. I hate every fucking thing about it. I wish I were dead. Wiping my eyes, I growl at Abby, who is completely unaware that I am openly crying. "Give me a break, Abby. You know you're gonna cheat on Everett eventually."

"Yeah, when monkeys fly out of my butt." Abby howls. As suit guy walks toward us, she shakes her hair and runs her tongue along her lips.

I watch her, my eyes burning from mascara. "Monkeys," I mutter, "start your engines."

6

I hold ice against my head and suck on a cube to make the rancid taste of margarita go away. My father slurps his coffee, making loud sucking noises like he's on a respirator. "Daddy, please. Can't you just sip it? Where's Mommy?"

"I don't know. She didn't check in with me." His tone is clipped. I wonder if he found out about Daniel.

"So how is Mommy?" I ask slyly. He grunts. My stomach gurgles and I swallow hard. I shouldn't have had that third drink last night. Or the Valium. Or the sausage biscuit. "Daddy, are you mad at me?"

"I would appreciate it, Frannie," he says, putting down a toast square, "if you didn't smoke in my car. I use that car for business. Do I eat in your bed?" He says this as if I use my bed for business which, to some extent, is true.

"I'm sorry, Daddy. But just so you know, it wasn't me. It was Abby. I'm sorry on her behalf." My head throbs. I wonder if I gave myself brain damage. "Hey, Daddy, come with me to see Shelly." He gets up and moves into the den. I follow him in. He flicks on the TV, balancing the clicker in his palm like an extension of his hand. "Daddy?"

He leans forward. "I'm planning to go this week."

"Well I really want to see Shelly *today*. She sounds terrible."

"So what do you want from me? Take the Subaru. It's been sitting in the driveway for months. Do I have to remind you again that it won't start if you don't drive it?"

"It doesn't have any air conditioning," I say sheepishly. "And Abby had to loan her car to her mom. Please can I have yours? I'll take it to the car wash." I feel rage toward him building in my head, but suck in air to calm myself. Frannie, I say silently, don't get mad. Don't do it. Don't. "Please? I promise Abby won't smoke."

"Move out of the way. I can't see." He waves, but I don't budge. Behind me, I hear Julia Child's shrill voice, and the sound of her hand slapping a chicken. "Come on, Frannie. This is my favorite show."

"You come on. I just want to see Shelly. Something you haven't done yet," I add casually.

My father starts to say something but instead tosses me his keys. Then he zones in on Julia again. "As soon as I get a job, Dad, I'll get a car. No joke." I continue to block his view. My father stares at the set as though he can see through me. "They invented microwaves so you don't have to cook. It's the nineties." He turns up the volume. What did I do? I apologized, my room is clean. What more does he want? "Your wife is fucking around," I whisper, wishing I could scream. "I bet you didn't know. But I do. And soon, you'll find out, too."

"Frannie, stop mumbling." He picks up a pen. "Don't you have to go already?" He doesn't take his eyes off the set but scratches notes on the *TV Guide*. "And no smoking. I'm serious. Let Abby smoke her stinking cigarettes in her own damn car."

"No smoking," I mutter. Then I race out feeling, for a second, not so sorry for him after all.

"Frannie, Frannie, Frannie. How *have* you been?" As much as I love her, Mavis Friedman can be unsettling. She calls Abby ten times a day, sends over her cleaning lady once a week, and tries to set her up with every Jewish boy she comes in contact with. The fact that her daughter is sleeping with a married man doesn't stop her from inviting Jonathan Lieberman over for drinks on the deck and not telling Abby until she walks out and sees a frizzy-haired guy wearing pointed cowboy boots and a pink Oxford button-down.

I let her set me up once. Abby and I refer to it as the Afta Disasta. "Marcus Afta," the guy had said, pumping my hand. "Afta Carpeting. Nice to meetcha." He seemed nice and very friendly. How was I supposed to know that four hours later, he'd wrestle me against the woolly carpet rolls in the back of his father's mini van? He came all over his linen pants, one hand on my breast, the other on his penis. "This is a disasta!" he cried, trying to squeeze out the come with his manicured fingers. "A fuckin' disasta!"

I take a Diet Coke from the refrigerator and walk into the living room. Mavis always plays music, which is comforting in a sad sort of way. "Do you like this?" Mavis points to the ceiling. At first, I think she's referring to the tiling, but then I realize she means the music. I cock my head like her and listen. "It's Yanni. Lonny and I love it. It does make a mood." She hums to herself and flits into the kitchen. I should suggest piping music into Shelly's ward. As I sip my soda, I marvel at my ingenuity. Maybe I should be a hospital consultant.

Abby flies down the stairs wearing a skinny leotard and leggings. "Wait a second, Abby. You can't go like that." I point to her chest.

"Fine." She pulls on a T-shirt. The shirt has no neck so her breasts hang out like rounded mounds of dough. "Jesus, Frannie, life with Mr. and Mrs. Cheerful is starting to show."

"I just don't want anyone to feel badly when they look at you."

"Why would they feel badly?" Abby grins. She turns toward the mirror. "Everett says he loves my breasts. He said they are two of his favorite things about me."

"Which shows you just how deep Everett is." I don't like Everett and it's not just because he's a stupid man with graying facial hair and no neck. He also has a wife and two kids, and despite what he moans to Abby in bed, he has no plans to leave them.

"Bye, Mom," Abby calls to Mavis, who sits, flipping through a magazine.

"Send my love to Shelly," she says without looking up.

When I was younger, I would come here just to see Mavis. I'd tell her about my mother and she would put her arms around me, dance me through the kitchen, and tell me that everything will work out, that mothers and daughters just have it rough sometimes. She always smelled good, a mixture of Poison perfume and Aqua Net hair spray.

She looks up from a magazine. "You never come around anymore, Frannie."

"I've been busy trying to find a job or a husband, whichever comes first."

"Don't rush yourself, honey. You practically just left school. In fact, Henrietta Baskin's son is moving back from Rome. I can introduce—"

"That's okay," I say quickly. But maybe she's right. Maybe it's not so bad to be me. She always makes me feel better. As we leave, I consider asking Mavis if I can move into Abby's room for a little while.

"Why does my mother like you more than me?" Abby asks in the car.

"I don't know. Probably for the same reason my mother likes you more than me."

"Your mother doesn't like anyone."

I shrug. I want to tell Abby that's not true these days. "She's not so bad."

"Since when?"

"Since she's still my mother, Abby. Shut up."

"Well, you don't have to get all defensive." Abby takes out a cigarette, but I point to the frog sign. "David says no smoking."

She lights up, blows the smoke at me. "Tell him I made you. Peer pressure."

We drive in silence. I look out. I wish people didn't go so fast. Doesn't anyone realize that all it takes is a flick of the wrist and it's doomsday out here? I slow down, let someone pass.

"Everett says he's leaving his wife," Abby says finally.

I signal, wave, and change lanes. Questions race: (a) did Everett really say that? (b) if so, was it in passing? (c) is his wife Sharrice the one leaving? and (d) are Everett and Abby still together?

"Did you hear me? I said Everett's getting divorced." Indignant, Abby holds up a bracelet. "He gave me this."

"He gave you a *diamond* bracelet?"

She shrugs and strokes the bracelet as if it's a live animal. "He says he doesn't love Sharrice anymore." She frowns. "Now he wants to be with me *all the time.*"

"So what's wrong?" I ask, so jealous I can barely breathe.

"I don't know. It seemed like a good idea when we met but now I feel so *pressured.*"

"Give me a fucking break, Abby. This was what you wanted." She pales. "Abby?"

"Wait a second," she snaps. "I'm thinking." She pauses. "I don't want to talk about it." She wraps the bracelet around her fingers. Cut in the shape of tears, the diamonds sparkle as they catch the light. Abby bites down on it. "How much do you think it's worth?"

"Depends on if it's real or not."

"Everett wouldn't buy me a fake bracelet. Just because he's unfaithful to a woman he doesn't love, doesn't mean that he'd lie to me."

I snort. "Right. If you married him, Abby, he'd do the same thing to you."

"I never agreed to marry the guy."

I think about my mother on the phone, giggling like an idiot girl, and my father, ignorant and alone in the dark, taking notes from a cooking show. Rage rises in my chest like vomit. "I can't believe you! That is so WRONG. You don't do that to people. He has a FAMILY!" I smack the steering wheel and start to cry.

Wide-eyed, Abby stares at me. "Jesus, Frannie, what's the matter?" I try to choke out words, but can't. "Did I say something? What did I say? Pull over, let me drive."

"I'm … fine." I slow down, blinded by tears. "Don't worry," I say, gasping, "I'm … okay." After a few minutes, I'm finally able to catch my breath.

I make my way to 75th Street. The city is empty on a summer Saturday, and I find a spot, shut off the motor, and wipe my nose. Outside the car, the hospital looms like a bad dream.

I whimper while Abby rummages through her purse. "Are you okay?" she asks. Sniffling, I nod. "Promise it's not me."

"It's not," I promise her. There's something not right with me, I want to say. I keep snapping like this. "It's hard to be at home. I always imagined that by the time I turned twenty-six, I'd live in a cute house and drive a nice car."

"But you do live in a nice house." She waves. "And this is a great car."

"I meant of my own, Abby."

"Frannie, I'm *trying* to add some levity." Two doctors pass by. "Hey, maybe we could meet some cute guys here. Now that would be great."

"Yeah, great," I echo hollowly. My eye catches the bracelet, which has fallen between the seats. If you ask me, the diamonds look like cubic zirconium.

Abby hugs me. "You sure you're okay?" she asks again and I nod. "I'll tell you what. I'm going to break up with Everett. I think it's time to move on, anyway. And don't you worry." She squeezes my hand. "I'll even give the bracelet back."

The first time Abby visited St. Mary's, she said it looked creepy. "It's a mental hospital," I had snapped at her, "not a health spa." Today, she rolls through the lobby without a word. Her silence bothers me. I don't want anyone too comfortable with Shelly being here. I want my sister to get better so things can return to the way they were when I could barely dress myself and Shelly was on the road to becoming a Supreme Court justice. One fuck-up in the family is embarrassing. Two fuck-ups is a made-for-TV movie.

"This place must cost a wad," Abby says. "Who pays for this? The Cheerfuls?"

"Shelly's insurance pays for six months, but she won't be in here that long."

When we get into the elevator, Abby nudges me. Standing with us is a tall, dark-haired guy. He's handsome and well-built, wearing a lab coat and a beeper, and holding a yellow folder. I stare at him, wondering if I've gotten too old to go to medical school.

Abby sighs loudly. "Boy, it's hot in here." With a flourish, she takes off her T-shirt. I roll my eyes as she arches her back, falls out of her leotard, and twirls a lock of hair around her finger. She winks at me, but the doctor doesn't notice her. Frustrated, she puts the T-shirt back on.

He gets out on Shelly's floor, and we follow him to her ward, where he goes into an office and shuts the door. As I look for Shelly, I wave at a few of the girls that I recognize. Cynthia Balducci is coloring at a table.

"Hi, Cynthia," I say softly. "This is Abby."

When she looks up, her blond hair falls away from her face. "I know," she says. "I haven't been lobotomized."

I stare at her. Something is different. It takes me a few seconds to realize that the tubes are gone. Without them, she is beautiful; she has luminous hazel eyes, high cheekbones, and full lips. She's also tall and willowy with long, sculptured legs and graceful hands that flutter around her face like pale baby birds. She nods listlessly as she moves the crayon back and forth.

"Can I color with you?" Abby asks, sitting down next to Cynthia, who shrugs and pushes a piece of paper toward her. Abby picks up a crayon. I stare at them, amazed by Abby, suddenly grateful.

"I guess I'll find Shelly." As I walk through the ward, I notice that it's extremely quiet today. No one is walking around or playing cards. Two girls sit on the couch, mesmerized by the TV. The silence is eerie and feels like my parents' house, ominous and depressing, weighted with the feeling of someone about to burst into tears. I wonder if something bad happened, or if all the girls' moods synchronized, the way women's periods do when they live together.

The cut-out flowers are still pasted on the wall. The air conditioning blows from underneath and the flowers are lifted as if by wind. Staring at them, I accidentally bump into one of the girls. "Excuse me," I say. "I didn't see you."

"It's okay," a male voice says. "I kind of snuck up on you." I look up to see that the voice belongs to the handsome doctor from the elevator.

I run a hand over my hair. "I wasn't looking where I was going."

"No, it was my fault." For a long second we smile at each other. I notice that his eyes are deep-set and black like melted tar. A moment passes between us, a very long moment, and I feel myself falling. Heat spreads through me, slow as honey, warm as wax, and I lose myself, not wanting to spoil the tension between us that is potent with movement held like a dare.

Slowly, I exhale. Someone turns up the volume on the TV. A door slams, which makes me jump. The doctor looks up. "That came from out of nowhere," he says, smiling.

I say shyly, "I thought it was just me."

"No, it scared me, too." He cranes his neck. "I wonder what they're watching."

"I'm looking for my sister," I say quickly, embarrassed that I'm flirting.

"And I was looking for you. I've been through the ward twice trying to find you."

"Yeah, right," I say, but I'm flattered. "You were looking for me. Right."

"I was. I wanted to talk to you before you saw Shelly. You're her sister, aren't you?"

"Oh." I'm quiet a second. "Yeah. I am."

"I could tell." He rubs his fingers across his mouth. I watch, wondering what he looks like naked, naked and leaning over me. I flush with desire. Barely breathing, I suck my lower lip, aching for this guy. I have *got* to get out more. "They rarely let residents on this unit," he is saying, "especially men, but they're short-staffed this weekend."

I try not to look at him—he's just too handsome. I always get apologetic around handsome men. I don't mean to look like this, I want to say. And I do have another pair of breasts at home if these aren't working for you.

The doctor licks a lusty smile across his mouth. He leans forward. "There was an accident this morning," he says quietly. His breath, warm on my neck, tickles. "Brought the whole ward down."

"Oh?" I panic. "It wasn't Shelly, was it? I spoke to her last night. She seemed fine."

He shakes his head. "No, it wasn't Shelly, but she isn't having a good day. No one is. One of the girls tried to hurt herself. She was moved upstairs." I must look scared because he puts a hand on my arm. "She's all right," he says. "But it shook up the ward, got every-one thinking. When you live here day to day, you forget what kind of hospital it is."

"I can't imagine that." I laugh nervously. "Seems to me you'd think about it all the time." We stand for a second in an awkward silence. "I guess I'll go find Shelly. I'll cheer her up. She asked me to come. I mean, I always want to come, but she asked me to. We're close. You know, sisters."

He smiles. "Look, I have to tell you—" His beeper goes off, which startles us both, him less than me. He holds up the beeper and squints at it.

"What?" I ask.

He doesn't answer immediately. Now he probably wants to tell me how to act around Shelly, that I shouldn't antagonize her. Like I don't know that. Well I'll be damned if I'm going to let him patron-ize me just because he's a handsome doctor.

He leans forward. I have to strain to hear him. He smells like mint. "You have an intriguing mouth. I rarely see women with such a full lower lip." And he turns away and leaves me standing with my mouth gaping open, mute.

The lights are on in Shelly's room. She's sleeping, bundled under the covers as if lost in a snowbank. I breathe deeply and replay the doctor slowly rubbing his lips. I imagine him licking my neck, making but-terfly kisses, trailing his fingers ... I catch a distorted image of myself in the fake mirror. My cheeks are red and damp with perspiration.

I brush a lock of Shelly's hair from her cheek. It feels like cotton on my finger. Shelly stirs. "Oh, I'm sorry," she says, "I shouldn't be sleeping." She rubs her eyes, which are glazed, either from too much sleep or from too much medication. "I'm really sorry. Have you been waiting long?" I tell her that it's no big deal. "Did you pick up the file from Lonny's office?" she asks.

"Oh, Shelly, I didn't have time. Shit, I forgot the magazines, too. I'm sorry."

She nods, but her eyes fill with tears. "It's okay," she says, turn-ing over.

"It's not okay. I feel awful. I'll pick up the file on my way home,

I swear." Shelly nods again. A tear slips out of her eye. "Shelly, I heard about the accident. You must be upset. Did you know her?"

She shakes her head. "Not really." We keep referring to it as an accident. Was it an accident that someone tried to hurt herself, or that she wasn't successful at the attempt? I look around and ask about Bernadette.

"She left," Shelly says. She continues to cry and I ask her what's wrong, but won't tell me.

"Please talk to me, Shelly. Please. I want to know."

She rolls over. "I can't," she whispers.

"But you can. Just try."

"I just feel so sad. This place just makes me so sad. Everyone's being so nice to me, and I'm still so fucked up. I feel so guilty I'm not happier or better or whatever I'm supposed to be." She wraps her long legs around a pillow. They are still so thin, it pains me to look at them. "Frannie, I wish I were dead so I didn't have to feel so ashamed of myself."

"Shelly, don't say things like that. When you're dead, you're dead. You don't get another chance. You have everything ahead of you. Mommy and Daddy are *proud* of you. You're so smart—you're going to Harvard Law School! How many people can say that?"

She tenses up. "Law school doesn't mean a fucking thing. If I was so smart, I wouldn't be in here, would I? You guys don't even know me."

"Of course we know you." I hate when she says this. It makes me feel like there's something I should be doing that I'm not; like if I made more of an effort, all this would go away. How else are we supposed to know her? I suddenly can't stop thinking about the doctor's black eyes. His sexy smile taunts me. *You have the most intriguing mouth.* What does *intriguing* mean? Maybe he said *incredible. The most incredible mouth.*

She keeps talking, her voice far away, as if she's forgotten about me. "It wouldn't be so bad to be dead. It's so exhausting to be here, thinking all the time, *all* the time. People don't see *me.* No one sees *me.* It's like being fat. No one takes you seriously. You just don't exist—you're so big, you're not even there."

"But Shelly, you're not fat anymore. Shelly"—I try to catch her eye—"look at me. You're beautiful. You've always been beautiful." *You have the most incredible mouth. Such a full lower lip. I wish I could kiss you.*

Exasperated, Shelly sighs loudly, "Why don't you *listen*? It's not about being fat. It's about being *me*. I don't even know who I am. What I am. Oh, forget it. I just want you to know that if you were in here, I'd bring you magazines every day."

Abby walks in. "Thanks a lot, Frannie. You abandoned me with psycho Cindy. Hey, you." She kisses Shelly, who sits up. "I come bearing gifts." Abby pulls out *Cosmopolitan, Mademoiselle*, and the new *Vogue*. I glare at Abby, who looks at me, bewildered.

"Thanks, Abby." Shelly smooths her hair.

"So what's up? How do you feel? My father keeps asking for you."

"He sent me those," Shelly says proudly, pointing to a bouquet of flowers. "We've spoken a few times. I'm helping him out on the Pennington case. Did he tell you?"

"We don't discuss work that much." Abby looks at me and I know she wants to change the subject. We've talked about this.

"If you speak to him, will you tell him I've reviewed the limited partnership documents? And if he asks, tell him that it might not make sense for Pennington to retain the corporate structure he wants. Will you tell him for me? I've been trying to work on it"— she looks at her hands—"but they keep me busy. And Frannie didn't pick up a file I needed."

"Shelly!" I interrupt. "You shouldn't be working in here. You know that."

"Shelly," Abby says, watching her, "Frannie's right. It will be there when you get out."

Shelly's mouth tightens. "I can work in here. They don't care." I can tell, by the way her eyes flicker, that she's lying.

I tell her I think it's a bad idea, but Abby plops herself on Shelly's bed and they start talking about lawyer bullshit, impressing each other with technical words. Occasionally, Shelly glances at me, but after a few minutes, I wander out.

I see the doctor sitting at the front desk. I walk slowly toward him with my head bent. I'll just make believe he didn't say anything. He probably flirts all the time. He flips through a chart. I take a deep breath. "I saw Shelly," I croak and quickly clear my throat, slow myself, start over. "She's not doing so great." He looks up at me and takes off his glasses. I move closer to him, but I'm careful not to look into his eyes. "I don't know what to say to her," I continue. "It's difficult, you know, to find the right words." He nods, but doesn't speak, so I keep rambling. "I mean, I want to talk to her, but it seems like I always say the wrong thing"—*Shit, would you SAY SOMETHING? Cut me off before I tell you how handsome you are and how lonely I am and*—"I mean …" I look down. "I feel like she's mad at me."

"She's not mad at you. Most of the girls in here are mad at themselves. It's a part of their pathology."

I look at him. "You know they *are* people," I say sharply. "And she *is* my sister." I turn to walk away.

"Hey wait," he calls softly. "I'm sorry. I didn't mean to say that. What I meant was that sometimes patients are angry and they lash out without meaning to—especially at the people they love the most." He smiles. "I really am sorry. It's been a bad day."

His eyes beckon like an abyss. I'm blinded, for a second, by their blackness. "It's okay," I say, softening. "You're forgiven." I smile. "I'm Frannie."

"I'm Bryan. Bryan Thompson." He clears his throat. "The asshole resident."

"You're not an asshole."

"You don't know me well enough to say that." He leans forward. "But if you want, you could get to know me. Shelly didn't tell me how pretty you are."

My face burns. "Do you always flirt like this? It's not very professional, you know."

He shakes his head.

"I don't believe you," I tell him.

"I don't blame you," he says, and grins at me.

Abby comes walking toward us. "Frannie, something's wrong with Shelly. She started crying and wouldn't stop. I mean, she was *hyperventilating*. She yelled at me to get out. I've never seen her like this. I feel like I did something to upset her."

"What did you say to her?" I snap, turning to go.

"I just *told* you I didn't say *anything*. We were just talking."

Bryan grabs my arm. "Don't go yet. Give her a moment to compose herself. I think everything that's been going on is overwhelming for her. She was very close to the girl who hurt herself. It was Bernadette, her roommate."

"Bernadette? Why didn't she tell me?" I look at Abby. "Did she tell you?"

Abby nods. "Bernadette took thirty-four laxatives. Apparently, her heart stopped."

"It was actually dehydration," Bryan interrupts.

Abby looks at Bryan and smiles. "Who are you?"

"Bryan is a resident," I tell her. "He normally doesn't work this floor, but he was on call."

"Well, Doc," Abby says, adjusting her T-shirt to expose the crack of her cleavage. "What should we do?" I immediately hunch over, feeling frustrated, first at Abby for flirting, then at myself for getting annoyed.

"Go in and say goodbye, but don't mention her hysteria unless she wants to talk about it. And keep coming back. Even though she says she doesn't want you here, she does. She just doesn't want to ask." He looks at me. "Come as often as you can, Frannie. Family is important. Especially now." He eyes Abby's chest. "You should put something warmer on," he says to her. "There's always a draft in here. I'd hate for you to catch something."

Abby turns away and Bryan leans over. "Maybe I'll call you," he murmurs, "to remind you that she wants you here." He lifts his hand in a half-wave and walks into an office.

Abby sneers. "What a fucking Rat Boy. And he kept staring at my tits, did you notice?"

"Oh Abby, stop it. Let's say goodbye to Shelly."

Shelly's room is dark and we tiptoe in. I hear the hum of the air conditioner and her quiet breathing. "Shelly?" I whisper. "Shelly, are you up?" She doesn't answer.

"I'm sorry if I upset you," Abby whispers, but Shelly still doesn't respond.

"I'll call you later, Shelly," I tell her. I want to say something comforting, something so she'll know how much I care. I fumble for a second until I have the right words, and I bend over to speak, but I can't quite reach them to say them aloud. Then, in a split second, they're gone, like a dream that is lost in the twilight of sleep. And the only thing that fills the void is Bryan's slow smile that he licks across his lips as if he can taste me.

On the way home, Abby and I stop at a diner. "Shelly looks terrible," she says.

"Yeah, she does, but that doctor seemed to think she'll get better. I hope he knows what he's talking about." I scan the menu. "What are you having?"

"The fucking left side. Being in that hospital makes me want to eat everything in sight." She shoves a roll into her mouth. As she talks, I can see the roll become pulp. "I'm getting tuna on a bagel."

"That's not a snack, that's a meal. Swallow," I hiss at her as flecks of roll fly from her mouth like pieces of ash. Tuna sounds good. Maybe I should just have tuna. Or a turkey pot pie. I think about Bryan. Maybe just a small house salad.

Our waiter clears his throat. "Frannie," Abby says, "the guy's waiting."

"Give me a second." The waiter tells me he can come back. "No, I'll decide." But what should I have? I think of Shelly's toothpick legs wrapped around the pillow. The chili? Maybe a nice bowl of chili. A turkey sandwich? I look up at the waiter. "What should I have?"

"How the hell should he know?" Abby screeches. "Order some fucking food, Frannie. We go through this every time."

"Hold on." What about an omelette? Apple pie? I don't know I don't know I don't know. "I'll have a bagel … No, forget it, I'll have the chopped steak dinner."

"The chopped steak dinner?! Are you from the fifties? What is wrong with you? Just order something normal!"

"Forget it," I tell the waiter, waving. "I'll just have toast." He stands a second. "Yeah, that's it. Just toast." I look at Abby as he walks away. "I couldn't decide."

"Obviously," she says. "Can you believe that shit about Bernadette?"

"I know. Why is everyone so fucked up?"

"Too many self-help books telling us how unfulfilled we are. Therapy has ruined our generation." She picks at another roll. "My mom's on my back to see someone. She says dating a married man is a sign that I have larger problems. Personally, I think she watches too many talk shows. Anyway, I told you I was breaking up with him and I am." She looks up. "You want the bracelet?"

I shake my head. "Don't break up with him just because I said something."

"Believe it or not, I'm breaking up with him because I don't love him." She smiles. "See, I'm maturing. I'm evolving. I don't need therapy."

As the waiter appears with our food, I ask Abby if she thinks I need therapy. In college, I went to the psych center. The counselor asked me questions from a pamphlet entitled *Are You Depressed?* that had a girl's face shaded in blue on the cover. When he got to "Do you lack interest in sexual relations?" I walked out, confident his questions weren't applicable to me.

"Of course not. You just need to get laid. Call my mother. She wasn't kidding about that guy, whatever his name is, Baskin."

"I don't think so." *Your mouth is so incredible.* I gnaw on my toast. "I think I'm interested in someone else."

"Since when?" She looks up. "Since we got our food?"

"I thought I'd call that doctor. He seemed to like me. We talked for a while."

"About what?"

I lick my lips. "How big your boobs are." Abby opens her mouth but I cut her off. "Abby, please. We were talking about Shelly."

"So what makes you think he wants you to call him?"

"He told me he thought I was beautiful. Or pretty. Something like that. I don't know. It's embarrassing."

"Some great-looking doctor tells you that you're beautiful and you're *embarrassed*? Have you no sense? There's a phone. Call him from here."

"He may not have said *beautiful.* Maybe just pretty. Besides, you think he's a pig."

"Yeah, well, looking at my track record, I'm obviously not the best judge. And that was before I knew he said something nice to my best friend." Humming the wedding march, Abby puts a napkin on my head so it sits like a veil. Then she pitches Everett's bracelet at me. "Here, you cunning little vixen. Wear it with Dr. Dolittle. And ask him if he's got a friend for me."

I smile and thank her. Then I point to her plate. "Are you going to eat that?" I ask. "I should have ordered the tuna."

I obsess about Bryan on the way home. I rent *Muriel's Wedding* and obsess through the movie. Then I obsess through *The Mary Tyler Moore Show* on Nick at Nite and the beginning of *Saturday Night Live*.

Before I go to bed, I sneak downstairs and pick up the phone. "What's up?" I whisper to Shelly when she gets on the line. "Is everything all right?"

"Everything's fine. How's everything with you?" Shelly sounds annoyed.

"Fine."

"Well then. We've established that we're both fine. Is that it?"

"Shelly, I'm sorry about Bernadette. You could have told me."

"I didn't feel like talking about it. She is a good person."

"So are you."

"I feel awful that I freaked out on Abby. I didn't mean it. Please tell her I'm sorry. I just couldn't contain myself." I try to focus on what Shelly is saying, but suddenly I find myself wondering when I'll see Bryan again. "Frannie? What are you doing?" Shelly interrupts.

"I'm listening to you. Shelly, I know I've been distracted lately with the fact that I have no life and may never get one, but I want you to know that even though you think you're fucked up, I think it takes a lot of courage to do what you're doing." I get up and walk with the cord. "I mean it. I'm proud of you for going into the hospital. I wouldn't just say that. Don't forget that you have everything ahead of you. You're only twenty-four. I'm the one who's in trouble here."

Shelly starts to cry. "I can't believe you just said that. That was so nice."

"You're my sister, Shelly."

She starts to cry harder. Before I can say anything else, she tells me that she feels like such a loser. "Everyone asks me all fucking day how I feel. I don't know how I feel. I hate all this attention. It makes me so tense. But I wish you were here with me, Frannie. Please don't forget about me." And she quickly hangs up.

It kills me to hear her cry. I want to call her back, but I'm all fucked up inside, so I sit alone with a carton of ice cream.

Hours later, I lie awake, still restless with fantasy, my blankets twisted around my legs like rope. I can't stop thinking of Bryan. I replay our meeting over and over and over. For the first time in months, I have a glimmer of hope, but I'm also worried. It's only been a day and he's already in my head.

I go into my bathroom and stare at my face. I lean toward my head which looms large and distorted and get as close as I can to my cyclops eye. I run my fingers along my lips, studying them carefully, and wonder what it is about my mouth that makes it so incredible.

7

I *'m worried about her, Marsha. She's so mixed up." Visiting for the* weekend, Aunt Lillian sits at the kitchen table with my mother, sifting through old photographs. I'm standing in the hallway behind the door, watching them through the crack.

"I thought she was doing better," my mother says. "Didn't she just finish that program?" I relax when I realize they're talking about my cousin Beth.

"She dropped out. Now she's living with Monte and me."

"How could you marry a guy named Monte? It is so Las Vegas."

"Marsha, please. I don't know what to do and all Monte cares about is taking pictures of cactus now that we're in the Great Southwest."

"She'll find herself. I'm going through the same thing. Although, you'll be proud to know that despite everything, I've cut down on my medication."

"Well, that's positive."

My mother shrugs. Whenever my aunt visits, she and my mother pull out the pictures. My father's parents died before I was born so we don't have many pictures of them, but we do have a ton from my mother's side of the family. She and my aunt can spend an entire afternoon shuffling through the photographs and pointing out people who have since died. It's their favorite pastime.

"Look at Mommy here," my mother says, brightening. "This was taken right before Frannie was born. Look, she didn't have that birthmark on her cheek. Remember? The one she had removed?" She looks up. "Actually, Frannie's been great, especially with Shelly. She goes to the hospital practically every day."

"Is she getting better?"

"Who knows? Her doctors think she's making progress although it's hard for me to tell. One day she's talkative, the next day, she won't even pick up the phone."

"She's a kid, Marsha. She'll grow out of it."

"I just think she's getting too comfortable in that hospital. I tried to talk to her about leaving, maybe seeing Marilyn again as an outpatient, but she wants to stay. End of discussion. Once Shelly makes up her mind, there's no talking to her."

"And we're so different? She's rigid. It's not like we don't know from rigidity." Aunt Lillian changes the subject. "So what are you going to do about this guy in your office?" Startled, I lean closer.

My mother lowers her voice, mumbling so I can't hear. "… he says he wants me to … but I don't know …" COME ON! I silently scream, Give it UP!!

"Maybe you don't believe him because you're afraid to," my aunt says quietly.

"I don't think it's that simple."

"By the way, is Frannie any closer to finding a job?" Aunt Lillian asks. I stiffen. Fuck you. Waitressing's a *job*. Not wanting to hear anything else, I walk into the kitchen.

"Hi, Frannie." My aunt smooths my hair. I kiss her and hold up a grainy picture of my grandparents wearing evening clothes. "When was this taken?" I ask her.

My aunt studies it. "At Ruby's wedding. Right before Uncle Bert died." She looks up at me. "Coronary. Beth was named for him."

"It's weird that Jews name their kids for someone who died."

"It's not weird to carry on a name. It's how someone who dies is remembered. Here." She hands me a picture of my grandmother. "Look at this. Don't you see Shelly?"

"No. Grandma and Shelly don't look anything alike."

"Look at her smile," Aunt Lillian instructs me. "It's Shelly's. You don't have to see a resemblance to know it's there. When I look at that picture, I don't see Shelly, but I feel her." She flips through the pictures and slides one toward me. "This is you."

I squint at an old black-and-white photograph of my mother taken when she first married my father, years ago when he was in the service and they lived in Rome. She is hugging a statue with one arm, her head flung back, her long hair blowing behind her like a scarf. Her other arm and leg are extended as if she's about to take flight. "Sorry, Mom. It doesn't look like either one of us. You look too *happy*." But the picture gives me a weird rush, and when they look away, I slide it into the pocket of my jeans.

"Daddy's worse," my aunt tells my mother. "We have to get him out of Florida."

"I *know*, Lillian. We've been through this." She glances at me, then back at her sister. "I told you I don't have the money right now."

"It's not about money, Marsha. I have money. You have Frannie here to help out."

"Must you always remind me how much money you have? That's why you're here, isn't it? To talk me into moving Daddy up here?"

"Of course not. But since I'm here, we may as well talk about it."

My grandfather only has 30 percent of his vision because of bad cataracts. When my grandmother died, my aunt hired a nurse to care for him. Her name is Tilly and according to my grandfather, she's "black as the ace of spades," which is really ironic because Tilly is white. Tilly is very tan so she looks dark, and she has a thick Mississippi drawl. My grandfather can only see images and he assumed she was black. In fact, when she said she wasn't, he said he didn't believe her. As far as I'm concerned, Tilly must be a saint. I can't bear to be around my grandfather. He calls the bank for his balance three times a day, he counts his pills ten times before swallowing, and he constantly asks me what line of work I'm in and why I can't find a husband. He's me magnified one hundred times.

"You are *so* manipulative, Lillian. Why do you always do this to me?"

I play with the pictures, suddenly reminded of Shelly's graduation from Cornell. I was very complimentary until after the ceremony when Shelly announced that not only were they holding her diploma to engrave *cum laude*, but Lonny offered her a paralegal job *and* he wanted to pay for her LSAT preparation. Everyone danced around and told her a million times how great she was. I, on the other hand, having taken the weekend off from Tom and Susie's Pet-O-Rama, asked if she was sure about law school. "What about being an anchorwoman?" I said, trying to act nonchalant. "Don't give up your dreams." When she answered, she sounded like she was about to cry. "Frannie, you always do this. I *told* you I switched out of communications."

"Stop overreacting," I told her. "I just didn't realize." I smiled fakely as my father pulled me into a picture. When Shelly threw her cap in the air, everyone clapped. I went to the hotel, claiming I was tired and afraid I might have mono.

Hating myself, I get up and grab an ice cream sandwich from the freezer. I tell my aunt that Shelly's thinking of applying to Columbia. "So she can continue to work for Lonny. Isn't that great?"

"Since when?" my mother cuts in. "I thought she had her heart set on Harvard."

"Since I don't know. I think *you're* the one whose heart is set on Harvard. Anyway, I think it's great. Can you believe Lonny's still paying her while she's in the hospital?"

"And why shouldn't he?" Aunt Lillian asks. "Shelly's a great investment." She turns to my mother. "She'll get through this. Everything's going to be fine."

"I know," my mother barks at her. "Stop saying that. You sound like a goddamn broken record. Turn off the older sister bullshit."

"Look at Grandma here," I interrupt, hating when they fight. I hold up a photograph of my grandmother. My mother fingers the picture absently, a faraway look in her eyes. She was very close to her mother, much closer than Aunt Lillian was. It dawns on me that at one point, my mother considered herself close to Shelly, too. Suddenly feeling very alone, I announce that I'm going to watch television.

My mom clears her throat. "Your aunt wants to see Shelly," she says. "I thought we'd take a ride into the city."

"Mom, I'd love to." I glance at my aunt. "But I have to work tonight."

"Oh, that's too bad." She seems genuinely disappointed. "Can you call in sick?"

"Marsha, don't ask her to do that," Aunt Lillian cuts in. "You said before she can't jeopardize this job." I look at my mother suspiciously. I thought you said I was doing *great*.

"I know, but it's not a *real* job. I'll tell you what …" She leans forward. "I'll call Paulie. How could he not believe me? Besides he adores you." She picks up the phone and dials Rascals. "I don't know," I say, but I'm warmed to the idea and don't want to break the spell of my mother's mood.

"Paul DiMartino," she says into the phone. "Hi, Paul? This is Marsha Hunter, Frannie's mother. No emergency. It's just that Frannie has a virus and it's not such a good idea for her to work tonight. Yes, she's sleeping. I know she'd feel terrible, but … Well, thank you so much, Paul. I'll tell her." She hangs up. "He's so nice. It's so nice to have a good relationship with people you work with." And she looks at my aunt who smiles at her mysteriously, like they're both in on a sisters-only secret they think I don't know anything about.

A week later, I spend the day at a law firm. I signed up with a temp agency and this is my first assignment. I have to smile and be nice and type letters and make copies, and the entire time I want to look at the pathetic little man who needs his copies ASAP and say, "Did anyone ever tell you that you look like a gerbil?"

I've been on a few interviews, but nothing's panned out. In fact, this Kelly Girl situation is forcing me to rethink my job search. As I was making the gerbil man's copies this morning, which weren't coming ASAP because the copier kept jamming and the pages kept sticking and it took me forty minutes to Xerox sixty pages, I wondered if, deep down, I am not a people-person. Lately, I seem to hate everyone.

The gerbil man kept *screaming* at me, "I NEED my COPIES!" like it was *my* fault they use some lame-ass copier. I couldn't stand it. So I slipped some papers from the garbage can into the final stack. I know it wasn't a nice thing to do, but it made me feel so much better.

On my way home from what will be, I'm sure, the last day of the assignment, I stop by the hospital. The nurses have relaxed the visiting hours for me, so I can come and go as I please as long as Shelly is up to seeing me.

"I finished my application to the big H," she says, walking toward me. "It took me three days." She leans to kiss me. Surprised, I kiss her back. She models for me. "What do you think?" She's wearing a silk blouse and black slacks. It's the first time I've seen her dressed in months.

"You look great. What's the occasion?" I try to appear nonchalant as I look around for Bryan. In a moment of weakness, I told Shelly about him, but she says she hasn't seen him since the day I met him.

"He's not here," Shelly says, watching me. "I already checked. I'm sorry, Frannie, but I promise I'll keep looking. Has he called you?"

I shake my head. "It's no big deal. Just forget it." I tug on her blouse. "How come you're so dressed up?"

"Lonny stopped by to drop off a file." As we walk into her room, I'm amazed to see her bed covered with open books, files, and legal pads. She starts to tell me about some case she's working on and how there's a possibility that they may try to publish a brief she's writing. It will be under Lonny's name of course, she says, but she'll get acknowledged.

"Sounds interesting," I say, hoping I appear enthusiastic. "Let me read your Harvard application."

Shelly blinks and looks away. "I don't want to jinx it. Mommy keeps asking about it. She's so fucked up. I think she's the one who wants to go to Harvard, not me." I laugh and tell her that I said the same thing. "Remember when she lied about going there?" Shelly asks. "When I went to that Princeton alumni lunch and Mommy told a group of women she went to Harvard, not realizing I was standing behind her?"

"I forgot about that. How do you remember shit like that? What did you say?"

"I didn't say anything. I wasn't going to admit to those bitches that Mommy never finished NYU. They're such fucking snots, anyway. I'm glad I didn't go to fucking Princeton." Her sudden hostility startles me, and I watch her closely. But then she brightens. "I'm drafting a letter for Mommy," she says. "Actually it's for Daniel. Let me ask you something, and I want you to be totally honest. Do you think I have a shot at Harvard? It's really gonna piss me off if I wasted all that time on the application for nothing."

"Of course you do," I say tightly, my mood punctured. "What kind of letter?"

Shelly paces. "A few years ago, he got into this real estate deal. Now he needs a letter certifying he was bought out. It's nothing major. Besides, Lonny checks everything I do."

"Have you been speaking to Mommy a lot lately?" I try to read her face, but she won't look at me. "Shelly, please sit down, you're making me really tense."

"I'm totally wired. I talk to Mommy every day. Hey, why did you tell her I was applying to Columbia?"

"I didn't! She always gets in the middle! So she just asked you to write this letter, just like that? Did you talk to Daniel yourself?"

She nods. "Briefly. Frannie, I know you have this thing against him, but he's harmless. Maybe too effusive, but he's a salesman ... Pia, Keisha, come here, meet my sister." She waves to two girls in the doorway. The waifish girl is black, wearing boxers and a T-shirt. She looks like she's a teenager, but when she moves into the light, I see that her skin is very wrinkled around her mouth and eyes. The taller girl is obese. She's wearing tight purple leggings, a turtleneck, and a sweatshirt tied around her waist. As she peers into the room, she holds one of her arms diagonally across her body as if it is a shield.

"Girls," Shelly sings, "this is Frannie. Frannie, this is Pia and Keisha. Pia's my new roommate. She's a poet." I remember Bernadette, and how Shelly introduced her as a bulimic. I guess this is considered progress.

Pia, the waifish girl, walks up to me. "I've heard a lot about you. You're really pretty." She touches her eyes, and plays with her shorts. "I should put something on."

"You look fine," Shelly interrupts. "Frannie, doesn't Pia have gorgeous skin?" I nod as Shelly looks at Keisha, who is still standing in the doorway. "You can come in," she tells her. Keisha inches forward. "All the way," Shelly commands.

Keisha moves some papers and sits on the edge of Shelly's bed. I sit next to her, but she won't look at me. Pia sits on her own bed. "Shelly's helping me with my poetry," Pia says. "She has a great ear."

"Shelly, what do you know about poetry other than 'There Once Was a Man From Nantucket'?" I ask. Keisha snorts, but her hand flies to her mouth. It dawns on me that she doesn't want to laugh out loud, as if afraid to call attention to herself. I'm hit with a sudden longing to cry.

Shelly looks at her hands. "Why would you say that? How do you know?"

"She's very talented," Pia says protectively. "She's read almost *everything.*"

"I was just teasing," I mumble, red-faced. "I'm sure she has." I turn to Keisha and ask her what she does.

"I was a physical therapist until I got so big," Keisha murmurs, wrinkling her nose. "And now I'm a ..." She hesitates. "... a transportation executive."

"What's that?" I ask.

"A bus driver," Keisha says sheepishly, looking at Shelly. "It's Shelly's idea to say that."

"I think it's a good idea, too," I tell her, looking at Shelly, who ignores me and walks to the door. "It's time for meds," she says. Keisha and Pia follow her like she's the Pied Piper. Finally she turns to me. "Frannie," she sneers like my name is a dirty word, "you wait here."

I sit on the floor and flip through a notebook, debating if I should leave. My eye catches the name Frannie. I read for a while before realizing it's Shelly's journal.

October 1—*Katie asked me to write about my favorite memory. I was in the seventh grade and I wrote my first term paper. It took me four months. I remember exactly how I felt when I turned it in. I was so proud. Mr. Hoffman said, "Rochelle, you really are something else." I remember how good it felt, not only to be something, but to be something else. I felt like a prodigy, like Galileo, like I could have discovered the meaning of life if I thought hard enough. I remember feeling like everything was ahead of me, I had a crystal-clear happiness. If I could have one day to relive again, it would be that one. When everything was neat and contained and I could rise above it and make it even better.*

October 3—Frannie was here. I'm getting used to her being here. Sometimes I feel like there's a vast expanse of land between us. Other times, I feel like she's all the way inside me. Is that what a sister is? Some girl who's been around your whole life, who, in one split second, is a stranger, and a second later, is the most familiar person you've ever known? Sometimes I hate her so much I want to kill her. Other times I love her so much, I want to cry.

October 4—Four nights without sleep. Please, God, please let me sleep. To sleep perchance to dream. To be or not to be. Maybe Shakespeare was anorexic [note to self: thesis topic, Eating Disorders of the Elizabethans—Bulimia With the Bard—maybe Ophelia wasn't mad, maybe she was hungry].

October 8—HARVARDHARVARDHARVARD Johnny Bennet's nephew called (finally) and says I'm in like Flynn. Is that the expression? Or is it "in like Flynt"? If so, who's Flynt (or Flynn for that matter?!). I'm in. I'm in. Yippee!!!!

October 8-PM—I just spoke to my mother. She's so excited about this Harvard thing. God, the whole FUCKING thing makes me sick. I don't want to go there. I hate those people. They're so snotty. It makes me hate myself for being like them. I can already hear my sniveling, whiny voice. Just like high school when I had no friends. "Hi, I'm Shelly and I'm sooo smart." Some therapist in college told me I wore my intelligence on my sleeve. WELL FUCK YOU. There's no way I'm going to Harvard. I'll just end up like all the bitches in high school who thought they ruled. My mother can take HARVARD and SHOVE IT UP HER ASSHOLE. I am not going. Why can't I just be normal? Please, God, let me be normal someday.

I hear voices in the hallway. "Do you really think so, Shelly?" Pia is asking.

"Pia, why would I lie? You're an incredible writer. Really. Your work is beautiful."

As they get closer, my heart pounds. I'm dying to read more, but they're getting closer. I hide the notebook under a T-shirt, but keep flipping through the papers, trying to find other things. I spy the Harvard application. Flip through it. And when I do, my breath catches. All the pages are blank.

"She's out," Carol says when I call to tell my mother. "She's showing houses with Daniel."

"I have something I need to talk to her about. Since when does she show houses?"

"They decided to ride together for a week. Teach each other what they know. Yesterday, he took us all out for lunch. He's such a nice man." She pauses. "What did you want to tell your mother?"

"Nothing," I say, hanging up. "It's not important."

The next morning, I wait for Abby at the gym. She called me, crying, begging me to meet her. "I can't go to work today," she said. "Everything's all fucked up."

The walls are covered with mirrors, and every time I move, I'm startled by my multiple reflections. I pedal on the bike, trying not to look at all my selves.

"Sorry I'm late." Abby sniffles, walking toward me. "I was with Everett." She stretches in front of me, so I talk to her ass. "And?" I ask. She sits on a bike next to me and pedals idly. "Well? What happened?"

"I did it. I broke up with him." Crying a little, Abby wipes her eyes, smudging her mascara. I don't say anything because I don't feel like dealing with her melodrama. "I just didn't think it would bother me so much," she continues. "You know, you can jump in at any time."

"What do you want from me, Abby? You know you're better off. I know a lot of people who cheat on their wives, or husbands, rather." I pause for her to ask me who, but she doesn't. "You never see it from the other person's point of view. I'd never do that to my husband."

"That's very optimistic of you, Frannie."

"What? Being faithful?"

"No. Being married."

"You don't have to be a bitch. I'm *trying* to be supportive and I *hated* that Rat Man."

"I'm sorry. I just feel like shit." Her face contorts. She buries her face in a display of sorrow, but I don't believe for a second that she's upset; deep-down, I think Everett disgusted her.

"Abby, come on. We'll go out Friday night. We'll meet new guys. Better guys," I add. "Then we can see Shelly on Saturday."

"How is Shelly?" she asks, changing the subject.

"Up and down. Down more than up." I start to tell Abby about the journal, but she's not looking at me anymore. She's staring at a jarhead lifting weights. Jarhead smiles at her and she smiles back. "I don't think I could deal with having a sister," Abby says absently, adjusting her bra top. "That's why I love being an only child. Everyone loves you most." She keeps staring at the guy.

"Do you want to meet him, Abby?" I snap. "I'm trying to talk to you. You could at least act like you're paying attention."

She glares at me. "I just broke up with my boyfriend. Would it kill you to be nice to me today?" We pedal in frustrated silence. "Frannie," she says. "it's obviously bothering you that that doctor didn't call. But you didn't give him your number. How is he supposed to find you? Jesus, if it's making you this unhappy, just call him yourself."

"That's what you think is bothering me? Thanks for your insight."

"What's a best friend for?"

I try not to look at Daniel as he scurries through the office. I told my mother I didn't want to come in, but she begged. "Carol's out sick and a temp can't make cold calls," she told me. "Please? I know you need the money." Apparently, she doesn't mind flaunting her affair. Maybe she's afraid I'll tell my father if she's not nice. She offered to pay me double, so for all I care, she can fuck the guy on her credenza.

I spend the morning writing my name on a legal pad:

Frannie Hunter Thompson Mrs. Frannie Thompson
Dr. and Mrs. Bryan Thompson ~~Dr. and Dr. Thompson~~

I hear my mother talking to my grandfather. She speaks slowly, as if talking to a child. She tells him that she and Aunt Lillian are looking into moving him out of Florida, that he'll eventually come live with her in New York. "Now just isn't the best time, Daddy," she says. "Frannie is home and there are a lot of people around … Yes, I told you that. Frannie moved home … About four months ago"—(*It's only been three, Mom, three and a half*)—"What? No, she doesn't have a boyfriend. No, it's Rascals, not Hooligans. And it's Houlihan's. No, she's not at Houlihan's, she's at Rascals. It's like Hooligans—I mean Houlihan's. Frannie!" she yells. "Pick up the phone. Grandpa wants to say hello." I make believe I can't hear her. "She must be busy, Daddy … Yes, Shelly is fine. Still at the law firm … That's right, just like Perry Mason. I know that's your favorite show … No, I like *Murder, She Wrote*." She doesn't speak for a second and I think she's hung up, but then she says, "Yes, you will move up here. I promise I'll talk to Lillian … I love you, too."

She walks over to my desk. "That was your grandfather. Honestly, I don't know what to do. He calls me every ten minutes."

"So does Aunt Lillian," I remind her, slipping my hand over the legal pad. I follow her into her office.

"I just don't think I can handle having Grandpa up here right now," she says, "but I hate the thought of leaving him alone in that house with his eyes so bad. Now Tilly's talking about moving in with her daughter in Tampa." She stacks some papers. "Anyway, he's becoming too much for Tilly to handle."

I try to appear nonchalant. "I think he should move in with us. You can't put him in an institution, Mom. It's so anonymous. I'll take care of him during the day, at least until I find a job." I can't even believe I'm saying this. My grandfather will drive *me* into an institution.

"He needs professional help, Frannie. I'll check out a few places. Not every nursing home has been on *60 Minutes*." She looks up. "I thought the same thing about Shelly, remember? But now I realize the hospital is the best place for her. She sounds great! Said she finished her applications."

"She said that? Are you sure?"

"Yes, Frannie. Why are you making such a big deal about this?" She tries to catch my eye. "You can go to graduate school, too, honey."

I shrug, but the urge to tell my mother the truth about Shelly's application is like a living force inside my head. "Shelly didn't—" I start to say, but I stop myself. If I tell her I read the journal, she'll just tell Shelly, and it will become a whole big thing. "Look, I just think you owe your father a decent place to live. I can't imagine him in a nursing home."

"When you're a grown woman with daughters and I'm aging against my will with nothing to do all day but call you, then we'll talk about who owes what to whom."

"Fine. Do what you need to do." The phone rings and I reach for it, forgetting I'm in her office. "Hi, Grandpa. No, I'm not sure what channel *The Price Is Right* is on. I didn't even know it was still on TV. Oh look, my boyfriend is here. And he's got flowers!!"

Johnny Bennet calls me into his office. While he finishes up a phone call, I glance at a picture of him standing in front of a rambling Victorian house, shaking hands with the new owners. Beaming, Johnny rests his free hand on a bright yellow SOLD sign. He's thinner in the picture than he is in real life, but looks just as dopey.

"My biggest sale." He gestures. "Four bills. That's when I was on fire. I was thirty pounds lighter." He pats his belly. "Then I got rich and fat. Not too bad a combination."

"Oh, you're not so fat." I wonder if this deflates the compliment he pays himself.

"Mrs. Bennet is constantly monitoring my cholesterol. What she doesn't know about are my after-hours martinis." He laughs heartily. His grandiosity amazes me. "So that will be our little secret, Frannie?" He smiles conspiratorially. "You won't tell the missus about my martinis?" I shake my head. I could give a shit about your martinis. I hear Daniel flitting around. I glance out and see him walking toward my mother's office. As I hear her stupid laugh, I want to race out there.

I realize Johnny is speaking. "The reason I called you in here is because I don't think Carol wants to come back full-time. Your mother and I have discussed it and we—well, *I*, since she told me she isn't sure if this is what you want to do—*I* was thinking that you might want to work here. Not permanently, but long enough so we can train someone. You could decide if you want to be an agent, maybe ride with Daniel." He sits back. The chair squeaks from his weight. "Think about it."

I look over at the picture. The thin Johnny Bennet looks at me. I bet my mother put up a fight about this. "God, Mr. Bennet, I am so flattered, but my mom's right. I *am* looking for something different. The more time I spend here, the less I have for my job search. But thank you." I move toward the door. "It's nice of you to even consider me."

I rush out of his office and turn to my mother's. Daniel's in there and her door is shut. It pisses me off that I didn't hear them close it. I'm so mad, I could spit.

After working at my mother's office, I have to go to Rascals. I can't believe I'm working two jobs. I don't know which one I hate more. On the way to the restaurant, I stop off at home to take a shower. There's a note on the kitchen counter.

> David,
>   Went to the gym. Will be home around 8:30. Eat without me.
>   M.

The note is written in my mother's looping, bold script. I study it for a few seconds. Before I leave, I grab a pen and scrawl *I love you* above my mother's initial, jabbing the pen into the paper, not even caring that my writing looks nothing at all like hers.

I don't make it to work after all. I take a chance and drive to Dr. Bryan's apartment. He's not surprised to see me, in fact, he's happy. We spend hours together, hours of sweaty, lusty, amazing sex. I lie in bed as he gets dressed. Slowly, I drop the sheet from my body. He crawls on the bed in his clothes and traces my nipple with his finger. "You are so awesome," he murmurs, his breath warm. "I want to kiss your incredible mouth."

I stare at the phone in the break room at Rascals. Call him. Just call him. He doesn't know where you live or where you work, thank God. How is he supposed to find you? It's been a month, maybe he forgot. But as much as I want to call him, I can't. I thumb through an old Manhattan phone book until I find:

THOMPSON Bryan 204 E. 79 . . . 555–9998

I write the number down on a blank check and put it in my wallet. Paulie sticks his head into the break room. "Frannie! Frannie, come on. You have food up."

"I'm coming. Jesus, you'd think I was late for a board meeting at General Motors." But like Pavlov's dog, I follow him out, gazing at the phone one last time.

Hours later, the dinner rush over, I walk toward the kitchen with a tray of plates. Behind me, Artie pulls the strings of my apron, which slips with the weight of checks, loose change, pens, and bills. "Tie the fucking apron, Artie," I say sharply. "My hands are full."

"Kiss me first," he says, breathing in my ear. "I'll do it if you kiss me."

"Artie, goddammit. This isn't funny." I jerk forward. Wine sloshes over the rims of the drinks. My apron and everything in it scatters all over the floor. As I bend over, Artie rubs my ass. "Stop it!" I hiss. "Just leave me alone." For a second, I stand paralyzed, not knowing if I should hit him or cry.

I walk past the couple at my last table three times, trying to appear as if I'm not watching them. Once they cash out, I can go home to my little bed and fantasize about Bryan. The couple huddle together, deep in conversation. It looks like the woman is crying. "Can I get you anything else?" I ask, trying to hear what they are saying.

They both look up quickly and shake their heads. The man is probably twenty years older than the woman and very distinguished. The woman is extremely pretty and talks rapidly, waving her hands in the air. For some reason, she strikes me as desperate. I notice the glint of a wedding band on the man's hand. He seems annoyed by the woman. He even glances away a few times as if she bores him. It bothers me to watch, but I can't help myself. I'm dying to know why the woman is suddenly sobbing so hard, and trying not to make any noise. When she holds up her hands to wipe her eyes, then rests them on his arm, it all makes sense: she's not wearing any rings.

I glance at Artie, who is counting bills in the waitress stand. I can feel his fingers in my hair, and a chill runs through me. The woman is still crying. I want to shake her, pull her away from that guy, scream that she should treat herself better. I inch up to the table. "Would you mind cashing out with me?" I try to sound sweet. The man looks up accusingly, like it's my fault his date is crying. "You're my last table. You can sit as long as you want." I feel like a trailer-park slut asking for the money, even though it's mine.

"We haven't finished yet. We'll leave when we're ready," the man says sharply. The woman doesn't say a thing, she just looks beaten.

"You can stay as long as you want, but I can't go until you pay me."

"I *said* we would pay you when we were ready to leave. You're a waitress for Christ's sake. Go get Paulie. I want to see him."

Anger explodes in my head when I hear him spit the word *waitress* through his teeth as if it's vile. I lean across the table and get right in his face. "Don't talk to me like that," I hiss. "You have no right to be such an asshole. I am still a *person*!" Dumbstruck, the man stares at me. He raises his hand and I jerk back, but he puts it around his date. Muttering, he digs a few bills out of his wallet and throws them on the floor. I look at the money lying at my feet. "Pick it up," he says. "You wanted it, didn't you?"

I hold his eyes. With images wrapped around my mind, Artie's sick smile, Shelly's blank application, Everett's diamond bracelet, and my mother giggling on the phone, I backhand a glass of red wine into the man's lap. "I went to college," I tell him. "And I'm going to law school. Harvard." I look dead-center at the woman. "He's a loser," I say. "Let his wife have him." An audible gasp comes from the woman, the man starts ranting about his suit, and I saunter away, triumphant.

"Hey, Artie," I call out, "I forgot to pick up the check from table seven, but I have to go to the ladies' room. Could you get the money?" Eagerly, Artie jumps up and scampers into the dining room. It dawns on me that the man knew Paulie's name. How does he know Paulie? Panic sets in and I wonder if Bryan Thompson will still consider dating me when he finds out I'm unemployed.

8

*T*he voice on the answering machine startles me. *"Mr. Hunter, this is Adele Reynolds, Daniel's wife, from On-Target. Could you please call me at home this evening? It's important. My number is 516–555–7575. Thank you."*

I rewind and listen again. She must be calling my father to talk about Daniel and my mother. I copy her number down, stick it in my wallet, and listen to her message again. This time I hear an undercurrent of depression, a hint of sorrow. She's been betrayed, she is beaten. I unwrap a piece of gum and chew it thoughtfully. Then I do what any normal person would if they heard a message like that—I erase it.

Later, I call Abby from the gym. "Are you there, God?" I ask. "It's me, Margaret." She doesn't pick up. "Abby, come on. It's Saturday. I know you're there."

"What's up?" She sounds groggy.

I force myself to stay calm. "Abby." I tense up. "You're not going to believe this. Promise you won't tell a soul."

"Promise. What is it?" She yawns, but I know I've got her interest.

"Abby, you have to swear. God, this is so fucked up." A woman jostles me. "Oh shit, hold on. I dropped the phone." I nestle it into the crook of my neck. "Okay, there."

"TELL ME ALREADY!"

"Calm down. Abby, canyoubelieve? My mother is having an affair."

There's a long silence. "Well I'll be damned. No wonder you were so freaked out about Everett. It's that handsome guy in her office, isn't it? Jesus, Frannie, I'm really sorry."

"He's not that handsome," I say sharply. "He's a fucking freak."

"How do you know?"

"Because I've met him."

"No, Einstein, how do you know about the affair?"

"I just do."

"Are you going to tell your father?" A woman brushes by wearing nothing but a turban. Her breasts hang like pendulums and she has sparse pubic hairs like a plucked chicken. Disgusted, I look away. "Frannie? Are you there? What are you going to do?"

"Nothing. We can't tell anyone—not my dad or yours. Especially not yours. God, imagine if Shelly found out. This would really fuck her up." She's silent. "Abby, this is serious. I mean it." Still, she doesn't say anything. "Look, forget I said anything." I get choked up.

"Frannie, you're my best friend. I won't say a thing. I feel *badly* for you."

"I feel badly for me, too."

Abby is quiet. Finally she says, "You know, there's got to be a better way to meet men. Do you think we should ask your mom for dating tips?"

Tuesday night is Family Night at St. Mary's. We haven't attended any Family Nights, but I was suspended from Rascals indefinitely and have nothing else to do. I've decided to spend the entire afternoon with Shelly. This Harvard thing has me all shook up.

My father walks into the kitchen as I'm about to leave and asks where I'm going. "To see Shelly. She's your other daughter. The one with all the brains." I eye him suspiciously, wondering if he has any idea about my mother and Daniel. "Is everything all right, Daddy?"

"Everything's fine. Have you spoken to your mother?"

"No. Why? You seem upset. Are you?"

"Am I what?" His back is to me as he rifles through the mail.

"Upset. Did something bad happen that I should know about?"

He sticks his head in the refrigerator and tells me he's making calf's liver lasagna for dinner. "Daddy, it's Family Night. I'm going to see Shelly." I inch toward the door. "What did Mommy want?"

"She said she'd be late, but wanted to know if you took her Liz Claiborne jacket." I tell him I haven't seen it.

He looks up. "Frannie," he asks, "why are you hovering? Am I missing something here?" His eyes are bloodshot and he looks exhausted. He must know something's going on.

"I just want you to come with me to Family Night. You've only been to see Shelly a few times."

He pats the mail. "I have a lot of things to do, Frannie. I'll come as soon as I can."

"Whatever," I say, and grab his keys. "But one day, you'll regret this."

I drive to the corner and stop. Then I make a U-turn and go back home. "Daddy," I yell, jingling the keys. "Come with me to see Shelly."

He's not in the den so I turn off the television and walk upstairs. At the top, I notice that Shelly's door is open. I peer inside. My father is sitting on the edge of the bed, holding the picture of us on the beach. He stares at it the way I stare at the photograph of my mother hugging the statue that I carry around, as if he's expecting her to step out of the picture and dance.

"Daddy?" I whisper. "You okay?"

He turns around, startled. "Yes, of course." He clears his throat. "I forgot about this picture. A lot has happened since then, hasn't it?" I nod. "I know … I … uh … Look, Frannie. I have a difficult time, you know, with hospitals. Your grandmother, my mother, spent a long time in the hospital before she died. I don't want you to judge me."

My throat constricts. "I didn't mean what I said before about you regretting this. That was an awful thing to say."

He waves. "Don't worry about it. I just … I don't know … it's no big deal."

"What? Say it."

"I …" He fumbles. "I was never smart like Shelly. Book smart, you know. Your mother's like Shelly. I'm people smart. So sometimes I don't know what to say. I guess … I, you know, I feel helpless, that's all. I just thought that things like this don't happen to people who are so smart. I always thought they'd be able to figure a way out."

"Daddy," I say softly. "I don't think anorexia has much to do with being smart." He says he knows, but keeps staring at the picture. "She's gonna be okay, Dad," I tell him. "She has big plans."

"I know." He manages a grin. "You girls always manage to pull through."

When I walk into the unit, I see Shelly curled on the couch in the day room. The television is on and people are milling through, but Shelly doesn't move.

"Hi, Frannie," Lucy, one of the nurses, says. "Here to see Shelly?" I nod. "I'll see if she's up to a visitor." She looks at my face. "Are you okay? You seem upset about something."

"I'm fine, thanks." You taking a poll, Lucy? As much as I like her, she's a little too concerned a citizen. I look around, hoping to see Bryan. He must not work at this hospital anymore, I guess. Shelly finally comes to claim me. Shuffling along, she looks at her feet as if mesmerized by the floor tiling.

"Hi, Shelly." I lean in to hug her, but she draws away. "Mommy and Daddy both had to work late. They said to tell you that they're sorry and they'll come next week."

"That's good because I called family therapy off." She trudges toward her room, not looking back to see if I'm following. As I walk behind her, I notice that her hair is stringy and thin, like it's falling out. She's wearing a bathrobe and two long T-shirts underneath the JUST DO IT sweatshirt. The once white sweatshirt is now gray and stained with what looks like vomit.

She turns on a radio and lies on her bed. "I see you're wearing Mommy's Claiborne jacket. You guys are sharing clothes?" She covers her eyes with her arm.

"You seem upset, Shelly. Did they change your medication?" I ask.

"So now you're a psychopharmacologist?" she snaps. "Why are you interrogating me?"

"I'm not. I'm just asking." Distracted by the radio playing in the background, I find myself humming.

We sit for a long time without talking. "Frannie," she says finally. "I have to tell you something, but you have to promise me you won't tell Mommy. She'll be very disappointed."

"I promise. I have something to tell you, too. And you can't tell Mommy, either."

"You go first." She sits up. "No, I'll go first. I didn't do any of my applications to law school." Tears fill her eyes. "I'm sorry I lied."

"It's okay, Shelly. I understand. Believe me, I understand." I pause. "I got fired from Rascals."

"How are you going to keep that from Mommy? Where will you go at night?"

I grin. "I figured I'd just come here."

Shelly doesn't smile. She reaches for a glass of water. When her sleeve hikes up, I spy long red marks, like cat scratches on her forearms. I grab the left one which she wrenches away. "Shelly! What the hell happened to your arms?"

"I cut myself. Don't get hysterical. It didn't hurt." She lies back and closes her eyes.

"With what? You're not supposed to have sharps in here. I'm calling Lucy."

"With a Scotch tape dispenser. They want me to move," she says slowly, as though every word takes effort. "A few floors up. They think I'll be happier. Here, I have to do activities, and upstairs, they won't make me do anything. It will be better up there, they said, and tomorrow we're expecting scattered showers, so bring an umbrella. Temperatures will fall. Tomorrow they're putting me on the tubes."

I stare at her. "What did you just say?"

"They're putting me on the tubes. I'm not supposed to know. I looked at my chart. If the tubes don't work, I'm going upstairs."

"No, about the scattered showers. And the umbrella."

"I didn't say anything about an umbrella. I said they're putting me on the tubes." She licks her fingers and runs them through her hair. Her mouth is so dry, I can hear the sound of her lips separating. Then she pulls out a strand and chews on it.

I flush with a wave of anxiety. "Shelly," I tell her, "I know you're in this place to get better, but lately, you don't seem like yourself." I say this gently, as if the two of us are in this together, and together we'll find a way out.

"I'm not crazy, Frannie. I just start to think about all that I have to do. And the only way I can contain it is to keep my patterns: my calories in order, my weight down. But in here, they fuck with my patterns. So my head gets all twisted and I have this constant whirring, like a fan is on inside it. I can't stop it. It's just going all day long, this huge fan, like a hum. But in my body, I can't feel anything. So I cut myself, just to feel *something*. They're making a much bigger deal of it than it is."

Shelly starts to cry without making any noise. Tears slip out of her eyes and run down her cheeks, but she doesn't move to wipe them. She just sits and looks at me through a catatonic glaze, as if waiting for her feelings to catch up. I don't think she even realizes she's crying. Late afternoon sunlight shines through the bars on the window, flushing Shelly's pale face with a beautiful golden light. Watching my sister glowing I wonder why, if the sun is so warm, it doesn't dry her tears. Sunlight is supposed to do that, I think, sunlight should dry all the rain.

October 9—*I miss the office. I miss the office. I miss the office. I miss my routine. I miss my routine. I miss my routine. I need to work. I need to work. I need to work. God, get me out of here!!*

October 12—*They ask me what I think of food. I tell them I don't know, but I do. I know everything about it. I feel like I'm at war. It's all about the battle. I am always aware of what I am doing. I watch myself watch the plate, I watch my hand lift my fork. I watch the mouth that opens like a cunt, the fork that slides in like a dick. That fucks me every time I swallow. I watch every second. I savor it all. The object, however, is to not let them know that you know this. Because if they do, they will take it away. Not the food, of course, but the knowing. Your absolute certainty that you will win. That's the real war, not the food, but the fuck and the desire of that fuck that I can control and I can deny. That I can destroy. You destroy the hunger, you destroy the desire, you destroy the need, you destroy the girl. The Me. And once I'm gone, what's left to fuck?*

October ?—*There's this place deep inside myself that I'm trying to reach. A calm, quiet place where I don't exist as a girl with a body that grows too big. A place where I can finally sleep. I'm trying to reach that place, every day I try, and I know there will be a point when I'll be able to slip through. I know the point, I've almost been there, the point when I'm so hungry, I can't feel it, the point of numb-ness, of suspension, the window of time when it's okay to say yes, to let go, to fly. That's the point I work toward, my own personal hunger point; a point when I feel everything and nothing at all. When all it takes is one more step and I'll be safe.*

"What are you reading?"

Startled, I wave the pamphlet I'd been holding in case she caught me. My heart raps in my chest. "Nothing …" I take a deep breath. "Well, actually, I was reading the hospital rules. It says here you're not allowed to go to the bathroom unescorted." I look up. "Ever?"

"I don't know, Frannie. Come on, I want to sit on the roof."

It's chilly out and Shelly trembles. "You're cold," I tell her. "Let's go inside. Shelly, I'm really worried about you."

"I'm fine. I like it out here. It's very peaceful." She looks at me. "How is living at home?"

"Are you thinking of leaving here?" I ask slowly.

"I don't think I'll be leaving here for a while. It's not so bad, really. I'm used to it now. How is it with them? With Mommy and Daddy? I can't remember."

"Shelly, I'm serious. I'm really fucking worried." My eyes tear. "Tell me what you're thinking. Please."

She sits up. The white lights overhead drain her face of color. "I can't feel myself anymore," she says. She leans forward. "I don't exist, Frannie, I'm a big black hole getting sucked into myself. And I can't stop the whirring in my head. It's there all the time."

"Shelly," I beg her. "Shelly, you've got to talk to someone."

"It's no use, Frannie." She rocks her head back and forth as if it's too heavy for her shoulders. "It's my brain," she says softly. "It's eating me alive."

In the lobby, I huddle against the pay phone. "Abby, I'm at the hospital. I just saw Shelly. She's worse than ever. You should hear her! And I read her journal. She's totally suicidal." I pause. "Look, I know it was wrong, but I couldn't help myself."

"What do your parents say?"

"What do they know? They're the reason she's here in the first place."

"What about Fatso?"

"Her name is Chubby, Abby. I mean Marilyn. And she won't tell me anything. All that shit is confidential."

"I don't know what to tell you, Frannie." Then she blurts, "Call that doctor! You have the perfect reason!"

"I can't use Shelly like that. Come on, this is important."

"You're not *using* Shelly. You're trying to *help* her. I care about her, too. Just call this guy. He's a psychiatrist, right? Maybe he can give us some advice."

"He's a resident." My mind races. "I don't know how much he knows about Shelly. Besides, even if he did, I don't think he'd tell me. What do you think? Do you think he'd tell me?" I roll the idea over and over.

"Call him. Shelly would, if the situation was reversed."

After we hang up, I start to walk away from the phone but change my direction mid-stride. I dig in my wallet and I pull out the paper scrap with his number. I dial quickly, willing the connection to go through before I change my mind. "I'm doing this for Shelly," I tell myself. When I hear the phone ring, I immediately hang up.

I take another breath, dial again, this time, much more slowly. I wait for Bryan's deep voice. "Hello? Hello? Who is this?" It's a woman's voice, one I can't place. When I glance at the number, I realize that I've mistakenly called Daniel's wife, Adele. Startled, I reach to hang up, but surprise myself by holding on. Adele gets more urgent. "Who is this?"

"This is Frannie. Frannie Hunter," I say quickly. "We got your message." There's silence on her end. "This morning, remember?"

"Yes?" Her tone is clipped. "Why isn't your father calling me?"

"I thought you might like ..." I stutter, "you know, to talk, about your husband."

"What's wrong with my husband?" Her voice rises.

"Nothing, I swear." It slowly dawns on me that she may not know what I'm talking about. "You did call about your husband and you know, my ... uh ... mother?"

"Of course not." She tells me she was going to ask my father to have his company print up 1,500 T-shirts for a muscular dystrophy benefit. "What did you think I was calling about?"

I think quickly, but not before an obvious, painful silence elapses. "I thought you were calling about the surprise party. You know, for Johnny Bennet. I'm on the invitations committee. Daniel and my mother are planning it."

"No," she says slowly. "Daniel hasn't said anything."

"Well," I race. "I wouldn't talk to him just yet. I think it's still being planned. Maybe they won't even have it at all."

"I'm sure he would have said something to me. I have a catering business."

"Oh. I did not know that. Wow. Huh. How 'bout that. Well, just goes to show you. Life is really funny. Well, I'm sure Daniel will bring it up when the time is right. Well, thanks. And, well, bye," I say.

"Goodbye, Frannie," she says. "Have your father call me, okay?"

The phone clicks, and I am left holding the receiver. I slowly hang up, my body pulsing. I lean forward and bang my head against the phone, once, twice, and then a third time until I feel it throbbing. The throbbing doesn't bother me. In fact, the only thing I feel is a sense of justice; that if anything, I have earned the pain, or rather, deserve it.

On the street I walk backwards and crane my neck. With all the bars, the hospital looks horrifying. Fuck it. I walk back inside.

"This is Dr. Thompson. If you'd like to leave a message ..." I hang up. He's not home. Then a thought strikes. "Dr. Bryan Thompson, please," I tell the hospital operator. She tells me she has to page him.

I wait a few minutes and then hear, "Yeah, Thompson, here."

"Oh ... uh ... hi. How are you?" I clear my throat, suddenly unable to breathe.

"Hello, Dr. Thompson here. I can't hear you. There's people talking behind me."

"HI, BRYAN!" I yelp. "IT'S FRANNIE HUNGER ... I MEAN HUNTER."

"Oh. Hello." He doesn't remember me. Fuck.

"I'M SHELLY'S SISTER. SHELLY FROM THE E.D. UNIT ON THREE."

"Oh, Frannie. Hi. How is everything?" He tells whoever's talking to move away.

"Well, I'm fine. It's Shelly who isn't doing so well. I ... I ... was like wondering if we could get together and talk. I thought maybe you could help me figure all this out."

"To be honest, I haven't been on that ward for a very long time."

"Oh well, then, okay." We sit in silence for a few seconds. Then he tells me he can meet me for coffee.

"I'm in the lobby," I blurt out. "How about now?" He says that now's not so good, and he's out of town the following week, but how about Monday the fifteenth? At the diner on the corner at noon?

"That's fine," I tell him. "I really appreciate it."

"Good," he says. "Frannie, don't worry. Sometimes patients slip, but she'll be back in med school in no time. Take care." And he's gone.

Med school? Who said anything about medical school? It's *law* school! And I'm Frannie, the girl with the incredible mouth. How could you forget me? You said you wanted to *kiss* me!

When I get home, Aunt Lillian calls from Arizona. "Mommy's working late," I tell her.

"I called to talk to you."

Wrapped in the phone cord, I lean into the refrigerator. "'Bout what?" I take out turkey, bread, tomatoes, mustard, Swiss cheese, and onions and build myself a Dagwood. Every time I lean into the refrigerator, I think about Shelly. I search for mayonnaise. Shit, my father didn't buy any mayonnaise. What is *wrong* with him? Mayonnaise is an essential household condiment. How could he forget mayonnaise?

"Are you there? Frannie, put down what you're doing. I need you to listen."

"I am listening."

"You're eating."

"No, I'm not," I say, swallowing. She launches into how she wants to sell Grandpa's condo and move him up to New York. Tilly can't take care of him anymore, and having both him and Beth in Tempe is too much for her to handle. "Grandpa needs us right now, Frannie," she says. "We owe it to him. I'll hire a nurse for the days you're working."

"Look, Aunt Lillian. Shelly's not doing so well. We have a lot going on, too." I bite into my sandwich and chew hard. With every bite, I make Shelly's face go away.

"But this is Grandpa. Don't you think we should get him the best care possible?"

"Of course I do. Jesus. Why would you even ask that?" *It's my brain,* she said. *It's eating me alive.* I crunch a pickle. The sound of myself chewing fills my ears. Is that possible? Can your brain eat away your sanity? Does it have that kind of power? "I don't know how much help I can be. Mommy and I don't always see eye to eye. And she's really worried about Shelly. Really worried."

"I am, too. Believe me. But maybe with Grandpa there, it will take her mind off things. We need to do this for him … And for Grandma," she adds solemnly. "They took care of us our whole lives, now it's our time to take care of them. Please talk to Mommy for me."

"Okay," I say, you manipulative fucking bitch. "I'll talk to her." Suddenly ravenous, I devour my sandwich, make another one, and eat that, too. And then I rip into a box of Oreos.

"A surprise party!! Frannie, what the hell is wrong with you?" My mother snaps on the light.

In bed, I rub my eyes to appear disoriented. "Huh?"

"Why did you call Adele Reynolds?" She stands over my bed. Her mouth is tight, and she looks like she's about to hit me.

"Frannie, look at me. What are you doing?" She leans over me and gets right into my face.

"I wasn't doing anything." I grope for words. "I was just trying to help out. Shelly's not doing so well, Mom. I mean, she's doing really bad. I'm scared ..."

She cuts me off. "I know that, Frannie. I spoke to the hospital today. They're adjusting her medication. But that's not what we're talking about, and you know it. I told you that there is nothing going on between Daniel and me. And even if there was, what right do you have to call his wife and make up some bullshit story?" She leans on my dresser, her hand in a fist. "Look at me, Frannie! I said LOOK AT ME!"

I quickly look up, then away. "I'm just worried about Shelly, Mom. Do we have to go into this right now? Do you think that just changing her medication will be enough? I think Shelly's getting worse in that hospital. Does Marilyn think that, too?"

"Goddammit, Frannie. Stop it. This is my house, I'm letting you live here as a favor. It is a PRIVILEGE, not a right. Do you understand?" I nod. "DO YOU?"

"I said yes, Mom. You don't have to yell. Maybe this would work a little better if we tried to have more respect for each other."

"And you've been showing respect? Making accusations? Calling the wives of my business associates? You're a grown woman living in *my* house and I tiptoe around on eggshells."

"Do you really think I *like* living here?" I ask. "That I *want* to live like this?" We both look around. Stockings and tights hang out of open drawers, sweaters are piled on the floor. I feel like I'm eleven years old and she's telling me how fat I am, fat and stupid, fat and lazy, fat and in the way. She acts like she hates me. Maybe she does. Maybe she hates the very sight of me, fat and smelly, living in my little room.

"I don't know what to do, Frannie. Tell me what to do. I have a daughter *wasting away* in a mental institution. Did it ever occur to you that I NEED you? I spoke to Aunt Lillian. I've decided to bring Grandpa up here, then move him into a nursing home after the first of the year. So if you're going to be around, you're going to help out. Otherwise, you can leave now. Then, when Grandpa moves out, you will, too. January first, I want you in your own apartment." She stares at me, but I don't say anything. "Do you hear me?"

I nod. Not knowing what else to say, I tell her that Aunt Lillian called me, too.

"Why did she call *you*?" My mother's still pissed, but she's calmed down a bit.

"She asked me to talk you into having Grandpa move up here."

"Jesus, that's so like her. Well, it's done. He's coming."

"I promise I'll help, Mom," I say, my eyes glistening. "You can depend on me."

"Fine. And are we clear on the January evacuation date?"

I mumble a yes. She stands in the doorway. "I know you make good money at Rascals and you haven't been paying rent since July, so please don't insult me by crying poor."

"Well, Mom, something's come up." I draw out the words. "I'm not employed at Rascals anymore." I look up. "But it was a mutual thing."

"What will you do for money? Forget it." She turns away. "I don't want to know."

That's good, I mutter, because I don't have the first fucking clue.

"Paulie?" I whisper. "Paulie, I need my job back."

"I can't, honey," he says. "Not yet. You pissed off someone important."

"What am I going to do?" I start to cry again. He tells me I have to go out and talk to people. His voice is stern.

"I'm talking to you," I whimper. I can hear the clatter of plates in the background and I sob, really let it go. I blow my nose in my sleeve.

"Frannie," he says, "call me in a month, okay? Things will have blown over by then. In the meantime, keep your chin up. This could end up being very positive for you."

"Yeah, right. I should step in front of a bus. That would be positive."

"Don't tempt yourself."

"It's too late."

I busy myself cleaning up my room. Screw it, if she wants me to move out, I'll leave now. She's totally overreacting, and I know it's because I found out about her sleazy affair. She doesn't have any respect for me. Calling Daniel fucking Reynolds in the middle of the night. Then I think about Shelly and start to cry, hating myself. I do make things worse. I deserve to die.

With no one else to call, I dial Chubby, but all I get is her service so I leave a message that it's an emergency. I sit on the edge of my bed and stare into space, wishing I had somewhere to go.

A half-hour later, the phone rings. "Frannie?" Chubby asks. "You called?"

"Well ... I'm not sure ... I don't know ... I guess I wanted to talk about Shelly." I sniffle. "I saw her today and she was totally out of it. She did this freaky thing where she picked up radio words as if they were her own thoughts. She like spliced them into her conversation."

"It was a mild psychotic episode, Frannie. It's scary, I know, but it's not dangerous. It's a symptom of someone who is detached from their feelings. Shelly's dealing with pain that she's buried for a long time. It's a way of checking out from feelings of sadness or loneliness. Recovery takes a long time. But she is doing better. I can't say much more. It may not seem like she's recovering, but she is."

"She seems worse than before she went into that place. Her insurance runs out soon. What will she do then?"

"Everything's okay, Frannie. She's where she's supposed to be. But how are you? That's what I'm interested in."

"I'm fine," I say, crying. "Just fine, thanks for asking. I'm just worried. You know, people worry."

"You don't sound fine." I can't stop crying. I know I'm making a fool of myself, but I can't help it. Then, in the kindest voice I've ever heard, Chubby asks me to come see her. "Sometimes it helps to talk things out." Her voice is like a pool of warm water and I feel as though I'm wading in it, my skin absorbing the water as if feeding on it. I tell her I don't know. "It may help, Frannie."

"Okay," I say, gaining strength. "I'll think about it."

"I'll be here," she tells me. As I listen, her warm voice fills my ear, flows through my body, soothes me all the way down, and holds me close, as if I'm a child.

9

I'd *like pizza for lunch,"* Shelly tells me as I sign her out. *"The* nutritionist and I planned it."

"Are you sure?" I wrap a scarf around my neck. She doesn't say anything as we walk to the elevator. "What's wrong?" I ask. "Are you upset?"

She shakes her head and chews on the string of her hood. We ride for a few floors in silence. For the past few weeks, she's been much better. She responded well when her doctors adjusted her medication, and they've stopped talking about giving her the tubes or moving her upstairs. In fact, they reinstated her privileges and now she's allowed to leave the hospital for outings. "So everything's okay then?" I had asked when she invited me to lunch. "I was really scared. I didn't know what to do."

"I was scared myself," she reassured me, "but I'm okay now. That was my last dip. A lot of patients have a dramatic mood shift before they start getting healthy. They call it the storm before the calm."

I look at her as the elevator dings. "Why aren't you talking to me?"

"I'm thinking."

"Fine," I say brightly. "Think." The elevator creeps down. It dings again and two patients and a nurse get on. The nurse turns

126

forward as the doors close, but the patients stop short, facing me. I smile sympathetically and pretend nothing unusual is happening. Shelly doesn't notice, not even when the taller patient sticks his hand inside his bathrobe and starts massaging his chest.

"I planned pizza," Shelly says finally. "I'd like to stick with my plan."

"I planned pizza." The short patient mimics her, licking his finger. "Pizza pizza."

I change the subject. "What will you do when your insurance runs out?"

She sucks on the string. "I expect to be out of here by then. Why? What do you think I should do?"

"Why are you asking me?"

"You're my big sister." She smiles, and I'm flooded with warmth. I miss the days when she asked my advice. When she was heavy in high school, she told me that I was her only true friend. Back then, I was a good friend to have, I guess. Once when she was a junior and I was already in college, she called me, crying. "I don't have a date for the prom," she said between hiccups. "And it's because I'm *FAT*. I don't blame people for not wanting to be seen with me."

We spent hours talking. I don't remember what I said, but it must have been nice because she stopped crying. I remember feeling good that she called me. In fact, I felt so important, I blew off a final and drove home to take her out for dinner and a show, just so she wouldn't have to be alone on prom night while everyone else got laid and threw up. It ended up being a nightmare because I ate some bad seafood and spent the entire show on my knees in the ladies' room, but at least I'd captured the spirit of the evening. Sometimes, when I remember times like that, I wish we were young again.

She's quiet as she waits for my answer. "It's a big decision, Shelly. You've been in what, five months? Give it another week. See how this medication does. Then if you feel good, maybe it *is* time to leave."

When we reach the ground floor, Shelly turns to me. "Guess who's getting out?" She stops to button her coat all the way to her neck. "Cynthia Balducci."

"No shit. God, she's the last person I thought they'd spring." I chuckle until I realize that Shelly's not laughing. "What? What did I say?"

"Would it kill you to have some compassion? Cynthia is a *survivor.*"

"Of what?" She was in combat?

"Of incest." In her newfound mental health, Shelly can be very self-righteous and I'm never sure what is acceptable psychoparlance. I try be sympathetic, but the hospital has become her whole world. Once we spent fifteen minutes debating if she should ask Pia to turn down her radio because Shelly didn't want to invade Pia's personal space. I hate myself when I lose my patience, but I thought therapy was supposed to move you away from your problems, not deeper into them.

"I'm sorry. I didn't realize." *You were the one,* I recall, *who said Cynthia fried her brain.* "You can still keep in touch, can't you?"

"I'm in a hospital, Frannie. Not a prison." We stop to collect ourselves before we tackle lunch in the real world. "Maybe it is time to leave," Shelly says wistfully. As we move through the lobby, her eyes dart around. She's looking for people she knows, I think sadly. Apparently the coast is clear because she puts her gloved hand on the glass double-door. She stops for a second, as if mulling something important.

"What?" I ask. "You've decided? You're going to check out?"

She turns to me. "I'm not going to have pizza," she says firmly. "I'm having a chef salad." Then she pushes the door open and moves into the winter afternoon, the string of her hood still wet where she was sucking it.

When the waitress walks toward us with our food, Shelly starts babbling. She tells me about the party they are planning for Cynthia, and how Keisha lost eleven pounds and is going to sue her old company for discrimination. She tenses up as the waitress places the salad in front of her and doesn't move until she leaves. "It's the anticipation," she explains, catching my eye. "I just can't stand the anticipation."

"Don't worry about it." I lean back in my seat. "So what are you going to be for Halloween?"

"Anorexic. You?"

"Unemployed."

"Good, so we won't have to spend money on costumes." She smiles. "Mommy told me you told her about getting fired from Rascals."

"God, does she tell you *everything*?" I attack my French onion soup. The thick cheese won't budge when I try to cut it, so I pull it apart with my fingers. I eat all the cheese and push the bowl away. Shelly is eating her salad very slowly, one item at a time. She chews each bite carefully, covering her mouth with her hand. I rummage in the empty bread basket and signal the waitress for another one.

She looks at my empty soup bowl. "Aren't you going to eat anything else?" she asks.

"I'm stuffed."

"Do you mind ordering something else? I don't like to eat alone."

"I had a whole bowl of soup and two baskets of bread."

"That's hardly anything, Frannie." She perks up. "Have a sandwich." She scans the menu. "A turkey club." She signals for the waitress and orders a turkey club with Russian dressing and fries. The girl moves away. "Oh, miss?" she asks. "Could you add onion? We love onion."

Shelly studies the menu as if memorizing it. "Do you remember the last time you had brisket? It's so weird to read a menu. They don't let us read anything that has food in it." I really want to change the subject, but it's nice to see her so bright and alert.

I groan as the waitress brings the sandwich. "Here it is," Shelly says. I take a big bite. Shelly pours ketchup on the fries. When I look up at her, it's like staring in a mirror. She hangs over the table, watching me eat her favorite sandwich. Her mouth moves slowly, as if she is chewing and swallowing every bite I take.

"If I ask you something, do you promise not to get upset?"

Shelly puts down her fork. "Depends on what it is."

"How come you never tell me what it was like at Cornell? Or when you lost your virginity? Or, I don't know ..." I pause. "What you talk about in therapy?"

She lights a cigarette. "It's not like you tell me about your life. I had to hear from Abby that you were meeting that resident for coffee."

A pair of junior high school boys sit at the counter. Occasionally, they swivel on their stools to stare at us. Despite two sweatshirts and a down jacket, Shelly is still painfully thin. Her neck is long and storklike, and her skin is pasty and broken out. The funny thing is, I don't notice it anymore unless I think about it.

The boys mimic Shelly, sucking in their cheeks and blowing out pretend smoke. I keep talking to Shelly so she doesn't turn around. For a second, I don't blame the boys for staring. Shelly takes dramatic drags, inhaling the smoke, then breathing it out in white clouds. The process pains me to watch. I ask her again what she talks about in therapy.

"About our family, I guess. Growing up with Mommy and Daddy."

"And how they fucked you up?"

She looks at me strangely. "The idea is to get past the point of blaming them for everything. They have their own problems."

I shrug. I hate when she defends them. I change the subject. "So when did you lose your virginity?" I ask.

"Why is that so important?" She looks at me nervously, as if expecting a punch line.

"It's not. There's just a lot about you that I don't know. You said so yourself."

She reddens. "A long time ago. It was with …" She trails off and looks at her hands. "Frannie, we don't have to pack everything into one lunch. We have an entire lifetime to learn things about each other."

"If we can't talk about your therapy or your sex life, what's left?"

"How about *your* depression?" she counters.

"I hardly think a few bad days constitutes a major depression, Shelly. There's nothing wrong with me that a good job and a long schlong can't cure."

"You get depressed," Shelly says indignantly. "Admit it, Frannie. You *are* depressed. I called Chubby, and she said she'd see you if you wanted. In fact, Mommy and I are starting weekly sessions when I get out, and I thought maybe you'd like to come. I thought it might help you. When I see what you're going through, it reminds me of how I felt when—"

"I am not depressed! Just because you're anorexic doesn't mean that I have a major thing, too. We're sisters, but we're *different*."

"I'm just making an observation."

"Observe something else."

"You didn't let me finish," she says quietly. "I was going to say that you're stronger than I am, Frannie. And I respect you. What you're going through is difficult, especially moving home."

"Don't psychoanalyze me." I bite into the sandwich and chew angrily. So what if I get depressed? Everyone gets depressed. And this therapy bullshit is like a cult.

"Okay, I'll tell you something," she says. "I don't believe I'm really anorexic."

"You're a compulsive overeater?"

"Don't be nasty, okay? I've been doing a lot of research. I admit that I deny my self, meaning me as a self, as a person. And that I deny my needs. I know I'm obsessive, but my mood swings are something else. In the hospital, they focus on the food, but the food is only a way for me to contain my thoughts. In fact, I'm more aware of food now than before. There's more to it than just food. Like why do some girls starve and others binge? I think it's something in the brain related to depression, some other mechanism … Forget it, you're not listening. *That's* what comes up in my therapy. About how you and Mommy and Daddy don't listen to me."

"Shelly, now don't take this the wrong way, but you're very smart. I do listen, but half the time I don't know what you're talking about. I'm not as smart as you. I can't get into your head and live there, you know."

She shrugs. "Guess not." For a second, she's in her own world. Then she tells me she's ordering a muffin and asks if I want coffee. I nod and she signals the waitress. "Two coffees and a bran muffin, dry please." She lights another cigarette, not looking at me.

I try to make her laugh. "Remember the time you had a bake sale with all the muffins Mommy bought for the PTA?"

Grudgingly, she smiles. "Remember the time you showed up

drunk at Mommy's office?" She laughs. "And you threw up in the reception area?"

"I forgot about that. God, I was fucked up." I laugh. "Remember the guy you brought home from Cornell? Sherman? The physicist with a lisp? *Hi. I'm Therman. A nuclear phthethist* …" She doesn't laugh. "Okay, Shelly," I ask. "What did I say this time?"

"You didn't say anything. Something just struck me."

The waitress comes back and accidentally puts the muffin in front of me. Shelly bites her lip. Then from out of nowhere, she snarls as if possessed, "The muffin is for ME. *I* ordered it. Have I suddenly disappeared? I also asked for it *dry*."

I clutch, awaiting a showdown, but the waitress just snaps her gum and grabs the plate. The stupid boys rise from the counter and walk out of the diner, snickering. "Shelly," I whisper. "It's just a muffin. We can get another one."

"I don't want another one. Just get the fucking check."

As we walk out, I turn to her. "I'm sorry if I said something to piss you off."

She smiles at me sadly. "It's not you. I was just reminded of that guy Sherman. I had a bad experience with him." I ask her if she wants to talk about it. "Not yet," she says quietly. "But someday."

Finally, finally, finally, my lunch date with Bryan arrives. I get to the diner forty-five minutes early and wait for him. When he walks through the door, my heart jumps.

"I forgot how pretty you are," he says as he approaches the table. He's a big guy, but moves through the diner like a cat.

I shred my paper napkin into little strips. "I didn't think you would remember me."

"Of course I remember you. I'm sorry I had to cancel last week, but I'm glad you called me to confirm. I wasn't sure how to find you. And I'm happy I could make it today. I've just been so busy lately."

"Yeah, me too." A waiter hovers as I stare at the menu. Shit, what do I get? Do I just order a snack or get a sandwich like this is a meal? If it is a meal, do I pay? Should I get the turkey with gravy and make it like a whole dinner thing or will he think I'm a pig? The waiter clears his throat and mutters that he can come back.

"No, just a minute." I feel Bryan fidgeting. I hold up the menu, but the letters blur. What if I get a salad? That's an in-between-meals snack which can also be considered a meal if that's what this is. "I'll have a plate of mashed potatoes," I blurt out, "with grilled onions and tomatoes on the side." I break into a sweat. What the hell kind of thing is that to order? I could just gag.

Bryan looks at the waiter and smiles. "I'll have black coffee." Figures.

There's a long beat of silence, then we both speak at once. "You go first," he says.

"I'm worried about Shelly. She's doing much better, don't get me wrong, but sometimes I feel like there's a whole hidden side to her."

"Shelly's not my patient so I really can't comment. But I do know that recovering from anorexia is a long process. Many times patients get worse before they get better. It's difficult to give up certain behaviors that become familiar even if they are self-destructive." As he talks, I find it impossible to pay attention. I wonder if he realizes how handsome he is. I want to ask him if he thinks I'm cute. No, I don't want him to think I'm cute. I want him to think I'm sexy. Drop-dead sexy. So sexy he obsesses about me. I realize he's still talking. "I'm working on a paper now about the relationship between rage and addiction."

"I don't know. Maybe it is rage. Sometimes she lashes out at me. It's like the smallest thing sets her off."

"Exhibiting anger is a good sign. Otherwise, she'd be directing it at herself. Just keep doing what you're doing. Learn about her illness, show your support." For a second, I stop thinking about his looks because he says something that strikes me. "Don't look at her symptoms," he tells me. "Get to know her as a person."

"I've been trying," I tell him. "Honestly, but she won't let me in."

"Be patient." He smiles a slow seductive smile, and I'm swept away again. "You know what you can do," he says, holding my gaze. "Come and see her all the time." He touches my hand. "And me. You can come and see me, too." At that moment, his beeper goes off. "Frannie, sorry, I have to take this. I'll be right back."

When he returns to the table, he's apologetic. "I have an emergency," he says nicely. "But I want to keep talking. Let's have dinner." He takes my number and kisses my cheek. "I'll call you," he says, but as he leaves, I have the feeling that he planned to have someone beep him so he could make a quick getaway.

The waiter comes with my vegetable ensemble. I mix it all together, pour ketchup on for flavor, and eat the entire thing. Then since it's a date, I order Black Forest cake and a scoop of ice cream. I can't stop thinking about Shelly the entire time I eat.

I spend the next few days organizing my meals. I'm gaining weight and it's showing. I write down everything I eat. Cereal for breakfast, a turkey sandwich for lunch, and a piece of skinless chicken with a salad for dinner. I don't allow myself more than 1,000 calories, and I count and recount all day long. I don't let myself fantasize about Bryan until after I've counted, as if he's the prize for all my hard work. After a few days I begin to feel better. Knowing I can get into bed and think about Bryan gives me something of my own to look forward to.

Two nights later, I hear my mother in the hallway with my grandfather. I'm watching the phone, sending call-me messages through mental telepathy and prayer, but Bryan isn't receiving them. If he is, he's not responding.

My mother taps on my door. "Grandpa's here!" Her voice raises an octave, as if she's about to burst into song. She's sedated, I'm sure.

My grandfather hobbles in. "Frannie! Where's my girl?" He has a European accent. It's not heavy, but he trills his tongue when he rolls his R's. He stands in the middle of my room, trying to see me. He's a sturdy old man with soft wrinkled skin. His eyes are bright blue like Shelly's, but loll in their sockets, and they're milky and glazed from the cataracts.

"I'm over here, Grandpa." I put my arms around him.

He touches my face. "You are so beautiful. I am so happy to see you. My one and only favorite beauty queen."

"Me too, Grandpa. I've missed you so much." I nestle my head in his neck and breathe deeply. He smells like baby powder and soap. "It's so good to see you." I turn to my mother. "Can I help make dinner tonight?"

"I was going to order in Chinese."

"I love cha mein," my grandfather says. "But I can't eat the brown sauce. I have to have the white sauce. Make sure you order the white sauce." He looks around the room. "Where's the little one? My other beautiful girl?" He squeezes my hand and whispers, "Don't worry, Frannie. You're still my favorite."

I kiss him. "And you're mine," I say.

"Shelly is out of town for a while," my mother says and I jerk my head up. She shrugs. "It's better this way," she says, mouthing the words behind his back.

"But he can't even see her!" I hiss. "What's the difference?"

"What are you girls shushing about? So where's the cha mein? Let's have Chinese. I can't have the brown sauce. Did you remember that?"

"Yes, Daddy. I remember. Come on, let's go."

My grandfather pulls me back. "Go ahead, Marshie. Go order the food, but no brown sauce. I only like the white sauce. And the big shrimps. Get some big, fat shrimps."

My mother smiles at me. "Yes, Daddy. Big fat shrimps in white sauce."

I touch his cheek. I watch his eyes roam the room. He takes my hands and holds them against his face. "I am so delighted to see you, *shaineh maidel*," he says. "So delighted, I'm excited. See? I rhymed." He chuckles. As he hugs me, I can feel the rhythm of his heart. "So tell me," he says, staring off, above my shoulder. "Tell me why you're not married."

"I've been waiting for you." I hold his arm as we make our way downstairs.

"Frannie, I must ask you something. Come close. It's very, very important." I bend my head. "Do you think she's gonna get the brown sauce? I don't like brown sauce. I hate to say this, but as much as I love her, I don't think your mommy listens to me."

"You know what," I tell him, smoothing his hair. "I don't think she listens to me, either."

A week later, I sit next to my father on the couch at St. Mary's, and watch him as he glances at the door. Shelly is to my left, also watching the door. My dad clears his throat. "Marsha will be here any second."

Chubby nods. "That's fine."

It's Family Night and Katie has bronchitis so Chubby's filling in. After a while, she says, "We should start. Marsha can catch up." Chubby looks robust in a shocking red suit. For a heavyset woman, she sure can put herself together.

Shelly is wearing a skirt, tights, and a pink blouse. She's filled out a little, although I don't look below her shoulders. Her cheeks are rosy and the warm yellow lights make her blond hair look like silk. "I want you both to know how much I appreciate you coming," she begins, smiling. "It means a lot to me."

"No problem." I look at Chubby. I wonder if she knows I was fired from Rascals. My father agrees. "Happy to be here," he says.

"Well." She turns to Chubby. "Marilyn and I have been discussing my recovery and—" At that moment, my mother bustles in wearing her maroon On-Target jacket. "What about your recovery?" she asks after apologizing for being late. She turns to me. "I found a spot two blocks from you and Daddy. I feel victorious!" Her face is flushed and her voice is lilting. She clutches her pocketbook to her chest as if it's a bouquet of roses. "Hello, Marilyn. Aren't you looking well?" She *must* have been with Daniel. She's never this happy just to see us.

"We were just talking about Shelly's plans," Chubby says. "For after the hospital."

"Oh," my mother cuts in. "Did you tell Daddy?"

"What plans, Shelly?" he asks. "I thought you finished your application to Harvard."

"Shelly's not going to Harvard. She's going to be a therapist. Just like Marilyn." Again, my mother is triumphant.

I look at my hands. I can't believe this. She's taking my idea. "What about law school?" I ask. I try to appear nonchalant but my mind's racing. I'm suddenly sick to my stomach with the feeling of being unemployed.

Shelly shrugs. "I think helping people with emotional problems is more important. I've got this theory about depression I want to explore."

"What?" I ask her. "Why are you looking at me?"

"I wasn't looking at you, Frannie," she says calmly.

"You keep giving me these looks." I turn to my mother. "Mom, you saw her."

"Frannie, really. Stop it," my mother says. "Try to be more adult about this."

I glare at my mother. I am so tired of Shelly's fucking anorexia. Who sits with her every day while she spouts all her bullshit? Who sits with Grandpa while you're at work? And who is hoarding your little love affair? That would be me, Mom. Or did you tell Shelly and now you don't need me? Face it, old lady. Without me, your life would be complete chaos.

"Marsha," my father says quietly. "I think you're being a little too hard on Frannie." Wow, I think, a voice from the dead.

"David—" my mother starts, but Shelly cuts her off. "I'm leaving the hospital in three weeks."

Startled, I look up. "That soon?" What about the way she acted at lunch with the muffin? Are they taking that into consideration? "Three weeks, how about that?" Who's gonna hang around with her all day? What if she needs to talk and I have an interview? I won't be able to just not go, I mean, what if she has a crisis? "It must be exciting, the idea of getting out. You can come live in my room. Daddy will make us bunk beds."

"That's terrific, Shelly," my father says. "We'll fix up your room. I'll put in a TV." I stare at him. You have *got* to be kidding. You never offered *me* a TV.

Shelly and Chubby smile at each other. "Thanks, Daddy, but I want to move into my own place."

"Your own place?" I blurt out. "Do you think that's wise?" I must have really hurt her feelings at lunch the other day. I rack my brain, trying to recall what I said.

"Frannie, I may have an eating disorder, but I'm quite capable of taking care of myself."

"I just meant that you may need some help, and moving home could be a better plan. I didn't say you couldn't take care of yourself."

"A second ago, you didn't think I should even leave the hospital."

"Stop taking every goddamn thing I say out of context," I snap.

I can't believe that Chubby is letting all this go. I imagine Shelly in a new apartment in the city, entertaining all of Abby's rock star and athlete clients while I'm stuck at home in my little twin bed. I should be happy for my sister, but I can't be. I can't. I just can't. My selfishness disgusts me, but right now, I hate her so much, I want to smack the smug little smile off her fucking face.

"I agree with Frannie," my father says tentatively, watching Shelly. "I don't know if moving into your own place is the best plan."

"Since when do you have any idea what is best for me?" Shelly says coldly. Jesus, she *has* been speaking to my mother. My dad slumps in his seat. "Nice way to talk to your father," he mutters.

"Shelly, honey, we're all just trying to help out," my mother tells her. "I think it's exciting to think about getting out of here, but I don't want you to rush into anything. I thought we'd decided to wait."

My sister shifts into her seat. I wish she'd throw a temper tantrum so Chubby can hustle her back upstairs and we can abort this stupid discussion about her leaving. "Mom," Shelly whines. "Mom, we said that a month ago. My insurance runs out in three weeks. We *talked* about this. You act like that conversation didn't even happen."

"I know we did, dear." My mother glances at Chubby, who sits stone-faced like a Buddha. "I'm not telling you what to do one way or the other. I just want you to be sure, that's all."

"I *am* sure for Christ's sake." Shelly looks at Chubby. "You know, I really wish everyone didn't feel the need to tell me what is best for me. I'm not asking for your approval. I'm *telling* you what I'm doing. I consider it a gift."

My father clears his throat. "I think we need to respect Shelly's decision."

"David, hold on," my mother interrupts. "What about Shelly coming home for a few weeks to get her bearings?"

"Hello, I'm here," Shelly snaps. "And I'm *not* moving home." She sits with her hands in her lap, totally relaxed. Her calmness freaks me out. I'm much more comfortable when she's hysterical. When she's so calm, she seems like a stranger. I remember her journal. *Is that what a sister is? A sister. What's a sister?*

"I'm only talking about a few weeks, Shelly," my mother is say-ing. "Not a lifetime."

"She said no, Marsha," my father says. My mother purses her lips and the two of them sit in a long, tense silence.

"Listen," I say finally. "I know we want to impress Marilyn with our harmonious family, but I think we're going overboard here."

"Shut up, Frannie," my father says and my mother agrees. "Yes, Frannie, please stop it." There's another long stretch until Shelly says, "Look, I love all of you, but I need to be on my own."

"We got that, okay?" I say sarcastically, breaking my vow of silence.

"Shelly," my father says, "we just want what's best. Just know that your room is there if you want it." I can't figure out why my father is urging her to move home. Maybe he wants me to leave. Jesus, he's always pushing me. I've only been there five months.

"I would just like to hear that you support me, that's all," Shelly says. "But even if you don't, I still have to do what I have to do." There's a chorus as we promise to support her. We talk for a while, then just stare at one another. "What I'm curious about ..." I say. Everyone turns to look at me. "... is how Lonny's gonna take the news that you're bailing on him?"

That night, I lie in bed, thinking of Bryan, when my phone rings.

"Frannie?" Shelly asks. "Did I wake you?"

"No. What's wrong?"

"Nothing," she says. "I just wanted ... look, I know you were upset tonight during our session and—"

"I was not," I cut in. "I'm happy for you."

"Thanks. I'm happy for me, too. I feel so much better about things. Anyway, I've been thinking. Why don't we get a place together? You and me ... roomies again?"

"You don't have to say that, Shelly. You've been talking to Mommy, haven't you? I can't believe she is using you to get me out of here."

"It has nothing to do with Mommy. I would like to live with you. I always wanted to hang out with you, but I never felt I could compete with Abby. You always had Abby. I never had anyone."

I consider that. "Shelly," I say slowly, "Abby is your friend as much as she is mine. And I'd love to live with you, but right now, I don't have a job." I mull over the idea. "Mommy wants me to move out. Did she tell you that?" Shelly mutters something, so I know the answer's yes. "Let me think about it, okay? I can continue temping, I guess. Temping's good, right?" I think about gerbil man and sigh.

"If it's about money, don't worry. I have some stashed away. Besides, I know something will come up. I believe in you. I just want us to be friends—like real sisters."

"We are real sisters, Shelly." I wait a long beat. "Why are you being so nice to me?" I ask her quietly.

"Because you're letting me," she replies.

Despite my anxiety, it makes me happy she asked me to move in. In fact, I'm so inspired, I get an urgent desire to go somewhere. I tiptoe downstairs and get into her car. I try to start it, but the engine's dead. I wrap my coat around my legs and sit for a while, watching my breath come out in foggy clouds. Before I get out, I blow a gust of air on the window and right smack in the center, I smudge my initials with the tip of my finger.

10

I spend hours fantasizing about Bryan. About him calling me. About our date. I won't make plans because I have to stay free. I know it sounds crazy, but I think I'm in love with him. You can't think about one person so much and not have it be love.

I get a call from Avalon Advertising, one of the places I sent my résumé. On interview day, I empty a briefcase and fill it with a legal pad; some pens; *Women Men Love, Women Men Leave*; and a can of Diet Coke to give it some weight. I'm about to prance out when my father walks into the kitchen and immediately asks why I'm wearing my mother's suit.

"She loaned it to me." I smooth the skirt. "For good luck on my interview."

He looks at the briefcase in my hands. "Dammit, Frannie, that's mine."

"Please let me take it. Today's important." I hold out my arms and model my mother's suit. "Well, what do you think?"

"The skirt is too long. It's not a good cut for you."

I walk into the den where my grandfather is lying down. "What do you think of my suit, Grandpa? I have a big interview today."

"Looks like a million bucks to me, kiddo," he says from the couch.

I go to a mirror. I roll the waistband of the skirt over a few times to shorten it. I consider stapling a hem, but the suit is too new. "James, get the car," I say to my reflection. "I have a board meeting at four." I smile at myself and feel a twinge of hope. You never know. Maybe this is it. Maybe this is the big one. As I walk back into the kitchen, the skirt unrolls.

My father is gathering the papers I dumped on the table. "Frannie, did it ever occur to you that I might have an important meeting of my own today?" He hovers over the briefcase. "At least put your résumé in a nice portfolio." He walks out of the kitchen, but first stops at the pantry and grabs a plastic garbage bag.

"Daddy, if you're going to put your papers in that, I don't have to take the briefcase. It's no big deal."

"Forget it, Frannie," he says, annoyed. I hear him pick up the phone. His salesman's voice booms, "Hey, babe, what's new?" Growing up, I marveled at my father. He always traveled to what seemed like very exotic places. He brought presents home for Shelly and me: plastic bubbles that made snow and pilot's wings we pinned on our T-shirts. It wasn't until years later, when he took me with him on a sales call, that I realized what his life was really like.

At the time he was selling paper products and we trudged through hotel basements, setting up black display cases of miniature paper cups, paper plates, and multicolored napkins. We talked to supply managers who all had the same greasy hair, pitted faces, and dirty Earth shoes. They smelled of Lysol and dried sweat and looked at me with piggy eyes as I helped my father set up the displays. What I remember most is the inside of the displays; how you could see the black staples that fastened the plates and cups to the frayed red velvet. I don't know if my father made any sales. I know he had to haggle and smile all day, even after we ate lunch in the car and he got terrible indigestion from a salami sandwich. I tried to make jokes on the way home, but I felt a pang of sorrow that still pains me every time I see my dad put on a coat and tie.

He hands me a leather portfolio. "For your résumé," he says.

"That's Mommy's. You gave it to her for her birthday. I can't take *that*."

"She hasn't even taken it out of the box yet." He holds it out and when I reach for it, snatches it away. "Think fast," he says, laughing. He hands me his briefcase and the portfolio and walks me outside. "Are you driving the Subaru?"

We both stare at Shelly's car. Dead leaves cover the hood, and the windshield is streaked with dried pollen. "I tried to start it the other night, but I think the battery's dead."

"I told you this would happen. The battery isn't dead. You just have to pump it." He gets into his car. "Knock 'em dead on your interview," he calls out.

"Oh Daddy, wait! I forgot to tell you Mommy called." He rolls the car forward. "She sold a house today and Big Man Bennet is taking her to celebrate. You should surprise her with champagne." Instead of agreeing, he hits the automatic window and drives away.

I slide into Shelly's car. It smells musty and damp. I turn the key, but the engine sputters. With my skirt hiked around my hips, I wait a few seconds, debating what to do. It dawns on me that my mother didn't ask my father to celebrate with her. I bet that hurt his feelings. "Get the car, James," I say aloud, "I have a board meeting at four." Suddenly depressed, I see myself hunched in a hot office while a scrawny man with piggy eyes reviews my résumé. I wipe my hands on my skirt and count to ten. I try to start the car, but it won't budge. This is an omen, I know it.

A cab ride, a train ride, and two subway stops later, I'm in an elevator, traveling up to the thirty-third floor. If this was St. Mary's, I'd be ascending into the world of schizophrenia. Truth be told, today I'd rather be there.

If a man gets in on the fifth floor, I tell myself, then this interview will go well. But if a woman gets in on the eighth, then it's going to suck. When the door opens on the fifth and a man gets in, I sigh with relief. I brace myself. We stop on the eighth and a woman steps on the elevator, but just as the doors are about to close, she gets off. Now I'm confused. She got in, but she didn't stay. Does that count?

"You must be Francine Hunter. Mizz Billings will be right with you." I sit down and scratch myself like an orangutan. Someone should tell the fashion world that wool suits are itchy, that people would rather wear clothing made out of ten-year-old sheets like the ones on my bed. Perhaps I should consider a career in fashion consulting.

"Mizz Billings is ready for you. She's the last door on the right."

I clutch my father's briefcase and tug on my mother's suit as I walk down a long hallway. I peer into her office and watch Mizz Billings talk on the phone. Her head is too small for her body, which is cloaked in a boxy suit that looks two sizes too big. I want to ask her why she's wearing a suit that doesn't fit her—even *I* read *Glamour Do's and Don'ts*—but seeing her lips purse in a thin, determined line and her long red nails tap her desk, I don't think my fashion tips are going to win her over.

She sees me and holds up a finger. I scratch my face. My skin's peeling because I sat in the sun bed. My face was breaking out from the anxiety I have doing nothing all day so I treated myself. I wanted to appear tan and rested. Instead, I look like a victim of radiation poisoning.

"Hello, Francine." She motions for me to sit. "Sorry I couldn't meet you in the lobby. I'm swamped. As I told you, my assistant deserted me to get married."

"You can call me Frannie. Francine makes me feel like a spinster."

"Oh?" She's reading what looks like my résumé. "That's too bad. I think it's a lovely name." She looks up. "It's my mother's." I start to say something, but she cuts me off. "So you want to work in advertising sales?"

I nod. "I was on the client side for a while, but I really want to work for an agency. I think the advertising industry is really gonna grow."

"You're right. I have my own theories, but why do you think so?"

Oh God, I don't know. Can't you just ask me to list my strengths and weaknesses? "I think," I fumble. "I think the economy is going to turn around. People will spend more money on advertising." I cock my head, awaiting her approval.

"It's too early to tell," she says, "but—" The phone rings. "Excuse me."

She talks for a few seconds, laughing occasionally. I slide off a shoe and curl my toes. I never know what to do when someone is on the phone and I'm not supposed to listen. Do I laugh when she laughs? Pretend I don't hear? There's got to be etiquette rules for this sort of thing. Someone has to know where to sit in a therapist's office, how to balance a plate of food and a drink at a cocktail party, and what to do when an interviewer calls you the wrong name.

Finally, she hangs up. "As you can see, I'm very busy and I need someone organized and conscientious. You're twenty-six, right?" She chuckles. "I don't think I'm allowed to ask you that."

"Go ahead. You can ask me anything except how much I weigh."

This sends her into gales of laughter and I'm suddenly warmed to the idea of working for her. Mandy, doll, I too want to wear boxy suits and pointed shoes and talk about diminishing returns. I want to be just like you. Shit, I want to *be* you. And go ahead, knock yourself out. Call me Francine.

"If I hire you," she tells me, "I'll work you to death. You'll work overtime and weekends without pay, but you'll learn so much about ad sales that in a year you'll be able to do my job. Can you handle it?"

I nod. "I'm very conscientious," I say. "I'm always on time so you don't have to worry. I don't mind overtime, I can use a computer, and I'm great on the phone." *(Just you wait, I'll man the lines like an AT&T operator.)* "I have a lot to offer, I promise."

She points to my résumé. "But Francine. You haven't done anything yet." *Well, you are wearing a suit that doesn't fit.* "In fact, your job history isn't very solid. Why did you stay with Jamaica Time Shares for only four months?"

"I wasn't sure what I wanted to do."

"And now you're sure? This is a very big commitment. Avalon wants people who will grow with them. I've been here five years. I came on board right after business school." Then it dawns on me. Mizz Miranda is only thirty years old. Oh God, I am such a loser.

"Where did you get your MBA?" I ask meekly.

"Wharton. I did my undergraduate work at Harvard."

"Huh," I say. "My mother went to Harvard." I clutch her portfolio.

"Funny, so did mine. She went to Radcliffe. Are you a legacy too?"

I guess that depends, Miranda, on what type of legacy you

mean. If you're referring to depressed, neurotic women looking for the right man to give their lives meaning, then yes, I am a legacy. Furthermore, if we're discussing the mother-daughter bond here, I didn't go to Harvard and neither did my mother. "No," I tell her. "I went to Syracuse."

"Good school," she says in the patronizing way that Ivy Leaguers always have.

"I really want this job, Mizz Billings, I'm ready for a commitment."

"I sense that you do. What are you doing now?"

Getting primed for Oprah and I'll be late if we don't speed this up. "I'm temping."

"Can I call for references?"

God no. I'll have to find someone other than Lonny to pretend he's a reference. When we tried it, he said I was sweet and would be conscientious if they can get me off the phone. Billings is waiting so I nod.

"Well then." She extends her hand. "I'm seeing other people, but I have a good feeling about you. Do you have any questions?"

"How much does it pay?" I blurt out.

"It's premature to discuss dollars, uh, Frannie, but we *are* very competitive." Her phone rings and she ushers me out. I turn away, wishing I could take back my last question.

As I walk out, I don't know if I should feel good or not. She *did* call me Frannie—that's a good sign, right? But panic strikes when I get on the elevator. She's going to check where my mother went to school! I know—I'll call her from the lobby and tell her that was only for a summer session and she won't be in the yearbook. No no no, I'll just tell her I lied so she'll see how honest and forthright I am. I walk to the phone, but someone is on it, and I can't wait because I have to make the two-thirty train to get home in time for Oprah. Face it, Francine. You're doomed.

"Hello, Miss Big Executive," my grandfather says when I walk into the den where he's sitting with my father. As I lean forward to kiss him, he whispers, "He keeps this place like an icebox. Could you ask him to turn the heat on?"

"Why can't you ask him yourself?" I whisper back, glancing at my dad. My grandfather rubs his arms. "I feel funny."

It's rough having Grandpa Max here. My parents and I constantly bicker about who will sit with him. My father cleared out his office so they could make a bedroom for my grandfather, and now all my dad's files are piled in the living room. He pretends that it's not an inconvenience, but he hung a sheet in the doorway to seal off his space. When it's dark out, and the desk lamp illuminates his body, he looks like the Wizard of Oz.

"Daddy, it's freezing in here, don't you think?"

He looks at my grandfather. "Max, if you're cold, why don't you say something?"

"I just did."

My grandfather follows me into the kitchen, his cane clomping like a horse. He sits while I rummage through the refrigerator. "Why hasn't Shelly been here to see me?" he asks.

"She just got back in town, you know that. She'll be here in a few days for dinner." I hate lying, but I'm trying to stay on the Cheerfuls' good side so they'll give me a loan toward my new apartment. My grandfather stares into space. "Did you eat?" I ask him.

"Franks and beans. Boy, I love franks and beans. That guy Kamps made a fortune with franks and beans. If we had stock with Kamps, we'd be millionaires by now, kiddo. Franks and beans is where the money is."

I spy an empty can on top of the garbage. "From a can?" I march into the den. "Daddy, what the hell did you feed Grandpa?"

"Van Kamps. He loved it." He clicks the channels anxiously.

"Why didn't you cook something?"

"If someone was around, I would."

"Grandpa's someone, you know." I block the TV, but he waves me away. I stalk out, muttering "Asshole, asshole, asshole" under my breath.

My grandfather has fallen asleep. I shake him slightly and whisper, "Grandpa, why don't you go upstairs? Come on, I'll help you."

"Frannie," he yawns. "Let's run away together. Just you and me."

"What will we do for money?" Sometimes I think I could kill my father, I really do. I could shove his head into the fucking TV.

Grandpa Max pats my cheek. "We'll live on love, kiddo."

"Someone named Vicky Tayborn called you," my dad says a few days later.

"Who's she?" I put a Pop-Tart in the toaster.

"I don't know. She wanted to talk to you about a job, I guess. I have her number."

"I'll get it later." I put my Pop-Tart on a paper towel. "Where's Mommy?"

"She took your grandfather to the mall. She wanted you to go, but I told her not to wake you." He looks up expectantly, as if I should thank him.

I break the Pop-Tart in half. They have 220 calories, and with milk, I'm up to 320. If I get the Avalon job, I have to fit into my suits and frankly, I foresee a problem.

"Did they ever call you from that ad agency?" my father asks.

"Not yet." I say this absently, but I've analyzed the interview for days, trying to find signs in Miranda Billings's every gesture, every inflection. She did say she had a good feeling, but I don't let myself focus on that. I focus on not getting the job, on having to call this Tayborn woman whom I don't know and could care less about.

"Daddy, if you're in an interview, and someone tells you they have a good feeling, do you think it means they're going to offer you the job? I mean, if they say it in a happy way, really gleeful like, 'I have a good feeling and here's your office,' can you think positively about it?"

"You should always think positively. You and your mother focus too much on the negative. I always focus on the positive, on getting the sale."

I try to think positively, but it doesn't get me anywhere. I should have called Shelly. She's great at interviews. I bet she would have gotten this job wearing the vomit-stained JUST DO IT sweatshirt, with her hair all stringy, weighing eighty pounds. It's times like these that I wish I were her.

I spend hours writing down the things Billings and I talked

about and the way she responded. I give myself a (+) for every time she laughed and a (-) for every time I fucked up. I count the (+)'s ten times, but I'm afraid to jinx it. Think positively, I tell myself, think happy thoughts. I count the (+)'s again, and with a giant burst of confidence, I tell my father to throw out Vicky Tayborn's number.

"I don't need it," I say firmly. "I feel good about this."

Later, in bed, I try to remember the number of (+)'s. Maybe if I hadn't asked about the salary, she would have offered me the job (-). She must think I'm greedy (-). How could I jump the gun like that (-)? Jesus, this is worse than waiting for Bryan to call. Did she like my suit? I think so (+). I hated her suit, the boxy thing. Maybe it bothered her I had a nicer suit (-). Maybe she noticed that it didn't fit (-) and now she thinks I'm a slob (-). But she did call me Frannie at the end (+) and she did say she had a good feeling about me (+++).

This is a waste of time; I never get what I hope for. I try not to think about wanting the job, but then I wonder if, since I realized the want, it's already jinxed. Can you discount a want if you've already admitted it? Eventually I fall asleep with my fingers crossed under my pillow.

The next morning I give myself a facial. I have a dark green avocado mask on when the phone rings. My face is really tight and cracks when I say hello.

"Is Frannie there?"

"This is Frannie." It's difficult to speak, so I open my mouth as wide as I can to loosen the mask.

"It's Bryan Thompson." Whoa! Panicked, my hand flies to my face and I claw at the mask, which flakes off under my nails. "Frannie? You there?"

"I'm here, here I am. It's me. Me, Frannie." I force myself to get a grip. Stop the fucking scratching, I tell myself. He can't fucking *see* you.

"You sound like you're out of breath."

"I just got back from a run."

"I didn't know you ran. How far did you go?"

It's two-thirty in the afternoon and I'm still in my nightgown, which is now covered in avocado flakes that look like soot. "Eight miles. I'm in training."

"For what?"

"The Olympics." The Dysfunctional Olympics for the Highly Neurotic.

He laughs. "How have you been?"

"Fine," I tell him. Then he asks if I want to have a drink with him. "And dinner," he says, "if you're not too busy."

"No, dinner is fine. Or a drink is fine. They're both fine."

"Good, how about next Friday night? We can meet in front of St. Mary's, if that's not inconvenient for you. I know you have to drive in."

"No, driving in is fine. Friday night is fine. Everything's fine. Really."

He tells me he'll meet me at eight and we can go to Amsterdam's first and then see how we feel. He asks me if that's okay and before I can stop myself, I tell him that eight is fine and Amsterdam's is … fine.

I leave a message on Abby's machine, then race to the hospital in Shelly's car. "Hi, Lucy. Is Shelly here?" I ask, gasping.

Lucy glances up from pasting Christmas decorations on the wall. "Hi, Frannie. I'll go get her."

"No, wait." I put on a Cinderella mask left over from Halloween. "I'll go incognito."

I walk toward Cynthia in the day room, who is calling out answers to *Jeopardy*. "It's photosynthesis, you idiot," she yells at the set. Her forehead is bandaged. "Hi, Frannie," she says. "What are you doing here?"

"What are *you* doing here?" I counter, smiling.

"I live here."

"I thought you were checking out. What happened to your head?"

Slowly, she peels back the bandage. Underneath is a long red gash that rises from her skin like a bloody worm. "I had a small accident," she says quietly. "I wasn't ready to leave."

Sobered, I take her hand. "Well, I'm happy you're still here.

Come on, let's surprise Shelly." We tiptoe down the hall to Shelly's room. When I peer in, I see Shelly sitting on her bed, holding court. Keisha and Pia are on the floor, listening.

"… so I said no. I'm sorry, but I'm not going to law school just because it's what everyone else wants me to do. I'll be a therapist. Maybe even a social worker. I'm not making any major plans."

"You have come so far," Pia says reverently. "When I first met you, I was so intimidated, but you're so nice. You really are."

"Hello, ladies." I walk in. "I hate to break up the love fest you got going, but I have some news. I also brought these." I pull five different magazines out of my bag. I even took the time to cut out pictures of food so the magazines won't be confiscated.

There's a chorus of hellos and thank-yous. Shelly hugs me. "What are you doing here?"

"Get this. Mizz Miranda Billings, a big hoo-hah at Avalon Advertising, called my reference, which is only Lonny but so what, it's a good sign AND …" I pause. "That doctor guy called me!!!" I dance a jig. "I gotta job, I gotta guy, I'm so happy, I could cry …"

"That's so great, Frannie!" Shelly claps and squeals like a ten-year-old.

Astonished, I look at her. "Shelly," I say. "Oh my God, you *squealed*!" She squeals again and I snap on the radio. "So let's celebrate, girls!" I shimmy to "Satisfaction" by the Rolling Stones. In two seconds, the room is alive with activity.

Singing as loud as she can, Pia jumps up and down, her arms and legs flailing like wings. Keisha writhes on Shelly's bed, kicking her legs in the air. Her weight makes the bed creak so loud, it sounds like a fart. "Hey, guys," she bellows. "I FARTED!" and she laughs and laughs and laughs. Cynthia slowly turns in a circle, holding her arms out and singing, "Keisha farted. She's retarded. I am Cindy. I break windy." Then she sticks out her ass and farts too, which makes everyone hysterical.

"Hey, Frannie," Keisha yells, "let me be Cinderella." She puts on the mask and stands in the center of the room, jerking her large body back and forth. Her sweatshirt falls to the floor. Completely unaware, she bites her lip and puffs out her cheeks. Then she shakes her boobs and pumps her hips as if she's having sex. She sings along with the Stones, and I nudge Shelly. Mesmerized, we both watch as Keisha struts her stuff.

Shelly jumps up. "Come on," she yells. "THE BAND IS HERE!!" She points. "Back up, please." While Keisha strums an imaginary guitar, Pia plays the drums, and Cynthia plays the trumpet. Shelly sings lead, using a hairbrush as a microphone. With Mick Jagger howling in the background, Shelly grunts and moans and squeals. And squeals again. I stand on the sidelines, watching my sister sing, and I marvel at how much fun it is, sometimes, just being a girl.

AVALON ADVERTISING
724 Fifth Avenue, 42nd Floor
New York, NY 10019
Telephone 212 334–9994
Facsimile 212 334–9997

Ms. Francine Vanessa Hunter
739 St. James Place
Lindsey Point, NY 11223

Dear Francine:

While it was a pleasure to meet you, I regret to inform you that we have found a candidate whose experience more closely meets our needs. I wish you the best of luck with your job search. I am confident you will find something more appropriate to your qualifications.

Sincerely,
Miranda Billings
Senior Vice President, Advertising Sales

P.S. Perhaps you should try the Harvard Alumni Association. I'm sure your mother has contacts from her days as a 'Cliffie. Good luck–MB

New York • Chicago • San Francisco
Atlanta • Santa Fe • Miami Beach

I crumple the letter and throw it out. Crying, I call my mother at work. "She rejected me. Avalon rejected me." I can't stop sobbing. "I felt like I had that job, too. I really wanted that job."

"I'm sorry, Frannie. I guess it wasn't meant to be. I don't know what else to say except that I'm sorry. I wish I could make it different."

"I'm such a failure. Everything I do turns out wrong."

"You are *not* a failure. But maybe you shouldn't want things so much. I've always felt that you girls want things too much. Honey, this is a terrible time. Can we talk tonight?"

"I just can't stand this anymore! I don't know what to do!"

"I don't know how to help you. What do you want me to do?"

This makes me cry harder. "I want you to know how bad it feels to get rejected. I want someone else to always be the failure. I want you to be me for a change."

"I can't stand to hear you cry, Frannie. Every time I see you and your sister so miserable, it turns me inside out."

"Why is everything about how I make *you* feel?"

"Frannie, please. I am very sorry, but I have a meeting."

Crying makes me feel better. Even when I get a call from Bryan who says that this Friday's not good, but next Friday, for sure. I sit with my grandfather and watch TV, waiting for my mother to come home. We talk about his bowel movements, his medication, and all his sore body parts. At seven, I'm panting at the window, but she doesn't show. By eight-thirty, I'm asleep on the couch. She calls around ten to say she got hung up. I tape the rejection letter to the phone, crawl into bed, and cry. When she cracks my door and leans in to talk, I pretend that I'm asleep.

"My dear, we've let ourselves *go*." Collette's hands are in my hair. My mother offered to pay for a trim as compensation for blowing me off. When I said that it wasn't necessary, that I didn't get the job so I didn't need my hair cut, she threw in a manicure. She didn't even utter a sound when I ate a Big Mac, fries, and a large Coke from my lap in the car.

"We've been neglecting ourselves, haven't we, Frannie?" Collette shuffles around the beauty parlor in bell-bottom jeans and platform shoes. I lean back while she rinses me. "My assistant has her own studio now so I don't have anyone to shampoo for me."

"It's hard to find good help these days." I wonder if she's telling me this because she knows I need a job. "What are you going to do?"

"Find someone else, naturally. I can't do everything myself."

What would be so terrible about being a hairdresser? I wouldn't have to get in until eleven, I could dress in cool clothes and listen to the radio all day. "I could help you out for a while, Collette."

She starts laughing. "You are so funny, Frannie."

"I'm serious. I could come in, shampoo, maybe give a trim. How hard could it be?"

"I am an *artist*, Frannie, not a barber. You go to beautician school, apprentice, sweep the floors while you watch me cut. You can't just walk in here and *do hair*." She sniffs, offended.

"Sorry," I say, my voice tight. My mother walks over, her head swathed in a towel.

"Frannie wants to be a hairstylist." Collette grabs a towel and massages my head. My mother laughs. "No, really," Collette continues. "She said she wants to *do hair*." That's not what I said! Collette's hands rub my head so hard it hurts. She smiles down. I smile up. You are such a fucking freak, I think, still smiling at her. Go find some decent clothes. It's the nineties for Christ's sake.

Abby's more excited about my date with Bryan than I am. "Third date, Frannie," she whoops into the phone. "You know what that means."

"What do you mean 'third date'? This is only our second."

"He called you, right? You talked for a while, right? So it's a date. A phone date."

"I don't think you can count the phone call."

"I can so. I make the rules. And this spells S-E-X to me!!"

"Calm down, Abby. I'm not having sex with him. I *like* him. I want to get to know him before we get up in the morning and the switch thing happens where I'm obsessing about him while he's telling me he can't be in a relationship, but it has nothing to do with me. I don't want to go through that. I can't get too attached."

"You're already obsessed. And we *all* get too attached, Frannie. You do it, some enzyme kicks in and he falls asleep with his hands covering his thing and you watch the ceiling. SO WHAT? It's not like you're going to *marry* this guy. Enjoy it for what it is. I would."

"You're not one to discriminate, Abby."

"If I recall," she says indignantly, "you were the last one to do the walk of shame. With that sleazy waiter Artie, right?"

The walk of shame is what happens when you stumble home after having sex with a Rat Boy—someone incredibly ugly, incredibly inappropriate, or with an unknown last name. You hang your head and moan, "I am suuuch a slut" while your friends promise that he really liked you and will definitely call.

"Abby, I'm *not* having sex. I'm going to maintain my dignity and go home."

"Why? Who needs dignity when you can roll around with a guy who's got a full-time job?"

"I just don't want anything to jinx this. What if he's the *one*?"

"Frannie, look at it this way. If you count the phone call, you've got two dates down and one date coming. And what's that expression? Three's the charm!"

11

Wearing the bodysuit was a mistake. The snaps are worn, so whenever I move even the slightest inch, they fly open. Then the whole thing rides up and bunches in my pants. I lean against the bar slowly so everything stays hooked.

Two hours ago, I had a mad try-on-a-thon in my bedroom. Frustrated, red-faced, and sweating, I settled on a navy bodysuit I filched from Abby, clingy black leggings, and a $45 Dior bra and underwear set bought specifically for tonight.

I sip my margarita and wait for Bryan to return from the men's room. I roll the glass between my palms. Who cares what I'm wearing? A few more of these and I'll be gyrating on the bar in nothing but my Dior ensemble.

Before I left the house I paraded in front of my mother, who was lying in bed. "You look nice," she said, her head bent. But then she looked up. "You're wearing that?"

I sat on the bed. "I have a date with that Bryan guy, the resident from St. Mary's."

"And then you'll be driving home? Do you think that's a good idea?"

"Well, hopefully I won't have to come home. It *is* our third date." I snickered wickedly.

"What's so special about tonight?"

"I might get lucky. You know how that goes." I tried to sound flip, but heard the edge in my voice as soon as the words flew out. Shit, I promised myself I wouldn't make any reference to her affair, or rather, the affair she's not having. "You know what I mean," I added quickly. "We might have a good time. Not a sleazy good time, but a good conversation good time."

"Don't forget Daddy has to take Grandpa to the doctor tomorrow. You need to be here."

I stopped in the den where my father was watching TV and asked him if I could take his Mercedes. "If you fill it with gas. But I need it first thing in the morning to take your grandfather to the doctor. And I'd really appreciate your going with me."

"I'll be here. I shouldn't be later than midnight."

"Frannie, I'm serious." He dug into his pocket. "Promise me."

"Back off, Daddy-man. I'll be here. Jesus, you'd think I was planning on spending the night with this guy." I tugged on my new underwear, smiling to myself.

"You're sexy." Bryan leans across the table, swaying and slurring. "Very sexy."

"Don't forget funny." I laugh. "And sweet. You forgot to say sweet."

I curl my toes. My mother should see me now, drinking with a handsome doctor who's hanging on my every word. I'm so happy. Happy, happy, happy. I say it so many times that soon it doesn't sound like a word. I chewed a Valium in the car and now I feel delightful despite my bodysuit unsnapping every time I lean forward.

Tingling, I teach Bryan how to drink margaritas. "You start with the salt." I lick the rim slowly. I let my tongue linger on the glass, then run it along my bottom teeth. As he watches, I slowly suck my bottom lip. I lick my fingertips and suck them slowly, one at a time.

Watching me, he croaks, "And then?"

"You take a big gulp and feel the burn as it slides down your throat." I tilt my head and gulp the drink. I feel my hair, long and full against my back. His eyes haven't left my face. "Suck the ice," he whispers. "Suck the ice for me."

I tilt the glass and a lone piece of ice slides into my mouth. I stick out my tongue and the cube dissolves. "There," I say softly. "I sucked it."

He licks his forefinger then runs it along my lower lip. A quiet rush fills my head. I love margaritas. I shake my hair, feeling so beautiful I can't believe I'm me. My thighs are taut in my leggings, my arms muscular underneath my bodysuit, which could be snapping open at this very second, but I can't tell and I don't care. I'm happy. Finally.

I hum idly with the jukebox as Bryan stares soulfully into my eyes. "The minute I saw you," he says, "I thought: that girl is sexy. You just exude sex, I swear."

I smile. "I'm just your average red-blooded, All-American girl."

"I love American girls."

"Have you had other kinds?"

He grins. "A gentleman never tells."

I want to dance. He is so handsome, so utterly handsome. I wonder if he likes me. Oh, but he must. I'm in control, this is my bus, and I'm driving. I imagine him pressing his mouth against mine, his tongue juicy in my mouth; warm, juicy, and sweet like caramel candy. I hope he means what he's saying; I wonder if he's falling in love. "Do you date a lot of girls?" I ask playfully.

He shrugs. "A few here and there."

"Pretty girls?"

"Always."

"Anyone special?"

"Just you." He rubs a piece of ice against my lips. I flush with desire, a feeling so overwhelming I almost fall over. "I love your mouth," he says softly and rubs another piece so slowly it melts in his fingers. I lean forward so he can kiss me, but a couple passing by accidentally jostle him and he jerks up.

"Sorry," the man says, holding his date's elbow. She stares at Bryan closely. A lock of golden hair hides one of her eyes and she grins at him, the corners of her mouth raised suggestively. The man propels her away.

Bryan rubs his head, watching the woman walk away. He plays with a plastic stirrer silently, as if contemplating something important. I shift in my seat. "Do you know her?" I ask finally.

"Who?"

"The blond woman. It seemed like you knew her." He shrugs and tells me he's never seen her before, but he glances over my shoulder, as if looking for her while he talks. "She was pretty," I say.

"I didn't notice." I wait for him to say something else, but he doesn't. I roll my glass between my palms, but it slips and I lurch to catch it. Then, when I look into it, I notice that all the ice has melted.

"Is something wrong?" The music has stopped between songs. My voice booms like a whine. "You seem like something is bothering you."

"What could be bothering me?" He's edgy. I wonder if I said something to make him mad.

"Have you ever been to Europe?" I ask. "Hey, I know, let's take a trip sometime. Let's just pack a bag and go to Italy." I'm spinning, and I hear myself talking too fast. My heart rocks like a ship on the open sea. "I'm a spontaneous kind of girl. I could take off. I could." Bryan looks at me as if seeing me for the first time. "I don't complain like a lot of girls." And I can cook and clean and I make all my own clothes. Jesus, Frannie, shut up. There's a dreadful lull. Unable to help myself, I blurt, "Do you ever think about getting married?"

"Not usually."

Oh God. Oh God. How could I ask that? And everything was going so well. "I don't think about it myself," I lie. "But my friends do. They're at that age."

"My friends do everything to avoid it. I guess *they're* at that age, too." He laughs so I lean forward. "I think you're so handsome," I tell him. I know I must look like a puppy in heat but I want him to kiss me so we can get this show back on the road.

He's suddenly solemn. "I'm nothing special, Frannie—not what you think."

I try to joke. "Then what are you?" I use a straw to outline my name in sugar. I get as far as F-R-A before the sugar runs out.

"You ask a lot of questions," he says abruptly.

"I was only kidding. Don't be so serious. Shelly's doing great," I say, changing the subject. "She's getting out of the hospital soon."

"Don't get your hopes up, Frannie. I've seen what happens to these girls when they get close to checking out. It's their most vulnerable time."

Abruptly, I stand. The snaps of my bodysuit fly open. "You're talking about my *sister*!" I squeeze my legs together. "You haven't even *seen* her! She's doing *great*!" I reach for my backpack, and my bodysuit creeps up my ass. Soon it will be bunched like a tire around my waist. "I'm going home," I say firmly, but I linger, watching him.

He looks up at me, then grabs my hand. "I'm sorry. I don't mean to be such an asshole. I'm having a difficult time with one of my patients." He brushes my hair off my shoulder. "I don't mean to take it out on you." He pulls me close. "You're much too pretty for that. I'm happy you're here," he whispers. "Please don't leave me." I slowly slide onto my stool. Maybe I should be more understanding. He is a doctor after all.

Bryan pulls my hand. "We should go. I told some friends we would meet them." He tugs playfully. "Come on. It'll be fun." What about dinner? I think. What happened to dinner?

Before we leave, I fix my bodysuit in the ladies' room and tell myself over and over that he wants me to stay. *Please don't leave me.* How could I leave you? I put lipstick on and flush with desire again, imagining his fingers stroking my lips. *You have the most incredible mouth.* I stare at my reflection, trying to imagine myself looking fabulously pretty, but all I see is the woman with golden hair smiling at Bryan, her breath escaping from her parted lips with the hint of a kiss. I blink and look at my face again. Don't leave me, I think.

"Do you want another drink?" Bryan asks. We're huddled in a dark and dirty bar that's packed with people. I'm sitting all the way at the end. It's amazing how quickly a good buzz can sour. I know I'm still drunk, but the tingle is gone and the fog has rolled in and I feel clammy and bloated and I think I might throw up if anyone jostles me.

I tell him I want a margarita. I had high hopes of making a nice impression on his friends, but they're too busy checking out women to acknowledge me. All I can do now is resurrect the more pleasant part of my buzz and not make a fool of myself. I am jonesing for a cigarette so bad. "Margaritas are my favorite beverage," I say. I lean back too far and quickly catch myself before toppling off my stool.

Bryan chews on the end of a straw and winks at his friends. "I'd rather drink Scotch." He smiles, but his tone is clipped. I wonder if he's moving into another bad mood he can blame on his patients. Well he can fuck himself. At this point, I could give a shit if his patients stood in a circle, sang "Kumbaya," and slit their wrists.

Bryan pats my arm. "This is Richard." Richard holds up a hand. He's short, with one eyebrow that stretches across his forehead like a furry shelf, and an eye twitch he can't control. He says something I can't hear, so I nod and smile.

I try to get Bryan's attention. "Do you usually date women who drink Scotch?" I imagine him fucking the golden-haired woman. She's lying on a gurney, her black skirt hiked around her waist, her naked legs kicking the air. I wipe away a bead of perspiration. My bodysuit, which unsnapped twenty minutes ago, has rolled up so far the crotch hangs out like a tail. My leggings feel really tight, like the material is bunched around my thighs, creating ripples of fat.

"I date a lot of women." Bryan stares into his glass. "Variety is the spice of life, don't you think?" Richard, whom I hate, snickers.

"I think variety is overrated." I try to sound flip but I feel sick. The Weight Watchers lasagna I ate earlier sits inside me like a cube of concrete. I put my hand on Bryan's arm to steady myself but he pulls away. Tears burn in my eyes but I refuse to cry. I should leave. We didn't have sex and I feel like shit. Bryan and Richard are talking, but all I can hear is the roar of the drunk inside my ears and the blare of the jukebox in the background. I lean forward. My head rushes to meet me.

I admit that I've never had much luck with sex. I lost my virginity in high school to Dylan McGuire, who had tattoos and was rumored to smack his mother, but whom I loved as much as my mother hated. "You'll never go anywhere if you stay with that creep," she said, which I find completely ironic because Dylan is now a bond trader on Wall Street. I, on the other hand, ended up in a dirty duck apron serving Mr. and Mrs. McGuire plates of fried cheese at Rascals. Used to serve, I correct myself.

The first time Dylan and I did it, I was really stoned. Part of me wanted to do it because I really loved Dylan, but the main reason was because being a virgin at seventeen was a bore, with all the stopping and starting and begging that went on, not to mention the endless discussions with Abby about what to do when. Dylan and I wrestled on the couch. The drugs wore off by the time we were naked. I stared at his head lolling between my breasts like a huge medallion, and squeezed my eyes closed, wishing he'd go away. He dug his fingers into me and I was really dry but afraid I'd sound whiny if I said something. I felt a pressure and a stab and wetness and I was about to tell him he was hurting me when he shuddered and fell into me, still kneading my breasts like they were dials on his car stereo. My head ached from banging it against the arm of the couch and my bare ass was raw from the tweed. There was a puddle of liquid between my legs so I sat on my T-shirt, aware that I was bleeding on the fabric. Dylan propped himself up and muttered, "How was that, Frannie baby?" I wanted to say something wildly sophisticated but instead blurted, "God, that was fast. Is that it?" Dylan got up and left without speaking to me and it was several weeks before I heard from him again.

I look up. Bryan and his friends are staring at a woman at the end of the bar. She's leggy and exotic, and from where I'm sitting, I don't see any signs of a rolled-up bodysuit underneath her clingy black tube dress. "... break her in half," one of the guys mutters. He smiles sheepishly but I shrug, trying to be a good buddy. Bryan says something and they all laugh. Very nauseous, I lay my head down, wishing I could drift off.

Bryan tells me he'll be right back. I watch him saunter away, and I think I see him sidle up to the exotic woman with the power body. I squint to see if she presses herself against him when he passes, if he smiles at her, cocks his head to say hello, holds her hand a beat too long.

Richard leans low. "Bryan and I have been friends since med school."

I sit up. "Are you a psychiatrist, too?"

He shakes his head. "Hematology and oncology–AIDS and cancer." He signals for the bartender.

I'm dying to ask a thousand questions about Bryan but don't. Men hate desperate women, that much I know, thanks to the talk I had with my mother when she gave me the pamphlet *Your Changing Body* a hundred years ago. "How long have you been seeing Bryan?" Richard asks. I tell him that we've been out a few times, trying to appear as if Richard is the most riveting conversationalist and I'm having the *best* time just talking to him.

"So what do you do, Fran?" He waves to a redhead across the bar who smiles and waves. "Sorry." He turns back. "What do you do?" he asks again.

I think of my Rascals apron, crumpled and unused, stinking up my closet. "I'm an equities trader," I say solemnly.

With that, Richard launches into a high-pitched discussion of his latest investment strategy. It's actually quite fascinating, the way this ridiculous guy with a unibrow has to tell me everything he's ever heard about Wall Street. As if oncology isn't enough. I wonder where Bryan is, if he has the exotic woman pressed against the wall, her long legs wrapped around his waist.

Richard's still talking. "So what do you think about Pfizer? I mean, as a way to go?"

"Pfizer?"

"Pfizer Pharmaceuticals. You know, for long-term growth. You have any tips?"

"Don't plant corn in the winter," I say just as Bryan returns. He whispers something to Richard before he sits down. I take out my lipstick and run it across my mouth. Bryan doesn't look at me. He's sitting close enough to touch, though, and I lean forward and press my bloodred lips across the back of his starched white shirt. Surprisingly, the impression my mouth leaves is that of a smile.

"I have to go to the ladies' room," I announce. I clutch my bodysuit and pick my way through the crowd. I wish there was a hole in the floor I could fall through so Bryan and his Rat Boy buddies don't discuss the size of my ass as they watch me waddle away.

*   *   *

I stumble to the back of the bar, and feel myself about to throw up. Miraculously, the bathroom is empty as I push my way in, head bent so I won't heave before reaching the toilet. I kneel on the floor and let 'er rip, gagging so hard, I almost dislodge a tonsil. My forehead is damp with sweat and my eyes fill with tears. I rest my face on the edge of the bowl and throw up again.

After gagging and gasping and drooling, I feel a little better. I know I should go home, but I refuse to admit that things can't be turned around. *Please don't leave me.* Admit it. This guy is an asshole. *Please don't.* I need to be more perky. That's what he liked about me. A string of saliva hangs off my chin. *Leave me.*

I hear voices as people walk in and out. I try to straighten up, but I'm so weak, I crouch with my elbows on the toilet. "Shit, that's my beeper." I listen for a second, wondering why there's a guy in the ladies' room. "Who the fuck is beeping me?" It's definitely a guy talking. In fact, it sounds like Richard, the Michael Milken of Medicine. What the hell is he doing in here?

"You gotta call in, Rich. If you don't, they'll beep Davenport and I don't want to be around tomorrow when you try to explain you were too fucked up to find a phone."

It *is* Richard. Oh shit. I lean forward. Shit, I'm in the *men's* room.

"In a minute. Check this out. Frankel calls me in on a consult, right? White lady, mid-thirties, IV drug user, end-stage AIDS, metastatic breast cancer. She's in septic shock. They're measuring her life span in days. So whaddaya think I say?"

"I don't know, asshole. What did you say?"

"Oak casket. Brass handles." They laugh and I panic. I have to get out of here.

They're obviously waiting for the stall because they keep talking. I rise from the floor and just as I am about to push on the door, I hear Richard ask, "What's wrong with Bryan's date?" I flush. *I'm Bryan's date. That's me!* Oh God, God, I promise I'll just go home if they don't say anything mean. "She seems like a bitch." Fuck you, Richard, you furry fucking Rat Boy. *FUCK* YOU.

"She's wasted. I think she's kinda cute. I'd do her." For a second, my heart warms. He likes me, I think.

"Did Bryan tell her about Leslie?"

"Would you?" They both laugh. Suddenly, Richard bangs on the door. "Come on, man. What's going on?" I grunt, hoping it's deep enough. "Shit," says Richard, "some guy's hurling. It stinks in here. Fuck it."

I hear the sound of paper ripping, then two snorts. "Good shit," one says, and the other obviously agrees because they snort again. Trying to steady myself, I stand up and use wads of toilet paper to wipe my face and hands. I fold the snap part of my bodysuit under and tuck it in my underwear. One of the guys raps again. "Jesus Christ, man!"

Straightening my shoulders, I open the stall door as wide as I can. I walk out and look right into Richard's eyes. "Hey, Dick!" I say, flashing a killer smile. "Who's Leslie?"

In front of Bryan's apartment, I cross and uncross my legs three times. I relax as he jiggles the key, then feel the pressure again and try to do the dance without Bryan knowing. The feeling passes, but only briefly because my bladder tightens and I squeeze my legs together, leaking droplets of urine. I rush inside when Bryan opens the door, then race into the bathroom where I pull the crotch of my bodysuit, situate myself, and release my muscles, the stream hitting the water even before I sit down.

What a grand entrance, I think to myself. I know I should have left him hours ago, but he begged me to go home with him, promising he'd sleep on the couch. "I know my friends are dogs," he'd said, quite proudly, when we left the bar, "but I'll make it up to you. Please, Frannie?" I looked at my dad's car. It was a long drive back to Lindsey and I had nothing to do the next day but watch my parents ignore each other. "Okay," I agreed, letting him take my hand and propel me home. "I'll stay."

I sit on the toilet, wondering if I did the right thing. I consider calling Abby, but lose the thought as I run the faucet and rummage through Bryan's cabinets. I find a pink Daisy razor. A clue to Leslie. There are a lot of pills, physician's samples, nothing good. Suntan lotion. Rogaine. Underneath the sink I find a few loose tampons.

She really exists. Disappointed, I stick them in my backpack.

In the glare of the light, I look old. Mascara is caked underneath my eyes and my cheeks are blotchy and tearstained. My hair is nappy. I make faces at myself. I hate you, you are so *ugly*. Ugly, ugly, ugly. I spray some of Bryan's deodorant into my armpits and think about the ice melting on my lips. Before I leave, I spray another squirt between my legs.

Bryan puts on a jazz station. A breeze blows softly into the room. I look around. If I wasn't so utterly uncomfortable right now, I'd probably be having a pretty good time. I sit on the edge of the couch next to him. "You met Richard in medical school?" I ask.

"Yeah, he's got it rough. He's in hemoc. I almost went into it, but it's incredibly draining. In psychiatry, your patients may be lunatics, but some have a chance. He treats AIDS and cancer; all his patients die."

"AIDS is scary." I turn over a pillow in my lap.

Bryan strokes my arm. "Ever been tested?"

I shake my head. "I know I should. I really haven't slept with that many guys."

"You should still get tested."

Even though he's right, I feel uneasy, as if he's telling me I'm inadequate, unclean. "How often do you get tested?"

"All the time. I have to. I moonlight at a clinic. One needle stick and my life is fucking over. Anyway, Richard's a hematologist. He tests me."

"You let Richard draw your blood?"

"We draw each other's blood all the time and"—he smiles as if remembering something pleasant—"women that we know. He sends it to the lab. It's free." A fire engine squeals by. "God, that's loud," he says, and gets up to shut the window. "I'm happy you're here, Frannie. Sorry tonight got so fucked up."

I reach for something to say. I feel the heat of anxiety. Sweating, I tug at my collar. Bryan is still talking, but I can't hear him. I can't focus. I shake my head. I notice that part of the wall is chipped. The plaster is white, bright white. White hot. My mind gets fuzzy. Hot, so hot. I pull my hair into a ponytail. In the background, I hear the radio: this evening, playing New York's favorite jazz, cool and easy. It's hot, too hot. I'm burning up. *Happy you're here. Kiss me.* "It's hot," I mutter. "Do you mind this evening playing New York's favorite jazz, cool and easy." Startled, I glance up. I said that. *I* did. Not the radio.

At the window, Bryan turns around. "Did you say something?"

Worried about everything now, I take a deep breath. It happened. I'm splintering. *It's my brain,* she said. *It's eating me alive.* "No," I say aloud, testing my voice. "I'm fine." I lean back, trembling. "You have a girlfriend, don't you?"

With his back to me, Bryan stares out the window and nods. "Richard told you?"

"Sort of."

He sits down next to me. We don't talk for a few seconds, and I tilt my head back and forth, waiting for more anxiety, but it doesn't come.

"I don't want to mislead you," Bryan is saying. "Leslie—my girl-friend—took a fellowship in another city."

"She's a doctor, too?" I groan. "So you miss her?"

For a second he looks very lonely. "I want to close that chapter. I don't know if I'm ready for another relationship, Frannie, but I like you, I do. I just can't make any promises." He looks so sad that I want to cradle him in my arms, make it right, bring Leslie back.

"You don't have to make any promises, Bryan."

"I know. I just want to be upfront about everything. I'm not the kind of guy who would just lead you on. But," he says, leaning forward, "you really are beautiful. And you have such an unbelievable mouth. I have to taste you." He kisses me, openmouthed. At first I hold back. I hear what he says, I really do: there's no promises, there's no promises, none, no promises, but I want him so much, God, it feels so good to have someone touch me, and hold me, and if I leave now, I'll be okay, I can do it. I can leave. I can say no. I tingle with desire and his mouth is so warm and when he rubs his wet wet fingers all over my lips, I lean forward and suck his tongue, and I'm flooded, absolutely flooded with warmth and relief and hot rich desire that fills my mouth like creamy soup, and I sigh and let him roll on top of me and the voices, all those voices, fade away.

*　　　*　　　*

"I want to be inside you," Bryan is saying. "Oh God, Frannie. I want to be inside you so badly." He runs his hands up, under my bodysuit.

"I think we should wait, Bryan," I hear myself say, but I'm moving with him and we've got a rhythm and I don't stop. "You're not over Leslie yet. Let's wait, okay?" My head pounds. I force myself to sit up.

"I just need some time, that's all, just time." He licks his finger, trails it down the length of my stomach, and reaches into my underwear. I want to feel him touching me, I do, but I can't stop seeing a woman in a white lab coat, wrapped in his arms, sobbing in the fog of a train station.

I push him off. "This isn't right," I say.

"I know." He clears his throat. "You should get tested."

"That's not what I meant." I look at him. "Okay, I'll get tested. Then we can start over. From the beginning."

"No, I'm talking about now. I can test you now."

"Now? Here? With what?"

"I have all the stuff. It won't hurt and I'll have the results in a week, maybe sooner. It's free. I'll take it to the lab at the clinic."

"It's not something I want to do right now."

"Why?"

I shrug self-consciously. Every time I think about AIDS, I replay all the sexual adventures I can remember, get petrified about the ones that I can't, and palpitate with anxiety, imagining myself alone in a hospice, ashen and shriveled with night sweats and diarrhea. "All right, maybe. Maybe." I'm really really tired. Maybe if I do it, he'll know that I trust him. Maybe he likes free-spirited girls. Maybe they let him do it. Maybe he'll forget about Leslie. The maybes run together and I close my eyes. "All right," I tell him. "Maybe."

"If you really don't want to do it, we don't have to," he says solemnly. "You shouldn't do anything you're not ready for. I'm serious, Frannie. I wouldn't just say that. But I know you'll feel so good when it's over." He gets up from the couch, tugs on his pants, and walks into the bathroom.

*   *   *

I sit on the bed in my bra. Bryan holds a small package and a tube. "You have beautiful skin," he says softly, tracing the curve of my chin. I shiver. He kneels beside me, and rips open the package with his teeth. "Really beautiful." I panic when I see the needle.

"I don't want to do this," I say quickly, turning away. "I really don't."

"It's your choice. A lot of people get nervous, though, Frannie." He tucks the sheet around me and strokes my bare arm. "Frannie, I'm a doctor. Let me do this for you. I want to do this for you."

I feel his fingers and allow myself to go limp. I look away. "Okay," I say very quietly. "But do it fast."

I don't want to watch, but can't help myself. He swabs my arm, then slowly runs his fingers up and down. "You're a phlebotomist's nightmare," he says. "You have no veins." I hold out my other arm. "No, I'm a magician. I'll find one."

He bends over me and I stare at the top of his head. The jazz music plays softly in the background and I am lulled. We both breathe deeply and I lose myself in the moment. Tenderly, he cradles my arm and stares into my eyes. "I promise I won't hurt you, Frannie." He smiles kindly and brushes my hair away from my face. Then he bends over me. The room spins and I stare at his balding scalp. "Make a fist," he says. I can't watch, but I do as I'm told. Then slowly, very slowly, as slowly as I could ever imagine, he pricks my skin and slides the needle into my vein. The needle stings a little, and there's some pressure, but it's not so bad. I open my eyes. Bryan's eyes are closed and he's breathing deeply, groaning with pleasure, as he draws my blood from my body. He smiles and his eyes flutter open. They're glazed, as if he's lost somewhere warm. He reaches up and strokes my cheek with his thumb and we both watch as my dark red blood, so dark it's almost black, fills the tube. He holds my arm where the needle sticks out, caressing me as if he's touching the most intimate part of my body. His fingers are long and thin, and I focus on each clear rounded nail as heat spreads through me. I can't believe that so much blood can come out of me but he's so loving and so gentle that I don't want it to end. He hovers over me so I lean forward, tingling, overwhelmed with feeling, wanting him to kiss me, but at that moment, at the moment when

I think how nice it would feel to have his wet warm mouth pressed softly against mine, he pulls out the needle, swabs my arm, and applies a Band-Aid.

"Good girl." He pats my shoulder, puts the rubber stopper on the tube, writes *Smith, Fran* in black Magic Marker, and tosses it into the pocket of his lab coat. Then he goes into the bathroom and shuts the door. I put my bodysuit on, get under the covers, and wait.

"You did good. Don't you feel better?" He gets into bed, kisses my cheek, and snaps off the light. Then he rolls over and curls up, his arms wrapped around a pillow. I lie on my back, wishing he'd grab me and hold me or at least say something. I wait a few seconds and the seconds become minutes. Just as I'm about to speak, I hear his heavy breathing. Unable to stop myself, I keep seeing the needle, rusted and bent, being slipped into my arm. As I feel my dirty blood flow through me, I reach to wake Bryan but slump back, petrified. In the darkness, I whisper rhymes to soothe myself, and in my head, where nothing's safe, I ride the radio music like a dream.

"It was great, wasn't it?" Abby sits on the edge of my bed. I nod, but tears well in my eyes and I look away. "Well tell me. Did you kiss at least?" I nod. "And?"

"And nothing. Look, Abby. I don't want to talk about it. He was kind of a jerk to me." I spent the day in bed, hung over and hating myself.

She picks up the navy bodysuit. "I can't believe you had this! I've been looking all over for it." She holds it up. "How was he a jerk?"

"I told you, I don't want to talk about it." I hear my mother and grandfather outside my door. "She's so pissed. I completely forgot I was supposed to take my grandfather to the doctor. They waited forever and my father had to take my mother's car so she missed some stupid open house and he missed some meeting. Like who has a meeting on Saturday? Anyway, neither of them are speaking to me."

"They'll get over it." Abby rummages through my closet. "So this guy didn't even take you for brunch? Jesus, he *is* a jerk." She holds up one of my favorite dresses. "Can I have this?" I nod. "Well at least you didn't fuck him." She peers at me. "You did, didn't you?

That's why you feel so bad? Frannie, listen." She sits on my bed. "We talked about this. It was what it was. He was a Rat Boy. Don't romanticize him."

"I didn't *fuck* him, Abby, for Christ's sake! And he's not a Rat Boy, okay? God, I hate that expression."

"Bite my head off, why don't you?" She picks up the phone. She always comes over and calls her other friends as if my friendship isn't enough. Annoyed, I ask her who she's calling. "I'm just checking my machine." For some reason, this bothers me more.

My mother taps on the door. "Frannie? Grandpa wants to say hello."

"We're kind of busy, Mom," I call out.

"It will just take a second."

She opens the door and they walk in. My grandfather inches toward my bed and sits down next to me. "Hi, Grandpa," I say and immediately turn to my mother. "I'm really sorry again, Mom, about this morning. I should have been here."

"Tell your father, not me." She reaches out. "Come, Daddy. Let's have supper."

"Frannie, you coming, too?" he asks. "We're having meat loaf. I love meat loaf. Especially with lots of onions. You like meat loaf, too, don't you?" I nod, thinking of Bryan and how nice it would have been if he had called me. "Frannie," my grandfather says, "I have to ask you one thing and it's very, very important. Come here." He crooks a finger at me.

I want to scream at him to shut up. "What, Grandpa?" I ask sharply.

"I want you to tell me all about this new boyfriend. Mommy says he's a doctor!"

I jerk back, glance at Abby and my mother, and then at my grandfather who is reaching out for me. I stare into his milky eyes and my chest constricts. And then without warning, I burst into tears.

M y mother's tranquilizers sit in a bag next to the phone. Lately,
she's been saying that she doesn't need them anymore; that
she only refills the prescription to have some on reserve. I want to
rip the bag open and scarf a few down, but I promised myself I'd
stay out of her stash. I know she watches me closely to make sure
I'm not taking her shit without asking. And God knows, I wouldn't
want to give her the satisfaction of catching me in the act.

Days go by, but Bryan never calls, not even to tell me the results of
my test. I beg Abby to come over and call him for me. "What am I
going to say?" she whines.

"Tell him you're with the phone company and you're checking
the line. I just want to know if he's home."

"Frannie, he'll know it's you."

"But it won't be me. It'll be you." After pleading with her, she
finally calls, but gets flustered when she hears his voice and hangs
up. Ten seconds later, my phone rings back. "Hello?" I ask suspiciously.

"Did you just call me?" It's Bryan. I'm so freaked out he's on the
line, I don't even disguise my voice. "Who's this?" I ask.

"Who's *this*?" he retorts.

"It's Frannie. Why are you calling me?"

"I have Caller ID. You just called me and hung up, so I called you back. It's a miracle of modern communications."

Some fucking miracle. I motion for Abby to listen in. We huddle over the receiver. "I was calling to find out my test results," I tell him. "I thought I got the wrong number." Abby snickers and I smack her with the phone.

"I got your results back." Bryan pauses. "I was going to call you."

"Why?" Wide-eyed, I glance at Abby. She doesn't move, but I know what she's thinking. My results came back positive. My body is riddled with disease. I am going to die.

"You're negative." Abby and I exhale at the same time. I start to say something, but Bryan cuts me off. "Frannie, I have another call. Congratulations on your test. I know it's good news. Send my best to Shelly."

"Sure. Well, bye I guess." My voice is hollow and small. Abby grabs the phone. "BYE, YOU VAMPIRE, YOU LOST BOY! YOU . . . YOU RAT BOY!" she yells and slams it down. Then she puts her arms around me. I don't have anything in common with Bryan. He's rude, arrogant, balding, and self-centered. But I bend my head anyway, and let myself cry for a long time over a guy I didn't even like.

The next day I stop by St. Mary's to pick up Shelly. She's having a trial overnight, and I'm helping her pack up some things to take home.

"I can't believe you're leaving," Pia sobs, rushing to hug Shelly.

"I'm just going home for one night. I'm not leaving for good until Tuesday. And you'll be fine without me. We can talk every day if you want."

"You promise?" When Shelly nods, Pia relaxes. She turns to me. "Oh hi, Frannie," she says. "How's your new job?"

"What new job?"

"I thought you got that advertising job." I stiffen and mumble that it didn't come through. "Oh. Sorry," Pia says. "You'll find something. People always get jobs."

I glance at Shelly. At first, it annoys me that she didn't tell Pia about the rejection, but then it occurs to me that she probably never talks about me. It reminds me, once again, that she has a whole other life that doesn't include me. Abruptly, I stand. "Is that it, Shelly? We really gotta go."

She nods. "I can't believe I'm leaving. It feels really weird."

"Yeah, well, we have a lot to do, so can we get this show on the road?"

"Why are you so pissed off?"

"I'm not, but you wanted to stop off at Lonny's, and we don't have that much time."

As we walk out, Keisha hands her a package. "I know we're going to have a formal goodbye in a few days," she says shyly, "but I couldn't help myself. I had to give you this." Shelly rips open the package. In a frame is a picture of all the girls standing, waving, and holding a sign that says WE LOVE YOU, SHELLY!

"Wasn't that so nice?" Shelly asks on the way to Lonny's office. "I can't believe they did this."

I sit in silence, stewing about my lack of friends. I haven't had any real friends since college. I certainly can't count on Abby anymore. She started seeing some guy from her office. She claims he's the *one*. She cancels plans all the time to be with him and talks about him nonstop. It makes me so sick, I refuse to meet the guy. And since I won't hang out with him, she won't hang out with me. So much for through thick and through thin.

I pull up in front of Lonny's office. "Please come in, Frannie," Shelly begs. I shake my head. "It will only take a second. I have a lot of books to carry."

Grudgingly, I park the car in a lot and follow her up. When we walk into Lonny's office, a crowd of people are in the reception area. The second Shelly walks through the door, they start clapping. I hear "Hi, Shelly" and "You look so good" about a million times.

"What are you? A fucking conquistador?" I mutter, hating them.

"Hi, everyone," Shelly says cheerfully. "How did you know I was coming?"

A woman wearing thick glasses pipes up. "Lonny told us. And what is this I hear about you going to grad school for psychology?"

"It's true. I hate to say it, but New York will have one less neurotic lawyer. This is my sister, Frannie." She nudges me, but I hang back, suddenly feeling too large to move.

"Hi, Frannie," Goggle-glasses says. "I'm Pamela Seaver." She holds out her hand.

"Hey, Frannie," Shelly tells me, "wait here. I want to say good-bye to Lonny."

"You must be so proud of Shelly," Pamela says as Shelly walks away. "Are you older than Shelly or younger?"

"Younger," I say. "Five years younger. I'm sorry. I have to go to the ladies' room."

When I get back, Lonny and Shelly are standing together. Lonny is holding a box of books. My sister is beaming up at him. You'd think he just fucked her, she looks so goddamn happy. I could never figure out how Abby got to be so pretty when Lonny's so homely. He has big jowls like a Saint Bernard and a pear-shaped body with an ass that could double as a billboard. But Shelly worships him like he's Don Juan DeMarco. And he worships her. They have this mutual admiration, MENSA, mind-fuck relationship that makes me feel like an idiot when I'm around them.

"You can always change your mind," Lonny says. "I shouldn't say this, but I hope you do."

"You never know. God knows I change my mind all the time." Shelly starts to well up.

"Shelly, don't cry. You know you can always come back. No matter where I am, you'll have a job." He turns to me. "Take care of her, Fran. By the way, how are you?"

I shrug. "Okay, I guess. Nothing new."

"Good, good." He rubs his stomach. "That's what I like to hear."

I grab the box of books and walk a step behind her onto the elevator. We ride down in silence. "Why are you crying?" I ask, feeling like I should say something. "Are you upset?"

"No," she says, crying harder. "I'm just really happy."

As we pass a garbage can on Fifth Avenue, Shelly tells me to hold up. She digs into her purse, takes out a notebook that I recognize as her journal, and tosses it in. "There." She wipes her eyes. "It's over. I finally feel free."

Even though I know, when we're almost home, I ask what she threw out. "My journal," she says solemnly. "The last vestige of the old me." I know I should feel happy for her, but instead, I have this nagging sensation that she's rubbing it in.

"Don't stand in front of the microwave, dear," my mother says to Abby. "You never know about those things." Abby moves to the left. Her boyfriend is out of town so she's graced us with her presence. "The table looks so nice, Marsha," she says to my mother.

My mother beams like she's Martha Stewart. "Thank you. But tell my husband. He did all the cooking."

My father looks around. "Frannie," he commands, "please go tell your sister and grandfather that we're about to eat."

When I get up to Shelly's room, she and my grandfather are talking on her bed.

"It's so weird to be here," she says as I walk in. "I feel like I'm back at the scene of the crime. I can't believe you guys talked me into moving home."

"It's only for a few weeks, Shelly. Then we'll get our own place. Make believe you're visiting another ward at St. Mary's."

"I just don't belong here anymore, Frannie. Things are different now. *I'm* different now."

"But I belong here?" I turn to my grandfather. "Grandpa, aren't you glad Shelly's home?"

"Why shouldn't I be happy? But I will tell you something. I'd go to my grave smiling like a goose if I could sing 'Here Comes the Bride' just once." Chuckling, he hums the tune as we move down the stairs.

When we reach the bottom, I whisper to Shelly, "Has he said anything to you about where you've been or anything?"

"He did tell me he thinks something might be going on that no one is telling him."

I smile. "He's pretty observant for a blind guy, don't you think?"

"I guess." She laughs. "He's upset no one will tell him why you act so strange. He's afraid there's something wrong with you, and if there is, he wants to know about it."

*   *   *

"I'm so excited to have both my girls home." My mother hands Abby a serving platter. "Abby, honey, pass this to my father. Daddy, have some more potatoes." Abby spoons potatoes onto my grandfather's plate. His head is bent. If he were any closer, his face would be in his food. "Well," my mother continues, "I just want to congratulate Shelly. We're all really proud of her."

"It's no big deal, Mom. Please don't talk about it. Let's just eat."

"But it *is* a big deal, Shelly. It's a very big deal. We're so happy you're coming home." Shelly groans. "I just think you look beautiful. Doesn't she look pretty, Abby?"

Abby nods. I feel her kick Shelly under the table. "Shelly looks absolutely ravishing. And I'd date her if she'd only give me the chance."

"But Abby's got a new guy," I announce.

"Oh?" my mother asks. She loves to hear stories of people hooking up.

"He's an attorney," Abby said. "His name is Randy. We work together. We've been out a few times. He's really nice."

"If you discount the fact that he's a skinhead," I interrupt. "And the hours he spends online in Courtney Love's chat room, and the pictures of naked children he has in a shoebox underneath his bed." I pause. "He also happens to be a midget. Although I wouldn't know for sure since I've never met him."

"You've had many opportunities to meet him, Frannie, and he's not a midget. He's just very short for his age."

"How old is he?" my mother asks.

"I don't know," Abby replies. "Thirty-one or something. A lot of boys have sudden growth spurts."

"All I know," I offer, "is the second Abby found out that his father was a plastic surgeon in Beverly Hills, he graduated from 'this loser midget guy who keeps bothering me' to 'I think I'll die if he doesn't call me.'" I turn to her. "No offense, Abiggirl. I mean, we all want to get married and drive Range Rovers, but you really need to take this one down a notch."

"I think you're jealous, Frannie," my mother says, smiling at Abby.

"I am not!" I yelp, my mouth full. I gulp my food so fast, I hiccup loudly.

"That's a lovely sound, Frannie. You're going to choke. And stop eating so fast."

"And so much. You can say it, Mom. I know it's what you're thinking."

"Frannie." She sighs. "I wasn't thinking anything."

I get up from the table to get more ice. At the counter, I pick at the crumby topping of a coffee cake. Without thinking, I jam my fingers into the dough to get at the cherry filling.

"Must you do that, Frannie?" Shelly calls to me. "You could use a plate."

"Sorry. I didn't realize you were on the coffee cake patrol. I just wanted a taste."

"We all have to eat it, you know."

"Like you'll be eating it," I mutter.

Everyone looks at me as I slide back into my seat. Feeling piggish, I wipe my hands on my pants. Shelly sips her water, and I feel the table reverberate with the rhythm of her foot bouncing underneath. She's wearing a denim workshirt with an open neck. Her collarbones jut out and the thin gold chain she's wearing accentuates the fragility of her neck. In the glow of the kitchen light, she looks like a shadow of the Shelly I grew up with. She picks at her food, lifts a string bean, inspects it, and puts it down. Just eat it, I want to say. Put it in your mouth and chew. I look over at the coffee cake, suddenly wanting to inhale the whole thing.

The phone rings and my mother jumps up, but I get there first. "It's for me," she says breathlessly. "I'll take it in the other room." I listen, but all I hear is someone breathing. "I got it!" she screams. "Frannie! Hang up!!" Slowly, I put the phone down.

My father tries to hold my gaze but I look away. "Who was that?" he asks quietly.

"MCI. It's a conversion call," I mutter.

"I hate when they call during dinner," Abby says too quickly. "It's so rude."

My father calmly sips his coffee. Shelly has no discernible expression on her face. I want to scream. Doesn't anyone see what is going on here?

Minutes later, my mother walks back into the kitchen, perky and happy. It must have been Daniel on the phone. I haven't been around the office, so I don't have any scoop. She and Shelly were talking earlier, but my mother immediately stopped talking when I walked in. I don't know if she's told Shelly anything, but I can't imagine that she would. Shelly's better, but I know she's not ready to handle that kind of information.

"So let's discuss our New Year's resolutions," my mother says.

"I'm going to fix up my new apartment." Shelly glances at me. "Our new apartment." Still smarting about the coffee cake, I ignore her.

"What about graduate school?" my mother asks. "I thought you were applying to graduate school."

"I am eventually. I think I'm going to spend a year doing research. Maybe even work at St. Mary's as a volunteer."

"But you're just getting out!" my mother exclaims. "Why do you want to go back?"

"I like St. Mary's. The girls are my friends. They're nice people."

"I'm sure they are, but you should be with people who make you *think*."

Shelly shrugs. "Nice people are smart, too, Mom. Anyway, Case Western and Stanford have good post-baccalaureate programs. I could take my sciences, then move into the Ph.D. program."

"I thought you weren't getting a Ph.D.," I interrupt.

"I said I *might* not. I just don't want to make any major plans right now."

My mother smiles at her. "Why don't you girls go into business together?"

"And do what?" I exclaim. "Open a donut shop?"

"I just think Shelly should keep herself occupied. If she could get into school by fall, it would be perfect. And Stanford would be wonderful. I've always wanted to live in a big beach house in California. To me, that would be the perfect life." She smirks. "Okay, so now that that's decided, maybe Shelly can help her big sister figure out what to do with her life." She pats my arm and turns to my dad. "Don't you think Shelly should go back to school?"

"We should let Shelly breathe," my father says quietly. "She just left the hospital."

"I thought Shelly was Wonder Woman." The words fly out of my mouth and I cringe at myself. I try to catch my sister's eye to apologize, but she won't look at me.

She lays down her fork. "Well," she says, sighing, "if Shelly—I mean if I"—she laughs self-consciously—"do commit myself, I want it to be the right thing. This time, I won't just jump into something."

"Well put." My mother turns to me. "And my dear Francine, what are your New Year's resolutions?"

"Since none of my suits fit me anymore, it wouldn't kill me to lose a few pounds."

"You and me both," my mother agrees. "Why don't we go on Weight Watchers together?" She looks at Shelly. "You can teach us how to eat healthy. They must have given you menus we could follow, no?"

"I'll go, too," Abby chimes in. "We'll have a contest."

I point my fork at Abby. "Girl, if I were you, I'd go on *Jenny Jones*: 'I Saved My Boyfriend From a Circus Freak Show.'"

"Yeah?" She laughs. "You could go on: 'I Dated a Vampire and Lived to Tell About It.'"

"Have you ever noticed how many fat people are on *Jenny Jones*?" my mother muses. "It's a very fat-friendly show." She looks at me. "What's she talking about, Frannie? What's this vampire thing?"

"Nothing, Marsha," Abby cuts in. "Frannie had a date with a guy that just about took everything out of her. Although, I don't think a pint of blood is too much to ask for a free meal. Do you, Frannie?" she asks sweetly.

"Shut up," I mutter. "Midget lover. Rat Boy's girlfriend."

"*You* shut up," Abby taunts me. "And don't dish it out if you can't take it."

"Girls, please." My mother looks at Shelly. "Do you know what they're talking about?" Shelly nods, but keeps her head bent.

"I don't have to tell you *everything*, Mom," I interrupt. "It's not like you don't have secrets."

"That's for sure," my father mumbles. He looks down at his

food as if expecting it to jump up at him. As he tugs on his tie, it dawns on me: it's true about Daniel. And he knows about it. He knows everything. I suddenly can't stop staring at him.

"*Please* don't mumble," my mother says to him, annoyed. He clears his throat and there's a long moment of awkward silence.

"No more food," my grandfather says sleepily. "I am too filled up."

"One more piece, Dad. Just a few more bites." My mother hovers over his plate.

"Dad," my father says, "wouldn't you like to go into the den and watch television?"

My mother snaps at my dad. "Leave my father alone," she says. "He's eating his dinner."

"Dad"—my father ignores her—"you'll be more comfortable if you relax in the den."

My mother raises a fork. "I *said* to leave him alone. He's fine."

"You're the expert," my father mutters.

I glance at Shelly, who makes believe she's not listening. She stabs a tomato half and leaves the fork standing up. She wrenches the fork out and stabs it again. Tomato juice squirts all over. I lean over her plate, grab the fork, and stuff the tomato into my mouth. "I'm sorry," I mutter. She shrugs and shreds her napkin with her knife.

When my mother speaks, her voice is strained. "Turkey, Abby?" she asks, trying to hand Abby the platter.

"Thanks, but I'm totally stuffed. Everything was so good."

"Shelly?" My sister shakes her head. "Come on, honey," my mother insists. "It's only turkey."

"Mom, I said no."

"But there's nothing on it. One more piece?"

"NO!" Shelly barks. "NO."

"Mom," I say, noting the pained expression on Shelly's face, "stop trying to feed her."

"Frannie, mind your own business."

"Marsha, leave Frannie alone—and Shelly for that matter," my father cuts in.

My mother looks at him. "I don't remember bringing you into this discussion."

"I'm just tired of you bullying the girls. She's my daughter, too."

My mother's face reddens. "You're suddenly realizing this?" she snaps. "Where have you been all this time? She's twenty-four years old."

"What is that supposed to mean?"

My mother's on a roll. "You sit there and mumble like I'm a stupid idiot who can't take care of her own family, like I'm a complete moron who does everything wrong. But let me ask you this: how many times did you visit the hospital? And how many times did you call her? Can you even count?" She turns to my sister. "Can *you*, Shelly? Can you count the number of times your father came to visit?" Shelly pales as my mother stops, waiting for an answer.

"I ... uh ... don't know," Shelly chokes out. She looks at me, as if begging me to jump in, but I'm mesmerized by my parents.

"Well *I* can," my mother snarls. "THREE!! THREE goddamn times. Don't you dare tell me what I'm doing wrong because you weren't even there!"

My father's eyes narrow. "I was there, Marsha. But who took care of YOUR father while you gallivanted around, doing GOD knows what? I hardly think you can judge me!!" Breathing heavily, they both glare at each other.

Suddenly, Shelly gets up. "I have to call the hospital." She moves across the kitchen to the phone. "I have to check in and let them know how everything is going."

"Tell Lucy I say hello," my mother calls out, but Shelly has already turned away.

Abby looks at her watch and gets up. "I really have to go," she says.

"Don't you want coffee?" my mother asks.

Abby shakes her head. "I've got so much to do tonight, but thanks for dinner. It was really good."

"And you can't beat the free entertainment," I sneer as I walk Abby to the front door. We say good night and make plans to go to the gym in the morning. On my way back to the table, I notice that Shelly is still on the phone with St. Mary's. She has the cord wrapped around her fingers so tightly, her knuckles are white.

She isn't speaking, although she nods occasionally in agreement with whoever is on the other end. She abruptly hangs up and stomps through the kitchen like a caged animal, opening and closing the refrigerator door. I reach out to touch her, to soothe her, but she smacks my hand away.

She glances up at me, but I get the feeling she doesn't see me. I am struck by the savage look on her face. Her eyes, gleaming in the yellow lights, dart wildly around the room, and her muscles pulsate beneath her clenched jaw. For a split second, she's the Shelly I hate, the moody Shelly who glares at me like she wants to fucking kill me. I weaken when faced with this Shelly; I weaken because I know she's going to turn everything I say inside-out. As she paces through the kitchen, I back up to get out of her way. All of a sudden, her very existence annoys the shit out of me. SIT DOWN, I want to scream at her. Just SIT DOWN with everyone else and behave like a normal human being.

When she finally returns to the table, she tells me that she refuses to stay here. "I'll move in with Abby until you're ready to leave. I can't believe Mommy said all that shit in front of everyone. Like HELLO, I'm here for Christ's sake. She is so fucking out of control. I can't believe it. There's no way I'm staying here."

"She didn't mean it," I say. "And it will only be for a few weeks. Listen, Shelly, I feel like an asshole for what I said before."

"Sometimes you are, Frannie."

"Well I'm saying I'm sorry, okay? Forgive me?"

My mother places a slice of coffee cake in front of her. "Sorry, honey." She pushes the plate in front of me. "I wasn't thinking."

"Would you like some more dessert, Daddy?" I ask my father, but he's staring into space. "Dad?" He looks at me like he has no idea who I am. "Coffee?"

"Uh, no thanks," he says dreamily. "I've had more than enough." He gets up without looking at anyone. I suddenly feel really badly for him, but I don't know what to do, so I just sit there.

My grandfather hobbles toward the bathroom. "You people are all meshugeh," he says. "All this bickering can drive a person to the nuthouse."

"Grandpa," Shelly says. "This place *is* a nuthouse. Here, let me help you."

My mother puts her hands on my shoulders. "Do you think I was out of line?" she asks. I shake my head. "It's just that your father drives me crazy sometimes. I should have said something a long time ago. You understand, don't you, honey? I am not the crazy one here." She walks out of the kitchen, shaking her head. "I am NOT the crazy one."

Left alone, my stomach is in knots. I look at the clock, my eyes misty. Ten forty-seven. There's a split-second interval between the act of looking at the clock and the act of pulling out the ice cream that I can't recall. But the next thing I know, I'm shoveling it into my mouth. The ice cream is soft and luscious and I'm filled with a gentle lift, a sweet release, and the creamy coldness slides down my throat and absorbs all my tears. I am soothed for a second so I eat another spoonful and then another, then jam my fingers into the leftover coffee cake, digging through the layers of crumby topping and flaky dough to get at the cherry filling. I stick my finger, blood-red with filling, into my mouth and suck on it. Then I cram a chunk of the cake into my mouth, but this time, I don't taste it. Nor do I taste the baked potato or the turkey or the string beans or the milk I use to wash everything down. When I look at the clock it is ten fifty-two. Everything forgotten, I ruminate about how much I ate. Although totally stuffed, I'm not the least bit surprised that my heart flutters in my chest as if I'm as hollow as a tube.

I wake up in the middle of the night in a cold sweat. My tongue is thick in my mouth and my head feels weighted with a food hang-over. I lie in bed and hug my bloated, distended rickets belly. I'm so full and so nauseous, I go into the bathroom and gulp water from the faucet. I kneel on the floor, lean over the toilet, and stick my finger down my throat, but I'm tired of fighting, and can't resurrect the energy to make the food come up.

I crack open Shelly's door and tiptoe into her room. "I'm sorry, Shelly, for what I said before. About you being Wonder Woman." I wait for her to say something, but she doesn't. There is a medicinal smell permeating the air, and it's difficult to breathe. I don't know where the smell is coming from until I see an open bottle of rub-bing alcohol on Shelly's nightstand. I want to put the cap back on the bottle to make the smell go away, but I can't find it.

I walk over to the bed. Shelly's wearing a white T-shirt and the moonlight shining through her window casts shadows of the blinds across the bed, illuminating her body. One hand is flung over her chest, as though covering her heart.

I lean in to tell her I'm sorry again when I notice a wadded paper bag. I tingle with anxiety as I uncrumple the bag that held my mother's tranquilizers. My eye catches an empty vial on the floor and heat spreads through me, lifts me, makes my head pound and my eyesight fuzzy, and I'm perspiring as I shake my sister's hand and listen for the sound of her breathing. But the only breathing I hear is my own panting and I start to yell for my mother, "MOM, IT'S SHELLY, COME, MOMMY, PLEASE?" and she rushes in and I point at the bed, my hand covering my mouth in horror. I can't breathe and I can't swallow and I watch, suspended in time, time that moves so quickly but feels like slow motion. My mother sticks her fingers into my sister's mouth and against her neck, then bends over and presses her mouth against Shelly's and exhales so loudly, I can hear her trying to force her own breath into my sister's. But nothing happens, so she shakes her head, and covers her mouth with her hand, just like me, and yells, through her fingers, for my father.

Suddenly all the lights are on and my father, who is so weak when it comes to opening jars, actually lifts my sister from her bed and rushes her down the stairs. We should call 911, I say or I think I say, but my father says, "NO, girls, there's no time, we have to go NOW." David, my mother keeps calling his name, over and over, David, David, David, what is happening? Is she breathing? David? Why isn't she breathing? My mother is actually talking to him, addressing my father in a frantic, plaintive voice I've never heard before. David, David. Help her, David. And suddenly he's the strongest man I've ever seen.

My mother follows close behind, but for one split second, and it is this split second that I will always remember, she turns to me and without any warning, my mother, my mother, who is so self-controlled with her perfect nails and perfect hair, opens her mouth and lets out a howl so full of anguish that I feel it travel through me. I force her down the stairs, saying softly, "Come on, Mom. We can do this. One step at a time. Hold on." Shelly is slack in my father's arms. This, I will learn, is one of the very last images I have of my sister alive. Her head is thrown back and her parted lips form a gaping hole, but Shelly, unlike my mother, has no sound at all coming out of her mouth.

PART TWO

THE
DANCING
STAR

13

When my grandmother died, it was very sudden. She had a heart attack at the kitchen table. The story became very undignified as it was passed around the family, and we all had a nervous laugh when we told it. Apparently the attack hit just as she swallowed, so the paramedics had to fish a piece of bran muffin out of her mouth, which for some reason, my grandfather saved. He rode in the ambulance with the muffin chunk wrapped in a paper towel that was soggy with her saliva, and refused to give it to anyone except my mother, whose flight from New York to Florida was delayed, and who didn't arrive until hours later. The funeral was sad, certainly, but it was altogether different from Shelly's. There was nothing funny about Shelly's funeral. My sister was twenty-four, ninety-eight pounds, and buried by her parents.

"Frannie, honey, wake up," my father calls from the bottom of the stairs. "I'm going shopping. Do you want anything?"

I curl up carefully on my side. When I made my bed, I pinned the sheets so I won't kick off the covers when I thrash in my sleep. If I move too quickly, the pins snap open and stick me, so I sleep with my arms close to my body. My sheets are faded and soft and when I

189

lie here, I feel like I'm carpeted in flower petals. I'm trapped in my bed, but I like it this way.

"Frannie, answer me. I'm leaving."

Two months ago, my mother put my grandfather in a nursing home and moved into her own apartment. Ever since then, I've had a fantasy. My father and I are on the golf course. I bend my knees, pull back, and drive the ball into the fairway. We both shield our eyes as we watch the ball sail through the air. But the best part is when I get home. My father had a queen-sized bed delivered that is so big, it takes up half my room. I lie in it spread-eagle, and realize that someone is in it with me. "Frannie?" Shelly whispers. "It's me. I'm here."

"Answer me, please. I've got a million things to do today."

I don't know why I fantasize about golf. I've never played in my life, but I wish my father would teach me. I brought up an ancient set of clubs from the basement. He didn't say anything, so now they're propped against the refrigerator, and I'm sure they'll just stay there until the cleaning lady moves them. If she didn't come once a week, my father and I would just sit in our own shit until the Board of Health came to cart us away.

I pick up my phone and dial the line downstairs. From my bedroom, I can hear my dad rush through the kitchen. I hear a loud bang. "Hello?" He breathes heavily into the phone.

"What fell?" I ask, knowing.

"I banged into the damn clubs. Why are they here?"

"I want to learn how to play," I mutter.

"It's really not a good idea to leave them in the middle of the kitchen, honey. Someone could break their necks. Hey, Frannie." He brightens as if the thought just occurred. "It's a beautiful day out. Why don't you come take a ride with me?"

"And sit in the car like some kind of dog? I don't think so."

"Come on. It'll be fun." His voice is loud and overbearing as though I'm a potential client. If he didn't sound so gleeful, I might consider spending some time with him if only to be with another living person, but I can't stomach his false happiness. I cannot be with him when he's yapping about how great business is, how tan he got, and how good it feels to be alive. I don't care how good he feels. The only thing I care about is Shelly.

"Come on. I'll buy you lunch. A turkey sandwich for my favorite roommate?"

I flinch. "Shelly loved turkey sandwiches, Daddy, not me."

He's quiet a second. "Well, then, I'll buy you whatever you want."

"No, thanks. I'm not hungry. Daddy, do you realize that it's almost been a year since Shelly checked herself into St. Mary's?" I know what I'm doing, how awful I sound, but I can't help myself.

"Frannie, I don't have time to stand around." He's getting edgy which makes me know that it's working. "Just get out of bed and take a ride with me. It's glorious out."

"You've already given the weather report. I'm staying here. I have things I need to do."

"But you'll be home for dinner?" he asks anxiously. "You have to eat, Frannie."

"I know, Daddy," I say as if he's the biggest fucking idiot. "*I* eat." Neither of us says anything for a few long seconds.

Finally he tells me he has to go. "Frannie," he says. "Have a *great* day. Ciao, honey."

Daddy, I tell him silently, wishing he hadn't said "Ciao" like a geriatric Italian playboy, go fuck yourself. Lying back, I can hear the sound of the garage door opening, his car roaring out of the drive-way, and his two honks of goodbye. I nestle my nose into the pillow and sigh heavily. I love my bed. Thank God I have somewhere to be all day.

It's been five months since Shelly died. I try to deal with her death as something final, but I can't. Every time I think about her, gaunt and hunched over, inspecting a string bean, tears cloud in my eyes like filmy contact lenses. The only way I can comfort myself is to imagine that she's on a tropical island, baking in the sun, planning to come home as soon as she runs out of money.

Her last few days were excruciating. We rushed her to the emergency room at Northside, the hospital closest to Lindsey Point. They pumped her stomach, but her weight was so low, she lapsed into a coma and they had to move her into intensive care. We gathered outside the glass. Chubby came to visit and stood with my mother for hours at a time, looking at my sister hooked up to tubes and machines. "She's young," Chubby said, taking my mother's arm. "She'll fight." I couldn't look at her, so I focused on everything else in the room: the feeding tube, the blinking lights, the monitors above her bed. I don't remember what I thought during that time, but I do know that it never occurred to me that she was going to die. If I had thought that even once, I wouldn't have been able to look at her. The entire scene was very intimidating, and it gave me respect for Bryan Thompson. I guess when you're forced to deal with this type of thing all day long, you have to be an asshole in real life. For most of the week, I wished he was around. I even tried to call him from a pay phone in the lobby. I didn't know what I was going to say, but I needed to hear some random guy's voice, pretending he cared. But the second I heard his voice, I started to cry and hung up. He knew it was me, I'm sure, but for once, I didn't care.

My mother slept in the hospital in a chair next to Shelly's bed. My father came every day with my grandfather, who spent most of his time in the cafeteria. I sat with Grandpa Max and held his hands while he ate bowls of tapioca pudding. "She's such a beautiful girl," he kept repeating. "Why does this happen to such beautiful girls?"

"She'll get better, Grandpa," I said. "She's just resting to give her body strength. Shelly's a fighter, Grandpa. She's just too thin."

"Ach," he said, swallowing his pudding. "Fat, skinny, fat, skinny, girls girls girls. What does it matter?" Spittle formed on his lips. "Your grandma … Grandma wasn't all skin and bones. She had meat on her. But she was beautiful, kiddo." He started choking. I patted his back until he caught his breath. "But no one asked how much she weighed. No one. 'Adoring wife, loving mother.' Not her weight, not 'too fat.'" At first, I didn't know what he was talking about. And then I realized he was referring to the engraving on her headstone.

"Marsha," my father said to my mother at one point, "come sit down, you look exhausted." Like a dutiful child, she sat in a chair next to him and he put his arm around her. Then she buried her face in the crook of his arm. Without saying anything, I sat in the chair next to her and she put her arm around me. I cried until I was gasping, thinking that this was the closest we'd ever come to being a real-life family.

Lonny and Mavis stayed close to my parents all week. It was weird at first since they'd never been a foursome before, but Aunt Lillian, Uncle Monte, and my cousin Beth carried on like they were at some primitive satanic spirit-raising, so it was a blessing that my parents had the Friedmans around. Mavis kept saying that our two families should take a vacation together next summer. "It will be fun. Maybe we'll go to the Bahamas, just to get away." Chubby came every day, too, and for a few fleeting hours, I thought she was a really great person. I loved everyone during those three days, and I kept telling people over and over until I guess I got annoying and my father asked me to please stop.

It scared me how everything was suddenly reduced. Shelly was in a little room in a little bed, being kept alive by machines. At the foot of the bed, there was a chart that gave her vital signs. It didn't say how sincere she looked when she smiled, how much she loved turkey sandwiches with onions, that she could have gone to Harvard. She, too, was reduced to a temperature, a heart rate, and a pulse that got fainter by the day.

My mother looked bad—her hair was never combed, her gray roots grew out, and her face was stripped of makeup. I tried to make her change out of her warm-up suit, but she wouldn't. She spent time reading aloud to Shelly, talking to Johnny Bennet at her office, and making lists. And taking a lot of medication. I tried to be around her as much as I could, but it seemed impossible for her to focus on anything, even me. Or maybe especially me.

"She looks so cold," my mother said to me when we were alone in Shelly's room. "Do you think she's cold? I'll get another blanket for her."

Left alone with my sister, I placed a hand on her ashen face, careful not to touch the tube in her mouth. I waited for her to open her eyes and apologize for sleeping so long. I have been a bad sister, I thought. I should have come to St. Mary's more, I should have talked to you more. And you were right: I don't know you. You never did tell me what happened with Therman. Or when you lost your virginity. It was with that fat guy with the curly hair, wasn't it?

The guy from Camp Galaxy you were so embarrassed about. "You shouldn't have been embarrassed even if he was a Rat Boy," I said out loud. "I'm your sister. Sisters don't care."

Shelly's doctors said that they wouldn't have worried about her pulling through, but she'd destroyed her resistance. "She would have been fine," one told us quietly. "We got the pills out of her system in time, but she's only ninety-eight pounds. She doesn't have much to fight with. When she gets out of here, she needs to go right back into St. Mary's and finish her treatment."

"Her insurance ran out. And I'll be damned if I send her back to that place," my mother said sharply.

The doctor flipped through Shelly's chart and shook his head. "She needs to go somewhere." His voice softened. "This is the *anorexia*, Mrs. Hunter. It's not the pills." When my mother and I were alone, she told me the doctor was afraid of the damage Shelly may have done to her heart, to her kidneys, as well as to her brain. "He treated another girl with anorexia last week," my mother explained. "She weighed sixty-two pounds. Sixty-two pounds!" I asked my mother what happened to her. "She had complete organ failure," my mother rasped, her voice thick. "She died in her sleep."

God, you fucked yourself over, Shelly, I thought, pulling the sheet up. But I couldn't shake a nagging feeling that all of this had something to do with me. "Shelly, listen, about dinner, you know, the Wonder Woman crack I made. Well I didn't mean it. I never mean half the shit I say. I'm just jealous, okay? You know that, don't you? I've always been jealous. I mean you're smarter than me, you're so much prettier, you can be anything. I'm just a loser. Once you get out of here, we're going to start over. We're going to spend all of our time together and really get to know each other. But if you could just forgive me, I think I'd feel better. Just give me a sign. Here." I grabbed her hand. "Press my hand." She didn't move. "Shelly, I can't stand to feel these things without you saying it's okay. Shelly, God, I'm going crazy. I ... I ... you know." I started to choke. "I love you." There was no sound but the hum of the machines. "Just say it, for Christ's sake, Shelly. Come on, just fucking forgive me already!"

"Frannie! Jesus!" My mother stood in the doorway. "She can hear you."

"I was just talking to her. The doctors said we should talk to her."

"Shelly, honey," she said, laying a blanket over her. "Frannie didn't mean to yell at you." She turned to me. "Could you give us a moment here alone, please?"

"Oh, so now you're the perfect mother, right?" Horrified, my hand flew to my mouth. But my mother wasn't paying any attention to me.

"I feel like this is somehow my fault, Mom," I said.

"How could this possibly be your fault?"

"I don't know. It's just how I feel. I feel like I should have done something different, you know I feel—"

But my mother cut me off. "It's no one's fault, Frannie. Sometimes life just deals a bad hand." She ushered me out of the room. "Please, Frannie, please stop talking like this. This really isn't a time to be philosophical."

On the morning of the third day, it seemed like Shelly was going to rally and they took her off the ventilator. Hanging over the bedrail, my mother yelled, "She said 'Mom'!" but when we rushed over, we realized she was gasping for air. She got worse by the afternoon, and could hardly breathe at all, even with the machines. And then the doctors asked my parents to consider turning everything off. "I won't kid you, Marsha." Chubby put a hand on my mother's shoulder. "There's been significant brain damage. They don't think she's going to come out of this." Chubby started to cry. "Marsha, the Shelly we know is dead."

My mother looked at my father who had his face pressed against the glass. A circle of film appeared where he was breathing. My mom opened her mouth to say something, but all that came out was a croak and the more she tried to speak, the worse off she got. She clutched her throat and waved her arms in the air. I thought she was choking, so I rushed over and lowered her into a chair, pushing her head down between her legs. When she finally calmed down, she tried to speak again, but all that came out was a few raspy sounds. For the next few hours, she and my father communicated by scratching words on the corners of magazines. *A week, David, just another week, they can't ask us to do this, isn't it against the law?— We'll sell the house.—Four days, then.—Don't be so goddamn proud, it's*

my sister. We'll take the money and move Shelly into a long-term facil-
ity.—I'm not giving up.—Then you be the one to say it. I can't do it. It
won't be me.

I brought her tea to soothe her throat and shared cigarettes with
my father in the parking lot. I'd never seen him smoke before. When
he took a deep drag, he coughed really hard and looked so much like
a teenager that I got a lump in my throat and couldn't swallow. He
wouldn't let himself cry, but I could tell he wanted to because his
eyes got wet, and he kept rubbing them, pushing his glasses away
from the bridge of his nose. "Damn cigarettes go right to my
sinuses," he said, crunching out the butt with his heel. It was difficult to look at him, but it was even worse to see my mother, hanging
over Shelly's bed, croaking "I love you so much." My mother never
did get her voice back in time to tell the doctors that there was no
way she'd turn off the machines, but it didn't matter. A few days after
we were told that Shelly had swallowed all my mother's tranquilizers
and washed them down with rubbing alcohol, my sister was gone.

The funeral was a disaster. It rained so hard, the streets flooded, and
when we drove to the cemetery, one of the limos got stuck in the
mud and it took fifteen minutes to pull the car out. The rabbi my
mother hired got sick at the last minute and sent his brother who
was extremely Orthodox and the service lasted ten times longer
than we had expected. Then, adding insult to injury, my mother
had a panic attack during the service and instead of crying, she
burst into such a hysterical, high-pitched cackle, it sounded like
she'd gone mad. Ironically, the one person who was sobbing uncon-
trollably was Lonny Friedman. It was a complete freak show. We are
such fuck-ups, we couldn't even do death right.

Everyone showed up, though; even my father's brother Edgar,
Edgar's schizophrenic wife, Jeanne, and all Jeanne's personalities.
My mother asked me to say a few words at the service. It was diffi-
cult to see through the tears in my eyes, and my throat burned, but
I forced myself to speak.

I walked up to the podium clutching the poem I was going to read.
I'd chosen a poem by Auden because when the actor read it in the movie
Four Weddings and a Funeral, I thought it sounded very beautiful.

I looked at the crowd then lifted the book. "I wanted to read this." I stopped. The silence in the room was deafening. I coughed, but no one moved. My throat tightened and I had a medicinal taste in my mouth. Panic stained my chest, and I couldn't catch my breath, convinced that someone in the room had poisoned me and it was taking effect. I need a doctor, I screamed silently. HELP ME! I coughed and blinked and the rushing stopped, and my heartbeat slowed, but I was left with a void in my head and I couldn't remember where I was.

"I want to read a poem," I started, "a poem that I saw in a stupid movie." I started to cry. "A stupid movie that doesn't have anything to do with today because it doesn't mean anything because it was just in a stupid movie. It's not about today, about Shelly, who … who … who … I, you know …" My mother rushed to the podium. She put her arms around me, but I shook my head. "No. Please. I don't think I knew my sister. Or that's what she said, and maybe I didn't." I heaved sobs, unable to breathe. "But I thought I did. All along I thought that. It's so difficult to know someone you love, but who can also make you so angry, even if you don't mean to be. And I wasn't angry all the time. I loved … love her. I love her. She's my sister." I stopped for good. "I'm so sorry," I kept saying. "I can't find my words."

And I ran out of the temple, into the rain, and cried until I was all dried up, ashamed of myself and embarrassed for being alive.

In the limo, I didn't speak to anyone. My mother sat between me and my cousin Beth, and her head lolled as we rode. Beth, who was more high on coke than my mother was on Valium, kept playing with the automatic windows. It got to be so annoying, I had to reach over my mother to slap Beth's hand to get her to stop.

"What is your deal, Frannie?" Beth whined, wiping her nose. "I've never been in a limo before."

My mother wasn't paying attention to either of us, and when she started talking, she was so zoned, I don't think she realized who was with her. "When Grandma died, I rushed to the airport, but all the flights were booked so I had to wait. Grandpa didn't tell me she had already died. It's weird, isn't it? She'd already died but I didn't know, so in my mind, she was still alive. I remember how frantic I was, how the strap on my suitcase broke, and I had to tie it in a knot to make the wheels go, rushing like a maniac, still thinking I had time. But she was already dead. So why does it matter to me that I wasn't there in time, when it didn't make a damn bit of difference?" She looked at Beth, who shrugged, hit the button, and the window went down.

By the time we got to the cemetery, my father was already there. He tried to help Beth, and had to lean his entire body in to wrench her out. When I opened my door, Johnny Bennet was waiting to give me a hand. "You're a terrific woman, Frannie," Johnny said as I turned to help my mother. "I wish I had a daughter like you." I started to cry, thinking at the time that he was such a sweet man. I hugged him and he helped lift my mother out of the car. Between her and Beth, we were a traveling Betty Ford relapse clinic.

My father didn't say much, but he held my mother through the entire service which got me all choked up. I was very moved by how nice everyone was. Until I saw Daniel Reynolds without his wife. "Why is he here?" I hissed at my mother.

It took her a few long seconds to lift her head. "Who?"

"Him." I pointed at Daniel, who wore a perfectly cut black suit and a rose-colored tie.

"To pay his respects, Frannie. Don't do this to me. Please, Frannie," she begged.

"I hate him, Mom. I hate him so much, I think I could kill him. I could take a gun and shoot his fucking head off." I felt wildly out of control. "I could. I could just kill him."

"Frannie!" I could tell she was about to get hysterical and I tried to back off. I walked over to Aunt Lillian and Uncle Monte who were huddled with my father. Beth was pulling flowers out of the ground.

Aunt Lillian put her arms around me. She didn't say anything, she just kept hugging me until I thought I would pass out. Over and over she said, "It's not fair, it's just not fair." Uncle Monte kept snorting and patting my head. "You come see us in Arizona, honey. Anytime," he told me. "Come in the spring. The cacti are beautiful, especially when the sun's setting and you capture them right in the shadows. It's religious, Frannie, I'm telling you." He sniffled and I couldn't tell if he was feeling sadness for his dead niece or reverence for the Arizona vegetation.

"Your mother needs you, Frannie," Aunt Lillian was saying. "No matter what she says, remember that. Try to be good to her, okay?" And she turned away, tears streaming.

Seeing her cry made me feel guilty about how obnoxious I was, so when I got back to the house, I rushed around, desperate to find my mother. I heard her sobbing in my father's office, and stood outside, wondering if I should knock. I was nervous, positive she was crying because of me, so I pushed the door lightly. I heard a man's voice. He was whispering so I couldn't make out who it was.

"I love you, Marsha. I want to help you through this."

Stunned, I glanced into the kitchen and saw Daniel leaning against the cabinets, talking to Abby. She was smiling, her boobs straining against the material of her dress.

"I told you before. I can't give you what you want," my mother whispered, her voice thick with tears. "I just lost a daughter, Johnny. Give me some room to breathe here."

Holy shit. Johnny Bennet. All this time, my mother's been having an affair with the fattest man in Lindsey Point. What kind of idiot am I? I looked up to see my father beckoning. I gave a half-wave, went into the bathroom, took off my clothes, and got into the shower, not knowing whether to laugh or cry. I turned the water on as hot as I could stand it. Curled on the shower floor, I let the water rain down, wishing I could hear my skin sizzle and that I could melt away like butter.

The first few weeks after the funeral, my mother wouldn't get out of bed. There is some truth, I think, to the idea that people are never the same after they've lost a child. My mother, always distracted to begin with, became detached, almost catatonic as she stared into space. She was quiet and her eyes had a glazed, hypnotic quality. I kept wishing she would break down and scream, but she barely moved.

Even though it scared the hell out of me, I couldn't stop watching her. For days, I didn't do anything but follow her around the house and analyze everything she said and did, trying to learn from her how I should act. I made her my focal point, thinking that if I was patient, she'd give me a sign and I'd know what to do, but the moment never came. Instead, she went to see Chubby and got a second wind. She started working sixty hours a week, leaving my father, my grandfather, and me alone in the dark living room where we stared at the flickering television. I wanted her to stay at home, that's what people do when they grieve. But she didn't. I kept waiting for her to explain what I was feeling, what I should do with myself now that Shelly was dead. But she wouldn't. She just got up in the morning, had toast with sugar-free jelly, and went to work every day as if our lives were totally normal.

I couldn't do much. I hung out with my grandfather, made all his meals, took him to the doctor, and watched television with him for hours. I wasn't ready to resurrect my job search, so I swallowed my pride and went back to Rascals. Paulie was very understanding when I confessed that Shelly didn't have a baby, she had died of a rare bone cancer. He got quiet. "Stop it, Frannie honey. I know the truth." He cleared his throat. "*You* could have told me, though. I didn't have to hear it from Artie." And he went out of his way to give me three moneymaking shifts a week.

Eventually, my dad abandoned our television vigil in the den and began traveling again. Since my mother was working late and I was back at Rascals, there was no one around to sit with my grandfather. I heard my parents fighting once, and stood outside their door to listen. I was amazed by their sudden willingness to confront each other. Consumed with rage, I stormed into the bedroom. "STOP IT, STOP IT, STOP IT NOW. MAYBE IF YOU'D TAKEN THE TIME TO TALK TO EACH OTHER ABOUT SHELLY, SHE WOULDN'T BE DEAD!" Jolted, they both stared at me. "OhmyGod," I muttered. "I can't believe I just said that." I tried to apologize, but they both turned away, from me as well as from each other.

Finally, I cornered my mother in the kitchen. "Grandpa can't sit around here by himself, Mom," I said. "He needs someone to talk to. I'm sure he just wants to die. Don't you have any feelings? He's so lonely." I started to cry.

"Frannie, Frannie, honey, I know you're hurting, believe me, I know …"

"I'm talking about GRANDPA!"

"Okay, calm down. I know Grandpa's hurting, but it makes me crazy to sit around. Don't you understand? I have to *do* something. Why don't you come to the office with me? You may feel better. I'll hire a nurse for Grandpa, a babysitter, someone to sit with him while we're at work."

"So I can see you hanging all over Johnny Bennet?" I held my breath, watching her mouth shrivel like a dried flower. "It's true, isn't it? I know, you know." She raised her hand and I flinched, but she just made a fist and walked upstairs. When I saw her the next evening, I mumbled an apology, but we didn't make up. I bet it was our fight that drove her away.

She sat me down a few days later. "I've been thinking about what you said, Frannie. Grandpa does need professional help." I started to cut her off, but she wouldn't let me. "Frannie, listen, we can't help him anymore." Her eyes filled. "This is too much for all of us." She took a deep breath. "Your father and I have decided to put Grandpa in the Jewish Home. It's very close." She looked away. "And I'm moving into my own apartment."

I panicked. "I didn't mean what I said about Johnny."

"Frannie, this has nothing to do with him or with you. I have to do this for myself."

"But what about me? You can't just leave me here."

"Frannie, you need help. We all do. I talked to Marilyn and she said she'd see you."

I screeched, "I'm not going to see Chubby. She's so … so … FAT! This is all her fault. If it wasn't for her, Shelly would be alive and we'd have our own place, and everything would be normal. You know it's true, Mom. You don't like her. You never did." I ached for her to agree, but instead, she started to cry. "You can come see me anytime you want, Frannie. I'm not moving far, I promise." She reached out for me, but I walked away, and vowed I would never speak to her again.

I roll over, pick up the phone to call Abby, then put it back. I start to get up, but overcome with a wave of exhaustion, I lie back, stare at the ceiling, and wait.

I calculated the other day that I am asleep more hours a day than I am awake. It's been this way since the morning my mother moved out. When I heard the garage door close, I went downstairs to the empty kitchen. There was a spoon in the sink with a blob of jelly still on it, and I just stared at the jelly sitting in a pool of water until my eyes blurred. A wave of anxiety hit me and I clutched the counter to hold myself up, afraid I was suffocating. When I finally caught my breath, the sun was still shining and the floor was still sticky but when I looked around, it was as if something suddenly shifted and the seams that held the world together were slowly unraveling. Rather than watch the wallpaper melt and all the pastel flowers run together, I went upstairs, got into my bed, and closed my eyes. Since no one was around to wake me up, I just stayed there.

The phone rings, but I let the answering machine get it. I'm sure it's my mother, calling to prod me again about seeing a shrink. "I'm not going to give up on you, Frannie. You can't get through this by yourself," she said the other day. When I didn't answer, she started interrogating me about my father.

"If you're so interested ..." I paused. "... call him yourself." Then I hung up without saying goodbye.

As I lie here, I kick myself for not telling her that my father's doing great, that he's happy she's gone, that he joined a bereavement group at some church and now he's thinking of dating.

"I talked about it in group," he said a few nights ago. I lay in my bed and stared at the wall. "We have to compartmentalize our grief and move on. Remain among the living. How does that make you feel, Frannie?"

I knew he was trying to—quote, unquote—reach out, but my rage and my silence are the only things that I have left.

I heard his pitiful, pleading tone, but I refused to acknowledge him. "I asked you a question, Frannie. How does that make you feel? We should think about clearing out the extra bedroom. To move forward. It's important to move forward."

I slowly turned over. "Which extra bedroom, Daddy? Which bedroom are you referring to?"

"Uh, your sister's. I've said this before."

The only reason I talk to him at all is because he lives here. Some days I don't talk just to see if people notice. Other days, it's because I can't stop the silence. The silence comforts me. If I don't speak, I can make believe I don't exist. The way Shelly believed. You destroy the voice, you destroy the desire, you destroy the need, you destroy the girl. The Me.

Right now I need relief. I can't breathe because my heart is tight inside my chest, I can't speak because my throat burns like it's on fire, and I can't see because my eyes always fill with tears. I feel empty, carved out, like a canoe floating downstream.

For the first time I understand what Shelly meant when she said she was a prisoner. If she were alive, I think she'd appreciate the irony: how ultimately free she became. Now I'm the one trapped. I'm haunted by her every second of every day that I'm awake. I don't know how it came to this. I never thought about her much before, and now I can't clear my head of her. Day after day, I relive her sitting silently in the backseat of my mother's car as we drove her to St. Mary's, dancing with Pia and Keisha and Cynthia in her hospital gown, chain-smoking cigarettes on the roof, lying in a coma with a tube in her mouth. The mornings are the worst because I wake up and my first thought is that I have nothing else to think about. My only relief is to sleep. When I'm sleeping, I'm not sad, I'm not angry, I'm not lonely, I'm nothing. When I'm sleeping, I can make all my memories of Shelly disappear.

I pick up the phone again and dial Abby's office. "Abby, please," I say to Corrine, Abby's new secretary. "It's Frannie."

There's a long beat of silent. *Oh, Frannie. How are you. I'm so sorry.* Everyone is so fucking sorry. "Frannie, can you hold? Abby will be right with you." She's very polite and I hate her for being so nice. Lately everyone speaks to me like it was me, not Shelly, who has brain damage. As I wait for Abby, I am aggravated that Corrine didn't tell me how sorry she is.

"Hey, Frannie. What's up?" I mumble something I know is incoherent. "Are you doing anything?" I don't answer. "Are you *going* to do anything?"

"No." I roll over and tuck the phone under my chin. "I don't have anything to do."

"So why don't you come into the city and meet me for lunch?"

I hang up the phone and just lie there. I do that lately—call someone then hang up. Part of me wants to talk and the other part of me just wants to hear a voice, the way all those anorexic girls at St. Mary's want people to eat without having to do it themselves. I call Abby back, but she went into a meeting, so I roll over and try to fall asleep.

It isn't easy, being alive. I hear people gossiping about me outside the 7-Eleven. They stop when I pass, but I know they're doing it. I called St. Mary's and asked for Shelly, but didn't realize my mistake until the woman on the other end paused before responding. I see girls who look like Shelly from behind, and I race to tap their shoulders, but when they turn around, none of them is. But the worst moment I've had so far was when I walked into Shelly's room a few months after she died. I got this eerie feeling like I wasn't alone, and I rushed out, unable to breathe.

It's my own fault. I wasn't prepared. But now I prepare every day. I plan my route to Rascals so I won't have to make a split-second decision when I'm driving. I won't drink water in restaurants because it might be poisoned. When I blow-dry my hair, I stand in the hallway so I won't accidentally drop it in the sink and electrocute myself. I have to protect myself. I have no choice. I may die in the end, but I won't die unprepared.

I don't know what it's going to take to get me out of bed for real. Seems like my parents are content with the arrangement. I assume Johnny Bennet will leave his wife and marry my mother, and my father will find a new woman, and everyone will live happily ever after. As for me, I'm trapped between my childhood sheets, a hostage of my own obsessing. My parents say they want to sell the house, but I'm not going anywhere. Every time they mention it, I march upstairs, rearrange my furniture, and dig in for the long haul.

A long time ago, I saw a made-for-TV movie called *Bad Ronald*. In the movie, a mother and a father build an infrastructure inside their house where they keep their mentally ill son. The parents die and another family moves in, and no one realizes that Bad Ronald lives there too until he appears one day and assaults their daughter. When I come up to my room, I feel like Bad Ronald, like I'm this insane teenager lurking in the shadows of a house that isn't mine. But once in my beloved bed, I can close my eyes and dream. In my dreams, a new family moves in and my new mother doesn't run away, my new sister lives forever, and my new father teaches me to drive a golf ball so that it soars over the green like a bird in flight. In my dreams, I belong to a whole new family. In my dreams, I can live my life all over again.

14

*F*ar off in the deep recesses of my dream, I hear the phone ringing, but I don't have the energy to roll over. Something white floats by, something of my grandmother's, and I reach for it. I hear Johnny Bennet's laugh. He has his feet propped up on my mother's desk and he's playing with a paperweight. On the microwave, there's a picture of Shelly. Johnny makes believe he doesn't see me, but I know he knows I'm here. Just as I'm about to move the picture, I realize that Shelly is standing behind me. "It just takes *discipline*, Frannie," she says in a witchy voice. She's a Halloween skeleton, and I reach out to touch her to see if she's real. "Get your hands off! Don't touch me." Just as I'm about to tell her that I want to make her feel better, I do, just give me another chance, I hear my mother's voice.

"Frannie! Get up!" She's shaking me. Her voice is high-pitched and tinny like she just heard bad news. "It's noon."

I refuse to roll over and she shakes me again, but she's not nervous anymore. "I've been calling all morning," she says angrily. "It's time to get *out* of bed. Enough is enough."

I cover my head with my arm, but she yanks back the blanket. I'm wearing my favorite nightgown. I've cut the bands around the arms so it will be more comfortable, and I've bleached out the stains. It fits me really well now, almost the way it did when I was in high school, especially since I've lost weight. It's not like I'm trying to lose weight. It just takes too much fucking energy to eat. Maybe this is how it happened with Shelly. Maybe living became too exhausting for her. Personally, I find suicide a comforting idea. Whenever I'm feeling overwhelmed, I remind myself that I can always kill myself and I start to feel better. These days, I don't have the energy to do it, but it helps me to remember that it's always an option.

"Frannie," my mother is saying. "You have to face this. If your father isn't going to involve himself, then I am. You're coming to live with me." She hovers over the bed.

"For Christ's sake, Mom. I'm just tired. Sometimes people get tired."

My mother opens the blinds. The intensity of the sunlight hurts my head. "Frannie, you have to get on with your life. I'm seeing Marilyn at four and you're coming."

"I'm meeting Abby at the gym. We have plans."

My mother sits on the edge of the bed. She tells me that she knows I'm lying, that Abby called her this morning, and she's very worried.

"I can't believe you're talking about me behind my back. Especially with Abby."

"Frannie, she cares about you. Now get up, get dressed, and we'll go see Marilyn. And I want to stop by Grandpa's place. He misses you, Frannie. He wants to see you."

Oh God no, I groan. I can't deal with my grandfather and his constant jabbering. Jabber jabber jabber. "Mom, I can't see Grandpa. I'll meet you at Chubby's. I want to remind her that she ruined this family."

"Fine. You can tell her anything you want. By the way, a woman named Vicky Tayborn called you. Who's she?" I shrug. "Well she left a message on the machine. Didn't Daddy tell you?" When I shake my head, she rolls her eyes. "Figures."

"What's that supposed to mean?" I snap. "Leave Daddy alone. And don't listen to his messages. You don't live here anymore. You're single and free now, remember?"

"Oh stop it, you're twenty-six years old."

"I'm almost twenty-seven," I remind her.

"Then act like it." She stops before walking out of my room. "Did it ever occur to you that I might be in pain, too?" As I look at her, I see Johnny Bennet propelling her out of her office in their matching maroon jackets, his hand resting on the small of her back. "Not really," I say, snotty. "Not lately."

"Well, just because you don't care about me doesn't mean that I don't care about you. Four o'clock. You better show up. Frannie! Look up. Promise me."

I look at her, then turn away. "I promise, Mom. Cross my heart."

I start to get dressed, but stop and get back under the covers. With the tip of my finger, I cross my heart again, but this time, hope to die.

I find a pair of jeans, smell them and wince, but put them on anyway. Downstairs, I listen to the answering machine. "Hello, this is Vicky Tayborn. I'm looking for Frannie Hunter. I'm with Cuisine America, and want to talk to Frannie about employment opportunities. Could you please have her call me at 212-555-2322?" I get a rush of excitement until I remember that Cuisine America owns several restaurants, one of which is Rascals. I hit the erase button and make Vicky Tayborn go away.

I get into Shelly's car. My parents put a new battery in it and now expect me to drive the car as if it's my own. It's creepy and weird and when they brought it back from the mechanic, I told them I couldn't. My father had looked at my mother, then quietly asked me why not. "Because I don't feel right," I told him. "It's Shelly's." I bent over the steering wheel and started to cry. I kept expecting one of them to reach over and stroke my hair, but neither of them did. After a while, they walked back into the house and no one brought up the car again.

Today, too tired to deal with a cab and a train and a subway, I'm forced to drive. The car starts perfectly. I strap my seatbelt tightly across my chest and hunch over the wheel. I drive slowly and stall a few times before I get going. By the time I'm on the highway, I'm panicked, imagining the 16-wheelers hooking onto my fender and dragging me to my death. I pull over twice to slow my heartbeat. I feel unprotected and foolish. I didn't prepare at all for the highway.

Deciding it might be nice to visit Abby, I pull into a parking garage by her office. Abby's firm takes up two floors of a Park Avenue skyscraper. The lobby has marble floors, cathedral ceilings, and a beautiful mural on the wall. As I wander through, trying to look as though I have somewhere to go, I get knocked in the arm with a briefcase.

The receptionist smiles at me sympathetically when I ask for Abby. Then she tries to act busy. I know she really wants to ask me things like how much Shelly weighed when she died, but she won't because it's inappropriate. I glare at her. Just ask me, you fucking bimbo. Just ask me.

Corrine walks into the reception area. "Abby's been in a deposition all day, Frannie," she says, extending her hand. "But I'll take you back to her office."

I haven't been to Abby's office since she started. The few times I walked through the gorgeous hallways where huge oil portraits and oak bookcases lined the walls, I felt like such a loser, I never came back. It didn't matter that Smitty, Forrest & Greenman's clients are the daily headliners in the *National Enquirer*. All that mattered was that Abby worked in a beautiful office, was on her way to being rich, and I was going nowhere.

Back then, she had a cubicle where she'd hung all her diplomas, a picture of her parents, and a small picture of me. Her father had taken it one summer when we were on his boat. When I saw it, it made me laugh to see myself, wind-tousled hair, my face sunburned. In the picture, I looked happy.

I wait in Abby's office, which now has four walls, a window, and a couch. Finally, she rushes in. "Frannie, I'm so sorry. I've been in a deposition all fucking day." She stops. "How could you wear those jeans? They look like they haven't been washed in two months."

"Sorry, I didn't realize I was going to take the stand today, Counselor."

Abby flips through a stack of papers on her desk. She's wearing a double-breasted navy suit that I haven't seen before, navy stockings, and high heels. Underneath the suit, she's got on a crisp white blouse with tiny blue polka dots. Her hair is clipped back and she's wearing granny glasses that I know are fake because she has perfect vision. She looks really good, all put-together and professional. I try to rub out a ketchup spot on my jeans. I realize I haven't washed these jeans in six months. The last time I wore them, I was eating a Big Mac from my lap. The thought of a Big Mac reminds me of Shelly. I start to well up.

"To what do I owe the honor?" She peers over her glasses and picks up the phone.

"I thought it was a good time to draw up my will. You know a good attorney?"

"Very funny."

Corrine sticks her head in. "Abby, they're calling for you."

"I have to go back into this meeting," Abby tells me. "Can you wait here for me?"

"No." I start to get up, but it takes a few seconds because I don't feel any bones in my arms or legs. "I have to go."

"Where?" she asks sharply. "Where are you going?"

"I have things to do today, believe it or not. You're not the only person with things. Or are you suddenly so great you can't imagine anyone else having a life?" A tear slips out, but I don't have enough energy to cry so I just wait for her to say something.

"Frannie, please. You're acting crazy. I can't deal with you when you're like this."

I lower myself to the couch. "Okay, I'll wait here. I won't bother anyone." I lie back. "I'm invisible."

She thrusts a magazine at me. "Here," she says. "Read this. I'll be back in a half-hour."

Tears burn in my eyes. "I'm sorry, Ab," I start to say, but I don't have a chance to finish. When I sit down, I realize that she handed me the *American Bar Journal,* which I stare at for a few minutes and then begin to pull apart, one page at a time.

I feel someone shaking me and I slowly rouse myself. There's drool on my hand. Magazine pages are all over the floor. A few cover my body. One is pasted to my cheek.

"Frannie, what are you doing here? Where's Abby?"

I look up. Standing over me is Baldwin Kendall, the Pilgrim with a last name for a first name who passed out on our blind date. Like Abby, he's all duded up in a navy suit and starched white shirt. And to think Abby took this job so she'd never have to wear a uniform again. I giggle, but make myself cough so I don't become hysterical.

I tell him that Abby's doing a deposition and I was reading. I sit up and cross my legs. "Why do you ask?"

Baldwin tugs on his tie. "I'll be right back," he says. I shrug, collect the loose pages around me, and try to fit them back into the magazine.

Someone else, a short guy I don't know, sticks his head into Abby's office and stares at me as though I'm inside a cage. "Oh sorry," he says. "I'm looking for Abby."

"She'll be right back. Had I known Abby was so popular, I would have brushed my hair."

"You must be Frannie." He extends his hand. "I'm Randy." He smiles broadly. "Abby told me all about you." I twirl a lock of hair around my finger and study him. Abby wasn't kidding. This guy is *short*. He almost looks like a regular person, but his small legs don't really fit his muscular torso. He's so top-heavy, you expect him to topple over. I can't stop staring at him. Maybe if his upper body was less filled out, he wouldn't look so dwarflike.

I try to fluff my hair, but my fingers get snared in the nest on my head. "Did Abby happen to mention that my sister died?" I ask Randy. Startled, he sucks in his breath. "It's okay," I tell him. "Don't look so horrified. Everyone knows." I sit down. "It's unfortunate we haven't met before this, but Abby was nervous that I'd steal you away. Since I am so pretty." I pause because I've caught a glimpse of myself in the mirror. I look pasty-pale and shrunken, my eyes are bloodshot, and my nose is running. My hair is matted against my head. "Well, I'm usually much prettier than this."

Randy doesn't know what to do and I love his discomfort. "I know what you look like," he says, "I've seen your picture." He points to where my picture should have been, where it must have been at one point, but isn't anymore. In its place is a headshot of him. We both stare at it. "Fortunately," I tell him, "I don't look anything like that. My head is much smaller." I cackle loudly, which makes him wince.

"I'm sorry about your sister," he says quietly. "It must be very difficult."

I nod. "I guess. I'm suddenly an only child. Only lonely, lonely me. But I've been keeping a journal, writing some stories, you know, expressing my grief."

"That's great," he says with enthusiasm I know is fake. "What kinds of stories are you writing?"

I glance at the picture of his big ugly head. I turn and stare him down. "Short ones." I wipe my nose with the back of my hand and hold it out to him. Since he doesn't take it, it just hangs in the air between us. He thinks I'm insane, I realize as he walks into the hallway. The thought just makes me laugh.

I walk down to the parking lot to retrieve Shelly's car. I watch the traffic whizzing up and down Park Avenue and decide to leave the Subaru in the lot. It's expensive, but I've dug myself into such a hole, I don't even care. In fact, I treat myself to a cab up to Chubby's office on 87th Street.

"I'm going to my sister's therapist," I tell the driver. "The one who had the bright idea of stashing her in a mental hospital. My sister is dead now." He just nods and sweats. His stink is all over the cab, and I breathe deeply. I lie back on the seat and let the smell seep into my pores. I give him a big-ass tip.

"You could thank me, you know," I sneer. "It's not like everyone in this country is rich." He narrows his eyes at me. "Go fuck yourself," I tell him, slamming the door. For a second, I think he's going to take out an Uzi and shoot me. I stand next to the cab. "Do it, fucker," I mutter. "Just do it." But he squeals off, and leaves me screaming, "You PUSSY. SUCK MY CUNT, you PUSSY."

I turn around. A woman is staring at me. "What?" I ask her. "You can suck my cunt, too, you prissy bitch."

I sit on the floor of Chubby's lobby to calm down. Whoa. I'm loose. It's invigorating and I laugh out loud. Suck my cunt. Suck it, baby. Suck it.

I cannot believe that after all that's happened, my mother still sees Chubby. I bet it was Chubby who told her to move out. Therapists always try to control your life. And everything was going so well, too. Right after the funeral, my parents spent time together. They went to the movies and out for dinner, and it seemed like their relationship was much better. But then my mother started going to Chubby, and they stopped talking to each other, and everything went back to the way it was.

I wasn't much help, either. Once, my father was sitting at the kitchen table with the Word Jumble, trying to unscramble YARBET. I studied the word. When a new word took shape, I casually suggested that it was pretty fucked up of Mommy to be working all the time, wasn't it, I mean, she's never around anymore, huh? He didn't say anything. He scratched his possibilities on a napkin. TEBARY. ETABRY. BYRETA. YAREBT. Daddy? I goaded him. Daddy? Don't you think? I guess, was all he said. I watched him work the Jumble. Suddenly, he filled in the new word. We both looked at it. BETRAY. Disgusted, he got up from the table.

The next day, I happened to mention to my mother that Daddy and I had talked about her. I tried to make it seem as if we were worried about her, that she was working so hard, and wasn't giving herself a break, but of course, she took it like we were plotting against her. "Why are you and Daddy talking about me?" she had asked sharply.

"We know you're having a hard time with … you know … with Shelly and your marriage … and everything." My words felt glued in with peanut butter.

"Jesus Christ!" she snapped. "I can't stand when your father decides what is best for me. He is NOT a GODDAMN doctor."

I tried to fix things, but it only got worse. "Well, he's concerned," I said quickly. "He said he wished he could spend more time with you. That's all he meant. He misses you, Mom." As she stormed out of the house, I got a panicky feeling. And I knew I fucked up because two weeks later, she packed her bags and moved out.

I sit in the corner of Chubby's lobby and stare at the people. I shouldn't have gotten involved. Maybe she moved out because she couldn't stand the sight of me anymore. It's not like she ever talked about me. How smart I am and how pretty, and how I could have gone to Harvard. She's probably ashamed of me because I'm this overgrown oaf like Bad Ronald, a retarded child who can't feed or dress herself. Maybe she's sick and tired of taking care of me. It's not like she has to take care of Shelly. Shelly was always so self-sufficient.

I get up from the floor. It's true, I realize. My own mother can't stand me. And now, she misses the only daughter she was proud of. I suddenly break into a sprint and leave the building quickly, rounding the corner as fast as I can. Without even thinking, I head straight for St. Mary's.

"Uh, hi, Frannie," Diana says as I walk into her office. Apparently, she's still working for Dr. Hoffman, which seems strange because I expected things to be different. You'd think that after losing a patient, the hospital would reshuffle the staff, if only to give the impression they regretted their mistake. "Is everything all right?" she asks.

I nod, touching my hair. I feel dirty. "I came to visit Cynthia. She's here, isn't she?"

She nods. "I'm sure she'd love a visitor. Are you alone?"

"Yeah." A few months ago, my mother threatened to sue St. Mary's. She called Abby and asked her to draft a letter, which was forwarded to Dr. Hoffman. Abby even went to her boss, who suggested that my mother hire a criminal attorney. There were conversations back and forth, but nothing came of it. I'm sure my mother knew she didn't have a case, but that didn't stop her from harassing the hospital. I think it was Chubby who talked her out of it because my mother stopped the process after only a few sessions.

"You don't need a pass, Frannie," Diana tells me. "Just go up and ask Lucy if Cynthia wants company. Don't be upset if she doesn't." She pauses. "She hasn't been the same since we lost Shelly. She misses her." She pauses again. "We all do."

Diana reaches out as I start to cry, but I leave her office quickly and get on the elevator. When I get to the third floor, my throat constricts. I get the same feeling I had when I walked into Shelly's bedroom. "Hi, Lucy," I say when she buzzes me in. "Is Cynthia here?"

"Frannie! Hi, honey!" She gets up to hug me. I stiffen, just because I feel so dirty and sweaty, and I'm sure that I smell. "Cynthia would love to see you." She pauses. "You look good. You okay?"

I shrug. "Fine and dandy, like sugar candy."

A handful of girls are sitting on couches, watching TV and reading. I look for Keisha and Pia, but they're both gone. I don't see anyone else I recognize, but I haven't been here in months. I'm sure the entire troop has changed. Except for Cynthia, I think, as she walks toward me. Her mother must have left her a bundle when she died.

Cynthia is wearing a faded pink warm-up suit and dirty yellow socks. She's filled out and her cheeks have softened, but her eyes are still cold and hard. She shuffles toward me. It's good to see her, and I tell her so.

Silently, she takes my hand and leads me to a couch in the day room. I glance at Lucy who nods. Tears slip from my eyes and I wipe them with my sleeve. As I settle in, I'm suddenly comfortable. It feels good to be here, like lying between clean sheets and listening to rain. I could spend the whole day here. Cynthia stares at the television. "Two weeks, Frannie." She sucks on her forefinger. "Or maybe three. Then I'm getting out." She stares at me. "You look kinda scrawny and your hair looks ugly."

I reach up self-consciously. "I didn't have time to wash it this morning."

She loses herself in some movie about World War II. "Have you ever been to France, Frannie?" I shake my head. "Have you?" I ask.

"No, frankly fry haven't been to France, Frannie." Despite my growing anxiety, I laugh. Cynthia puts her dirty socks in my lap. "So is your mother still fucking her boss?"

"What?" I ask sharply.

"I was just wondering if you ever went to France, Frannie."

"How do you know about my mother?"

"How do you know about my mother?"

"Please stop repeating me, Cynthia."

"Please stop repeating me, Cynthia."

I start to get up, but Cynthia pulls my hand. "Don't leave, Frannie. Will you live with me when I get out? I have an apartment, you know. I'll make us lots of baked potatoes."

I think about the time Shelly asked me to live with her. It seems like another life, someone else's. "How do you know about my mother?" I ask again when I think Cynthia has calmed down.

"Shelly told me."

"How did Shelly know?"

"Your monster told her—that's what Shelly called your mother." Cynthia laughs. "She used to call every day." She pauses. "Shelly told us about it in group. Everyone knows." She smiles, trying to act sweet but instead she looks sinister. "We read each other's journals to share our deepest thoughts and desires and hopes and goals. We don't keep secrets. We have a club. Nothing that is said in here can leave these walls."

"I don't believe you." I feel clammy. *We don't keep secrets.* The room shrinks. I search for something to count. I see flowers on the wall. I get to three. *We don't keep secrets.* Why was my mother confiding in Shelly? It's a mistake. Cynthia made it up.

"Your monster said that you were in your own little world. That's what she told her. And since Shelly was getting better, I guess, she told her all her secrets. I hate her."

"Who? My monster?"

"No." Her voice gets small. "I hate Shelly. She never did see my new place. And I don't care what anyone says. She didn't get any better." Cynthia leans over and whispers to me. "Shelly said this place will make you crazy if you're not careful. But I'm careful, Frannie. I'm very, very careful. Shelly said that if it gets too much, you can always check out. Shelly said that and she meant it. I don't have any friends anymore, Frannie." Abruptly, Cynthia stands. "I have to go now, Frannie France," she says, suddenly crying. "I can't take this anymore." And with a wave, she's gone.

I walk to the phone, my heart pounding. *We don't keep secrets.* This can't be true. I call my mother to scream at her, but remember she's with Chubby, so I try Abby. "Uh, Abby please. It's Harriet the Spy."

"Hold on, Frannie." I feel as though I've made a vital connection. I make a mental note to ask Cynthia when she first heard about Johnny. How could my mother have done this? I thought *I*

was the only one who knew. I *told* her not to tell Shelly. I've been
YARBETTED!

Suddenly I hear Abby. "What do you want?" Her voice is tight.
She sounds mad. I look up. Four, I count four flowers. Four and
then five. Five comes too slowly. "Frannie?"

"Abby, something major has happened."

"Look, I don't have time. And I don't appreciate your behavior
this afternoon."

"But this is important. I'm at St. Mary's and I was talking to
Cynthia, remember her? Well, she said my mother was calling Shelly
every day. Abby, do you know what this means? My mother was confiding in her and then she died! Do you get it? Shelly couldn't handle
knowing about my mother's affair! And my parents fought about it
at dinner that night. That very night! It's like all connected." I hear
Abby's breathing. I expect her to say, "God, Frannie. What did she
say?" but she doesn't. She just sits there. "Abby?"

"Frannie, I've tried to be a good friend, I really have, but I can't
do this anymore."

I get anxious. "What? You mean this afternoon? I'm sorry about
that." I try to sound sheepish and contrite, but I'm dying to get her
opinion about my mother.

"It's not just me that you've offended, although that should be
terrible enough. But also my business associates. I've worked hard at
this firm. People finally respect me, even a boyfriend whom you
offended."

"I was just joking. Besides, since when do you care about being
professional? You're fucking your so-called business associate." I let
out a fake laugh. She doesn't say anything so I continue. "Anyway,
this is important. This is about Shelly."

"Did you or didn't you say something mean to Randy?"

"I didn't say anything, Abby. He said I was crazy!"

"Randy would never say something like that. Were you rude to
him?"

"Why would I be rude to your boyfriend? So now you believe
him over me?"

"Were you rude to him, Frannie? Just answer the question."

"Fuck you, Abby. I am not your client. I am your friend. Your best friend." Or I was. Envisioning the picture of Randy's big head makes me want to ram the phone into the wall.

"Frannie, you've got to get help. I know you can't talk to your mother ..."

"What the fuck is wrong with my mother all of a sudden? My mother has been nothing but good to me. She lost a daughter, for Christ's sake! Her daughter is dead! Don't you get it?"

Abby's voice is firm. "Frannie, you aren't making any sense." Her voice softens. "I can't watch you fall apart like this. You need help. I love you, Frannie, please?"

"You fucking CUNT!! You stood me up twice last month to go out with Randy."

Her voice cracks and she starts to cry. "We've been friends our whole lives, Frannie. You're like my sister. Please go talk to someone."

"YOU ARE NOT MY SISTER!" I scream. "My sister is dead and all you care about is your fucking boyfriend. Well fuck you, Abby. I was there for you. Every time some guy fucked you over. Who sat with you when you studied for the LSAT? Who was your friend when everyone hated you? Fuck you, FUCK YOU! I hate you and I wish you were dead, too."

I slam down the phone and hug myself because I'm shaking. Lucy rushes over. "Is everything okay?" I curl into a ball and she strokes my hair. "Are you all right?" I nod and let her help me to my feet and walk me over to a chair. "Who was that on the phone?"

"Just a dumb girl." I hear my voice but it feels like it's outside my head. It doesn't matter. I'm not sure if I said that out loud. My eyes burn, but I don't give in. I will not cry over Abby. Will not will not will not. A few warm tears slip out and I lick them with my tongue. They taste salty. Margarita salty. Where has everything gone? I wasn't prepared. I should have taken the train. "I'm so tired, Lucy." I try to lift myself.

"Just relax a little, Frannie honey. It's okay."

"Just two minutes." I lie down across two chairs. I feel myself drifting. It occurs to me that I have to ask Cynthia something, but I can't remember what it is. It's something about Shelly and I know it's important, but it seems far away, like my voice, like the salt. Eventually I feel my whole body go limp like I haven't allowed myself in a long time, maybe months, maybe years, maybe ever, and across the empty chairs of a group therapy circle in my dead sister's mental ward, I give in to sleep all over again.

15

"You really let me down," my mother says the next day. "Marilyn and I waited for you until four-thirty."

I nestle the phone in my neck and take out a carton of milk from the refrigerator. "I went to visit Abby and then to St. Mary's."

"What the hell did you do there?" I tell her I watched television with Cynthia, saw Lucy and Diana. Remember them? "Vaguely," she says. Then she launches into her speech about how worried she is, how I need to see someone, how Marilyn blah blah blah. I put the phone down while she talks. "FRANNIE?" she screams. "WHERE ARE YOU?"

"I'm right here. Calm down. Once I get a job, everything will be all right."

"Did you call that Vicky Tayborn woman? She sounded like a good lead."

"I left a message," I lie, "but she never called me back. Hey, Mom, can I ask you something?" I pause for emphasis. "When Shelly was in the hospital, right before, you know, did you tell her what was going on between you and Johnny?"

I hear the pitch of her voice change slightly. "Of course not, why?"

I put away the milk and hang up without saying goodbye.

Then, with nowhere to go and no one to talk to, I get into Shelly's car and head for the Jewish Home where Grandpa Max is stashed away.

If it weren't for the smell, this place wouldn't be so bad. It's a combination of mothballs, urine, and sauerkraut. The building itself is nice; high ceilings, hardwood floors. I approach an old lady sitting at the front desk.

"Maxwell Swartzberg is in Room 617," she tells me in a mousy voice. "Sarah will show you around. Why don't you wait in reception?"

Sarah is very friendly. She's in her forties with frosted hair. Her chewed-off cuticles make me like her immediately. When she tells me she's wearing a wraparound skirt because nothing else fits, I'm in love.

"Look at this, Frannie," she says. She holds her ass. "This is kreplach and pastrami and Black Forest cake. I'm gonna take a picture of this"—she squeezes tighter—"and put it on my fridge with a sign that says *This is what you get, Fatty, when you feed yourself like a skinny person.* That's what I'll do. I'm gonna take a picture of my fat ass." I laugh out loud, startled by the sound of my voice.

She leads me through the gardens where there are weeping willows, rose bushes, and tulips. Benches line the walkway. I notice lights running along the ground. "What are those?" I ask, pointing down.

"The lights come on at sunset. They run all through the garden to give the impression of a stream. It's very beautiful."

"No doubt." I marvel at who would think of something like that. I could think of something like that if I tried. I glance around. And some music would be nice. Maybe they need a consultant here.

Sarah leads me through the gift shop, the synagogue, the physical therapy rooms, and then stops in front of the beauty parlor. She points at a sign over the door that says *Dames and Gents.* "Come in. There's someone you should meet."

Standing in front of the mirror, sucking an unlit cigar, is a rotund man with no neck. He munches on the cigar, muttering to Sarah about how busy he is and could she please leave him alone?

222 ❦ JILLIAN MEDOFF

"Freddie," she tells him. "There's no one in here but you."

He speaks in a heavy Russian accent. He winks at me. "There vill be, Big Shot. You vait. They svarm like locusts."

"Frannie, this is Freddie. Freddie, this is Frannie. She's Max's granddaughter."

He waddles toward me. Without warning he hugs me, crushing my body against his big belly. Instead of stiffening, I surprise myself by relaxing. I nestle my nose in his shoulder. He smells of cigars and aftershave. As he releases me, he asks, "Who's Max?" and holds his arms out so he can hug me again.

Sarah smiles. "Freddie and Grandpa Max are roommates. They spend all their time together."

"And now that *chazzer* owes me $15 from poker. *Chazzer.*" He makes a spitting sound. "Such a pig, that man."

"Freddie!" Sarah says sharply. "Stop it now. I mean it."

"Ach, mind your own business, Big Shot." He turns to the counter, takes a comb out of the canister, and pushes it through his two strands of oily hair. "I'm an old man, Sarah, living with a *chazzer*, a *chazzer* who plays cards and steals from me." He snaps his scissors and leans in. "You know, for a good-lookin' girl, you have vone hell of a mop. Maybe I should give you a trim?"

I touch my knotted hair. All my curls are limp. "Okay," I tell him. "Maybe later."

Freddie eyeballs me. "I've heard all about you. All day long, Max talks. Someone should shut him up. You're Max's favorite. Says he can't stand the others, but Frannie, Frannie is the vone he likes." Freddie sucks his cigar. "Ve've been vaiting for you, honey," he says softly.

"I'm here," I tell him and reach out to squeeze his hand.

"It's nice that you let him cut hair," I tell Sarah in the elevator. "It must get boring to just sit around, anticipating your next meal." I should know, I want to tell her. I do it every day myself.

"It is nice for him. He's there on Tuesday and Thursday afternoons, when the regular barber is off. People stop by to kibbitz with him, keep him company. He was so happy when Grandpa moved in. They immediately became buddies. There are more women than men here and most of the men are very confused. When you do get a man who's able to feed himself and hold a conversation, the women swarm around him like moths."

"Kind of like college."

She laughs. "Kind of like anyplace." She smooths her skirt. The elevator dings and we get off. "Freddie takes good care of Grandpa Max. They do everything together: they eat together, watch television, play cards."

I'm suddenly desperate to call Abby. This is the worst fight we've ever had. I bet she hates me, though. And I don't blame her. "How do they play cards?" I ask, trying to focus on something else. "My grandfather can't see."

"Freddie tells him which cards to play."

"No wonder he owes Freddie $15."

I glance down the hallway. People are everywhere. I hear a television and music from other parts of the hall, and as we stop in front of my grandfather's room, a phone rings next door and someone picks it up, laughing. "This is so different from what I expected."

"Getting old doesn't have to be a death sentence, Frannie. Most of these people come from wealthy families, but can't take care of themselves anymore."

"My grandfather is very lucky to be here." I wonder what will happen when my parents get to that point. Whenever I imagine them old, they look exactly the same except they're shorter. I suddenly see my mother wrapped in a bathrobe, shuffling to the dining room. Her face is wrinkled, her hands liver-spotted. "Frannie, I hate this place. Frannie, don't leave me here." Her voice is shrill and quivering. "Frannie? Where are you?" I swallow hard and look around. I see walkers, a wheelchair, bedpans. I have to go. I'm running out of time. The heat starts, lifting me, my heart palpitates. My parents have nothing. I've been so stupid. They're going to die. I reach for the wall. They're going to die and I'll be all alone. Oh God, Shelly. How could you leave me? You were supposed to be here. I can't do this myself.

"Frannie?" Sarah is touching my arm. "Are you okay?"

I take a deep breath as she calls to my grandfather. "Maxwell! You have a visitor." He's facing the television, which is blaring the theme for *Wheel of Fortune.* I can see the top of his head over the chair. She nudges me into the room, tells me to call if we need anything, and walks down the hall to the reception desk.

I suddenly feel timid. "Hi, Grandpa." I kiss his head. "Guess who's here?"

"Frannie? Is that my girl? Sit down." He starts to get up, but I tell him to stay where he is. I pull a chair over and sit Indian-style next to him. We both stare at the set while we talk. "Look at that idiot," he says. "Pick a vowel. A-E-I-O-U. Stupid jerk. I thought you forgot all about me. I don't like to watch the shows with anyone but you."

"How could I forget about you? You're my best friend." My eyes mist.

He chuckles. "You hungry? The food here is very superb. I like the breakfasts. I don't eat the lunches but I have to pay for them. I keep telling your Aunt Lillian to stop paying, but it's a package, she tells me. Today is Tuesday so they have the Sloppy Joes. You like the … the whatchamacall … the Joes?"

"Nah. I'm not really hungry right now. Maybe later. I can't stay that long today, but I can come by tomorrow if you'd like."

He shakes his head. "Busy busy busy. Just like your mommy. She's an executive. Does she drive the same car? That's a big car, boy. Why should she drive such a big car?"

"I ask myself the same thing all the time." I can't believe how good he sounds. He was so depressed before coming here. Either this place works, or he's on a very impressive drug. If so, I wonder if he can get me some.

"Your dad gave me a watch." He extends his arm to show me. I lean over and listen. He pats my head. "It doesn't tick, kiddo. What kind of car does he drive? A Ford?"

"A Mercedes."

"That's German. I wouldn't drive German for all the tea in China."

I notice that other than the hospital beds, the dresser and chairs, even the lamps look like they're from a regular living room. I don't recognize anything. Aunt Lillian sold all of my grandparents' furniture. Everything in the room must be Freddie's.

Charts hang from the foot of his bed. I try to envision the room without the curtain that separates my grandfather's side from Freddie's, and for a split second, I imagine I am back in the intensive care unit where Shelly died. I suddenly have that feeling of reduction; I feel taller and stronger and louder than everything around me. I spy a vase of flowers. I don't remember flowers in Shelly's room, but there must have been. I don't know why I can't remember. Of course there were flowers. Or maybe there were flowers in her room at St. Mary's. I remember her pointing to a bouquet. "Lonny sent me those," she said proudly. I wonder if she was in love with Lonny, if they flirted madly and once, late in the evening when all the other lawyers went home, he kissed her. Shelly never once told me she was in love. Did she die without ever being in love?

"You want the Joes?" As my grandfather hunches to get closer to the TV, his nose almost touches the screen. For some reason, this makes my heart ache. "They say they're delicious, but I don't eat lunch. I try to tell them I don't want the lunch, but they don't care. It's a package, they tell me. Then I feel badly because I badger people." He turns to me. "I don't mean to, you know."

"I know, Grandpa." My throat burns with tears. "I miss you being at home. From now on, I'll come here and watch the shows with you." I can't believe I haven't been here yet. I've been a selfish, selfish, selfish girl. "I'll come every day." I promise I won't let you down, Grandpa. I'm silently crying, and I want to say more, but can't. "Do you like it here?" I finally choke out.

"I've been better. I like my new watch. I can almost see the numbers. I wish I didn't have to pay for the lunches. But the watch was very nice. Your father's a nice man. It's a shame." He's quiet and I wonder if he's fallen asleep. I lean over but his eyes are open.

I walk over to Freddie's dresser and look at the pictures of his family. In one of them, there's a guy wearing a cap and gown. He has nice features: piercing blue eyes, wavy black hair, a strong jaw. But it's his smile that really gets me. His smile is cocky, but engaging, as if he knows something I don't, but if I leaned close, he'd tell me all his secrets. "Who is this?" I show the picture to my grandfather.

"Freddie's grandson. You should meet him. He's single and eligible and Jewish. Frannie," he says longingly, "why aren't you married, my favorite Frannie? It's such a pity. You're a very beautiful girl." He zones in on the TV again.

I start to say something sarcastic about marriage, but instead I change the subject. "Freddie seems very nice," I say.

"He's a Mister Know-It-All. But I'll tell you, Frannie. His people are rich as, as, as … rich people. He can eat lunch or not eat lunch, they don't care." I glance at Freddie's bed. There's a New Kids on the Block sleeping bag at the foot. "I got nothin' bad to say about Freddie 'cept he's a cheat in cards. He thinks I don't know what he's doin', but I do." He rearranges himself in his seat, which seems to take a lot of energy. I ask him if he wants to sit on a pillow, but he says no. "And the women kvetch all day long. Your Grandma wasn't anything like that."

"No," I say slowly, thinking of my grandmother and her glasses that were so dirty, you couldn't see her eyes. Afraid I'm going to bawl again, I tell my grandfather that I have to go, but I promise, cross my heart, I'll be back tomorrow.

"I hope so, Frannie. I miss you so much. Like I miss Grandma."

"Me too, Grandpa," I whisper.

I let Freddie trim my hair before I leave. I can't help myself. He covers me with a sheet and introduces me to the men and women who ooh and aah. I give him a $15 tip. Not so much because he tells me ten times that my grandfather, the *chazzer*, owes it, but because I'm feeling unusually generous. In the lobby, I stop by Sarah's office. "Hi," I say. "Thanks."

"For what, honey?" She looks up from her desk.

"I don't know," I stutter. "For taking care of my grandfather. I … uh … I'll be coming by a lot now, and I was hoping there were things I could do, you know, volunteer work, I don't know, answer phones, whatever."

She sits down. "We could always use help in the cafeteria. Unfortunately, though, I can't afford to pay you."

"I don't need the money." I linger in her office, wishing I didn't have to go home. Sarah looks up at me and we smile at each other. I feel a glimmer of hope; it's as if for one fleeting moment, I could learn how to live again.

*   *   *

As soon as I get home, in what feels like the most impulsive thing I've ever done, I call Chubby. When she calls me back, I tell her that I want to come in and see her. "I'm not committing myself to anything," I say. "I just have some questions I need answered."

Two days later, I sit in her waiting room, flipping through *Entertainment Weekly.* I look at the models in the ads, marveling at their long, firm legs and narrow hips. I hunch over. My legs feel swollen, like tree trunks covered in cellulite. I think about Abby. "I don't know if I believe in God," she told me once. "I mean, we all have cellulite, right? What kind of god would do *that* to people?" I wonder what she's doing right now, if she's thinking about me. As Chubby opens her office door and beckons me in, I feel like the loneliest person alive.

Chubby looks up as I sit in the seat directly across from her. "That's where Shelly used to sit," she says softly.

"Is that supposed to mean something?" I snap. "Because if it does, I'd appreciate it if you said what it is without any psychobabble bullshit where I have to guess what you're really saying."

"It doesn't mean anything," she tells me. "It's just the truth." She leans forward. "So how can I help you? You said you had questions?"

"Look, uh, Marilyn. In terms of people I respect, you're not at the top of my hit parade, if you know what I mean, but I do have questions about my sister." She sits patiently, which pisses me off. "Aren't you going to say anything?" I bark.

"I was waiting for you to ask me questions."

I glare at her. Then I blurt out, "Doesn't it bother you that I think you're responsible for what happened to Shelly? I mean, how can you just sit there and take it without defending yourself?"

She's quiet a long time. She scratches something on a pad of paper and shifts in her seat. "Frannie, in my profession, you do the best you can with the information you're given. But sometimes we make … I make mistakes in judgment. I don't blame you for being angry at me. I've been angry at myself." She holds my gaze. I'm the one who looks away first. "I've spent a lot of time trying to figure out what I should have done differently, why I didn't catch her in time, how she managed to slip away."

"She slipped away because no one was watching her."

"That's not true, Frannie. We *were* watching her. That's what makes it so difficult for me. I was watching every move she made. I didn't think …" Chubby looks down at her hands and I am struck by how badly she feels.

"Look," I tell her, shifting awkwardly. "I didn't come here to be mean to you."

"You don't have to protect me, Frannie. I do have a certain amount of responsibility, and right now, I'm in the process of finding ways to deal with it." She smiles. "Therapists are people, you know. We have the same guilt and anger that our patients do."

As I think about that, I wonder what it was like when Shelly was here, the things she talked about. "Did Shelly cry a lot when she was here?" I ask.

"Sometimes. Sometimes not."

"That wasn't a very specific answer."

"You didn't ask a specific question."

We sit in a silence that makes me edgy. Say something, I scream at her. Just talk already. Finally, I blurt, "She's in my head all the time. There are so many things that I want to know about her. Like if she was better, if she was getting out, why did she do it?"

"Sometimes patients are most vulnerable when they're preparing to leave the hospital, or the first few weeks after they're home. In the hospital, they work very hard to deal with their problems, and sometimes they have high expectations for returning to their normal routines. There's often a 'now what' feeling, which can be troubling for some patients who are just starting to recover."

"So she wasn't really better? I mean, it was all an act?"

"I believed Shelly believed she was better. But Frannie, St. Mary's isn't designed to 'cure' an eating disorder. It's a place where patients can live without starving or bingeing. It's a first step. I do believe that people can recover from anorexia and bulimia, but sometimes it takes a long time to live without engaging in self-destructive behavior."

"But what was she *thinking*? I mean, she had all these *plans*. Why did she pick that particular night? Why? I mean, even if she had the 'now what' feeling, she could have just stayed in the hospital. I don't understand why she had to ..." Frustrated, I trail off.

"Shelly left you with a lot of gaps, didn't she?" I nod. "Frannie, I'm afraid there isn't any one answer. Her anorexia, her depression, and ultimately her suicide were the product of a lot of factors. Depression is an elusive, insidious disease. It manifests itself differently from person to person. Anorexia is a symptom, but again, the reasons differ from person to person. For some, it has to do with control over the self, or denial of the self. For others, it's about rage and self-destruction. But regardless of the reasons, it's always a battle. And the battle is a very fierce one. As a psychiatrist, I grapple all the time with the *whys*."

"I bet if Shelly had gone to graduate school, she would have figured it out."

Chubby smiles. "I bet she would have," she says softly. "But if you're looking for answers about her, what you can do—what I try to do in my practice—is not look at her symptoms, but find out who *she* is. Shelly, the woman." She pauses. "And to do that, you have to go backwards."

I remember Bryan Thompson telling me the same thing. "But what do I do? Talk to my family? Yeah, right. Thanks for the advice." I start to get up.

"I don't mean just about her. Look at your own life, your own history, and the role Shelly played in it. Examine how your paths crossed and where they diverged. Then try to see your life from her vantage point."

"And how do I do that? Just sit and think about it?"

"You can always talk to me." She checks her watch. "Frannie, our time's not up yet. Why don't we talk about you for a while?"

"What about me?" I ask. I stare at her for a long time. "Well, Marilyn. I think our work is done for now. But thanks for meeting me." This was a waste of fucking time, I tell myself. She's just trying to hook me in, so that I'll come every week and give her all my money so she can decorate her fucking office, which, the more I look at it, doesn't look so *tasteful* after all. It just looks dreary. Before I go, though, I hand her the *Entertainment Weekly*. "I was going to swipe this," I tell her sheepishly. "But I felt guilty."

She takes the magazine. "You know, one thing I can tell you

about Shelly. She used to steal my magazines all the time." She laughs sadly. "But she never thought I knew."

When I get home, I look around for my father. I hear him on the phone in his office. I really want to talk to him about Shelly, so I stand in the hall outside his door and wait for him to hang up. While I'm waiting, I rummage through the closet. I spy my mother's coat, an ankle-length faux fur. I wrap myself in the long coat and breathe in her perfumy smell. I walk into the kitchen and from the wallet in my backpack, I take out the picture of my mother when she was first married to my father. I study it for a long time. She looks so happy in the picture, she looks young and free. I wonder if my father was laughing with her when he took the picture, if he also felt free.

He finally hangs up and I walk into his office. "Do you remember this picture?" I ask.

"Why are you wearing your mother's coat?" I shrug and thrust the picture at him. He looks at it and smiles. "Jesus, that was a long time ago. We were in Italy, when I was in the service. Where did you find it?"

"In a box. Let me ask you something. Do you think I look like Mommy?"

"When you're upset, you wrinkle your face like she does."

"Aunt Lillian told me I have Mommy's smile."

"I haven't seen your mother smile in a long time." He bends over his desk as if to dismiss me.

"When this was taken, did you ever think you'd have kids like me and Shelly?"

"I don't remember. It was a long time ago. Please, Frannie, I have a lot to do here."

"But I just wanted to ask—" My father cuts me off. "Frannie, I'm busy. I really can't talk to you right now, okay? Maybe later."

I leave him in his office and go upstairs to my room. I get hot in the coat, but don't take it off. I imagine my mother dropping her father off at the Jewish Home. "Bye, Daddy," I bet she said. I bet she also promised to visit all the time. And now he just sits by himself, watching *Wheel of Fortune*. But she's all alone, too. I pick up the phone and call her. "I went to see Chubby," I tell her. "And Grandpa. His place is really nice."

"I'm proud of you for seeing Marilyn. Was she helpful?"

"Not really, but seeing Grandpa was. I really missed him."

"And he missed you. He kept asking for you." She's polite with me, as if purposely watching herself to make sure she doesn't say anything wrong. Realizing this makes me sad and ashamed.

"Look," I tell her, "I know I've been a major bitch lately, but I just want you to know that I think you did the right thing for Grandpa. It must have been hard, huh? To put your father in a home?"

"Yes," she says. "It's very hard." I realize she's crying. "It makes you feel old. And hopeless. Like your whole life is passing you by and you're powerless to stop it." She changes the subject. "I'm thinking of taking a trip for a few weeks. To Arizona to see Aunt Lillian. Do you want to go?" I tell her no. Then I feel her hesitate. "Do you want to have dinner with me?" she asks slowly.

"Okay," I say, just as slowly. "Mom?" I pause. "You really did do the right thing. I know it was hard, but Grandpa seems so much better off. I'm going to spend a lot of time with him, too. You don't have to worry anymore."

"Thanks, Frannie. I appreciate that."

After we hang up, I lie back on my bed and stare at the ceiling. I roll over and wrap my mother's coat around me, making sure the arms hold me tight, and I breathe in her smell; a smell so pungent, so much like her, that it makes my eyes sting with tears.

W hy are you wearing Mommy's coat?" Shelly snaps. "You guys are sharing clothes now? Now you're a psychopharmacologist? Now you know everything?" I shake my head and say no, but she doesn't believe me. She rolls over and faces the wall. I walk over to her bed. "You think you're everything, Shelly," I scream at her. "You're the one who thinks she's so great!" And I'm suddenly falling, falling, and I wake up in a panic, my heart pounding.

My father sticks his head into my room. "Come here, Frannie," he says like a giddy little kid. "I have something to show you."

I look at the clock and see that it's one in the afternoon. I feel groggy and thickheaded, and it takes me a while to get out of bed. I lumber into his bathroom where he's looking at himself in the mirror. The fluorescent light hurts my eyes. "Daddy, what is it?"

He pushes a newspaper across the counter. It's a recent copy of the *Christian Times*, a newspaper for singles. There's a middle-aged man on the cover with blue eyes, sandy-blond hair, and a go-get-'em grin. Underneath is a short description of his habits and hobbies, and an address for how to reach him.

"He's very handsome, Daddy. You gonna call and ask him out?"

"Ha ha. Nope, even better." He picks at his hair. "I'm going to do it myself."

"You're going to put in a personal ad? Are you crazy?" I stare at our reflections. My father's all Dapper Dan, suited up for work. I, on the other hand, look like a fifty-year-old woman on a three-day bender, drawn and pasty, clutching my stained bathrobe. "If you're going to do this, Daddy—which personally I can't believe—then use a decent picture, something professional, one that shows your personality," meaning, of course, he should put on a tailored suit, not the plaid jacket he wears with a striped green tie.

"That's a thought." He tugs on his tie. I swear I see him wink. He draws in his breath at the sight of himself. "Actually, that's a terrific idea. A picture is worth a thousand words."

The phone rings just as I am about to go to visit my grandfather. "Hello? Is this the Hunter residence?" a woman asks.

"Depends," I say. "Do you need money?"

"No," she laughs. "My name is Lauren, Lauren Weist." She pauses when I don't say anything. "I was Shelly's roommate at Cornell."

"Oh yeah, hi. This is Frannie, Shelly's sister." I'm confused. Why is she calling me? "I was just about to walk out, Lauren. Can I call you back later?"

"Actually, I was calling to talk to Shelly. I'm home for the summer from business school. I called Shelly's apartment, but someone else answered. Did she move?" I try to say something, but can't get any words out. "Frannie?"

"Shelly's not here. Lauren," I say slowly. "Shelly had an accident."

Lauren's breath catches. She starts to ask questions. No, I say to myself. No. Sweating, I hang up. No. Not now.

Lauren immediately calls back. "I think we just got disconnected. What happened to Shelly?"

"I can't say," I mutter.

"Is Shelly okay?" she asks. I don't answer. "Frannie, what's going on?! Why aren't you saying anything?" I know she's frustrated, but I can't speak. "Frannie, is Shelly okay?"

"No," I say finally. "No, Lauren, Shelly's not okay."

"What happened?"

"Like I said, she had an accident." I take a deep breath. "Lauren, she died last December."

Lauren is quiet for a very long time. Finally, she says, "I'm so sorry. I didn't know. Jesus, no one told me." Her voice catches. "Oh, shit. I don't know anyone our age who died. I really don't know what to say." She starts to whimper.

Suddenly calm, I tell her that it's okay, that Shelly had anorexia and got thin, really thin. "She had complete organ failure," I say. "She died in her sleep."

All I hear is silence, and then a rush of words: "God, Frannie, I didn't know. I really didn't know. How's your mother? Is she okay? I can't imagine ... God, if there's anything I can do. Why don't I stop by your house? Say hello to your mom?"

"Actually, my parents have split up, and my mom's not living here anymore."

"Jesus, Frannie. I am so sorry. This must be so hard for you."

Tears spring into my eyes and I let them slide down my face. "You never think that something like this is going to happen to your family, but when it does, it feels so weird. You're part of it, but you're also watching it."

"Is there anything I can do? I have some of Shelly's books, I can bring them over."

"Nah, don't worry. You could send my mom a note, though. I think she'd like that. But keep the books. Shelly would want you to have them. I'm sorry you had to hear it like this."

"Frannie," she keeps repeating, "I am so so sorry."

We're about to hang up when I think about Chubby. *Go backwards*, she told me. "Lauren," I start. "I know you probably want to make believe you didn't hear this, but ... I know you don't know me, but ... would you mind meeting me? Just to talk? I totally understand if you're too uncomfortable. You can say no, I mean it."

"Of course I'll meet you, Frannie. I'll do anything I can."

"I have some questions, I guess. But if you're uncomfortable, we don't have to." She tells me it's fine, that she'd love to meet me, and we agree to have a drink tomorrow in the city. But before we hang up, she says something strange. "To tell you the truth, Frannie," she says softly, "I was afraid for Shelly when we graduated. I was afraid that something like this could happen."

"Hey, Frannie, could you take out the salads, please?" The dining room manager on my grandfather's floor points to a huge bowl of salad. I put plates on a tray, fill them all with salad, and wheel the tray into the dining room where I distribute them.

From the corner of my eye, I see a line of old women eating. They chew almost in unison; their jaws drop from their faces as if manipulated by strings. Someone makes a hacking sound and phlegm is pulled from down deep. This pains me so much, I turn away.

I've gotten used to being here. I tell all the women that I'm Max's granddaughter. "My name is Mattie," one women said once. "And I love Maxwell. He's my favorite." I beamed with pride as if he were my son. She beckoned me to lean close. "Find out what his plans are for next Friday night," she whispered. "I'd like to escort him to dinner." So, in addition to helping out in the kitchen, I arrange dinner dates for my grandfather and Freddie. I'm like the Heidi Fleiss of the Jewish Home. But I don't care. I am so happy to have somewhere to go during the day, I don't even mind wearing a hairnet all afternoon.

Right before dinner, I walk into my grandfather's room to say goodbye. Some guy is sitting on Freddie's bed, mesmerized by the TV. I look around the darkened room, but I don't see my grandfather or Freddie. When the guy doesn't acknowledge me except for a slight lifting of his eyes, I walk back into the hall. One of the nurses tells me my grandfather and Freddie are in Friday night services, so I sit on my grandfather's bed to wait.

"Do you mind if I turn on a light?" I ask, studying him. I've seen him before, but I can't remember where.

The guy glances over his shoulder, then back at the TV. "Suit yourself."

I snap on the light on my grandfather's side of the room. It doesn't do much, but at least I can see him. He's a stocky guy wearing a dark suit and polished loafers. The top button of his shirt is open and his tie is unknotted. His thick black hair is cropped short and he doesn't have much neck to speak of. He's handsome in a careless way: blue eyes, strong jaw, well-defined cheekbones, and a five o'clock shadow. I've seen hundreds of guys that look like him roaming the city: guys that went to Lafayette or Drexel, guys I danced with drunkenly at keg parties, that I pushed off me in bed, that I yearned would call me, but didn't. I know I know him. Is he from college? God, I pray silently, please don't let him be some guy I've slept with.

I get up and stand next to Freddie's bed. The guy has kicked off his shoes and is sitting on the edge, the clicker hidden underneath his palm. He presses the buttons quickly, not even blinking as he changes the channels. His face is bathed in fluorescent light. "You look like someone I know," I say, watching him. He glances up briefly, then turns back.

"People always say that," he tells me, transfixed on the set. "Sometimes I think there are only fifteen people in the world and everyone is just a variation of them." He doesn't even look at me as he speaks.

"Oh yeah? Well, then I'm Madonna." I walk back to my side and sit down in a chair.

The guy laughs. "Sorry to be rude." He gets up. "But I just finished a really long day and I'm totally exhausted."

Shrugging, I flip through a book, wondering where the hell my grandfather is.

"No, really. I'm sorry." He walks toward me. "You could forgive me or something." I ignore him. "Fine." He mutters under his breath. "Be a bitch. This is great. This is just what I need."

"You know," I say after a while. "You really shouldn't sit so close to the television."

"So now you're an ophthalmologist?" *So now you're a psychopharmacologist? So now you know everything?*

"I was *trying* to be nice. God, you're really a dick. Who are you anyway?"

"Richard Gere."

"You can't be Richard Gere. Richard Gere has much more hair and," I add, hopping off the bed, "a much nicer ass." I grab my backpack and walk out the door. "Could you please tell Max that Frannie stopped by?"

He jumps up behind me. "Hey, Madonna," he calls to my back. "Nice hairnet. Really does wonders for your image. And you didn't even see my ass."

"Thank God for that." I walk toward the elevator, remove the hairnet I forgot I was wearing, and lift it in a good-riddance wave. What a Rat Boy.

The next day, I drive Shelly's car into the city to meet Lauren. I park and walk around. Soon I'm at Lonny's office. In fact, I'm in front of the garbage can that Shelly threw her journal in. I know it's not here; Shelly threw out the journal months ago, but I pick through the can anyway, just for a second, figuring it doesn't hurt to look. I also look in the gutter and up and down the sidewalk. I know I won't find it, I mean, there's no way, but it makes me feel better knowing I tried.

Lauren walks into the bar wearing a gray suit and high heels. She's a pretty girl with curly blond ringlets that frame her face. We stand for a second, but it feels awkward to hug, so we simply shake hands. We both order vodka tonics.

"That's a nice suit," I tell her. "Although I thought Shelly's friends would end up working at a women's shelter in Harlem, not a business school."

"A girl's gotta eat," she says wryly. "What do you do?"

"Not much." I gulp my drink. "I'm in between jobs right now."

"What were you doing before?"

"Watching television." I look at my hands. "This past year hasn't been easy for me."

"I can imagine." She pauses. "Actually, I can't imagine. I have two sisters. I don't know what I'd do if anything happened to them. It must be the most painful thing in the world."

"Are you close to your sisters?" I ask, wondering if I sound jealous.

"When our medication kicks in, sometimes we manage." We both laugh. "We're each very different. My older sister, Jessie, is totally stoic, nothing ever gets to her, but I cry when I read Hallmark cards. I'm sorry, but some of those cards just choke me up."

I smile. "I never used to be that way, but now I cry all the time. I was watching a rerun of *Family Affair*, and when I heard Buffy screeching 'Uncle Biw, Uncle Biw,' and Mr. French was comforting her, I started fucking bawling. But you know what really gets me? It's an old Gillette commercial."

"I know, I know!! It's the one with the guy running toward this beautiful woman and he sweeps her up and twirls her around. And in the background is the song—Gillette, the best a man can get—that one?" I nod and Lauren sits back in her seat, shaking her head. "That one always got me, too. It's funny. Shelly hated those ads. She thought they were such bullshit."

"She was lying," I say, smiling. "I've seen Shelly totally lose it over an AT&T commercial."

Lauren takes a sip of her drink. "I hadn't spoken to Shelly since graduation," she starts. "I knew she was working for a law firm, but I was away, and we lost touch."

"Shelly isolated herself," I tell her. "I doubt she was talking to anyone from Cornell. Not that she would have told me anyway. We drifted apart when she went up to school. Or maybe we weren't that close to begin with. It was just ..." I trail off, but Lauren finishes for me. "A Sister Thing. Frannie, like I said, I can't imagine what you're feeling, but I do know that the Sister Thing is hard to explain to anyone who doesn't have one. One time Jessie and I were driving somewhere and she asked me to hold her sandwich. And I said no. I don't know why I said no, I just did and suddenly, we're having a major world war. I'm bringing up shit she did to me when she was twelve and she's pinching me. I mean, she's like twenty-five, and she's *pinching* me. We didn't speak for three weeks. But she called me and we went to the movies and during the movie, she asks me to hold her popcorn and we just laughed. The Sister Thing is an inexplicable force of nature."

I listen to Lauren, thankful I asked her to meet me. I'd always ignored Shelly's friends in the same way, I guess, that I ignored Shelly. "The truth is, Lauren," I tell her, my courage building, "I don't know much about Shelly's life at Cornell. Like how she felt about things, her boyfriends and stuff. I mean, was my sister ever in love?"

For a second, Lauren looks pained. "Shelly and I talked a lot, Frannie, mostly during freshman year. You should know that Shelly was a genuinely warm, funny woman who everyone admired. And she was brilliant." Lauren signals the waiter and orders us another round. I'm beginning to feel the liquor, and I think Lauren is too because she keeps rambling. "I could tell you so many stories of her generosity and kindness, and—"

I interrupt her as the waiter brings our drinks. "It's not that I don't want to hear those stories, Lauren, because I do. But I really want to know why you said you were afraid for Shelly."

Lauren chews on her straw. "That was a stupid thing to say. I should keep my mouth shut."

"No, it's important. I have to know."

She takes a deep breath. "Shelly was pretty fucked up about food during school, but I had my own issues, so we never discussed it. Besides, who our age isn't fucked up about their body in some way? Anyway, Cornell was difficult for her. She put so much pressure on herself to pick a profession and 'get on a track.' She always said that, as if 'getting on a track' was going to solve all her problems. When I said that I was afraid for Shelly, I meant it in a general sense. That if she didn't stay in therapy, she could get out of control. She's the kind of person who *had* to have a plan. I mean, most people feel that way, I guess, but for Shelly, it was life or death. She couldn't just *be*. She had to *be something*. When we graduated, she seemed happy about law school, but I also felt that if she felt overwhelmed, she'd self-destruct."

"Huh." I suck my lime. "Lauren, I have to tell you ... I wasn't completely honest on the phone. You were right about Shelly self-destructing." I stare at the television in the corner, high up, above Lauren's head. "Shelly committed suicide."

"Holy shit." Lauren blinks. "Holy fucking shit."

"We don't have to talk about this anymore if you don't want to."

"No," she says, shaking her head. "No, it's okay. I just need some air." She grabs her purse, excuses herself, and rushes outside.

I wait a long time. I'm disappointed when she doesn't come back. I don't blame her, I think as I dig into my wallet for cash. Just as I'm about to grab my backpack, Lauren walks toward the table. "I'm sorry, Frannie. I just couldn't breathe."

I tell her that it's okay, that I'm glad she came back. She studies me. When she finally speaks, her voice is even and controlled, as if she is carefully choosing each word. "Frannie," she says, "I always thought that Shelly was really angry about something. She tried to hide it by studying or exercising, but underneath, I felt there was another person raging inside. I'm no psychiatrist, but I think it had to do with those boys when she was young. It's as if she created all these diversions to help her forget, to contain her guilt or anger or whatever, but sometimes the smallest thing set her off. I always felt that Shelly was very fragile, and that she could collapse at any time. Is that an awful thing to say?"

"What boys?" I ask slowly. "You mean like Sherman, the physicist?"

She shakes her head. "No, before college. When she was in junior high. Sherman loved Shelly, and I think she loved him, but I don't think ... well, I don't know, but I don't think she was capable of being close to a guy, especially when she was having problems with her weight. Sherman used to talk to me about it, not to betray her, but to understand her. Once, right after they had sex, she screamed at him that she hated him, that he was vile, and she never wanted to see him again. He never got over it, he felt like he'd raped her. They couldn't connect again after that. Sexually, I mean." Lauren pauses. "I'm uncomfortable talking about her this way. You have to know that everyone really loved Shelly."

"I loved Shelly, too, Lauren," I say. "Which is why I have to know." Lauren tries to tell me that I shouldn't focus on the bad things that happened to Shelly. "She was a really good person, Frannie. Why can't you just leave it at that?"

"Because, Lauren, I can't. Aren't there things you don't know about Jessie? Personal things she would tell her friends, but not you. Imagine if she died and you didn't know them. Imagine how left out you'd feel."

"But sisters don't always share everything, Frannie."

"Lauren, you can say that because Jessie's alive. And one day, maybe you *will* share everything." I look at her. "Shelly's gone. I don't even have a chance of that happening."

Lauren looks at me as if considering something. "Sherman tried to talk to Shelly about sex, but all she could hear was that he wasn't attracted to her. So she broke up with him. Her rationale was completely convoluted. She broke up with him, but *she* was the one who felt rejected. She couldn't deal with the sex. The intimacy. Whatever you call it." Lauren's getting looped, so when she raises her hand to call the waiter, I tell her I don't want another drink.

"I know this is hard," I say, "but I have to know about the boys from junior high."

"I need another drink." Lauren reaches into her purse. "Shelly and I took a creative writing class together. We wrote poetry and stories, most of which sucked. But she wrote this one story that flipped me out. I don't know if it really happened, and since you don't know about it, it probably didn't. I always thought … fuck, I don't know, I thought it was true. It really bothered me and I just stuck it with Shelly's books and figured I'd ask her about it one day. Anyway, I went through my college stuff last night. Here …" She thrusts some papers in my hand.

I skim the pages. I'm dying to read them, but Lauren is watching me, and I feel woozy from the alcohol. "What's it about?" I ask.

"Just read it. You'll see."

Reluctantly, I fold the story into my backpack. "Did you ever *ask* if it was true?"

She shakes her head. "I thought that if she wanted to tell me, she would have," she says, then she grabs my hand. "Let's get fucked up, Frannie. I mean, really shit-faced." I call the waiter over. "We'd like two more vodka tonics," I tell him and Lauren adds, "just hold the tonic," and for some reason we suddenly can't stop laughing.

"That Therman. What a guy," Lauren says. "Hello, I'm Therman and thith ith my girlfriend, Thelly." Lauren and I howl like it's the funniest thing in the world. Soon, we're laughing and crying and hugging. "I'm so sorry," she whispers, her arms around me. "You can always call me. I can be a pretend sister. Any time you want."

I squint. In the glow of the lights, I keep thinking that with her blond hair and creamy skin, Lauren looks like Shelly. I can't stop staring at her. "Thanks," I say, "I'm so tired of being alone."

"You're not alone," she says. She rummages through her purse and finds a safety pin. "Frannie, give me your finger," she commands. I hold out my hand, and she pricks my finger, then her own. We press them together. "Now we're blood sisters." We giggle. "God," she says finally. "I sure as shit hope you don't have AIDS."

"*Smith, Fran,*" I mutter. "Negative." Even though she doesn't know what I'm talking about, Lauren laughs like a hyena. And I laugh too. Because if I didn't, I'd be bawling like a baby.

The next morning, massively hung over, I go into the kitchen to carve up a cow and make hamburger meat. I'm so fucking nauseous, I need beef. But the minute I open the refrigerator, I lose my appetite.

On top of the microwave, there's a picture of a strange man wearing a turquoise ascot and horn-rimmed glasses. He's smoking a pipe. As I get closer, I recognize the man's eyes, which peer out like those of a bunny caught in headlights. I stare at the picture closely and groan. The man is my father.

I walk into his office. I look around and see another picture of my dad on his bookshelf. In this one, he's wearing silver-rimmed aviator sunglasses and a shiny white racing scarf. He holds up two fingers, making a "V." I shove the picture in his face, but he waves me away. "I'll move the cards. Right. Ciao, babe." He turns to me, beaming. "So what do you think?"

"Daddy, who are you? What the hell are these?"

"You told me to get a professional picture. I wanted something different, so I went to that place in the mall where they dress you up and take pictures. You know—Glamour Shots." He frowns. "They told me these were terrific. You haven't seen the best one." Apprehensive, I follow him into the den. Next to a picture of Shelly, there's another shot of my father. I blink so I don't have to look at Shelly.

In the picture, he's wearing a Western shirt with fringe, a red bandanna, and a ten-gallon hat that he's tipping as if to say howdy. "I got some eight-by-tens and a few wallet-sized. But wait, you haven't seen the best part." He hands me a piece of paper. "I put this together for the *Christian Times.*"

Howdy, cowgirls! This issue's bachelor of the month is **David Hunter**, a salesman from Lindsey Point. Dave is looking for a single, divorced, or otherwise uninvolved woman who's outdoorsy, likes the smell of a campfire, and riding bareback through moonlit fields. Dave's a middle-aged cowboy with an Achy-Breaky heart lookin' for a pistol-packin' mama who ain't afraid of the call of the wild. David enjoys good books, fine wines, and two-stepping to Garth Brooks. For a rootin'-tootin' good time, call David at ext. 2453 or write to the *Christian Times*, 405 State Street, Lindsey Point, New York, 11225. Yee-haw!!

"This is your personal ad?" He chuckles. "Dad, you want a nice lady from the Junior League to honey-bake some ham and watch *The Way We Were*. You don't want a woman who rides mechanical bulls." I look at him. How can you be so weird and still live in your own body?

"It's a gimmick, Frannie. Everyone loves a gimmick."

"Daddy ..." I pause. "Women don't like gimmicks. You're a nice guy. Just be yourself."

"Too late." He snatches the paper back. "It comes out next week." He reads it again and laughs. "I happen to think it's very clever."

"But it's not clever, Daddy. It's a very strange thing to do."

"I can't sit around brooding my life away. It's time to move on. Carpe diem. Besides," he adds, "this would drive your mother *crazy*. Imagine her face if she saw this."

"Yeah," I say, a hollowness carved in the pit of my stomach, envisioning my mother looking at the cowboy picture and rolling her eyes. "Imagine."

17

*S*hell*y's story opens with three sisters sitting with their mother at the* kitchen table, counting calories. It's upbeat and funny. Then it takes a turn, and all of a sudden, it's not so funny anymore.

Hannah wishes she could fly. At night she jumps out of her bedroom window, just a little jump, but one that makes her feel weightless and free. She is young: ripened and juicy like the blue plums she sucks in the summertime. On the hill behind her house, she meets boys from her school. Sometimes there's one, sometimes there's two. Sometimes there's more. They lodge their tongues in her mouth, unbutton her blouse and squeeze her breasts, they put their hands down her pants and stick their dirty, sticky fingers into her vagina. They laugh and smell their fingers, stick them into her mouth, make her taste herself. The taste makes her gag and Hannah lies on her back and stares at the stars, wishing she was airborne, far away.

They pull off her pants and one of the boys straddles her. He puts his rubbery dick in her face and she smells him. He smells fishy and sweaty and she keeps looking up at the stars. When he jams himself into her, the other boys watch, mesmerized. Hannah hears a car door slam, but it is drowned out by the voice in her head, the voice that says he shouldn't do this, Hannah, he shouldn't, tell him no, but Hannah doesn't. She feels him inside her and her mind shuts down and when the other boys take their turns, she feels herself floating upward, up and far away, as if she's been levitated from her flesh. She floats above the boys and above herself and watches as they enter her and pull out, their creamy white come covering her stomach like a soft woolen blanket.

"Let's go," one of the boys says. "Get up!" He shakes her but Hannah won't move, not when he kicks her, not even when he drags her by her hair down the hill. As they race away, their laughter echoes behind them, naked and ugly like the baying of a drowning cat. Hannah lies on her back, closes her eyes, and lets the night envelop the body she used to inhabit. It wasn't like they forced me, she tells herself. I didn't say no. I didn't say anything. And she no longer feels like a summertime plum.

She sticks her fingers in her mouth and sucks on them, wondering why she feels so empty when, just seconds before, she was filled. She feels a soft breeze waft slowly over the houses, deeper and deeper into the trees. She lifts the body that is merely a dead weight and rises from the ground. The sweet summer breeze blows softly away and she looks up at the stars and makes a wish. But she knows that wishes aren't meant to come true, and for girls like her, flying is impossible.

Horrified, I lie in bed, trying to connect this story to Shelly. I try to remember her in junior high. She was so pretty back then, but I can't remember anything significant that could make this story real. It's difficult to picture her at twelve or thirteen. In my head, she's blurry like a photograph that's out of focus. I remember she had nosebleeds and silky hair and loved red barrettes. She went to a school for gifted kids and ate hot honey sandwiches and Rice-a-Roni. It was in junior high that she first gained weight, wasn't it junior high? Was that the beginning?

I read the story again. If it's true, why didn't she tell me? It's not like you told me about *your* life, she would have said. But this is different, I say silently. How? she retorts. How is this different?

I remember my own clumsy experiences with boys, their groping hands, sweaty kisses; their fat tongues pushed into my mouth, always tasting of beer and cigarettes. And the endless panting, like fucking dogs, begging and panting and begging and panting and ... Suddenly sick, I go into the bathroom, kneel over the toilet, and gag until I'm dry-heaving. In my head, I'm confused and I can't make connections, but it hurts too much to think about so I take two Valium, get back into bed, and will myself to fall asleep.

I spend my days at the home until my shift at Rascals. My grandfather and I don't talk much. Sometimes we watch TV, sometimes we play cards. We just do what old people do. We sit.

When I walk into his room, I see Rat Boy sitting on Freddie's bed, watching TV.

"Have you even moved since I last saw you?" I ask him.

He shakes his head. "I've been sitting here all week, waiting for you."

Despite myself, I smile.

Suddenly Freddie rushes in. My grandfather hobbles behind him, cane in hand. "Look who's here!" Freddie calls. He grabs me in a big hug. "Hello, *shaineh maidel.*"

My grandfather pumps Rat Boy's arm. "Such a good-lookin' fella!" He turns to me. "Isn't he good-lookin'?"

I look at the guy. "He has no idea what you look like," I deadpan. "He's blind."

Freddie tugs on my hair. "This is *still* too long. Ach, such a ragamuffin."

Rat Boy raises his eyebrows. "We know *he's* not blind." Indignant, I smooth my curls.

Freddie pushes the guy toward me. "Say hello, vill you? I've been vanting dis day to come for months. Dis is my grandson. Charlie. Charlie, say hello already."

Charlie forces a smile and sticks out his hand. "Nice to meet you. I'm Charlie. And you must be ..." He glances at my chest. "Madonna?"

I shake his hand. "Actually, my name is Frannie. Madonna's just my stage name." With my arms at my sides, I squeeze my breasts together to create cleavage. "You're the guy in the picture." I point to Freddie's dresser.

"That's me." Charlie beams. "Major stud material, huh?"

"SO?" Freddie claps. "Vhat do you tink?"

Charlie puts his hands on his grandfather's shoulders. "Grandpa, calm down. It's too early to call the caterers."

I help my grandfather to a chair. I put a pillow underneath him and adjust his feet. I feel Charlie watching me. "I can't stay long," I announce. "I have a date tonight."

"Vith who?" Freddie barks. "Your mother said you've been alone for months." Charlie grins. "So, let Grandpa and me watch TV vile you and Charlie get to know vone another. Here, Max, you blind fool, get out of Frannie's vay. Let her sit."

"Get your hands off me, you *mamser*, ya bastard," my grandfather snaps at him.

"Ladies," I interrupt. "You two sit. Charlie and I will sit on Freddie's bed, okay?"

My grandfather leans toward the TV. "So Charlie," he says, transfixed on the set. "Why aren't you married? Such a good-lookin' fella."

Charlie laughs. "Max, watch TV."

"I'm watching. It's just a question."

"You're thirty-one, kiddo," Freddie cuts in, also facing the TV. "You ain't gettin' any younger."

"You're thirty-one?" I blurt out. "I didn't realize you were so old … I mean, I thought you were closer to my age."

"Since when is thirty-one *old*?" He stares at me. "You're hardly nineteen."

"Frannie's twenty-six," my grandfather cuts in. "Her birthday is coming. So Charlie, you can take her out for a Happy Birthday to You dinner." He hums a few bars of "Happy Birthday."

"Grandpa," I cut in quickly. "Charlie probably has plans."

"What plans? Charlie, you can't cancel these plans? Why? It's Frannie's *birthday*."

Charlie looks at me and shrugs. I just roll my eyes. Finally engrossed, my grandfather and Freddie bicker about which program to watch. "Grandpa," I tell him, "don't be so selfish." I get up and kiss his head.

Charlie watches me as I sit down. "Twenty-six is hardly nine-teen, Madonna," he hisses at me. "Face it, you're about to hit the wall."

"I have years before thirty. And stop calling me Madonna, *Chuck.*"

"Time's running out," Charlie whispers. "They say that women over thirty are more likely to get killed in a plane crash than find a husband. If I were you, I'd snag the first man who'd have me."

"If you're going to quote a statistic," I hiss, "get it right or better yet, read a book. You might learn a thing or two about your *own* marketability."

"Oh God," Charlie rolls his eyes. "A feminist."

"What's wrong with that? You're one of those guys who hates women? Problems with a domineering mother? Confused about your own masculinity?"

"Hardly," he says. "But believe me, I know what you're all about. For starters, you won't let a man hold a door open for you because it's patronizing, but you'll allow him to pay for dinner. You combine your salaries, but *you're* allowed to spend 25 percent more. You order him around like a drill sergeant in bed; you expect to be on top 50 percent of the time so you can control *everything*; and then you wonder why I want to sleep with the pretty young thing at the gym who wears sundresses that show off her voluptuous breasts and pink-passion lip gloss and who smiles at me like I have a ten-inch penis!" Charlie takes a deep breath. His face is beet-red.

I stare at him, wide-eyed. "Someone you know?"

"My girlfriend. Excuse me … woman friend."

"Well," I say slyly, "I don't expect to be on top 50 percent of the time, although once in a while is very nice. So how long have you been dating her? This feminist?"

"Six months, maybe seven. Actually, she just dumped me. I hate her." He smiles. "Hate her with me."

"I'm bonded with her in sisterhood. I can't hate her because I hate *you.*"

"The truth is," he tells me, "she scares the hell out of me." Leaning back, he almost topples over, but he grabs my shoulder to catch himself. He lets his hand linger.

"Now, about my marketability," I begin. I haven't been this close to a guy in a long time. My mouth's suddenly dry and my heart's pounding. I wish I had a Valium.

"Almost thirty," Charlie clucks. "No man, no kids. I'd stock up on cat food."

"I could get married if I wanted. Besides"—I lower my voice—"I don't know if I want kids. Seems like it's easy to screw them up. Look at you. Who refers to a woman as a 'pretty young thing'? This is the nineties and you're Ricky Ricardo."

His voice deepens. "You'd make a great mother. I see how you dote on Max."

"You're making fun of me, aren't you?" I glare at him. "I can't tell when you're kidding and when you're trying to hurt my feelings." I get up. "I have to go," I tell everyone loudly. "Or I'm going to be late for my date. With a rich, handsome Jewish doctor."

"It was good to see you again, Madonna," Charlie says. He grabs my hand. "Trust me," he whispers, pulling me back. "I wouldn't hurt you." He squeezes my hand, and as I leave the room, it pulses like the gentle beating of a heart.

I'm ready for business at line-up. Paulie runs his fingers along my dry-cleaned shirt. "Nice creases, Frannie," he murmurs. He turns to the other servers. "Guys, this is a dry-cleaned shirt. I suggest you study it and by tomorrow, make sure you're wearing one just like it."

Artie rolls his eyes. "Thanks, Frannie. Since when do you dry-clean your shirts?"

I shrug and jam my hands into my apron pockets. I don't have much time. I need this job. I have to care about something. This morning at the home, I watched Ben, a physical therapist, help a woman walk down a narrow hallway. Clinging to her walker, she hunched over as she took a first step. Ben was behind her, patiently coaxing her. "Come on, Roberta, honey, come on." Roberta tripped and I held my breath.

"Tonight's specials are mahi-mahi, which can be blackened, broiled, or put in a blender for all I care." Paulie rubs his mustache. He looks tired, and he's wearing glasses, something I hadn't noticed before. Someone said his wife, Tina, is divorcing him. In fact, she's supposed to be his second wife, his first wife left him for another man, or so the story goes. Since all this is passed from waiter to waiter, it's hard to know what's true. "The pasta is pasta primavera and the soup is tomato basil. We're low on soup, so don't push it. Also, we're out of vinaigrette dressing but Cecil is making some. It'll be ready in five minutes." Paulie leans against the counter. "Anything else?" He waits. "No? Good. Now go out and make some money."

"I have something to add." Artie lifts a finger. Paulie peers into the dining room and tells him to make it quick. "I want to know if anyone can trade stations? I need to get out early tonight." Artie looks up, expectantly. No one says a word.

"I guess you're shit out of luck, Artie my man. Okay, let's go, guys." Paulie claps. "Come on. Chop chop."

Artie pulls me aside as ten duck aprons file out of the kitchen. "Come on, Frannie. Trade?" He lets his hand linger. I think of Roberta's hands on the walker, tense from the fear of falling.

"Okay, I'll close for you." I wrench my arm away.

"Frannie," he asks suddenly. "Why don't you like me?"

"I do like you, Artie," I say slowly. "We're friends."

He stares at me. "Why don't you want to be with me?" He tries to kiss me. I pull back. "But why, Frannie?"

Why? The image of three teenagers straddling the girl in Shelly's story flashes in my head. I want to tell him that he's pathetic, that when I'm with him, I hate myself, that sex isn't supposed to be about fumbling in the dark to make parts fit. "I don't know, Artie," I tell him honestly. "I really don't." I bite my lip as he slinks away. I'm sorry, I tell him silently, but I can't be with you anymore, not that way. Not right now. I see Artie, the dewy eyes, the hopeful mouth. Or is it me? I blink.

There's a woman sitting at the bar. When I look at her, she smiles at me in recognition, but I can't place her. She is thin but shapely and her eyes are such a deep blue, it hurts to look at them. She has flawless skin and perfect lips. I wish I could be that beautiful. The bartender puts a soda in front of her. She squeezes a lemon wedge into the glass. I look away, then back. She's still smiling at me as if I'm supposed to know her.

Back in the dining room, I place three waters on a table. "My name's Frannie." I smile. "I'm your waitress. Anyone want to start with a drink?"

A heavyset man leans forward and points to his wife. "This is Ann and I'm Bert and this is Bruce. We're your customers." He chuckles at himself.

"Dad!" Bruce moans. He sticks his fingers into the water glass then sucks on them. I watch him suck his fingers and suddenly feel like gagging.

"A glass of red wine for my wife, a Coke for Bruce, and a Bud for me. Got it?"

"Red wine for Ann, Coke for Bruce, and a Bud for Bert." I head for the bar. "Got it."

The woman is still in the bar but this time Paulie's with her. Her eyes travel over the bottles, squinting as though counting, then rest on me. She smiles again but this time doesn't linger.

She's wearing a tailored taupe suit and sling-backs. I feel like I've seen her before but maybe I've only seen women who look like her, women rushing through the city holding leather briefcases and the *New York Times*. I shred a bar napkin. Seeing her poised and pretty makes me feel oafish, like I'm not trying hard enough. A memory nags at me, a mental image of this woman sitting somewhere else. In the image, the woman nods her head, rests it against a bench, a booth maybe, a wine-colored cushion.

"Who's she?" I whisper to a waiter.

"She's with corporate. I don't know her name. But watch Paulie. He's crawling all over her." From the corner of my eye, I see her gesture. She rests her hand on her face. Her hand. It's her hand that I recognize. Her hand on a dark gray suit.

I make my way back to Bert, Ann, and Bruce and put their drinks down. I'm distracted when they order, thinking of the pretty woman's hand, her hand on an arm, fluttering in sadness, clenched in anger.

Bert holds the menu as if reading a book. Ann turns in her seat, reaches up, and rests a hand on his arm. He pulls away. For a second, Ann's hand is suspended in mid-air. Then I know. I waited on the corporate woman! She was with that married man the night I got fired!

"Excuse me," I say. "I have to check something."

The woman is standing next to Paulie, looking out at the parking lot. I can't see her face but I'm positive by the way her hair swings, that it's her. Shit, she's gonna ask Paulie if I'm the obnoxious girl who yelled at her date. She'll want to know why I'm still here, we have a policy about that sort of thing. She turns slightly and I get a profile. I can see the shape of one full eye; a narrow, fine-boned cheek; the soft curve of chin. She lifts her hand to wipe a lock of hair out of her eyes. In my mind, Roberta almost makes it with her walker. There's a group of elderly people huddled together, beckoning to her. "Come on, hon." They hold out their hands. There's a flutter of a purple scarf, the clomp of her walker as she takes another step.

I purposely avoid the bar. I wonder when Paulie will ask to see me, when he'll close his door, sit on the edge of his desk, kick his foot, clear his throat. "I'm sorry, Frannie," he'll murmur, fidgeting with some papers. "I have to let you go. It's from corporate. You'll find something, honey." He pats my arm. Each of his gestures makes me want to cry.

Around eight-thirty, I'm really backed up. I have six tables going. One's a party of eight with special orders. I've gotten their salads and am going over their order with Cecil who can't stand to be bothered on a busy Saturday night.

I lean over the pass-out bar and stand on my toes to watch his hands. He works fast, leaning over to grab a stack of plates which are already garnished, the buns lying open-faced in a circle made of a lettuce leaf, a tomato wedge, an onion slice, and a sprig of kale. "I'm sorry, Cecil. But eighty-six the nuts on the chicken. And only a little glaze, hardly any, okay?" I glance behind me. The dining room is full. I flush with exhilaration. Cecil sticks a brush into a bowl of glaze and slathers it on a piece of chicken. "Cecil! That's too much!"

"Frannie, let me cook and I won't bother your tables. The lady won't know the difference. If I don't do this, she'll say it's bland and send it back. Trust me." Minutes later, I watch the woman eat her glazed chicken. She lifts the fork to her mouth, chews thoughtfully and swallows. She licks her bottom lip and cuts another piece.

"Frannie?" Paulie grabs my apron strings. "Take care of the lady on two. She's a friend."

I'm not really paying attention, so when I get to the table, I stop short. It's the woman from corporate and she's still smiling that same fucking smile. "Hi." I falter. I lean on the edge of my foot so my ankle turns under. "I'm Frannie."

"I'm Victoria Tayborn." She extends her hand. "I've wanted to meet you."

Her handshake is firm. I swallow. "I've had a busy few months."

"So I hear." She smiles. Her smile really isn't so bad.

"I have a business proposition for you," she says. "We have an opening on our marketing team. If you're interested, why don't you call me next Monday?" She hands me her card. "We can meet next week to talk about it."

"Okay, thanks." I study her card and drift back to this morning, to Roberta and Ben. Roberta reaches the crowd. They take away her walker and someone lowers her into a chair. "Oh, my Gawd!" someone screeches. "Roberta, look at you!" Ben and I applaud. As I look into Vicky Tayborn's face and her eyes glint with kindness, it is this sound, the soft sound of Ben's hands coming together, that echoes in my head.

"Grandpa tells me you've been spending time with him." My mother tears at a crust of bread. "I appreciate it, Frannie, I haven't had a chance to see him lately."

I shrug. "I like being there." I pick at a roll. "I've been helping out in the kitchen."

"Maybe they have something for you full-time."

"I don't know about that." I laugh. "It's not really what I had in mind for myself."

She tells the waiter that her veal is undercooked. As he walks away with her plate, she grabs my hand. "Did you see that?" she asks. "I'm Grandma." We laugh and sit for a few seconds. The silence isn't uncomfortable.

"How's your father?" she asks.

I put down my fork, not really hungry anymore. "He's okay."

Some woman called my father about his personal ad. In fact, they went out tonight. He told me about it when I mentioned I was having dinner with my mother. It was so obvious he wanted me to tell her. "I thought you guys spoke every day."

"Not every day, but we speak often. I meant how are things going between you two?"

"Good. He's changed, he's more mellow. You should come by. What's up with you?"

"Things are better." She thanks the waiter who returns with new veal. "I've cut down on the Valium. Marilyn's helping me." She stops and I wait for her to tell me I need help, but she doesn't. Instead she smiles. "I'm sure you consider me a drug addict."

"I never paid much attention," I lie. "Congratulations, I guess." We're being too nice. It's like a first date. My mother picks absently at her veal. "Have you and Abby made up?"

I shake my head. "I guess we weren't meant to be best friends for life."

"You know Abby's volatility. She'll come around. I wouldn't let it go just like that."

"Maybe some things in life are better off let go." I say this quietly, tracing the rim of my wineglass with the tip of my finger. I drink from it, staring at my mother. Her head looks distorted through the curve of the glass. I have to blink to get her in focus. "Mom, I've been thinking. Did Shelly ever tell you about anything that happened to her as a kid? With some boys?" She shakes her head and asks me why I want to know. "I don't know. Just wondering. Did Shelly ever—"

My mother interrupts me, her face crumpled into an expression of pain. "Frannie, honey. I'm not ready to talk about Shelly. I don't mean to cut you off, but I just can't." Her eyes get wet. "I also want you to know that no matter what happens with Daddy and me, it has nothing to do with you."

"Mom, you're acting like I'm twelve. Don't you think I know this?"

"I just wanted to make sure that you heard it from me." A waiter comes by and asks if we want dessert. My mom asks me if I want to split something.

I shake my head, but the fact that she asked me if I want dessert registers. It may be the first time in my life that she's asked me. I think this is supposed to mean something. "So you and Daddy may get a divorce?" I calculate my tone, try to sound mature.

"I don't know. We'll see." She looks up. "What do you think I should do?"

Surprised, I look up. She never asks for my opinion. "Why are you asking me?"

"I don't know." She laughs self-consciously. "It just came out." She plays with a spoon. "I wish you'd consider going to Tempe with me."

Suddenly I can't help myself. "Are you still seeing Johnny?" I ask, not maliciously, just because I'm curious.

She stares into the candle on the table. The light illuminates her face, softens her cheeks, makes her glow. "Johnny and I never really had an affair, not the way you think. He was just someone to talk to and he let it go too far. I liked talking to him. He made me feel like I made sense, like I mattered. Your father always blows me off."

"You slept with him, though, didn't you?"

She rests her fingers on her mouth. Speaking through them, she says, "I don't think that's any of your business."

"So you did." I rub my legs under the table, thinking of my dad and Shelly. And me.

"I know you're not going to understand this—" she starts to say.

"Please stop telling me what I understand. I'm twenty-six years old."

"Okay, Frannie. Yes. Once. It was uncomfortable and I knew it was wrong. But I was lonely." She pauses. "Despite being your mother, I'm still a woman. And I make mistakes. I'm not apologizing. That's between Daddy and me. I'm just trying to help you understand."

I'm about to crack a joke about Johnny's size, but listening to her talk to me as if I'm a woman, too, not just a dopey girl who eats her food and uses her towels, makes me stop myself. "You always talked to Shelly," I say softly. "You never talked to me." I start to cry.

She smooths my hair away from my face and her eyes fill with tears. For a few seconds, we sit and size each other up. "It was awful," she tells me firmly. She stirs her coffee. "Just awful. The man really should get some exercise." She smiles through her tears.

I wipe my eyes. "I'll bet," I say because I know just how awful it can be.

My mother excuses herself to go to the ladies' room. When she returns, she's followed by a crowd of waiters holding a chunk of cake with a candle, and singing "Happy Birthday." "By the way"— my mother smiles—"you're not twenty-six, you're twenty-seven. Happy Birthday."

Imagine that. I close my eyes to blow out the candle. I make a wish. I'm twenty-seven. In two months, Shelly would have been twenty-five. She didn't make it. I'm sure my mother's thinking the same thing, because she's crying and we're holding hands.

I'm sorry, I want to tell her. I'm sorry I made it and Shelly didn't. And I can't help but think about the girl in Shelly's story, lying naked in the dirt, sucking on her fingers, wishing she could fly.

18

One night, I dream about St. Mary's. Shelly and my grandfather are sitting on her hospital bed, watching television. I try to walk into the room, but can't. Shelly is really fat, obese like Keisha, the bus driver, who suddenly appears. Then, Pia, the poet, also appears, and she tells Shelly how well Shelly writes. In the dream, I know that they're not letting me enter the room because I read Shelly's story. "We have secrets," Cynthia says as she whirls in a circle, whirling, whirling so fast, she becomes nothing but a blur. Shelly is a skeleton, lying on her bed, and she's covered in dirt. Little boys tickle her toes. She screams for them to stop, but they won't. Then it's me, not Shelly, who is in the bed. I hear a deep voice, a man's voice, telling the boys to go away. I look up. Standing in the doorway, still yelling at the boys, is Charlie.

"I was in the city," I tell Diana the next day when I stop by St. Mary's. "I wanted to say hello to Cynthia."

"Cynthia checked out," Diana says. "She went home to live with her aunt. I can give you her number. I'm sure she'd love to hear from you."

"She checked out? Wow, that's great." I feel a pang of sadness. "Yeah, give me her number. I'll call her," I say, knowing I won't.

As I walk out of the hospital, I hear someone yell my name. "Hey, Frannie! Wait up!" I turn around and behind me, in all his baldheaded, needle-sticking splendor, is Dr. Bryan Thompson. "Uh hi, Bryan," I say. I stand for a second as he walks toward me. Then, not feeling much like talking to him, I turn away.

"Wait, Frannie! I want to talk to you."

"I'm late, Bryan." I walk faster. "I don't have time." Then I start to run and I'm practically down the block when he catches up to me. He puts his hand on my arm, which I shrug off. "I said I gotta go."

"Frannie, I just wanted to tell you I heard about Shelly. I'm really sorry. I was going to call you, but I didn't think it was appropriate."

"Appropriate? What the fuck do you know about appropriate?" I'm sweating and panting, and feel like spitting on him.

"I'm sorry," he says again, picking at his slacks. "I was an asshole. I'm sorry."

"Are you sorry about Shelly or how you treated me? There's a difference, you know."

"Both." He shades his eyes from the sun. "Would you have coffee with me? I'd like to talk to you, to apologize."

"You just did." I start to walk away again, but he won't let me go. "I'd just like to see you," he tells me. "Please?" I shrug, but then I think about Shelly, and how maybe he can help me. I nod. "Okay. You can call me."

It doesn't dawn on me until later, when I'm driving home in Shelly's car, that I almost blew off Dr. Bryan Thompson. Jesus, I think. That was big. That was like major. I smile, proud of myself. How the hell did I do that?

The following week, I'm in Vicky Tayborn's office on Fifth Avenue. I took a lot of time getting ready this morning. I washed my new shoulder-length hair courtesy of Freddie. He cut it one afternoon when my grandfather and I had a special Spa Day at Dames and Gents. Afraid I'll jinx it, I haven't told anyone except my grandfather and Freddie about this interview.

I haven't spoken to Abby, which makes me wonder if we'll ever be friends again. I want to tell her about my grandfather, about

Freddie and Vicky Tayborn, but I'm still ashamed about my behavior and I can't bring myself to call her. My life is so different now, it almost feels like she was never in it, although I'd be lying if I said I didn't miss her.

I sit in one of the chairs facing Vicky's desk. Her card says she's the vice president of East Coast promotions. I don't know what that means, but I do know it warrants her a corner office with a huge desk, a couch, two chairs, and a small table for conferences.

"I'm so happy you could make it today, Frannie," Vicky says. She brushes away a lock of hair. Every time I look at her, I wonder what she feels like when she stares into a mirror, knowing that the face staring back is her own. She must love herself every day. "I really wanted to meet you." She's wearing a form-fitting hunter-green suit. I smooth my own suit, arrange my legs. She speaks so softly, so sweetly, I feel like her beauty deepens and is extended to include me.

"Well thank you for inviting me. I know I've been difficult to get hold of."

She waves her hand. "Well? Where do we begin?" She sits back in her leather chair. "I've learned a lot in the past few years," she says. "I always thought that if I did well in school, I'd get a good job and if I got a good job, I'd have a nice life. But it doesn't always work that way. I was fired from my first job because of politics. Business—and life, I guess—isn't always about fair play. I couldn't find a job so I went to Reggie's, another one of Cuisine's stores, and started my career as a waitress."

"Like me," I break in.

"Yes"—she nods—"like you. I got my MBA at night. I moved into corporate and as I got promoted, I made a point of hiring women with drive and ambition. It became a personal mission to help foster their careers. Don't get me wrong"—she laughs—"I get something out of it, too, but I feel that if we can create a network of women like men's good-old-boy cliques, then our business lives and our personal lives will prosper."

"What does this have to do with me?" I ask, not daring to hope.

"The first night I saw you ..."

"I am so sorry about that. I was going through a hard time. Shelly, my sister ..."

"I know, Frannie. Please don't apologize. You just reminded me …" She trails off. "As your career evolves, you will learn that a business life and a personal life are not mutually exclusive. Paul DiMartino told me about Shelly," she says, and as I look at her, I feel her sympathy. "And since I know about Shelly, it's only right to let you in on my own personal history." The phone rings. "I'm sorry, Frannie, but I've been waiting for this call. Do you mind?"

Are you for real? I shake my head. As she picks up the phone and starts speaking, I cross my fingers. Please please please don't let this be a joke. She looks up. "Again, I'm sorry. That was our Wall Street store. They're having a theme party and—"

Without thinking, I blurt out that they should set up a bar outside. "Every time I've been there, it's like a nightmare getting a drink. You have to stand like an idiot while whoever you're with goes inside and of course, there's no one decent to talk to …" I realize I'm rambling and sit back, startled by my enthusiasm.

"That's a good idea, Frannie," she says, hanging up. I beam. Finally, trolling in bars has served me. "So," she continues, "where were we?" She gets up and closes her door. Then she launches into a story. Apparently, the man she was with that night is a big shot in operations and she was having an affair with him. "His name was Ed Morgan," she says, then pauses before continuing. "He was my boss. I knew he was married. And I knew he'd never leave his wife, but I didn't care." She tells me that she just kept seeing him, that she was crazy about him. "When you threw that wine, I suddenly felt so foolish being there, what with the way he was treating you." She pauses. "And the way he was treating me."

"You're so beautiful," I tell her. "I can't imagine you being crazy, especially about some guy. Seems like men would be crazy about you."

"Believe me, love can make anyone crazy. And when it's not love, when it's something else, it can assume a life all its own." I nod and cringe, remembering Bryan. "To make a long story short," Vicky says. "That evening brought me to my senses. It took courage to do what you did. I admired you for that. You left quite an impression." She plays with a pen. "A month later, I requested a transfer and was promoted to this position. I thought about you a lot, Frannie. That night was a turning point for me."

"So you kept calling me to *thank* me?"

"In a sense. I called because I knew I would need an assistant." She waits a beat. "I want you to come work for me. You have spunk and charisma and if you're as smart as Paul says, I know you'll do a hell of a job."

And? Keep going. I'm also quite attractive, no? Giddy, I almost laugh out loud.

"I'd like you to start in two weeks. I'm in promotions, which means we develop theme parties for Happy Hours, Monday night football, that sort of thing." She leans forward. "What do you think?"

I can't believe this: a job developing food parties in bars. "It sounds like a dream come true," I say. "I only have two questions." I pause. "What's your mother's name and where did she go to school? I like to know these things in advance so I don't make any stupid mistakes."

"Virginia," she replies, not even stopping to question me. "And she didn't go to college."

"Perfect." I look up. "Where do I sign?"

When I get home, there's a letter by the phone.

From the Desk of Abigail Lynn Friedman
Attorney-at-Law

Dear Frannie,

    I feel like I should be there to wish you a happy birthday, but since we're not friends anymore, I don't think it's appropriate to just barge over. I know how sorry you are. If you want to call me and apologize, I think I can be a big enough person to accept.

    I miss you, Frannie. I miss you so much, I feel like my heart's been carved out with a spoon. In some small way, I think I understand what it felt like when you lost Shelly. Maybe it's presumptuous of me to think that I can feel something that painful, but remember that I'm an only child, and you're the closest thing to a sister that I've ever had.

    I hope that you will call me so I can lavish you with gifts and get you drunk and help you pick up men. I know you must be chomping at the bit to get back to the bars. You don't have to say it, but I'm sure life is no fun without me.

So happy birthday, big girl. I'm waiting for you. I don't have anyone to talk to anymore. Life without you is boring and lonely and just takes too long to live, if you know what I mean.

I love you. I need you. Please forgive. I remain,

Abby Lynn Friedman Junior, Esquire, the First
Queen of the Planet

P.S. If you've found yourself a new best friend, disregard above.

My father walks into the kitchen. "I got a letter from Abby," I tell him. "She wants to make up."

"Good. Are you going to call her?"

"Tomorrow. I think I'll sit with it for a little while." As he walks back into his office, I start to tell him about Vicky Tayborn, but stop myself. I think I'll sit with that, too. I notice a package on the table. I open the card. There's a girl on the front, looking out a window. Her chin rests on her hand, and she looks dreamy-eyed and far away.

Dear Frannie:

Happy 27th!! Try to remember that when a door closes, somewhere in the world, a window is opened. Have a happy day. I hope all your wishes come true.

Love, Your dad

I open the package figuring he got me a T-shirt and a mug like last year. The box is from Neiman Marcus. I lift the cover and my breath catches. He got me a leather portfolio, the expensive kind that women like Vicky Tayborn carry. I slip it under my arm and march around the kitchen. "James, get the car," I say. "I have a board meeting at four."

As I walk to his office to thank my father, I notice a Glamour Shot on the microwave, the one in which he's holding a pipe. I smile at him smiling at me, and I can't help but think that the man is really much smarter than he looks.

* * *

"I stopped by the house the other day and saw a picture of your father," my mother says as she folds a blouse into a suitcase. We're packing for her trip to Tempe. "Why is he wearing a cowboy outfit?"

I avoid her eyes as I work through her underwear drawer. "He's got a couple of different poses. You know, for different moods. He's been going to group therapy. I think he's dating his inner child." And some woman named Eleanor.

My mother laughs. She holds up a lavender dress. The dress has short, puffy sleeves. "What do you think?" she asks. "Too young?"

I stare at her as if examining the dress, but I'm really searching her face for clues. I wonder if she and my dad are getting divorced. "No," I tell her. "I bet it looks cute on."

She hands it to me. "You take it. I feel funny wearing it. Besides, it's too dressy for Arizona." She walks into her closet and comes out holding a purple blazer. "It will be nice for work. You need shoes, too?" She turns to her closet again. "I may have a pair that'll go."

"No, I'm fine, Mom. I don't need them."

She walks over to me, leans as if to hug me. I stiffen, although I don't think she notices. She takes the outfit from me and shakes it. "We should put this in plastic," she says. "You're not careful enough with your clothes, Frannie." She noticed. Guilty, I want to hug her, tell her I'll miss her. She hands me a slip of paper. "Here's Aunt Lillian's number. If you need anything, call me. Also, call Grandpa every once in a while. I know you'll be busy, but he's going to miss having you around."

"I'll spend a few nights a week at the home. You know, to make it easier." I say this as if I'm only doing it for him.

She eyes me closely. "How are you feeling? Are you okay? I won't go if you're not okay." She pulls a scarf out of her drawer. "You *seem* better." She says this with more urgency than she probably means.

"I'm fine, Mom," I tell her. I'm quiet a beat. "I miss Shelly though, even more than at the beginning." My throat burns. "I dream about her. Sometimes I'll be going about my day, not really thinking about anything and all of a sudden, I realize she's gone and I become paralyzed. And every time is like it's the first time, you know? The pain, I mean. It's always a punch in the stomach." I choose my words carefully. What I really want to do is ask my mother if she understands why Shelly killed herself, but out of a rush of love for her, I don't ask for anything.

My mother sits on the bed. She winds the scarf around her hand as if she's binding it. "I miss her, too. It's very difficult without my pills. I have a sharp pain that never goes away. Sometimes I can't catch my breath, it hurts so much. Before it was a dull ache, as if I was living under water. Seems I've surfaced. The world's not murky anymore, but living in it, as you say, 'sucks.'" I sit down next to her. She wraps the scarf through my hair. "Collette can trim this if you want. For your first day."

I shake my head. "I just got it cut. I let Freddie do it."

She holds up the ends. "I thought maybe Collette could fix it up." I'm aware of my mother's hands on my shoulders, the pull of her fingers on my collar, the tickle of her nail on my neck. I feel every inch of her touch, which is tentative at first, but then grows stronger, more possessive.

I let her play with my hair. I look up. She draws back and lets her hands drop. I take them in my own and squeeze. "I'll miss you, Mom," I tell her.

"You will?" I nod. We sit for a few seconds, eyes forward, not speaking, but not in such a hurry to leave, either. I kick my heels beneath me, like a girl, like a daughter. Finally, she speaks. "The picture of your father made me laugh. Sometimes he can be a funny man, don't you think?"

I take the scarf off my head. "Sometimes." It's the only thing I can think of to say.

Abby and I agree to meet at a diner. When I get there, she rises from the booth and hugs me. I hug her, too, but hold back a little.

"You look great," she tells me. "I can't believe how much weight you've lost."

"I haven't been trying. I just don't seem to have an appetite lately."

"Are you okay?" she asks tentatively, searching my face.

I nod. "I'm fine. It's not like that. I've just been busy." I tell her about my new job and the home and seeing Bryan.

"You saw him!" she screeches. "OHMYGOD. How did he look?"

"Not so good. But the funny part is that I started to run away from him, like really run. He had to chase me. I was practically down the street."

"You go, girl!" she says. As we laugh, it feels good to see her. She looks beautiful, as usual, and I tell her so. "Thanks," she says, suddenly self-conscious. "I'm still seeing the midget. He wants to take me to Bermuda." Then she launches into a long story about Randy and how they broke up for a while, but now she thinks they're ready to make a commitment, maybe get engaged. "But what if we have short kids?" she rambles. "What if they all grow up with Napoleon complexes?"

I start to feel edgy, and try to tell her about the things I've learned about Shelly, about the story I read, but Abby keeps cutting me off. I hold in my anger and completely stop listening. I shift in my seat and signal for the waiter. I never should have done this, I think. She's the same.

Suddenly, I can't help myself and blurt out, "I can't believe how fucking selfish you are! I'm trying to talk to you about Shelly. Shelly, my sister. What is *wrong* with you?"

She looks at her hands. I see a tear fall. Slowly, I realize that maybe she's upset about Shelly, too, that maybe she also lost a friend. "I'm sorry, Abby. I didn't mean that."

"No, you're right. You're so right. It's just ... just that ..." She can't talk because she's sobbing so I hold her hand and let her cry. She blows her nose. "I don't know how to deal with it, Frannie. Shelly was your sister, I understand that, but I also grew up with her. I—"

"I know," I cut her off. "She was your friend, too. And I never once asked you how you felt. I never cared how much *you* hurt. I can't take that back, Ab, but I can listen now." I pause. "Please forgive me for being such a bitch. It was a Sister Thing." She looks at me blankly.

I explain, "It's something you can't define. Like when you're cruel to the people you love the most, but you don't know why."

"Maybe you're cruel because you think they'll always be there." Abby wipes her tears. "When Shelly got sick, I felt so helpless. I couldn't help her, and then I couldn't help you. I felt like I was the worst friend in the world. To both of you."

"But you're not. You stuck by me the whole time. You took a lot of shit. You're my best friend, Abby. You always have been. There will never be another you in my life."

She waves me away, but not before holding my gaze for a long moment. In her eyes, wet with tears, I see everything I've missed. "It's so good to see you," she whispers. Then she changes the subject. "So what do you think, Frannie? Should I go to Bermuda with him?" I nod, smiling. "If it makes you happy, Abby, then go. You deserve to be happy."

"It's a free trip. Frankly, I knew he'd come around. He said he didn't want to lose me." She smiles sheepishly. "You blame him?"

When Bryan calls, I agree to meet him for a drink. I drive Shelly's car into the city and park on the street.

"Thanks for meeting me," he says when I walk in. "I wasn't sure if you'd show up."

"I wasn't sure if I would, either," I tell him honestly. We order drinks, then sit for a while and talk about nothing. I suck my drink quickly. I chewed a Valium on the ride over and the drink warms my stomach. "It hasn't been easy," I tell him, referring to everything.

"Losing a sibling has got to be painful. The grieving process can take a long time. Even when you think you're better, it can hit you again like a ton of bricks."

"You have sisters or brothers?"

He nods. "One brother."

"Are you close to him?"

"Close enough."

"Huh." I signal the waiter for another drink. "I've been thinking a lot about Shelly. I mean, about her life." I pick at the lime in my glass. "I was wondering if there was anything you could tell me about Shelly? I mean, something that may help me to understand why she kill … why what happened happened?"

"I read her chart. I don't think there was anything in it that could give you any more answers than any of us have. From a clinical perspective, she was still depressed, but the doctors who treated her believed she was stable and ready to leave. If I'd been her doctor, I would have done the same thing."

The waiter brings us fresh drinks. I watch Bryan as he hands him some bills. "But was there anything in her chart about a specific event that may have happened a long time ago?"

"Nothing specific. Only that she had problems with intimacy, with sexual relationships." I can't tell if he's lying or not, but I let it go. "Frannie," he starts, "when something tragic happens, it's normal to try to pinpoint one event or one reason to help you make sense of it. But in situations like Shelly's, there's rarely one reason; it's much more complex than that, and you can go crazy trying to figure it out. Don't do that to yourself."

"I'm already crazy." I feel the liquor and the Valium kick in and my head starts to buzz. When I scratch it, the buzzing increases. I take another gulp.

Bryan takes my hand. "I don't think you're crazy," he says slowly. "I think you're very beautiful."

I wrench my hand away and try to stand up on my Jell-O legs. "I don't think this is such a good idea," I tell him.

"Wait, please. Don't go." He reaches over and his T-shirt sleeve hikes up. His arm is muscular and hard. It would feel nice to have his arms around me. Really nice. And he's so handsome, with those sexy, sexy dark black eyes. Woozy, I sit back down. I want to slide to the floor into a puddle of myself. I clutch the edge of the table for support.

"Want another?" He points to my glass.

"One more and I won't be able to get myself home." I giggle and Bryan grins. "I'll be happy to take you home."

I consider it, feeling myself slip away. "I live out in Long Island. It's a long drive."

"I didn't mean to *your* house."

"Oh. Well."

Bryan leans over. "I know I fucked up the first time," he whispers, "but give me another chance." His face is against mine, so close I can feel the warmth of his mouth. He trails my arm with his finger. "Come home with me, Frannie." I smooth his hair away from his face. It's soft, like baby hair. Aching, I sit up. I can't hear anything except the rush in my head. I run my finger down my arm to feel what Bryan felt when he touched me.

I wonder if he's telling the truth; if this is a new beginning; if he'll call me every day just to say hi; if he'll want to be my boyfriend; if he'll turn to me one day when we're in the kitchen and tell me that he loves me; if, when he says it, he'll mean it.

Bryan looks at me. "Do you want to?" he asks softly. When he smiles at me, I feel the ache of desire. I imagine us in bed, his body covering mine, his hands on my face, on my neck, whispering sweet things in the dark. I imagine my legs wrapped around him, letting him inside me, so deeply inside he becomes part of me.

I grab my backpack. "No needles?"

He shakes his head. "No needles."

Back at his apartment, I lie on the couch. "You can stay over if you want," Bryan tells me, holding my head in his lap, playing with my hair.

"I have to be somewhere tomorrow," I say. "I have my car here." I hear myself refer to Shelly's car as *mine*. I called it *my* car. I feel a slight chill, the faint stirring of a memory fading.

"It's up to you." Holding my chin, Bryan pushes my bottom lip with his thumb. "I love your mouth," he says quietly. "When you're excited, your lower lip trembles. It's unbelievably erotic." He leans over and kisses me, a long soulful kiss, and I reach up and put my arms around him and kiss him back for what seems like forever.

He runs his hands over my breasts, caresses me as if I'm the most beautiful woman in the world. I'm with him at first. When he tells me how good he feels, how much he's wanted this, I feel myself ache for the moment he'll be inside me. He rips open a condom package with his teeth and puts on the condom with one hand, murmuring how good this will be, just wait, Frannie, he says, just wait. But when he moves inside me and we find a rhythm, he stops talking. And something inside me shifts.

He hangs over me, his eyes glazed, his mouth open, as if unaware I'm beneath him. I get cold. In my head, I see him slide the needle into my arm, toss the tube with my blood as if it were a dirty tissue, snap off the light and roll over. Completely disengaged now, I watch the top of his head as he bends it to lick my breasts, and for a split second, he's a teenage boy, bony and clumsy, laughing as he sticks his fingers inside me. I clutch the sheets. Get the fuck OFF me, I scream silently. Get OFF. Then I lose all my thoughts as he trembles and jerks and comes in spasms inside me. Finally, I push him away, feeling dirty and empty, and absolutely alone.

I gather my clothes. "I have to go," I tell him, my voice edged with rage. He nestles my head against his shoulder and tells me how great it was, how good it felt, how much he wants to do it again. "I'll call you," he tells me. "I'll call you."

Later, when I'm alone in my bed, I wrap my arms around a pillow and hold it against my chest. When we were kids, Shelly would climb in my bed and we'd describe the husbands we'd have and what our marriages would be like.

"Do you think we'll end up like Mommy and Daddy?" Shelly asked. "Will we sit across from our husbands at dinner with nothing to say?" And I was so sure back then, so positive that we'd never end up like them, that I said no way. "Our husbands will be rich and famous. They'll treat us like queens."

"But I don't want someone rich and famous," she said. "I just want someone to talk to." At the time, I thought she was so stupid, that at eight years old, she'd already given up.

My fingers smell of sex, even though I washed them. I run them through my curls, slowly, tenderly, as if they are Bryan's. I feel so lonely. I am reminded of the way I felt with the original Rat Boy in my junior year at Syracuse. He was a poet—pale and scrawny with underdeveloped arms, a blurry tattoo of Zeus on his bicep, watery brown eyes, and a face like a rat (hence the name). He was in graduate school so he was older than me and I thought he was the most romantic boy I'd ever met. He talked about Kant, Nietzsche, and Kierkegaard, people I'd never heard of. He was so smart, he didn't think modern art looks like Spirograph, he understood things about the world. And he wanted to fuck *me*. I was spellbound.

He told me he didn't want a relationship, that he didn't have those types of feelings for me. Deeply wounded, I was incapable of speech. But the more he said it, the more I craved him. I fantasized about him; I waited for the phone to ring; I was constantly irritable, moody, and depressed. But I couldn't help myself. I wanted him to want me, I wanted to be the love of his life, I wanted to be the one woman he couldn't live without.

Instead, I became his beck-and-call girl. Whenever he wanted to see me, I'd be there, even if it meant skipping classes or breaking plans. He took other girls out for dinner, then called me just to have sex. Sometimes he'd show up in the middle of the night, come over, fuck me, then ignore me the next day. Of all the things Rat Boy did, his refusal to acknowledge me in public—like I was a dirty, shameful secret—was the worst.

After a few months, I started to notice things about him. He talked about himself all the time, he wasn't particularly insightful, he was really insecure, and, I'm no expert, but I'd heard better poetry from Bazooka Joe. Also, despite the fact that I moaned when he touched me, Rat Boy was a *terrible* lover, even for a twenty-five-year-old. He tweaked my nipples like a kid, flattened my breasts like pancakes, and rubbed my body as if he were using it to wipe his hands. He wanted to tie me up, slather me in oil, get me down on all fours. He had a habit of pulling out just as he was about to come. It was frustrating, God, it was frustrating. At first I thought it was some technique he'd misunderstood in *Playboy*. After a few *very* disappointing encounters, I asked him what he was doing. He said he was *preserving his chi*.

"It's not good to spill my chi," he told me, "my seed. You know, like a boxer. Boxers can't fuck before a fight because they have to stay focused. I need to do the same thing for my Art."

At first I thought he was kidding but when I realized he was serious, rage grew inside me, crystal-clear and voracious. Not only was this guy the lousiest lover I'd ever had, but he actually believed he was Michel-fucking-angelo. GET OVER YOURSELF, I wanted to howl. YOU ARE A FUCKING JOKE. Instead, I faked an orgasm, and made him feel like he had the biggest dick on the planet.

I cringe, thinking of Rat Boy. I still hate myself for that, especially since I had no right to be angry. I had a choice. He didn't force himself on me. All I had to do was say no, but I didn't. I didn't say anything.

As I lie in bed, haunted by my lack of voice, I think about Rat Boy, Bryan, and Shelly, and slowly, slowly, I make a connection. "Shelly," I tell her—or maybe it's myself I'm telling—"I understand now. Whether your story is true or not doesn't matter. What's true is Hannah, the girl in the story, and the feelings she had about herself; her need to have a voice and her inability to find it."

I get an itchy feeling between my legs, as if Bryan's fingers, or Rat Boy's fingers, or all the fingers of all the guys I've fucked, are poking me. I scratch myself until I'm raw and bleeding, until I can feel pieces of my flesh underneath my fingernails. I jab myself with my thumbnail so hard it hurts. I want to yank my cunt right out of my body so that I can't use it anymore to damage myself.

I turn over. My vagina aches. To soothe it, I wet my fingers and softly stroke myself. "I'm sorry," I tell myself, and softly cup my hands. My pubic hair is matted and wet. I continue to stroke myself until I tingle, until I can't stop, until it feels so good, I close my eyes and the tingles become ripples and the ripples become waves, and the waves keep coming and coming and flood me with delicious heat, delivering me, gasping, all the way home. When it's over, I'm pulsating with warmth and exhaustion. Then, as if it will help me to sleep without sorrow, I put my fingers in my mouth and suck them like I'm a little girl.

19

Y*our mother called," my dad tells me at breakfast a few days later.* "She wants you to call her. Frannie? I'm talking to you."

"I heard you." For something new and different, I'm depressed. Bryan didn't call me. Deep down, I knew he wouldn't call, but it would have been nice. I can't fucking believe he's in my head again.

I find the wedding announcements in the *New York Times* and pick out a husband. After discarding Blake Harrison Tweeter, Schlomo Blatstein, and Reginald Lloyd III, I find him. The dark and swarthy Pepe Alvarez Mantilla Garcia. Bond trader. Harvard undergrad. Wharton grad. Father a diplomat, grandfather a Spanish politician.

"You want some eggs?" My father pulls out a frying pan. "I have Havarti and chives." I shake my head. There's a piece of unbuttered toast on my plate. "You ate already?"

The interrogation has begun. He's been on my back to eat for the past few months, and I keep telling him I'm not trying to lose weight. I'm just not hungry. Especially the past few days, after fucking Bryan. I just don't have an appetite. Studying Pepe Alvarez Mantilla Garcia, I imagine my own wedding announcement.

Frannie Hunter graduated from Syracuse University prepared to do absolutely nothing, which she now does with aplomb. Her estranged parents, Marsha Swartzberg Hunter, real estate agent, and David Hunter, giftware salesman extraordinaire, give kudos to the Garcia clan for finally moving her out of their home. Since the Hunters are footing the bill, the couple will honeymoon in Frannie's bedroom and take a weekend trip to the Poconos Twinkle Lake Motel. Donations for the wedding may be sent to the Jewish Home in Lindsey Point, where the reception is being held, c/o Max Swartzberg, wedding coordinator and menu adviser. Frannie's dress will be a Donna Karan knock-off discovered in a fit of panic in the Back Room at Loehmann's. Invitations by Collette. Hair by Freddie.

My father cracks two eggs over a bowl and throws the shells into the sink. He turns on the burner and spoons margarine into the pan. "This is your brain," he mutters. Then he pours on the runny egg mix. "And this is your brain on drugs." The eggs sizzle as they hit the heat. I look at my father and try to imagine the honorable Juan Alvarez Mantilla Garcia, Pepe's padre, cooking eggs. "You want some, Frannie?"

"You asked me already. I said no."

"Okey-dokey." He bustles through the kitchen like Donna Reed. He arranges his silverware, pours juice and a mega mug of coffee, and places margarine and three jelly jars on the table. He sticks two pieces of bread in the toaster and glances at me. "Toast?"

"No, Daddy." I lie. "I ate already. I have to meet Abby. We're going shopping." I ignore the growling in my stomach. I like my hunger, the emptiness. "Daddy?" I ask as he settles down with his eggs. "Do you think I'll ever get married?"

He looks down at the paper. "If you put your mind to it, of course you will."

"But what if I never find the right person? What if I'm alone forever?" I tug on his sleeve. "Daddy, what if I die a virgin?" I try not to laugh as he gulps his coffee. I hear it gurgle in his throat. Finally he says, "Frannie, you worry too much. You'll meet someone when you least expect it. You can't look for love."

"How can you say that? You put in a personal ad!"

He doesn't answer. With the edge of his knife, he slowly cuts his toast into four perfect squares and spreads them with jelly. The sound of his scraping drives me mad. I fold the paper and get up from the table. "See ya, Daddy."

"Frannie, wait." He chews thoughtfully, swallows dramatically. "I've shared your situation in group." He looks up. "Love, people said, is locational. You can't expect the boys to come to you. Go where the boys are." He chuckles. "Location, location, location." Fatherly wisdom imparted, he stretches with a flourish and hunches over his paper.

I try not to think about Bryan, but I can't shake him. It's like Rat Boy all over again. I know he's wrong for me. I mean, I don't even like the guy, but once again, he's lodged in my head like a tumor. I can't believe I fucked him. I simply can't believe it.

"I can't, either," Abby says in the car on the way to the mall. "What the hell were you thinking?"

"I just thought it might work out, you know, we could start over."

"You start over with a drink and a good-night kiss. You don't start over in bed. You know that better than anyone."

"Since when did you join the Moral Majority? You're like the biggest slut I know."

She sneers. "I'm *trying* to give you advice, Frannie. And I'm a reformed slut. And now I'm allowed to be self-righteous."

"Well, keep it to yourself. I liked you much more when you'd fuck anyone."

An hour later, she studies me in front of a three-way mirror at Ann Taylor as I try on suits for my first day of work. "I don't know. It hangs wrong." She hands me another one. "Here, try this."

In the dressing room, I take off my clothes and stare at myself in the mirror. I see a girl in a black bra and faded underwear. I focus on the underwear so I don't have to see the body. Reluctantly, I look up. The girl in the mirror traces her ribs, which are visible underneath the tight skin. Her flat stomach moves in and out with the rhythm of breathing. Her waist is pinched, her hips stick out like knobs, and her calves are thin with a muscle the size of an orange. The girl in the mirror is skinny, but she's not me. I feel a current of anxiety work its way through my system as I stare at this stranger. I realize that the girl is smiling mischievously, like she has a secret.

I take off my bra and underwear and stare at the naked body. I cup the little breasts, arch the back. *You are so beautiful.* Bryan's voice echoes in my head like a call down a canyon. I trace the leg, marveling at the long taut muscle. I feel myself floating. As I stroke the stomach, it rumbles, soothing me like the rocking of waves. My heart races and I feel a glimmer of glee. I'm skinny. This is me. Ha. This is my body. My hunger lifts me. My head rushes as if from a strong drunk and I feel myself reeling. My thoughts collide. I can get thinner, I think, even thinner, I can cut it all off, I can wear low-slung Levi's and cropped tops and long, straight dresses like willowy models, and I gasp with the breathlessness of being airborne.

Then I look up. The girl in the mirror kneads her skin, detached, as if her hands don't belong to her. I suddenly see Shelly, skeletal and ashen, dead in a hospital bed. I glance away. When I look back, I see myself, me, Frannie, staring, wide-eyed with terror.

I dress quickly, but the girl's eyes, my eyes, haunt me. I back-track through the past few months, wondering when I got so skinny. I've been lonely, I tell myself, I've been depressed. I look again at the girl in the mirror. I promise myself that I will make her go away, but that moment of taking flight, that easy freedom, lingers like a sweet tang on my tongue. "Jesus, Shelly," I say out loud. "I never realized just how easy it was."

I don't notice the wrapped gift until I am on the highway. I can't open it because I have to fumble with change for the toll, so I slide it into my new portfolio. I'm on my way to my new job. To work. Heigh-Ho, Heigh-Ho. I try to whistle, but all I get is a spray of saliva.

I open the present before I go upstairs. I laugh when I see my father's face. It's a Glamour Shot. In the picture, he's wearing a sailor's uniform, complete with epaulets and a row of medals across the right breast. He's saluting. I open the card.

Ahoy from your loving Captain. Good luck on your first day. Love, Dad.

The fun never ends. And in five short days, I'll be forced to deal with this face-to-face. My father informed me that he has a date with Eleanor, the pistol-packin' mama looking for a rootin'-tootin' good time. He wants me to meet her for a drink. Get to know her. I can't get a date to save my life and my father's already *involved*. I get into the elevator. I can't believe my father's dating. And I can't believe Bryan hasn't called.

"Vicky isn't here yet," the receptionist says. "Would you like a cup of coffee?"

"No," I say, thanking her.

Minutes later, Vicky strolls in wearing a gorgeous burgundy suit. "You're here!" We walk through the office and I trail behind and look around.

Rows of offices line the outer corridor, all of which have windows overlooking 47th Street. Outside every two offices is a secretary's desk. The inner offices are smaller, but they're just as nice. They have desks and chairs, lamps and pictures. I remember the scene in *Working Girl* when Melanie Griffith unknowingly sits in her secretary's desk. Not wanting to make the same mistake, I continue standing, clutching my portfolio.

"This is you," Vicky says. She has her hands on the small desk outside her office. It's a secretary's desk, complete with computer terminal, typewriter, and telephone. On the front of the desk is a nameplate with FRANNIE HUNTER written on it.

"This is so great," I say, "I can't believe that's my name." I try not to be disappointed. I know it's unrealistic to think that I'd have my own office, but I can't help being upset. I keep comparing my life to Bryan's. He's a *doctor*, he saves lives, and I am a fucking secretary. Of course he didn't call me. Why should he? I'm a nothing.

"Relax a few minutes, then come into my office. And lock up your purse. Even though everyone's friendly, this *is* New York."

She walks into her office and picks up the phone. I take out the picture of my father and prop it up next to my computer. His smile embarrasses me, so I turn it over and put a coffee mug on top. I stroke the phone with my fingertip. Abby called this morning to wish me good luck. "Call me the minute you can," she said. "I want to hear everything about everything." I notice a headset hooked over the computer keypad. "Figures," I mutter. I take a deep breath and put the headset on as a tear slides down my cheek.

I take out my phone book. After debating five long minutes whether to call Bryan, I put the book away. I can't stop thinking about him. Why does this always happen? And why does it make me so upset? A few days ago, *I* was the one who could have cared less. Now *I* am the one crying. Strangely enough, the only person I feel like talking to is Chubby. Go figure.

I walk into Vicky's office with a legal pad and sit down.

"Hi, Fran. Hold on a second." Vicky finishes up a phone conversation and hangs up. "We have a meeting tomorrow at the Reggie's in Parsippany. They want us to do a Labor Day promotion. They should have called in May, but here it is August and they expect me to work miracles." She looks up. "Thank God you're here. I don't know what I would've done if you hadn't taken this job." She smiles at me, but I don't smile back. She's gushing and her effusiveness makes me nervous.

"What would you have done?" I ask.

"Probably freelanced the job out. Why?"

I take a deep breath. "It just seems that this is too good to be true. Why would you hire someone with my track record? You saw my résumé."

"I thought you had spunk. You also came highly recommended."

"From who?"

"Paul DiMartino. We worked together ten years ago. In fact," she says slowly, watching me, "he was my first husband."

"Paulie? You were married to Paulie?"

Vicky nods. "We met at the Reggie's in Weehauken. He was a bartender and I was a cocktail waitress. We had a child together. A little boy." She pauses. "Tommy, our son, died when he was only a few months old. After a year, I went to business school. Then Paul and I started to fight and, eventually, our marriage fell apart. We're friends now, though."

"I don't know what to say. I'm so sorry. It must have been so painful."

"It was the worst thing that ever happened to me. I still love Paul and I suppose he loves me, but he's married to Tina and we each have our own lives."

"I don't think things are going so well with her." I don't know if this is appropriate, but I want to say something to let her know how sorry I feel. I'm struck by how awful it is to have to comfort someone like this. Everything seems so trite.

Vicky tells me that Tina's trying to get pregnant, but can't. "He calls me sometimes to talk. Anyway, he knew I was looking for an assistant and recommended you. He adores you, despite your track record, or if I know Paul, because of it."

"Why didn't he say anything to me?"

"For several reasons. One was that he wanted you to feel as though you were doing it on your own."

"So," I say quietly, "everything you told me was bullshit."

She shakes her head. "No, I said that was *one* of the reasons. Paul was going to tell you, but you weren't working at Rascals when he first got the idea. When you didn't return my calls, I made an offer to someone else. She turned it down and Paul suggested I call you again. He told me about Shelly and how difficult losing her was for you, something we both are painfully familiar with, and he decided to let things work out—or not—without getting involved. When I finally met you, I thought you were terrific. I was happy, you seemed happy, and the sequence of events that got us there didn't make a difference."

"But it does make a difference. I feel like you hired me because you felt sorry for me."

"You're not listening, Frannie. You *did* do this on your own. Paul just gave you a push. And the truth is, waitresses are rarely promoted into management. Paul wanted to keep it quiet for that reason as well. I told you during the interview that you made quite an impression. That was the truth, Frannie. You have to trust me on this."

I did trust you, I want to say. This was so much easier when I thought she was just some beautiful woman I wanted to look like. "I never realized about Paulie," I tell her. I want to haul my ass to a phone right now and tell him how great he is. For a long and sad moment, I wish I was back at Rascals.

"You didn't know." She pauses. "Frannie, you never know where people come from. Everyone has a story, and a lot of those stories are very painful." Then she tells me that my desk is only temporary. "Regina is moving upstairs. I want you to move into her office. Then Sue will move to your desk so we can both be close to her. It might take a few months, but it'll happen."

"That's great," I say. "Thanks a lot. I'm just happy to be here." I stare at the floor, feeling very naive. I keep having to relearn everything, and it seems like I'll never catch up.

I wonder if this is what Shelly was feeling in St. Mary's or back at Cornell, or even before that, in junior high. There are so many choices, but each choice has an overwhelming number of implications. It occurs to me as I force myself to forget about Paulie and his dead little boy and pay attention to a job that I can't afford to lose, that Shelly must have been scared as hell of growing up.

"Okay, what about this?" My father walks into my room wearing a camel's hair jacket, a forest-green shirt, and a red tie.

"It's ninety-five degrees out, Daddy. You can't wear that jacket. And lose the tie."

He comes back a few minutes later wearing a green linen blazer and a pale green tie.

"You look like the Jolly Green Giant, Dad. What is with you?"

"I don't know what to wear, goddammit, and Eleanor's going to be here in fifteen minutes." He looks tired and frustrated. "I just want tonight to be special. I made drinks and hors d'oeuvres. Then we're going to the Rainbow Room and back to her place, and—"

"Whoa, big guy," I cut him off. "Keep the festivities to yourself. Come on, we'll find you an outfit." I search through his closet until I find a tailored navy blazer, a white shirt, and an old rep tie. I hand them to him, but he shakes his head.

"I'm not wearing that shirt or that tie. I want something with pizzazz." When he takes out a yellow tie with pink flamingos to go with his green shirt, I excuse myself to get dressed.

I'm having drinks with my father and Eleanor, then I'm going to the home to eat dinner with my grandfather. Abby and Randy are in Bermuda so they're not around to hang out with, but I'm exhausted from my first week at work and looking forward to something sedate. It's nice to be exhausted at five after being somewhere other than my bed.

In the bathroom downstairs, I'm suddenly stricken with nausea. I can't believe my father is going on a date. I crouch on the bathroom floor and lean over the toilet. My father walks in on me. "What the hell are you doing?" he accuses me. He sounds frightened. "Are you sick?" I shake my head and look into his eyes, which are wild with panic. "Are you making yourself throw up? Is that what you're doing? Frannie! Tell me the truth!"

"No, Daddy," I say softly. "I wouldn't do that. I promise."

"You've gotten so skinny, and you don't ever eat. I will not ... I can't ..." He looks away.

"Daddy, I promise. Don't think those things." His sudden concern touches me, and I put my hand on his arm, but he walks away. He takes a deep breath. "Frannie, I don't think I could survive if something happened to you."

My throat closes. "I'm fine, Daddy, I swear." I pat his shoulder and he sighs.

He looks at himself in the mirror. "I hate this tie. I look ridiculous." The doorbell rings. "Oh God. It's her."

"Get a hold of yourself, Daddy. You look very handsome tonight." I turn to open the door and mutter, "Let the games begin."

Expecting a young hot mama in thigh-high cutoffs, teething on hay, I'm surprised to see a short, stout woman wearing a yellow linen duster, a silk pantsuit, and sensible shoes standing in the doorway. She has a face like a fox and bright blue eyes that peer into the house. She smells like mothballs, which startles me. Eleanor looks old enough to be my father's mother or at least a great aunt. "You must be Frannie." She holds out her hands. "My gosh, you're pretty. I'm Eleanor. I've heard so much about you." I take her hand and usher her inside.

We sit in the den and pick at the oyster dip and the shrimp puffs my father whipped up this morning. I shove a glob of oyster dip into my mouth. I immediately gag from the fishy taste, spit out the cracker, and stuff a napkin in my mouth to make the oyster wang go away. Instead of relief, I am suffocated by wet paper.

Eleanor tells me she saw the picture of my father in the *Christian Times* and couldn't pass it up. "Did you see the picture?" she asks. I nod and gulp my wine.

"I never pictured him as much of a cowboy," I tell her, "but what do I know?" I try to relax. The taste of salty fish lingers in my mouth like the smell of dirty feet.

Eleanor smiles at my father. "I just thought it was the cutest thing, the way that hat just sat on his head. I just had to write him a letter. The next thing you know, we're having coffee." She leans forward. "I must tell you, Frannie. Your father is nothing like my husband, Walter, may he rest in peace. He'd never make jokes about himself."

I look at my father, who has cupped his hand over Eleanor's, and is leaning back with relish, listening to her talk about him. "How long were you and your husband married?" I ask. I have so many questions: her real age, for example; how her vital signs are holding up, but I hold back. I remember my mother asking Dylan McGuire why he wasn't going to college. She must have wanted to ask him so much more. I'm suddenly sad for my mother; sad that this is happening while she's in Tempe, that it has to happen at all.

"Walter and I were married for thirty-nine years. He had a myocardial infarction."

"A heart attack," my father interprets.

"That's right," Eleanor squeezes his hand. I study her lips. They're thin and her lipstick is smeared in the corner. I wonder if they kiss on the mouth. Stop it, Frannie, I tell myself. Don't go there. I hear my father chuckle as they study the Glamour Shots. I try to remember a time when he and my mother looked at pictures together and laughed, but can't.

"I better be going." I shake Eleanor's hand and tell her how nice it was to meet her.

"It was wonderful meeting you," she bubbles. "You are just darling." Slow down, Bessie, I want to say. This isn't the fucking Miss America Pageant.

"Be careful driving," my father says. "I'll call you tomorrow." I remember he has big plans for the evening. The sudden image of him lying in Eleanor's bed, sunlight streaming through the curtains as they cuddle, rocks me with a burst of rage.

My father walks me to the door. "I just want you to know …" he starts.

"I know, I know. This is only a date, you're not getting remarried, and you will always love Mommy. I know, Dad. You don't have to tell me."

He smiles. "Actually, Frannie. I was going to tell you that I think you're terrific."

When I walk into my grandfather's room, Charlie is sitting on Freddie's bed. "Hi, Madonna," he says and I ignore him.

"Vell," Freddie says. "You're here. Good. Now ve can eat."

I look at Charlie. "We're all having dinner? Together?"

Freddie hits me. "Of course ve're having dinner together. Vhat is wrong vit you?"

As we walk down the corridor, I hold on to my grandfather. His eyes are very watery, and the right one, the one with the cataract, stares off, glazed and idle, in the wrong direction. I wonder what he sees, if it's dark like being without lights or murky like being under water. One night, I tied a scarf around my eyes and tried to walk through my room. I couldn't go two steps without stubbing my toe. Ever since that night, I'm careful with my grandfather, making sure I call things out so he'll know what's ahead. It's not much, but it makes me feel better.

"Give Max to me." Freddie pushes me forward. "Charlie, you are Frannie's escort. Vhere are your manners? You vere raised by volves? It's no vonder you're all alone."

"I guess I'm your date, Chuck," I say to Charlie.

"Looks that way." He studies me, picking at his lip with his forefinger and thumb. His expression is hidden behind his hand. "Can I buy you a drink? A straight shot of tequila or how about Sex on the Beach? A Screaming Orgasm?"

I look into his eyes. "How about a Slow Comfortable Screw Up Against the Wall?" He raises his eyebrows and takes my arm. "What's the matter, Chuck? Cat got your tongue?"

He doesn't answer. Slowly, we walk arm-in-arm toward the dining room. Behind us, I hear Freddie's loud stage whisper, "Max, look at zat. Zey like vone another!"

Charlie holds my elbow. I glance at him just as he checks to see that the boys are okay behind us. Under his breath, I hear his faint humming and despite myself, I smile. He is serenading me with a slow rendition of "Like a Virgin."

"Ve need a toast," Freddie says, holding up a glass of wine. "To Frannie and Charlie."

"A toast," my grandfather echoes. "More wine for me, please." He holds out his glass for more wine.

"Grandpa," I say softly. "Take it easy."

"I take it easy all year. For one night, let me not take it so easy."

"So how is business?" Freddie asks Charlie. "Not so good, huh?"

"Business is great, Grandpa," Charlie tells him, stretching.

"So vhy should you vork so hard? Vhen business is good, you should be out vit girls." He glances at me. I turn my head slightly as if I'm not listening. "What's wrong vit you you're not married? Here's a beautiful single girl."

"So you're a lawyer?" I ask loudly.

"Sat's right," Freddie says proudly, smacking Charlie's shoulder. "Vent to Princeton. Top of his class."

"What do you do?" Charlie asks me, red-faced.

"She's a waitress," my grandfather says, just as proudly. "At Hooligans." He licks his lips, which are purple from the wine.

"Grandpa," I tell him softly, "I got a job, remember?" I look at Charlie. "I'm in promotions for a restaurant corporation."

There's a lull as we eat. I can feel Charlie watching me, but I don't look at him. I excuse myself to go to the ladies' room. As I get up, Freddie asks Charlie vhen he's goink to ask me on a date. I rush away.

I look at myself in the mirror and groan. My hair is all ratty. I can't even believe I care. I mean Charlie's nice I guess, but Jesus, he's, I don't know, he's just whatever. An elderly woman comes out of the stalls. She peers up at me. "The chicken is dry," she screeches. "I can't eat this garbage."

"Maybe they can give you cottage cheese."

"For what I pay I'll choke it down. You're Max's girl, right? That your boyfriend at the table?"

"No, that's Freddie's grandson."

"Is he married?" I shake my head and inch toward the door, trying to escape. "So what's wrong with him?" She lowers her voice. "He's a *faygeleh?*"

"I don't think so. I just met him, though, so I don't know for sure."

She puts her hand on her hip. "And you're hiding in here like a scared little rabbit? He's a handsome boy and he's *Jewish,* and from what Max says, you're not getting any younger."

"I'm only twenty-seven," I say meekly.

"Go out there," the old woman says. "It's not every day you're in a place like this, having supper with a nice Jewish boy." She nudges me. "Go!"

Location, my father said. I look around at the cracked linoleum floor, the steel bars along the walls, the wheelchairs lined up at the entrance to the dining room, and the smell of old age that covers everything like a blanket. Location, location, location.

I walk back to the table. Charlie hovers over our grandfathers, pouring them coffee. He is completely unselfconscious, as if he genuinely likes to do this. He leans forward to talk to Freddie, tilts his head back, and laughs. He suddenly looks so handsome, I can't catch my breath.

My grandfather is still drinking wine. "Grandpa," I say. "Maybe you've had enough." Drowsy, he mutters, and lets his eyes close. Quickly, as if he's startled, they flutter open. "How about a nap?" I ask him softly.

"Come on, Maxwell, my man." Charlie gets up from his seat. "Let me help you home."

I move toward my grandfather. "I've got him," I tell Charlie.

"No, it's okay. You sit with Grandpa Fred. Let him grill *you* for a while about your marriage plans."

"Call me a cab," my grandfather whines, holding his head.

"You're a cab," Freddie says. "Und you're a gut-for-nottin drunk cab, you old man. Now get to bed." When we're alone, he turns to me. "So, vhat do you tink?"

"I thought it was good. The chicken was a little dry, but I'd come back."

He isn't amused. "Sat's not vhat I mean. Vhy do you play games? I'm an old man."

I shrug. "Okay. Charlie's very nice. I like him. Why? Did he say something?" Freddie shrugs, but he smiles coyly. "What, Freddie? What did he say?"

"Max is fine," Charlie says, returning to the table. "He's out like a light."

We all get up. "I'd better be going," I tell them.

"No, Frannie," Freddie says. "It's Shabbos. Zey have dancing."

"You can't leave yet, Madonna," Charlie whispers. "Give him one dance. You're all he talks about."

In the auditorium, chairs and tables have been pushed to the sides to make room for a dance floor. The lighting is dim and the music is extremely loud like at a heavy metal concert. The score from *Fiddler on the Roof* is playing. Women in wheelchairs line up around the dance floor, clapping their hands to the music. Not one of them claps in time to the beat, most of them can't even get their hands to connect. Out on the dance floor, four or five women waltz with each other, their movements jerky and uncoordinated. A lone old man stands in the middle of the dance floor as three women sway around him. My eyes fill with tears as I walk inside.

"Excuse me." Charlie walks to the dance floor. He takes one of the women in his arms, waltzes her slowly across the floor. All the other women giggle.

"Shall ve?" Freddie holds out his arms. "Get me now before ze vultures do." He puts his arms around me and we waltz clumsily across the small wooden dance floor. I nestle my neck in the crook of his shoulder. He smells like roast chicken and sweet purple wine.

"May I cut in?"

Freddie releases me too quickly, and I stumble toward Charlie. I try to get my balance, but I trip first over his foot, then over my own. "Great moves there, Madonna," he says, laughing.

"You think you're so great, don't you?" I blurt out.

"Yeah, don't you?" He pulls me toward him. As we move together, I slowly relax. He reaches down and pulls my arms around his neck. He's stocky and sturdy and great to hug. I reach up and run my hands through his hair. Horrified, I pull back. "It's okay," he says softly. "It's clean. My grandfather made sure I was all decked out just for you."

Across the room, I see the woman from the bathroom. Her little body sways to the music, her hands clasped in front of her. She waves at me with a scarf like I'm on the deck of a steamer and she's seeing me off. "Who's that?" Charlie asks.

"A fan." I wish my grandfather was awake. It would make him happy to see me dancing. Charlie pulls me close, his hand pressed against my back. As he waltzes me slowly across the floor, I feel weightless and luminous and rich with youth. I hear the clomp of a cane, but with my eyes closed, I imagine it is something else, far away. The lights in the auditorium are pretty. In fact, if I close one eye and squint through the other, I can pretend I'm on a beach in the South Pacific, being held very close by someone I love. So I do it. And as we sway with the magical rhythm of an unspoken connection, I feel like I'm finally moving to a place I've never been.

20

F*rannie." My father walks into my room. "The mail's here. Abby* sent a postcard."

In my closet, I finger an orange jacket, wondering what possessed me to purchase such a heinous color. "What does it say?"

"I didn't read it. How was last night?"

"Fine. Good, actually." Charlie walked me to my car. We hugged awkwardly. "I'll call you sometime, Madonna," he said. Famous last words. My father stands with his hands jammed into his pockets. "How was your date?" I ask. "The Rainbow Room?"

He shrugs. "We didn't make it there." He looks down, as if embarrassed. "We started talking and filled up on that oyster dip. That dip was good, wasn't it?"

"Delicious. I can still taste it." His hair is matted and his eyes are puffy. "Daddy, is something wrong?" He shakes his head. Then he tells me in a sad, somber voice that he can see I'm busy so he'll leave me alone. "You want to have dinner with me one night?" he asks.

"Sure. Eleanor too?"

He shakes his head. "I don't think I'll be seeing Eleanor anymore," he says. "I like her. I like her very much. She's very smart. I just don't think I'm ready for the kind of relationship she's looking for. She's a bit ... intense."

I look at him. I can't fucking believe this. My dad can't commit. I can see it now. He'll father hundreds of babies who won't know him, he'll be hit with paternity suits, he'll beg me for refuge from teenage girls with big bellies. "Daddy," I say slowly, "you've been married a long time. It's not easy to jump into a new relationship when you're still working out an old one. Maybe this separation just proves that you and Mommy are meant to be together."

"Has she said anything to you?"

"Mommy's been in Tempe, Daddy," I say, cringing at the sound of his voice. "We really haven't discussed it."

"Oh." When he walks away, I notice he's limping. "What's wrong with your leg?"

"Nothing. Just old age." He lingers in my doorway, reaches down, and absently rubs his calf. After a while, he stands for a very long moment and stares ahead at Shelly's bedroom.

On the front of Abby's postcard is a naked woman with long blond hair buried in sand up to her waist. Across her bare tits is the message *Greetings From Bermuda*. Her erect nipples look like pink pencil erasers. I turn the card over:

Some beach in Bermuda—Hell on Earth

Frannie:

    Been here three days and can't wait to leave. This place is for honeymooners and Texans. Randy is on my nerves in a big way. We're breaking up when we get home, but I don't want to tell him here 'cause he already sunk a grand into this trip. I'm not ready for a big commitment. I miss being a slut (like you). C'est la vie. (That's French for "another one bites the dust.") I'd call you, but Randy's already pissed that I ordered room service ($37 for Diet Cokes and chips. Who knew?). I know you're lonely without me, but I'll be home soon.

    The weather is here, wish you were beautiful.

Love and kisses,
Your Spinster Friend

    P.S. That's me on the front. I colored my hair. Maybe blonds do have more fun. Check out those nips. Vavavoom!!

I grab two suits to take to the cleaner's, bills to mail, shoes to reheel, and a *Glamour* magazine that has the article "Thinner Thighs in Thirty Days" that I plan to read to my grandfather and Freddie this afternoon by the pool. I throw everything into the car and drive off. Instead of feeling invigorated by an entire August weekend, I feel frustrated at having to do everything by myself all the time.

When I get home, my father is watching television in the den. All the lights are off and the curtains are drawn. "Daddy?" I call out softly. "Is something wrong?"

"No."

"You want to go to the supermarket with me? I need to get some things." He shakes his head and I snap on the light. "You can't just sit here, Daddy. You have to get out."

"Let's just go tomorrow, okay? I don't feel like going tonight. By the way, Mommy left a message on the machine," he says sadly. "She wants you to call her."

"Is that why you're upset?"

He shrugs. I glance over his shoulder at Shelly's graduation picture. I look back at my father, hunched forward, shoulders drawn, and I want to cry. This is all your fault, I scream at Shelly in my head. This is all because of YOU! She stares at me, her eyes fixated on something in the distance. I walk over to the mantel and take her picture down. I want to smack her smug expression off her face.

"Hey!" my father calls out. "Where are you going with that?"

"I'm just moving it."

Alone upstairs, I open Shelly's bedroom door and peer inside. Everything looks the same. Her furniture is pushed against the wall, her bed is made, luggage is piled in the corner. A lamp sits without a shade. I put her picture on her dresser. I can't look at her bed, so I sit on the floor in the closet and slowly open a box marked *Hospital.*

I pull out a few bras, some T-shirts, and four pairs of black leggings—all size one. My sister's shrunken face burns on my retina as if she has appeared in the room and then vanished. I shake out a T-shirt. LINDSEY POINT 10K RUN. I ball up the shirt and stuff it back into the box. I spy Shelly's yellow bumblebee coat pushed to the back of the closet. I pull the coat down and also stuff it into the box.

I think of my family and how unhappy we are. My mother's alone in a pathetic apartment, my father's alone in this ugly, old house, my blind grandfather is living in an old-age home, and I'm still stuck in my little twin bed. I can't believe how unfair this is. Maybe things weren't perfect before Shelly died, maybe we had problems, but sometimes we laughed. Sometimes we even had fun.

I hold up my sister's leggings again. They look like they were made for a little girl, not a grown woman who goes to college, works for a man who worships her, and could have gone to Harvard Law. HOW COULD YOU DO THIS TO US? I pull on the leggings, trying to rip them, but they won't tear. I hold up a leg and gnaw on it until I finally make a hole. Then I shred it into little strips. I'm sweating and panting, but I pick up another pair and gnaw on the crotch until I have a hole big enough to rip. I grunt like a big, fat pig. My gums bleed from the friction of the fabric and I tear my cuticles, but I keep ripping my sister's leggings until I have ragged pieces of black fabric piled by my feet.

When I'm done, I lie down in my sister's bed and smear her pillow with the blood from my mouth and fingers. I bury my nose in the pillow, and missing her, I cry myself to sleep.

"Are you coming with me to the supermarket?" I ask my father the next morning at breakfast.

"I guess. What were you doing in your sister's room?"

"Nothing, just cleaning up." I rub my mouth where my gums ache. When I got up this morning, I was startled to find myself in Shelly's bed. But when I began to get spooked, I made myself sit in her bed and count to ten. Then I cleaned up the floor, picked out some clothes that I wanted, and put the box in my bedroom to take to the home. I got into my own bed and slept peacefully without dreaming.

In the car on the way to the supermarket, my father is quiet. He sits in the passenger side as I drive and stares out the window. "Are you hot?" I ask. He shakes his head. "I can turn the air higher if you're hot." I glance at him sideways. "Mommy's coming home soon. I'll pick her up. Unless you want to."

"I think it's better if you go."

I pull into the parking lot and turn off the engine. "Do you think you guys will work things out?" I ask.

"That's up to her. I haven't thought about it." He looks away.

"I don't believe you. Come on, Daddy. Why can't you talk to me? I'm your daughter."

He stares in my direction, but doesn't look at me. "I want," he says slowly, as though each word pains him, "things to be the way they were. I don't think our life was so bad."

"But maybe it will. Maybe it will be the same, just different. And the different things will be good."

"I guess." He opens the door and begins to get out.

"Wait a second, Daddy. I want to talk. I know you miss Mommy. I know you do."

He looks at his hands. "I ... uh ... I wish your mother and I ... I wish we could start over ... that may sound foolish, but that's what I wish. I think about how things are and how they got this way ... Frannie, I know I shouldn't be telling you this, but I think it's important that you know."

"Know what?" I clutch the steering wheel. "What else do I have to know?"

"Remember last fall when you had that date with that doctor from St. Mary's?" I nod. "You took my car and didn't bring it back?" I nod, slower this time. "Well, I borrowed your mother's car to take Grandpa to the doctor. I stopped at the cleaner's. When I handed the girl your mother's On-Target jacket, a note fell out. It was a love note from Johnny Bennet to Mommy." He takes a deep breath. "Frannie," he says solemnly. "Your mother is an adulteress."

I stare at him. That's it? That's the whole thing? How could you think that I didn't know? You're such a Martian! "You've known since then and didn't say anything?" I ask.

"I didn't want you girls ... uh ... you, to know. I'm your father. I try to protect you from unpleasant things."

"It must have been hard," I tell him gently, thinking I should explain how sometimes women do things for the wrong reasons, how sometimes it's hard not to say no even when you don't mean yes, when yes never crossed your mind. "Maybe you're wrong," I say, calculating every word. "Maybe you misunderstood."

He shakes his head. "No, I talked to Mommy about it, and she said—"

I cut him off. "Dad, I'm really hot. Let's talk inside where it's air conditioned."

Stone-faced, he gets out. I feel guilty cutting him off just as the dam was about to break, but I can't hide what I know. And then I'd really fuck up their chances for reconciling. Before I get out, I reach into the backseat and pull out the JUST DO IT sweatshirt I took from Shelly's room.

"Where did that come from?" my father asks sharply.

"I went through Shelly's things last night," I tell him. "I'm making a donation to the home. Why are you yelling at me?"

"You cleaned out her room?" He barks. "Why didn't you say something to me, goddammit?"

"Someone had to clean her room, Daddy. All those things were just sitting there, collecting dust."

"Well you could have said something. She was my daughter, Frannie. You just don't go into her room and give away her things. Maybe there was something I would have liked to keep. Did you ever think about that?"

"I'm sorry, Daddy. I didn't realize. Everything's still there."

"Sometimes you need to think about someone other than yourself, Frannie. What about her diploma and her books? Are those still there?" I nod. "I was so proud of Shelly," he continues. "Proud that she had graduated from Cornell, that she was gonna be a lawyer. I want to remember those things. Those things are all I have left. I couldn't have done those things. It meant something to me."

"I understand, Daddy. I couldn't have done them, either. Everything's still there. You can go through it all when you're ready."

He doesn't answer. He gets out of the car and walks into the supermarket, five paces ahead of me. All the way in, he limps as if lame.

I lean on the handle of the shopping cart while my father walks ahead. "Why are you moving so slowly?" he asks sharply.

"I didn't know we had a time limit." I pause. "Daddy, I'm sorry I took Shelly's things. I really am."

"I know. I shouldn't have gotten so upset. I didn't mean to yell at you."

A little girl walks next to me. She looks up at the shelf. "You want cereal?" I ask. "Which one?" She points to a box of Count Chocula. I hand it to her and she almost topples backwards.

"She's cute, isn't she?" my father says idly. "I remember when you were that little." He doesn't say anything else except to murmur something to the toddler. He touches her head and it seems like it's agony for him to draw his hand away. I realize, as he watches her stumble away with the box, that it's Shelly he's remembering. Shelly as a little girl, who went to Cornell, who killed herself and left us all behind to wonder what we did wrong. You didn't do anything wrong, Daddy, I whisper to his back.

An hour later, we move toward the checkout counter. I notice the *National Enquirer*. WOMAN GIVES BIRTH TO BABY BABOON. As I inch the cart forward, I spy the little girl walking through the maze of carts, still holding the cereal box. Her eyes are wide and rimmed with tears. She walks to my father.

"Are you lost?" he asks her in a high-pitched baby voice I've never heard before.

She bursts into tears. I look up from the magazine and see that my father is smiling but his face is tight, as if he has gas. He picks up the girl and weaves his way through the carts until he sees her mother racing toward them. The mother scoops up the girl and hugs her. "Thanks," she tells my dad. "I got scared."

He waves his hand, as if to say it was nothing, and returns to the checkout counter where I'm standing. As he takes out his wallet, I lose myself in the birth of the baby baboon.

"Are you okay?" I hear the checkout girl's voice. I look up to see her leaning toward my father, but he's staring over her head, his face ashen. I can see beads of perspiration on his forehead.

"Daddy? What's wrong?"

"I'm fine," he whispers to the girl. "It's my daughter. My little girl." A sharp honk escapes his lips, and he doubles over as if punched in the stomach. Red-faced, I pat his shoulder as more weird-sounding sobs rack his body. "My daughter is dead." He looks up at the check-out girl, who stares at him, wide-eyed. "She graduated with all A's, she was going to Harvard, but she's dead." He continues to cry. "I'm sorry," he says to the girl, then to me. "I just miss her so much. I never had a chance to tell her how proud I was."

I'm aware that this is a breakthrough moment, but instead of feeling therapeutic, it's awkward and uncomfortable. In my haste to reach my dad, I dropped the *Enquirer*. I stare down at the picture of a bewildered man cradling his monkey baby. I step on it so my father won't see and pat him some more, wishing I knew what to say.

On Monday at work, Sue stands over my desk. "Frannie," she asks. "Do you mind covering the phones during lunch?"

"Be happy to."

"Thanks. By the way, Abby called again. At least I think it's Abby. She said it was Ronald McDonald."

"It was Abby." I move to Sue's desk and put on her headset. I'm working on a holiday promotion for a Rascals in Connecticut. We plan our promotions months in advance, so the theme I'm working on is "Christmas Cocktails." I envision all the servers wearing elf hats or reindeer horns serving drinks called Santa's Schnapps and Rudolph Rum Runners. I begin to brainstorm. Elf ears and reindeer horns are just the beginning.

"Good afternoon, Cuisine America."

"Frannie, why are you answering the phones?" It's Abby. This makes call number five.

"Sue needed me to fill in. I'm a team player. What's up?"

"I'm still hung about whether I should have broken up with Randy. Did I do the right thing?"

"You weren't ready to make a commitment. You saved him a lot of heartache. I mean, you didn't have to do it on the plane back from Bermuda, but … hold on, incoming." I switch lines. "Good afternoon. Cuisine America."

"Vicky Tayborn, please."

"She's out of town this week. Would you like to go into her voice mail?"

I click back to Abby. "Okay, continue."

"But I like him. And he's very smart. And handsome. I mean, for a guy who's so short. But he constantly talks about himself. It's like a psychosis. I don't think he realizes he does it. Like anyone really gives a shit about his stupid life. I mean—"

"Hold on again, Abby. I'm sorry."

"Jesus, what are you doing that is so import—"

"Good afternoon, Cuisine America."

"May I speak to Frannie Hunter?" At first I can't place the voice, but then it hits me. My heartbeat quickens. Oh God. Kill me now. Let me die. It's him. It's Charlie. "She's not in," I say in a falsetto voice. "Would you like to speak to her personal secretary?"

"I'll just call back later."

"But I'm sure she wants to talk to you. In fact, I'm positive. Why don't you leave your name and I'll have her call you?"

"No, thanks. I'll just try back."

"Okay." I try not to sound disappointed. "Well bye, I guess."

"Bye, Madonna," he says and hangs up. The click sounds like a burst of laughter.

My father avoids me for two days. I avoid him, too, figuring he's embarrassed about his outburst. Finally, he walks into the kitchen to tell me that a guy named Charlie called.

My heart flutters. "What did he say?" I follow my dad into his office. "Okay, Daddy. Take it from the top. Phone rings. BBR-RING! 'Hello?' you said. And he said, 'Is Frannie there?' and then what? Try to remember, Daddy. Please?"

"Frannie, get a hold of yourself." He rummages through his desk. "I'm not your Girl Friday." He holds up a Post-It note. "Here. This should make you happy."

"It does. Thanks." Before I leave, I turn to him. "Look, Dad. You don't have to be embarrassed ... you know ... about Sunday."

He looks at me blankly. "I'm not. Why would I be?"

"I don't know. Call me crazy, but some people get embarrassed when they have an emotional outburst like that. I mean ... every-one, you know ... understands. Losing Shelly was probably one of the worst things that ever happened to you. I totally understand."

"Personally, Frannie, I think you're the one who is embarrassed." He hunches over his desk and starts scribbling on a piece of paper.

"Why would you say that? I am not embarrassed. You're my

father! I'm perfectly comfortable with your emotions. You can feel any way you want."

"Well thank you. That's very big of you. But maybe it's not my feelings you're uncomfortable with." He turns to look at me. "Maybe it's your own."

The phone rings. Please be Charlie. Please please. "Hello?" I say, holding my breath.

"Hi, Frannie. It's Bryan. Bryan Thompson. Sorry I haven't called, but I've been really busy. I've been thinking about you, though."

"What have you been thinking?"

He lowers his voice. "I can't get our *date*"—he snickers—"out of my mind. I'd like to do it again."

"Huh." I pause. I start to tingle a little at the thought of him kissing me, his sexy black eyes, but a thought strikes. What about *me*? You didn't say anything about *me*. "Actually, Bryan," I tell him, "I'm busy. So no, I don't want to do it again. NO." I roll the word in my mouth as if it is a salty nut.

"Well okay," Bryan stutters. "But if you want to, you know, if you want—"

"I'll call you, okay?" And I hang up on him. "Hey, Shelly," I sing. "Didja see that?"

I'm so invigorated, I call Charlie. "Hi," I say. "It's Madonna."

"You sure this is Madonna, and not her personal secretary?"

"Okay, cut it out. You got me." I pause. "How are you?"

"Fine. I was calling to see if you could fit me into your busy schedule."

"If you wait a second, I'll check my book. Oh look at that! I'm totally free."

"So how about the Mets game on Saturday? They're playing the Phillies."

"A baseball game?" I'm quiet.

"You don't like baseball, do you? I thought it would be fun to do something different."

"I love baseball. I go to games all the time." God, I hate activity dates. Especially ones that involve sitting outside and sweating. "Sounds fun."

"Great, so I'll pick you up about nine?"

"In the morning?"

Charlie laughs. "This should be fun. See you Saturday, Madonna."

The next evening, my father walks into my room. "It's from your mother," he says, handing me a postcard. "It came yesterday. Sorry I forgot to give it to you."

"Thanks," I tell him. I look at the postcard. There's an Arizona sunset on the front and her big, looping handwriting on the back.

Dear Frannie:

Been here two weeks and I hate to leave. The weather is beautiful every day. Aunt Lillian and I went shopping and I bought you a new outfit which I hope will fit. If it doesn't, we can send it to Lillian and she can take it back. Beth is doing better and Uncle Monte sends his love. He wants you to come out as soon as you can. I can't wait to see you. Miss you tons.

Love ya,
Mom

P.S. We went to the Grand Canyon and I rode a donkey. It was really fun.

P.P.S. I lied about the weather. I hate this damn heat. I've got a rash.

I turn the postcard over a few times, studying it for clues. *Love ya.* It's weird to see that. *Love ya, Mom.* It's the kind of thing that girls at camp write to each other. *Sealed With a Kiss, UR2Sweet 2B4Gotten, Love ya like a sis, XOXOX.*

I imagine her riding a donkey down the Grand Canyon. She tries to hold the reins without losing her hat. "Look at me, Lily," she screeches. "I'm riding a donkey!" I look at myself in the mirror. I'm wearing a navy suit, pantyhose, and high heels. I don't see a girl anymore. I see a woman who goes to work while her mother rides a donkey.

I look at the picture of her in Italy that I put in a frame on my dresser. I stare at her long hair being lifted in the wind and hear her squealing in delight. I tell her to be careful, that sometimes she behaves foolishly, that you never let go of the reins when you're on such a steep hill. Exhilarated, she laughs at me and tells me to lighten up, that I shouldn't worry so much. But I would. I'd watch her donkey from behind, its fat ass waddling down the hill, and I'd flush with anxiety until she had her feet on the ground.

I look at myself again. My mother is suddenly me, a girl on a donkey with her hands in the air. And I'm her, a woman in a suit who worries too much. She's coming home soon. We're having dinner together and I'm sleeping over at her apartment. I suddenly can't wait to see her. It feels like she's been gone a very long time.

21

There's a corner office on my floor that has panoramic windows, a huge couch, and a conference table that seats eight. It houses the Grand Poobah, Mr. Henry F. Waddel, AKA the Waddler, executive vice president of Cuisine America. He's Vicky's boss, which makes him my boss once-removed. When I see him walk briskly through the halls, I avert my eyes, trying to award him the dignity that is his due. Usually he ignores me, too, but just last week, he cracked a half-smile, which indicated that he's either warming up to me or had terrible indigestion.

His office suite is partitioned by two sliding doors made of tinted glass through which you can see silhouettes. When he has people in for informal meetings, he shuts the doors and sits next to them on the couch. When I look through the glass, it's like watching a cocktail party. People sit with pads balanced on their laps like plates, their heads bobbing in agreement. Sometimes, I can't help but feel that they're talking about me. "She was late again today," I imagine the Waddler saying to Vicky, who bleats like a sheep to defend me. "And get her off the phone, Victoria. I have no time for slackers."

I stand outside the Waddler's office, trying to hear because Vicky's inside, having a couch conference with him. When she comes out, she smiles at me, but then looks away, as if she's hiding something.

Back at my secretary's desk, I call Abby. "I think I'm in trouble," I whisper.

"For what?" Abby's distracted. She told me Randy's begging her to get back together. She doesn't want to talk about anything else. "Did you do something?"

"No. I just *feel* it. Well, I did leave early last Friday to get my hair cut. And then there's the limo." I gnaw a cuticle. "I called a car to take me home and they just sent out a memo about cutting expenses. They couldn't have seen the voucher already, could they?"

"Since when did you start taking cars home to Long Island?"

I dangle my headset. "Since I became such a big executive."

"Look, are we going to the beach on Saturday or not?"

"Can't. I'm going to a Mets game with that guy. Charlie."

"I can't believe he's taking you to a baseball game on a first date. What is wrong with him? That's so *involved*. Why can't he just get you drunk and jump you like everyone else? Then you can fuck him and hate yourself when he doesn't call. Jesus, men these days. Listen, Frannie, go stand by the fax machine. I want you to read a letter I wrote to Randy."

"I thought you weren't going to call him."

"I'm not calling him, I'm writing him. There's a difference."

The limo couldn't have been that much, I reassure myself as I lurk outside Vicky's office. There's no point in even thinking about it. Vicky motions for me to enter. I fold my hands in my lap like a lady. I'm calm. I'm in control. The second she hangs up, I blurt, "I'm sorry about the limo."

"What limo?" The phone rings. She picks it up and says she's in a meeting.

"I took a car home. I was afraid Mr. Waddel, I mean Henry, was mad."

"At you? Frannie, he barely knows *I* exist." She waves. "Forget it. Just don't make a habit of it." She looks down at some papers.

"What's wrong?" I ask.

"I'm worried about next quarter's sales. Two stores closed in Maryland and they're reducing our budget." She drones on about all the programs we have to pull.

I listen for a while, then I drift, trying to decide what to wear on my date. It's the end of the summer and it's hot as hell, but shorts are so unflattering. Shelly used to have a dress that would be perfect. It was a black linen wraparound dress that tied in the back. It was sleeveless with a deep V in the front, not too revealing to be slutty, but just enough to show you had promise. The last time Shelly wore it must have been three years ago when we went for dinner and to see *Cats* with my parents.

The phone rings again. Vicky picks it up. "Sorry, Frannie, but I have to take this."

I smile and nod as if I care but understand, and lose myself in the memory of Shelly's black dress. She was just beginning to get thin, but was far from emaciated. In fact, my mother asked if I noticed how good Shelly looked. "Don't you think, Frannie? I didn't realize what a pretty bone structure she had." She turned to Shelly. "Your cheekbones are a gift from Grandma," she continued. "And from me, of course." Then she laughed. "One day, you'll almost be as pretty as I am."

Shelly shrugged. "I don't care so much about what I look like."

"You should care," my mother told her. "When you're a big-shot lawyer and your picture's on the front page of the *New York Times*, you'll want to look nice."

"I think it's more important to be a good person." Shelly smiled at me, but I had looked away, stewing about how my mother wouldn't stop bringing up Shelly's plans for law school. Law school law school law school. Between her and Abby, I wanted to scream.

"Well," my mother smirked, "it's nice to be nice, but if I had a choice, I'd rather be *rich*. Then you can afford to be nice."

Shelly picked at her fish. "Sometimes I think I'm going to die young," she said suddenly.

"What kind of thing is that to say?" my mother snapped.

"I don't know, it's just what I think." She put down her fork and went to the ladies' room. When she returned, her eyes were red and puffy. My mother asked her if she was all right. "I think I have food poisoning," Shelly told her. "I just threw up."

My mother looked at me. It was a long glance. Then she looked at Shelly. "Do you want to go home?"

Shelly shook her head. "I'll be okay." She became very boisterous after that. She told dirty jokes that made my mother blush and my father roll his eyes. I remember thinking it was weird she got sick; that it was the exact same thing that happened on her prom night when she and I had gone to a show and *I* got sick. In fact, I was marveling about the coincidence so intently, that it was fish *both* times, I don't think it even crossed my mind that she made herself vomit. But now, looking back, I realize that the glance my mother gave me was one of knowing, and I guess I knew it too on some level. I wonder if my mother remembers that night. I wonder if, when she thinks about it, she feels as guilty as I do that nothing was said, that for some reason we tried to protect Shelly. But maybe it was all of us, the family, that needed the protection. Jesus, I think, *was* it our fault? If we had said something, could we have saved her? And then another thought strikes me: maybe she died because she was trying to save *us*.

Vicky's voice interrupts my reverie. "That was Henry," she says. "He wants us to check out a new advertising agency. They're cheaper, but supposedly just as good. They want to meet you and me for dinner tomorrow night. Are you okay with this?"

"A free feed? I wouldn't miss it." I try to get back to Shelly, but I lost my thought. Vicky asks me another question and before I know it, I'm back at work.

Abby calls me while I'm lying in bed. "What did you think about the fax?" she asks.

"What fax?" I'm groggy, lost in that murky place right before sleep.

"The fax I told you I was sending. Shit, Frannie, you don't want it free-floating!!"

I sit up. "What did it say?"

"Don't ask. I just hope whoever finds it has a sense of humor."

At seven the next morning, I flip through stacks of paper. I check the floor, the garbage cans, and all the in-boxes. I could *kill* Abby. When Sue arrives, I ask her if I got a fax yesterday, but she says no. "It was busy in the afternoon," she tells me. "Mr. Waddel's personal fax jammed, so Adrienne used ours. In fact, we ran out of paper just as a twenty-page document came through." She shrugs. "Maybe they sent it when we ran out of paper. Why don't you just ask who-ever sent it to refax it?"

"Good idea, Sue. I'll call them." *Hello, Sue. Maybe I've thought of that. I'm only panting like a dog here.* "Is Mr. Waddel's fax machine still broken?"

"The guy came and fixed it last night." She smiles. "Really, Frannie. I wouldn't worry. I'm sure if it came through, you'd have it by now."

If it was anyone else, Sue, I'd agree, but you don't know my luck.

By one-thirty, the fax still hasn't shown up. I call Abby who tells me that she went through the garbage and couldn't find the confirma-tion receipt, so it probably didn't go through. "You want me to send it again?" she asks.

"No way. Just wait until this weekend and I'll read it in person."

"But by then, my feelings may have changed."

"I'll risk it."

Vicky calls me into her office at three. "Frannie, I want to see your ideas for the Philadelphia promotion." She glances up at me. "Nice suit. I talked to Henry. He thinks these guys are going to come on strong, so be friendly, but don't say too much."

"I wasn't planning on saying anything."

"You can talk." She laughs. "But don't offer any information about our current projects. Henry will do most of the talking, I'm sure, but if they direct questions to you, remember that the less they know, the better."

When I leave, I immediately call Abby. "What if I say some-thing I shouldn't?"

"Just talk about how much you like your job and how good your salmon is. Don't get too technical or too personal. Besides, if you're at a loss for conversation, you can always bring up a topic that's funny, titillating, and relevant to everyone."

"Which is?"

"Me."

*   *   *

I sort through my in-box, looking for the pad that had my ideas for the Philadelphia deal. With one hand, I open my mail. With the other, I dial my grandfather. I have three messages—all from him.

He picks up on the eleventh ring. "HELLO?"

"Grandpa? It's Frannie. I'm calling to say hello. How are you feeling?"

"HELLO? Who is this? Hold the wire. Freddie, listen, can you hear?"

"Freddie? It's Frannie. I'm calling to say hello."

"Vell vhy the hell didn't you say so? Max, it's Frannie."

My grandfather and I speak often, but lately he's been out of control. One day last week, he called me seven times. He's as bad as Abby. If I had any sense, I'd give him *her* number so they could talk to each other all day.

"Grandpa, hi, it's Frannie. How are you?"

"Not so good. No bowel movements and I had a terrible breakfast. My eggs were all wet. I think they're out to get me. They tell me I talk too much."

"Well you do talk too much. But I don't think they're out to get you." I look up to see Sue standing in my doorway. She has a strange look on her face. "Grandpa, I'll call you back."

"When?"

"Soon." I hang up. "Sue, what's wrong?"

She hands me a piece of paper. "Adrienne found this. We wanted to make sure you got it." She turns to leave.

"Thanks." Panicked, I flush with heat, and my stomach cramps as if I'm having a painful bout of diarrhea. It's Abby's fax. And there's no note.

From the Desk of Abigail Lynn Friedman
Attorney-at-Law

Frannie,

Here's the letter to Randy. I know it's sentimental, but I'm sick of being perceived as the type of girl who doesn't give a fuck about romance and who only wants a massive member (a jolly Johnson?) and a house in the Hamptons (however true that may be).

P.S. Has the Waddler said anything about the limo? If he's as cheap as you say, it's probably a good idea not to do it again. But you really should stop sending a car every week to pick up your mother in Hartford. How can you hide that in your expense reports? Furthermore, there's nothing wrong with using petty cash every once in a while for incidentals. I can understand lunches, a dinner sometimes, maybe even toiletries (you can rationalize those by saying that if you didn't have a job, you wouldn't wash your hair). But a suit? From Saks? And a cashmere coat? Are you out of your mind? You're gonna get snagged.

OKAY—HERE IS THE RANDY LETTER:

Dear Randy:

I haven't returned your calls because I don't know what to say. I think if we're ever going to work this out, we need to establish a few things. I will concede that you are not solely responsible for our problems. I can be demanding on occasion. But that's only because I give a lot. I know I came on too strong about getting engaged. I just panicked. So I'm sorry I made you crazy. I'll stop talking about it, but you have to promise to stop teasing me about things I can't control— like being beautiful (ha ha). No, really, you have to stop teasing me about other women. It hurts my feelings. If you want to be with someone else, fine, but I refuse to be with you if you're seeing other people. That's the bottom line. I also promise I won't cut you down anymore for smelling so bad (I do suggest you see a doctor, but I swear, this is the last time I'll mention it).

I miss you so much. I just want you back. I love you.

Abby

I stare at the fax for a long time before I call Abby. In fact, I'm so engrossed, I forget I have no idea who else has read this. From the time they started dating, Abby's been telling me how much Randy was pushing her to make a commitment, but she kept stalling. Well, that's obviously not true. I'm surprised she let me read this, but then she probably forgot she lied about it.

"I am so furious," I tell her when I get her on the line. "How could you send a fax like this to my office? Is there something wrong with you?"

"So you found it. What do you think? Pretty queer letter, huh?"

"No, *I* didn't find it. The Waddler's *secretary* found it. Are you on drugs? What if people read it and they *believe* it? Abby, I could really be fired. This is not a joke. Jesus, *you're* supposed to be the professional here."

At first, she's indignant. "You were supposed to be standing by the machine," she says. "I never thought it would fall into enemy hands!! Besides, who would believe all that stuff? If it were true, would I *fax* it to you? I thought you'd think it was funny." When I don't say anything, she begs me to forgive her, but I'm so mad I can't speak.

"Oh God, Frannie, I'm sorry." She starts to cry.

"Abby, stop crying. *I'm* the injured party."

"But they're gonna fire you and it will all be my fault. What can I do? Please let me do something to make this up to you. I'll buy you a new outfit. I'll pay for you to go to law school. You can be a lawyer. Fuck that place, you don't need them if they can't take a joke." Now she's frantic. "Why don't I call the Waddler and tell him it was just a joke. Please?"

"I don't think he'd see the humor, Abby," but I imagine him reading about Abby's desire for a massive member and I have to smile. I never imagined that I'd keep this job for long. I mean, really, who are we kidding?

I avoid Vicky and the Waddler for the rest of the day. I don't have my own office yet, but I finally realize why it's so important. It's more than just having privacy to call your friends; it's also the only place you can avoid the people you work for without raising suspicion.

At six o'clock, Vicky stops by. "Are you ready?" She looks at her watch. "We're supposed to meet them at seven, but I thought we'd get together first and talk."

I glance at her face, checking for signs indicating that she knows about the fax. She's her same smiling self, all perky and professional, but I'm not convinced. "I'll meet you in the lobby," I tell her. I rummage through my desk. I consider clearing it out, but decide to wait. Even if they demand my immediate resignation, they have to let me come back to gather my things.

In the restaurant, I order a glass of wine that comes in a goblet the size of my head. I gulp my wine while Vicky talks. "I know you've been under a lot of pressure lately," she says.

"It hasn't been so bad," I mumble, reaching for my wine. "I'm really happy at Cuisine."

"Well, it's been busy as hell for me." She laughs. "What have *you* been doing all day?" You don't want to know, Vicky old girl, I wouldn't know where to begin. "Anyway, Frannie, I've been meaning to talk to you about something, but I haven't had the time."

This is it. This is the big talk. I'm sorry, Vicky. I'm sorry about everything. About the limo and my dirty suits and the fax, especially the fax. You know it was just a joke, right? I may be a bit loony, but I'm not a thief. And it'll never happen again. Please, Vicky, don't make me leave. I have nowhere else to go. I can't go back to Oprah. I kicked it once. I don't know if I can do it again. "What is it?" I say quietly, looking away. Just say it. Just get it over with.

"Regina's leaving!" Vicky sings. "You're getting your own office!"

"That's it? That's the whole thing?" I try to resurrect some energy, but it's like French-kissing at a funeral. "Wow, that's terrific. Oh, thank God, that's good."

"Oh, look. There's Henry!" Vicky waves as the Waddler walks toward our table, flanked by two men wearing flashy suits. The one carrying a cellular phone has a bouffant hairdo that looks like a bee-hive. The other has his hair slicked back in a ponytail. He has a weird stringy thing around his neck, a cross between a bolo tie and a cameo with two silver-tipped shoelaces hanging down. As the three men move through the restaurant, I feel like I'm being approached by a firing squad.

"You must be Frannie Hunter!!" The bouffant man pumps my hand. "Alvin Meyer, account exec." As he pulls out a chair to sit down, he nods at Vicky but doesn't say anything. Then he shakes her hand as if he could give a shit.

The other man sticks out his hand. "Hugh Vandermire," he says quietly. He takes a seat, but not without first wiping it off with his pocket handkerchief.

I open the menu, close my eyes, and point at an entree. I open my eyes. Swordfish. When the waiter stops by, that's what I tell him I want.

Vicky excuses herself to go to make a phone call. While she's gone, Alvin fires off questions to me: how long I've been with Cuisine, our current advertising budget, our plans for the future, and where we'd like to be positioned in the next five years. I smile politely and try to answer him honestly without revealing too much, but he's got me all befuddled. I'm grateful when our food finally arrives.

The Waddler is engaged in discussion with Hugh, who, I've noticed, wipes off every piece of silverware. This wouldn't be so odd, but then he doesn't even use it. He eats everything, his fish, his vegetables, even his rice, with his fingers.

"So Frannie," Alvin says. "I know you told me, but tell me again. How long have you been with Cuisine?"

The Waddler speaks up. "Two months. Not long." I look at him. For a second, he holds my eye. Then he looks away. He's read the fax, I know it! Hank, I don't think you're cheap. And if you are, so what? We're all idiosyncratic.

"Only two months? What kinds of immediate changes do you foresee?"

The Waddler smiles slightly. "Go ahead, Frannie."

"Well," I say slowly, wondering what's going on, "first I need to evaluate my own position and adjust to corporate life."

"Where were you before?"

"Operations." I look at my hands. "I've made some minor mistakes in my first two months, mistakes I *know* I can learn from." I look at the Waddler, who raises an eyebrow. Oh God, what does *that* mean? It wasn't like I *killed* anyone. I flash him my best smile. "This is a whole new ball game for me, but I have a decent, honest head on my shoulders, and I believe I can rise to the occasion."

"I like humility in a boss." Alvin punches my shoulder lightly. "You must get it from Henry." He turns to the Waddler. "Hank, I hear you had a hell of a year. Profits up by 25 percent. If you let Littleton & Branise handle your ads, I bet we can raise that another 15 percent. Easy." Alvin is practically in the Waddler's lap.

"What are you talking about?" I cut in. "Henry's not my boss. I report to Vicky. She reports to Henry."

The color drains from Alvin's face. Hugh coughs. "Vicky's your boss?" he chokes out.

I nod. "She's the vice president. I'm the coordinator."

"I thought the coordinator oversaw the entire division."

At that moment, Vicky returns to the table. "Well, Frannie has *some* responsibility, Alvin, but we haven't given her the entire division yet. We're still working on moving her out of our secretary's desk."

Obviously embarrassed, Alvin tugs on his tie. "Well, Henry, had I known, I would have waited for Vicky before I started interrogating Frannie."

Henry shrugs. "Looks to me like she was holding her own."

I beam at the Waddler, but he turns and says something to Vicky that I can't hear. Then he excuses himself and leaves the table. While he's gone, we make small talk as we eat. "So Vicky," Alvin says at one point. "Guess who I had lunch with last week—your old boss, Ed Morgan. You guys speak often?"

Vicky looks up. "No. Why?"

"No reason, I knew you were friendly."

I watch Vicky. I can't tell if Alvin is baiting her because he knows about Ed, but Vicky seems totally cool. She's amazing. If someone asked me about a guy from my past, I'd completely decompensate. "Anyway"—Alvin leans forward—"he brought some little blond who had no idea how to act during a business lunch. Here I was pitching our agency and she's trying to *cuddle* with him. You gotta wonder about some women." Alvin winks. "That's why it's so great to deal with you, Vicky. You are the *consummate* professional."

Vicky jams her fork into her trout, takes a bite, and gnashes the fish between her teeth. "Alvin," she says, "cut the bullshit, okay? It's not the women you have to worry about, it's the goddamn men. Why was Ed bringing her to lunch anyway? You don't find that even the slightest bit inappropriate? Regardless, if you're trying to get Ed's business, stop gossiping. He and I are on the same side, you know."

Two bright red puddles stain Alvin's cheeks, as if his skin was cut underneath and he's bleeding from the inside out. "I didn't mean to offend you," he mumbles. "I was just making conversation."

The Waddler returns. "What did I miss?" he asks. The table is silent. He turns to Alvin. "So, you were saying? You think you can raise our profits by how much?"

"Fifteen percent." Alvin takes a deep breath. "I really think Littleton & Branise is the right firm for Continental. Hugh, show him your concept board."

Henry interrupts him. "We're Cuisine," he says dryly.

"That's what I meant. Cuisine. Cuisine American."

"America."

Alvin looks like he's going to cry. There's a long silence while we all pick at our food. Alvin swallows his pork loin and mutters a small "Sorry" to no one in particular. He looks around the table meekly and runs a hand across his bouffant do. I suddenly feel pity for him and for Hugh, whose face is contorted as he sucks on a lemon wedge. Sitting next to him, I'm the only one who hears Alvin mutter, "I guess I fucked this one up," under his breath. I shift in my seat. God, this is really awkward. I wish someone would say something already.

Suddenly, I blurt, "One time when I was in college, I worked for a public relations firm." I'm speaking quickly, running my words together, not even realizing they're coming until they're out there and there's no way to get them back. "I worked a few days a week while I was in school, so I was juggling courses and work assignments and boyfriends. My life was very hectic and I was often distracted. But I was hired to type and file and do general office work, so I didn't think it would be too stressful. And the work wasn't stressful, but the man that I worked for was very old-school and he had an antique intercom, and he would buzz me when he needed me. The buzz was very loud and he buzzed me all day long, and every time, it made me jump out of my skin.

"Anyway, I began to make mistakes. Nothing major, just misfiling letters or forgetting to take messages. But every time I did something, this guy went ballistic. He'd *scream* at me, which got me all uptight. And the more he screamed, the more I screwed up. A lot of times, though, things weren't my fault, but because I was already in the doghouse, he was convinced I was sabotaging him. Once, he told me to send a contract to a really important client. Two days later, the CEO called to ask him why we'd sent pamphlets for luxury time shares and cruises with the contract. Apparently, I didn't check the Jiffy bag I'd sent the contract in. We always reused Jiffy bags and this particular one had twenty brochures stuffed at the bottom!! The CEO was already annoyed that our firm's fees were so high, and now he got all these brochures addressed to my boss for luxury vacations!" I relax to catch my breath. The Waddler checks his watch, but his head is cocked and I know, instinctively, that he's listening.

"Anyway," I continue, "this guy keeps yelling at me and buzzing me and yelling and buzzing and I'm making more elaborate and more costly mistakes. And then there's the rose fiasco. He asks me to call a florist for him and he gives me an address and a message. No big deal, right? Just call a florist and have some roses delivered. I mean, a chimpanzee could do this, right? So he gives me this address and just as I'm calling the florist, he buzzes me, 'FRANNIE, DID YOU SEND THE FLOWERS? I NEED THE FLOWERS SENT N-O-W!!' And I'm fumbling with the phone and he mutters something over the intercom like 'Rush those flowers to my wife. She and I had a fight.' Anyway, as I said, I'm flustered and he buzzes me *again* to remind me to include the note, and I suddenly can't find the paper with the address on it. So to save time, I flip through the Rolodex for his home address, and send a dozen roses with a note that says, 'You are incredible. I loved yesterday and I love you. And yes, I can get away to Paris.' Okay? No big deal. Well that night, he calls me and starts screaming that I am fired, that I ruined his life and he never wants to see me again.

"I'm totally perplexed and I demand to know what he's talking about. It turns out that I sent roses that were intended for his *girl-friend* to his *wife*. So I say, 'But over the intercom, you told me to rush the flowers because you and your wife had a big fight,' to which he replies, 'What I said was: Rush the flowers, Frannie, and for once in your *life*, do something *right*.'"

By this point, everyone is laughing, even the Waddler. In fact, he's the one who asks me to continue. "That's it," I say. "I mean, I got fired."

"So what's your point?" the Waddler asks.

I look at Alvin. "Sometimes you have to say, 'Today's just not my day.'" I shrug. "That's my story."

Alvin's forehead is drenched in perspiration and his bouffant is matted in the front, but he smiles. "Did you ever see the guy again?"

I laugh. "Actually, when I interviewed for my first job after I graduated, I called him and asked him if I could use him for a reference."

"What did he say?"

"He didn't know what to say. He was completely baffled, like I was the biggest moron. So we sat there for a second in silence until I said, 'Just kidding,' and hung up on him. It may not have been proper etiquette, but it made me feel better."

"Well he shouldn't have told you to send flowers to his *girlfriend*," Vicky says indignantly.

"He shouldn't have done a lot of things," I say, "but you know, you win some, you lose some. And the world keeps spinning, I guess."

By the time dessert comes, conversation has picked up a bit between Vicky and Alvin. As we walk out of the restaurant, Mr. Waddel sidles up to me. "Well, Frannie," he says. "That was some story." I look at him. Well that was *some* dinner. He's thoughtful a second. "You know, we have a policy at Cuisine ..." Oh boy, here it comes. "I like to have lunch with all the new hires. I'll have Adrienne check my calendar and get back to you."

"You want to have lunch with me? Is everything okay?"

He laughs. "It's supposed to be a positive part of the Cuisine Experience."

"Oh," I say quickly. "I'd love to have lunch with you." I shake my head, marveling at myself. God, I am so neurotic. "Henry, can I ask you something?" The Waddler nods. "You knew from the beginning that Alvin had Vicky and me mixed up, didn't you?"

He shrugs and smiles slyly. Then he says, "I'll let you in on a little secret, Frannie." He turns to hail a cab. "If you don't have a sense of humor in business, if you can't have fun once in a while, there's just no point in doing it."

"I think the same way!" I say, pumping his hand goodbye. "How about that!"

The Waddler gets into the cab and waves goodbye. I lurch forward. "Hey, where did you go to school?" I ask, but it's too late.

He closes his door and leans forward. The cab speeds away. Through the window I can see the back of his head, but he doesn't turn around to wave, which, now that we've bonded and all, sorta disappoints me.

22

"*Have you ever thought about how much an anxiety attack resembles an orgasm?*" Charlie asks as I dig into my Cracker Jacks.

"No, but I'll remember that the next time my heart's palpitating and I feel like I need to be rushed to a hospital."

I look at the field where the players are warming up. There's no one in the bleachers yet because we got here two hours before game time. "I like to get here early," Charlie told me. "I don't like to miss anything." I knew then I should have brought a book.

By the time the teams assemble, I've had two giant beers, and I'm ready to go home. I look around at the women wearing tank tops and skimpy cutoffs and I feel hot and sweaty and really stupid in my linen shorts and little heels. Abby, as usual, was wrong. "Wear something cute," she said. "Just because he doesn't know proper dating protocol doesn't mean you should suffer."

"Get up." Charlie nudges me as the National Anthem starts. He takes a deep breath and slowly exhales. I can't believe he's going to sing. But as the music plays, Charlie doesn't sing. He fucking *bellows*, wrenching every word from his gut in a soul-filled baritone, swaying with his eyes closed like he's surrendering to Jesus. By the end, he's screaming. "And the la-haand of the freeeee and the hooome of the ..." He holds the final notes. "... bah-raa-ave." He

314

looks at the field in reverence, then yells, "LET'S PLAY BALL!!"

A red-haired guy high-fives Charlie. "Great set of lungs!" he says, knuckling Charlie's head. "Simply awesome. PLAY BALL ALREADY!"

I watch Charlie staring at the field, his blue eyes glistening with the lunacy of a psychopath. I tug on his shirt. "So what are the odds here? What's the spread?" He turns as if to say something, but quickly looks away. "Well don't worry about me," I mutter. "I'll just sit here by myself. Would you look at that! A spaceship!"

"Did you say something?" He glances at me sideways.

"I just thought that this being our first date, we'd have a chance to talk."

He looks at the field. "We are talking. Frannie, baseball's very important to me."

"Well, I never got into it. I mean I've been to a few games, and I dated a few ballplayers in school." All right, so they weren't exactly *dates*.

"I think Jennifer and I broke up because she hated baseball." He watches me out of the corner of his eye. "I'd say our differences about the sport cost us our relationship."

"Actually, baseball is quite compelling. It's all in—"

Suddenly Charlie jumps up, waving his fist. "Go, go, you moron," he yells. "Go HOME. Go FUCKING home!"

"You are so weird!" I stick my finger in my ear, positive he's deafened me.

Later, as I make my way up the long steps toward the bathroom, I hear a crack and watch a batter round the bases. When I look down at Charlie, he and the redhead are doing a victory jig, their arms thrown around each other's shoulders, kicking their legs like can-can girls. Charlie spots me and waves. He looks so boyish and cute, I could eat him alive.

"What did I miss?" he asks, returning from the men's room.

"A hairy guy hit a home run and another guy got smacked in the head with a bat." I look up. "Nothing special."

"Thanks for the recap. Here, I bought you a present." Charlie slips a cap on my head.

"A Mets cap! Love it." Shit. Hat hair. "You know, Charlie, it's so cute, why don't *you* wear it?"

By the fourth inning, the game has calmed down. No one is scoring and everyone is striking out. Charlie has his head bent, gulping his beer in frustration. When I ask him what's wrong, he points to the field. "They're fucking up."

"And you take that personally?"

"I try not to." He squeezes my hand. "You know, I didn't tell you how pretty you look."

"You don't have to." I smile coyly.

"You already know?"

"No." I laugh. "I just meant that you don't have to say that because there's more to me than my being pretty. Not that I'm pretty, but I don't want it to be the only reason you like me." Having finished my third giant beer, I'm not quite sure what I'm trying to say.

"I didn't say I liked you, I said you were pretty. You want another beer?" He waves a concession guy over.

"If I have another beer, I'll be dancing in the aisle in my underwear." I'm trying to pace myself. I can't get out of hand; he's practically family.

He smiles. "I can think of worse things that could happen." Gently, he lifts my hair off my forehead. His touch is soft and careful and I can't stop smiling as we look at each other. His eyes are so blue. And his face is so handsome. I lean forward. He's got a really nice smile. And he was on time and showered and God, I wish he'd kiss me. Maybe I should kiss him. He's right there, and he looks like he wants me to. I lean in. "HOLY SHIT!" He blinks. Whips his head around. Damn.

I hear a crack. Charlie jumps up. When the player reaches home plate, Charlie grabs me. His skin, warm from the sun, smells of musky cologne. He releases me, but I don't want to go. When we sit back down, he asks how I'm doing.

"Great." I smooth my shorts. "Just dandy."

"You're not having fun."

"As compared to what? Getting a cavity filled? Having a Pap smear? Now put me in a department store the day the Wonderbra is on sale, and I'll show you fun."

He squeezes my hand. "You are so funny." I flush. Yeah I am, aren't I? A regular riot. But do you wish I was naked? I gulp my beer and glance at him over the rim of the cup. I could be, you know.

"You have to go to the ladies' room *again*?"

"Yes, Charlie, *again*. It's what we do."

At the concession stand, I spy a phone. "Abby, this guy is no Rat Boy. He's totally hot."

"So what's the problem?"

"I don't know if he's attracted to me. He hasn't kissed me and he's had a lot of opportunities."

"Frannie, you're still *on* the date. You don't get to the kissing part until the date's *over*. This isn't college. You can't expect him to just grab your tit. Besides, if he *had* kissed you, you'd be whining that he's all over you already."

"But we've been together for five hours. This is like a whole *relationship*. I just want to know if he thinks about me in *that way*."

"So bring up something sexual. If he likes you, he'll talk about it. If he doesn't, he'll change the subject. Jesus, Frannie, how do you function when I'm not around?"

"This is called a squeeze play." Charlie points to the field. "There's a guy at third, no one's at second. When the batter bunts, the guy on third goes home. They'll tag the batter out at first, but … whoa, there he goes. Told you."

"To tell you the truth," I say, "I think my favorite sport is football." I squint at the field. "I love the uniforms. Most football players have really tight asses."

"Personally, I like the asses at baseball games." Charlie is staring at a woman standing a few rows ahead of us wearing mini shorts cut so high, her cheeks hang out. "You're not laughing," he says.

"I didn't think it was funny." I *had* to listen to Abby.

"Oh? You can comment on men's asses, but I can't comment on a woman's perfectly formed, heart-shaped behind that's practically in my face? Isn't that a double standard?" I don't say anything. "You're mad? Frannie, you can't be mad. It's not like I asked her to go out with me." He looks again. "Although …"

"It's obvious that you're not interested in *dating* her," I snap. I try to laugh as if I'm joking, but my face is burning. We sit in silence.

"Okay," I finally concede. "She does have a perfect ass."

He smiles. "So do you. Is that okay? Can I comment on your ass?"

"No, we can't comment on anybody's body parts. Besides, my ass is far from perfect." He doesn't say anything. "So you agree with me?" I ask. "About my ass?"

He holds up his hand. "Truce, Frannie. Don't drag me into this."

He leans to watch the game. I wonder if he thinks I'm psycho. And he still hasn't kissed me yet. It's probably because he thinks I have a fat ass.

I spend the next two innings learning about baseball. Charlie teaches me strategies, rules, etiquette, player biographies; everything from their batting averages to their wives' names.

"So"—I point—"the batter is just out of rehab and his wife left him?" Charlie nods. "And the pitcher used to be his friend, but now they don't speak because they were partners in a bar that went belly-up." He nods again, and I settle back. "I can deal with this. It's like *Melrose*." The crowd boos and hisses. "That's mean," I say.

"The guy's an asshole. I bet he strikes out. He's fucking dead out there."

"Charlie, I'll bet you dinner this guy hits a home run."

"You're on. The guy's a loser."

Ten seconds later, I'm on my feet, yelling at the batter who smashes the pitch into left field. "GO, GO, RUN, you moron!" At first, it doesn't look like the ball's going to make it, but the out-fielder slams against the wall, and the ball sails out of the park. "YES!" I dance around until I'm winded. I hug Charlie. "God, I LOVE this game!"

"That was fun," I tell Charlie a few hours later as he rummages in the kitchen.

"Yeah, it was." He hands me a Diet Coke and picks up the phone. "Chinese?"

I nod. "Nothing too spicy." Charlie sits down next to me and dials. After he orders, he makes another call. "Who are you calling now?"

"Hey, Grandpa," he says. "There's someone here who wants to say hello."

"Hi, Freddie," I say into the phone. "How are you?"

"Frannie?" Then he yells, "Max! Max! Frannie and Charlie are on the vire!! So, darling," he purrs, "are you havink a good time? Is Charlie behaving?"

Charlie's massaging my thigh. His fingers trail along my skin, which rises in goose bumps. "Charlie's being a perfect gentleman." Making slow soft circles, he draws on my leg with his fingertip, then leans forward and lightly kisses my neck. I lean back and sigh. "Here, Charlie, you talk," I murmur. God, this is so great, this is finally like a real date.

We eat from cartons on his living room floor and watch a rerun of *Bonanza*. Charlie tells me about going to Princeton on a wrestling scholarship. He shovels lo mein noodles into his mouth. He swallows without chewing, gulping his food as if breathing it. "Are you going to eat that?" He points to the chicken and broccoli next to me. I shake my head. "Then hand it over." I pick it up. "Please," I say.

"Please," he repeats, taking the carton.

I bite into an eggroll. "You must be incredibly smart." I lick my fingers.

"I am. I'm also incredibly handsome and incredibly athletic and incredibly strong."

"And incredibly humble. People say that if you have an overly inflated opinion of yourself, you're probably very insecure."

"They also say that if you have to analyze everyone, you're probably very horny." He cocks his head. "And of course, I don't blame you."

"Well aren't you glad you're you?"

"Truth is, Frannie," he says suddenly, flipping through the channels. "Hey, have you ever seen *Saved by the Bell*? There's some very good acting on that show."

"Truth is what?"

He walks to the kitchen. Over his shoulder, he tells me he's pretty nervous.

What am I supposed to say to that? Shit, if *he's* nervous, who's driving this bus? "Please don't be nervous," I say shyly. "Knowing you're nervous makes me *really* nervous." He walks back with an eggroll in his hand. "Charlie, I've never seen anyone eat so much."

"You should have seen me in college. I'm 180 now but I wrestled at 135. To make weight, I ate nothing but applesauce and Ex-Lax. I was a skeleton, man, fucking *ghoulish.* Now I have to watch myself. I work out for an hour and a half five times a week."

Shelly was a skeleton. Shelly was fucking ghoulish. I imagine her cheekbones as her jaw clicks away. "That seems a bit excessive. To me, a solid workout is breaking out in a sweat going from my bed to the bathroom." Suddenly anxious, I glance around for the door.

"I get up at five-thirty. I work out from six to seven-thirty, I'm in the office by nine."

"Sounds like a full life. You know, it's really hot in here. Don't you have air conditioning?"

"What's wrong?" He flexes. "Aren't you impressed by my discipline and massive girth?" He reaches for another eggroll, lifts it like a torch, and swallows it in two bites.

"I just hate listening to people drone about weight and food and exercise. All I hear is 'I really want this, *but* I shouldn't'; that *but* ruins everything. I wish being fat was a good thing. I wish we were all fat cows."

"So you're *not* impressed by my massive girth?" He smiles, but I look away.

"I really gotta go."

"What's wrong?"

Words gush out of me like vomit. "You're making all these jokes and I'm trying to talk! I'm trying to talk, to *talk* and you're not listening to me. My sister *died.* She is *dead.* She was anorexic. Her last meal was a bottle of Valium. And they could have saved her, but she was too skinny. Her lungs *collapsed* and she *suffocated.*" My throat burns. "OhmyGod. I can't believe I just said that." Shaking, I start to cry.

Charlie stares at me. For a long time, neither of us moves.

Finally, he puts down the carton. "I'm sorry," he whispers. "I don't know what to say."

I breathe deeply. "No, I'm sorry. I just got all uptight. God, I hate myself right now."

"It's okay, Frannie. You're right. I know you were trying to talk and I made it all fucked up." He reaches for me and I lean against him. "But I know all about Shelly. My grandfather told me, but I thought you'd want to tell me yourself. Maybe that was stupid. I don't know why I say stupid things, Frannie. I'm just not very good at this." I squeeze my eyes closed so no more tears can slip out. Charlie hands me his Diet Coke. I take a sip and try to swallow but can't get it down. For a while, the soda sits in my mouth. Charlie's eyes glisten. "Max talks about Shelly, too."

"My grandfather? He hasn't said one word to me about her."

"He doesn't want to upset you. He talks about it a lot. I don't think he can make sense of it."

"Charlie, none of us can. I've been through hell trying to figure it out."

"When my grandfather told me, I wanted to do something, send a card, I don't know, *something*."

"But what could you have done?" I can't stop crying. "You didn't even know me. And it was obvious you hated me."

"What are you talking about? *You* wouldn't give me the time of day. And I knew about Shelly, too. I just sat there like a fucking idiot, but I couldn't think of anything to say. I should have acknowledged it—you, I mean, I should have acknowledged *you*. I wanted to meet you the first day I heard about you. You've been through so much and you have your shit together. From the first day, I had a crush on you. You seemed so sure of yourself."

"You think I have my shit together? I spent the last year in a major depression. Who are you talking about? I'm like the poster child for the American Psychiatric Society."

Charlie shakes his head. "Frannie, look at yourself. You're smart and funny and compassionate. I could never have survived what you've been through. You're the strongest woman I've ever met. You have everything going for you."

"I used to think that about Shelly." I lay my head against the couch. "I thought she had everything. Look at her now."

"But you and she are different people, Frannie."

"Sometimes I'm not so sure. You don't know me that well."

Charlie and I sit for a long time. As he strokes my face, I slowly relax. The room is lit by sunlight that eventually fades. We don't speak; he just wraps his arms around me and in the dark, we listen to the sound of each other breathing. "Are you okay?" he asks after a while.

I reach for his hand. "I'm embarrassed. It's our first date and I yelled at you."

"I deserved it."

"Maybe I should go," I say quietly. "It's been a long day." My voice comes out in a croak and I'm afraid I'm gonna start crying again. I start to get up, but Charlie tugs on my hand. "Look," he says softly, "please don't leave." He clears his throat. "I don't want you to go." He pulls me into his lap. "I don't know much about relationships. Believe me, I've fucked up every one I've ever had, but I'm happy right now. You were like a fantasy at first, but now that I've met you and spent time with you, you're even better. You're like my idol, you're great with Max and he loves you so much and I know why.

"I'm rambling, I know," he continues, "but I haven't been in love in a long time and I'm not saying I'm in love, but if there's anything that can resemble love without actually *being* love—because you can't be in love with someone you just met, I mean, you can be infatuated, but it's not actual love. But if there's anything that resembles love, then I'm in it. And I'm sorry about Shelly, I really am and I'll do any-thing to make it better for you. Please don't leave, Frannie. Not tonight. I can't believe I'm saying all this. I feel like an idiot." He stops short. "If you were me, what would you do now?"

I answer by pressing my mouth against his.

Later, in the dark, his voice covers me like mist. "I feel like I've known you my whole life." We're under the covers, but we're both fully dressed.

"You have. I'm just like all the girls you grew up with. We both were. Me and Shelly. But Shelly was really special. She was going to do great things with her life." I pause to see if Charlie's listening and when I realize that he is, that he's really listening to *me*, I keep talking. And the things I talk about surprise the hell out of me because I've never told them to anyone, much less a guy. I tell him about Camp Galaxy. I tell him about diet days and guava jelly and the first time I caught Shelly making herself throw up. I even tell him about Rat Boy, well not everything, but enough to give him a general picture. I also tell him about how I've been searching for reasons why Shelly died, how I dream about her and how the pain eats at me, how it hits me at work when I'm supposed to be concentrating and I can't do anything but go into the ladies' room, sit on the toilet, and cry.

"The thing that I'm the most ashamed about," I whisper, "is that I didn't pay attention to her when she was alive, but now that she's dead, she's like everything. Maybe if I'd made her more important to me, all this could be different."

I look at Charlie. Tears run down his face, but he doesn't make any noise. "You did the best you could," he says. "We all do. You have to say that to yourself every day." I feel like he means it. And for a few wonderful minutes, there's no shame.

He tells me about his childhood, about growing up with an overbearing mother and his father who was always angry, and his older brother Eric, the doctor, who has a life complete with wife and son, something he's always wanted. We keep saying over and over how easy this is. And it is Charlie who says how lucky he feels to have finally met me. "I've always wondered where you were." He sighs. Then he's serious for a second. "I have to ask you something, Frannie."

"What?" I sit up, suddenly anxious.

"It's really embarrassing. I mean, really embarrassing, like the most embarrassing thing I could ever ask a girl." I don't say anything. "Okay," he says. "I can do this. Okay." He takes a deep breath. "When we first met, you told me that you thought I had a fat ass. Do you really think that?"

"I'd never say anything like—" Then I remember my Richard Gere comment. "All I said was that Richard Gere had a *better* ass," I tell him, trying to reassure him. "I'd never say you had a fat ass because you don't. You have a great body, I swear."

He laughs. "I'm being ridiculous. It's just something my brother used to tease me about. I knew you were just kidding."

"Yeah, I can tell," I say, hugging him.

We talk until the sun shines into the room. And when I try to hide my face because I know my makeup is dry and cakey and my mascara is smeared like raccoon rings under my eyes, Charlie tells me that I'm the most beautiful girl he's ever seen. And then he kisses me; a warm hopeful kiss that's shared between us like a secret, and wrapped around each other, we finally sleep.

"So how was it?" Abby asks Monday morning. "Tell me everything."

"How was what?" I'm packing my things in a box so I can move into my own office.

"Saturday. You didn't call me at all this weekend and I called you four times! Randy and I decided to work things out. I've been *dying* to talk to you. You shacked with Charlie, didn't you? You are suuuuuch a slut. Did you have sex?"

I smile. "No, Deep Throat." She sighs like she doesn't believe me. "I swear, Abby. We stayed up all night and talked and he kissed me. Well, actually, if we're going to get technical, I kissed him first."

"So? Do you like him?"

"Yeah. I do, I guess. I like him." I say it again. "I like Charlie." It never dawned on me to think about that. If a guy wanted me, then of course I wanted him; I never questioned whether I actually *liked* him. "He asked me to go out Friday night. A week in advance. Can you believe?"

"Charlie, Charlie, Charlie. I'm already sick of his name. I can't believe you have plans already! I *hate* this guy. I bet he called you this morning to tell you what a great time he had this weekend."

"Twice." I can't stop smiling.

"So what are you guys doing Friday?" Abby asks.

"Drinks after work. Actually, I'd like you to come. I want you to meet him."

"Does he have friends?"

"What about Randy?"

"He's not invited. He's suddenly getting on my nerves."

"I met a guy," I tell my mother as we walk toward the baggage claim. She's holding a sombrero and a new straw purse.

"I know. I spoke to Grandpa. When were you planning to tell me?" She hands me her luggage stubs and starts looking for her bags.

"You just got here," I say, but she's already turned away. Aunt Lillian had called to warn me that my mother was going through changes. She's very depressed, Aunt Lillian told me, she started again with the pills.

"There's one," she says and points to a bag. I pull it off the carousel. "I've decided to see Marilyn twice a week for a while."

"Are you sure that's what you want to do?" I ask.

"Frannie, not now. Don't start with me now."

"I was just asking a question."

She ignores me as we walk through the parking lot. When we put her bags in the trunk, she hands me the sombrero. "This is for you."

"What am I supposed to do with it?" I put it on and shake my hands as if I'm holding maracas. I make a move to hug her, but she inches away. "I thought you'd like it," she says.

"I do, but am I supposed to wear it or is it just for show?"

"I don't know. It's a souvenir. If you don't want it, don't take it."

In her apartment, she immediately goes into the bathroom. I can hear her crying over the sound of running water. I open her pocketbook and take out a plastic bag filled with photographs. There are pictures of my grandparents and my aunt and uncle. There are also pictures of her with my father, looking tanned, happy, and much younger. In the back of the stack, there are pictures of me. I rummage through the bag. Tucked in a small envelope, separate from everything else, are old photographs of Shelly.

"What are you doing!?" she exclaims as she walks out of the bathroom. She snatches the pictures away. "Please don't go through my things, Frannie." She tucks the Shelly pictures into a drawer.

She flips on the television and we sit on the couch. Cautiously, I ask how her trip was. "Hard. I mean, it was nice to be out of the office, but being with my sister is enough to put anyone away. I caught Beth going through my pocketbook and Lillian got all defensive, as if I'm the one who's crazy. Is that it? Is it me? Am I the crazy one?"

"Maybe we're all crazy."

We both chew on that for a second. "Maybe," she says finally. "Maybe we are." She plays with my hair. The feel of her hands on my head makes me shiver. "So nothing's new?"

"Nope. Can't complain. In fact, I've been looking at apartments."

She drops her hand. "Have you talked to Daddy? Maybe he doesn't want to be alone in that big house."

"A month ago, you were selling it. Mom," I say softly. "We've talked about this for a long time. I want my own place."

"Who's telling you not to get your own place? You're an adult. Live where you want."

"I thought you'd be thrilled." I put on the sombrero in a feeble effort to make her laugh. She turns away and gulps a Valium without water. I see her as though watching an old movie.

"Take that thing off," she insists. "It looks ridiculous and it's probably filled with bugs." But I've already walked away and am standing in the kitchen where I can turn my back and make believe I can't hear her.

During the night, I dream about Shelly. She's in the hospital but she's in my twin bed. She's wearing sexy underwear, a bustier and lace garters, and her legs are so heavy, the fat ripples over the tops of her stockings. Curled on her side, she strokes herself and writhes on the bed, but I can't tell if she's feeling pleasure or pain. I walk over to the bed and she laughs in a high-pitched cackle that makes me shiver. When I get close, I realize it isn't Shelly. It's my mother.

Friday night, I meet Charlie and his friend Evan at a bar. I keep thinking about my Shelly dreams. They always make me feel empty and depressed the next day. "We don't have to stay," Charlie tells me when I explain that I don't feel well.

"No, I just need a drink." I signal the bartender and order a margarita.

"I'm nervous about meeting Abby," Charlie tells me.

"Charlie, she's going to love you. Oh … there she is. Abby! Over here." Abby walks toward us wearing a skirt so short, it looks like a scarf. Her hair is shiny, her makeup is perfect, and her boobs are hanging out of her sheer blouse. When I see her, I'm annoyed that she went home and changed when she knew everyone else was coming right from work.

"Frannie!" She kisses my cheek. She turns to Charlie. "Well, you must be the man of the hour." When she turns to introduce herself to Evan, Charlie asks me if her tits are real. I eye him suspiciously. "What do you think?"

"I think yes."

"Then it's obvious how you got into Princeton, isn't it?"

"I'm excited to meet you," Abby gushes. "Frannie hasn't stopped talking about you."

"Okay, Abby, have a drink or I'm going to get you a muzzle. What do you want?"

"I'll have what you're having."

When Charlie turns to order her a drink, she gives me the thumbs-up sign. "Cute," she whispers. "Very cute."

Charlie smiles at her. "Frannie tells me you're an entertainment lawyer."

"Yeah, we did work on the O.J. case. Our firm set up the 900 number for people to call in and say whether they thought he was guilty or not. I ran the switchboard."

"She's just kidding," I cut in. "Abby's a great lawyer. She plans to go into politics."

"I'd like to," Abby says, "except I inhaled." She smiles. "A lot. Actually I hate being a lawyer. You?"

Charlie sips his drink. "I hate being a lawyer, too. I think the only people who actually like to practice law are the ones who write novels about it."

Evan tells Abby she looks familiar. Abby turns to him. "Fire Island," she says. "My mother set us up two summers ago. Brunch, remember? Then we went back to your house and spent the entire day in bed. You were terrific."

"Oh, I'm … sorry, I don't remember …"

328 • JILLIAN MEDOFF

Abby laughs. "We work in the same building. Don't look so nervous. I'm just kidding."

"You want another drink?" Charlie asks me. I shake my head. "What's wrong?"

"You told me you loved being a lawyer," I hiss.

"I was just being nice." Abby and Evan are laughing at what must be the funniest joke ever told. "Look at me," Charlie commands. "You're smart and beautiful. Don't you dare be jealous of Abby or anyone else in this bar."

"That's such a college thing to say. Like 'You're the prettiest girl I'm with right now.' What about the rest of the world?" I smile and order another drink.

"Well, that might be a problem. The world's a big place." He kisses my cheek. His mouth lingers next to my ear. I pick up my margarita and lick the salt off the rim of the glass. Then I drain my drink so there's nothing left but ice.

I begin to get really buzzed, so buzzed I think I feel better. I run my fingers along his chin. He clenches my finger in his teeth and softly sucks it. I kiss him, openmouthed, feeling the softness of his lips, the sweetness of his tongue. I suck on an ice cube and transfer it from my mouth to his without using my hands.

"Delicious," he mumbles. "Do it again."

Hours later, alone in his apartment, Charlie leans over me. His mouth is on my face, his hands are on my hair, on my breasts, between my legs. "You are so special," he whispers. "I can't believe I met you." I love how he whispers to me. I feel like I'm completely with him. As we start to make love, I lose myself in how good it feels, God, he keeps touching me, and I'm so warm and so wet and I ache for him, but when I open my eyes, I see Shelly's pale face, my mind shuts down, and I panic, feeling like Charlie's suffocating me.

"Charlie, Charlie, wait." I push him off me and sit up. "Stop, okay?"

"Is something wrong?" he asks. "What did I do?"

I shake my head. "I promise, cross my heart, that it's not you. It's me. I'm not ready. I need more time. I can't do this yet."

He lies back and cradles me in his arms. "That's fine," he says, kissing my hair. "Just don't bail on me."

"I almost did," I say softly. "But I'm here."

And during the night, for reasons I can't explain, I cry in my sleep.

23

I dream about Shelly almost every night. I wake in a cold sweat, my face wet with tears. When I fall back asleep, she always reappears. My dreams are sequences that are completely unconnected, split-second images in vivid colors, but I can always make out my sister's face, or her arm, or the back of her head. In all my dreams, Shelly is dead.

I wonder if I'm going crazy; if this is how schizophrenia starts. I'm afraid I'm splintering for real this time, that I've reached that point of no return. And because I'm so frightened, I don't tell a soul.

"Are you all right?" I'm in my new office-ette, talking to my mother on the phone. I didn't get Regina's office, but I did get a smaller version a few doors down. I christened it with my diplomas from Syracuse and Lindsey High. At the time, I thought it was funny since I don't have a graduate degree. Now I think it looks ridiculous, as ridiculous as the stuffed bear that Charlie brought to cheer me up. "Frannie," my mother says, "you seem so depressed lately."

"*You're* the one whose been depressed, Mom. Not me. Why do you always do this?" I rip out pages from *People* magazine to Xerox so I can read at my desk and look like I'm working. Vicky's been working on budgets and hasn't had time to review my projects. I don't have much going on, which is just as well since I'm not interested in doing anything anyway. "You always make me feel bad."

"Frannie, I don't *make* you feel anything. Marilyn says—"

"Fuck her. If she was so goddamn smart, do you think Shelly would be dead?" The words spew like lyrics lodged in my subconscious. "In fact, did it occur to you that if she had talked Shelly out of leaving the hospital, she might have been okay?"

"Shelly was leaving the hospital because all the doctors—*not* just Marilyn—felt she was ready. I refuse to have this conversation with you. I'm hanging up now."

"Oh that's great. Just cut me off when you can't deal with something."

"Don't you think I have any feelings?" She starts to cry.

"I'm sorry, Mom." My eyes fill with tears. "I don't know what's wrong with me."

"Then make an appointment with Marilyn. Or someone. You need help."

"I can't afford it. I'm trying to save money to move into my own place."

"Then *I'll* pay for it. You act like it's a prison sentence. It's supposed to be a positive step. Maybe you can figure out why you're so unhappy."

"I'M NOT UNHAPPY!" I scream into the phone and start to sob.

At lunchtime, I play with my sandwich. I nibble a crust of bread, then throw the rest of it out. My stomach is in knots. And all my skirts are hanging on me. The image of the skinny girl in the three-way mirror flashes in my head, but I will her away. I like the emptiness in my stomach, how lightheaded I feel. I call Charlie, who has already called me three times and counting. It's amazing how much can change in six weeks.

"I can't come over on Friday," I tell him. "I got a call from this girl Pia, someone Shelly knew at St. Mary's. She's giving a poetry reading at the 92nd Street Y."

"Do you want me to go with you?"

"I think I should go by myself. I'll bring my gym clothes. If it's boring, I'll just work out. Hey, Charlie," I ask slowly, "have you noticed anything different about me?"

"Well you've been a little depressed and can't sleep. Is that right?"

"I was wondering if you noticed anything weird about my body."

"Do you mean your weight? Your shape? What?"

"Do you think I'm fat?" I ask.

"Of course not. You know you're not fat."

I sigh. "But if you had to name one part of my body that wasn't perfect, what would it be?"

"Frannie, why are you doing this?"

"I'm just wondering." I sip my soda. "We should be honest with each other. If you were getting heavy, I'd want to be able to tell you. It's part of being in a relationship."

"Do you think I'm getting fat?" he asks quickly. "Because if I am, just say so. I mean, I'm not eating any more than usual."

"No, Charlie, for Christ's sake. And we're not talking about you, we're talking about me. So tell me. What part of my body needs work?" He groans. "Charlie, no one is perfect."

"I think you're perfect. You're beautiful. You're the most extraordinary woman I've ever seen."

"Buuut ..."

"I don't know, your legs, I guess. You could tone your legs." I squeeze them together. I'm silent. "Frannie," he begs, "please say something. You *made* me pick something."

"Did you notice I had fat legs when we first met or is this something new?" When Charlie laughs, I tell him that I'm not kidding.

"Frannie, stop it," he tells me. "I'm starting to get mad."

"*You're* mad? *I'm* the one who was just told she has fat legs."

"I didn't say you had fat legs, goddammit! I said you were beautiful! And you are! You're fucking beautiful and you're fucking crazy! What is wrong with you?"

"You're only saying I'm beautiful because I made you! Fuck you, Charlie. Why don't you date a skinny girl instead of a fat pig like me!"

"Fine!" he yells.

"Well, I'll tell you something, Charlie. You're a fucking RAT BOY!"

He's silent a second. Then he says quietly, "I can't believe you called me that." Silently, he hangs up. I hold the phone for a long long time. It's over, I say to myself. And in a strange sort of way, I'm relieved.

It dawns on me about mid-afternoon when I'm standing on the toilet in the ladies' room, trying to see my body in the mirror over the sinks, that Charlie and I may have broken up. I stare at my piggy face, hating myself. Hysterical, I call Abby, who orders me to spend the night. We stop off at the supermarket and everything reminds me of Charlie. I can't stop crying, even when we're standing at the checkout counter behind a handsome guy and Abby combines our Diet Cokes and cigarettes with his stuff and tells the clerk we're all together. She turns around and sees the tears streaming down my face. "Jesus, Frannie." She hustles me outside. "At least wait till we get home."

I lie on Abby's couch and wail. Randy calls and Abby tells him that we're in a Code Blue and she can't talk. When he calls back, Abby tells him to get a life. He hangs up on her. She tries to call him back to apologize but he won't answer.

"I'm really breaking up with him this time," she swears, handing me a tissue. "Our lives were so much better when we didn't have these stupid guys." I make her examine my legs under the bright light in her bathroom. "Tell me the truth," I beg, "do you think they're fat?" Over and over she promises me that my legs aren't fat. With no boys to talk about, we smoke cigarettes, order pizza, and pick at the crust. I lie on her floor, watch *Fast Times at Ridgemont High*, and eventually doze off to the sound of garbage trucks. I wake up in a panic with Abby shaking me. Apparently, I was screaming in my sleep.

I don't hear from Charlie for a day and a half. I walk around in a trance. I tell myself I don't need him, that this break is good for us. When I remember how he installed a phone in my car, I cry in the bathroom at work, knowing I don't deserve him.

"I don't think we should see each other for a while," I tell his answering machine. "I need time to figure things out. I'm sorry for making you crazy. Please don't call me although I'm sure you weren't planning to." The second I hear the beep, I want to erase my message, but I can't. And of course, he doesn't call back.

On Friday night, I walk into the 92nd Street Y. I find a room where a bunch of chairs are set up. Pia just started reading, so I take a seat and try to listen. It's difficult to concentrate because there's a buzzing in my head.

"My next poem ..." As Pia drones on, I study her. She looks healthy and filled out; her brown skin is clear and her hair looks lush and full. She's still small, but she doesn't look anything like the waif I met in the hospital. She looks absolutely beautiful.

She reads her poem with a rhythm that goes up, down, up, down, and I am soothed by the beat. "AND then WE went TO the ..." I say the words silently "AND then WE went TO the ..." Suddenly I hear the name Rochelle Hunter. I look up. Pia is peering into the crowd. Instinctively I know that she's looking for me. I lift my hand and she smiles.

"As I said, I'd like to dedicate my last poem entitled 'Hunger Point' to Rochelle Hunter. But first, I want to share something she wrote." Then she reads, "'There's this hidden place deep inside myself that I'm trying to reach. A calm, quiet place where I don't exist as a girl with a body that grows too big. A place where I can finally sleep. I'm trying to reach that place, every day I try, and I know there will be a point when I'll be able to slip through. I know the point, I've almost been there, the point when I'm so hungry, I can't feel it, the point of numbness, of suspension, the window of time when it's okay to say yes, to let go, to fly. That's the point I work toward, my own personal hunger point; a point when I feel everything and nothing at all. When all it takes is one more step and I'll be safe.'"

The crowd is silent. Pia takes a sip of water. "Shelly Hunter was a friend of mine who, instead of attending Harvard Law School or studying psychology at Stanford, killed herself last December." She pauses. Someone in the room gasps. "I don't want to turn this reading into a polemic, but it's important for me to say aloud that mental illness is a dangerous disease. And just because you can't see it, doesn't mean it isn't there. It *is* there; it exists. And it can be deadly. Shelly helped me with my lifetime struggle with anorexia. She was probably one of brightest women I've ever met, but she was vulnerable, like we're all vulnerable, to self-hate, self-denial, and self-destruction. So now she's guiding me in other ways, a star above, if you will." Pia pauses. The room is silent. "So Shelly, baby," she says, looking up, "this one's for you." And she begins to read.

I can't concentrate on the poem because I'm reeling from the shock of hearing Shelly's journal entry. It stays in my head like a mantra. *All it takes is one more step and I'll be safe. One more step to say yes, to let go, to fly. One more step. One more step.*

Pia comes over after the reading. She hugs me. "I was going to tell you about the journal," she says, "but I decided not to. I hope you're not angry with me."

"Angry? Why would I be? I'm very flattered that you asked me to come." I smile at her. "You really look awesome," I tell her. She thanks me and turns to some people who congratulate her. I want to talk to her, but she's surrounded. "Can you wait a second, Frannie?" she calls to me.

Ten minutes later, she leads me to a chair. "I've wanted to call you," she says, "to see how you've been."

"I've been okay," I tell her. "Some times are easier than others. By the way, do you have the rest of Shelly's journal?"

"No. Only that part. She read it once to me and I asked her for a copy. Why?"

"I've just been trying to figure out stuff, I thought it might help. Shelly threw out her journal when she left the hospital." I pause. "Can I ask you something, Pia?" She nods. "Why do you think Shelly killed herself? I mean, she was getting better, right?"

Pia takes a deep breath. "I don't know, Frannie. She always said that for her, there was a tenuous link between life and death. Shelly walked a fine line." Her eyes mist. "It's crazy, isn't it? She was a great person, I mean I don't want to martyr her because what she did was awful, but she really did make a difference in my life."

I start to cry. Pia hugs me. "Frannie, I'm so sorry. This must have been so hard for you."

"It's been very hard," I tell her. "But I thought I dealt with it. I grieved, I was depressed. What else is there to be? But now she's in my head all the time."

"You probably did deal with it on some levels, but Frannie, it's very complex. With Shelly, I don't know. She was very rigid. She made up her mind to do things and there was no stopping her. Sometimes she'd say that she wanted to die, that it would be so much easier than the struggle. We'd all get pissed off at her and tell her that the struggle is all you're given and when you're dead you're dead, and all that bullshit, but Shelly didn't buy it. I don't have any answers, Frannie, certainly no more than you've probably come up with. But I do feel that some people, people like Shelly, are born with more sensitive souls. And they can't soothe themselves no matter how much you love them or will them to live."

"But Shelly's death was a choice."

"Shelly may have had a choice, Frannie, but truth is, she may not have had a chance."

Vicky takes me out for a business lunch to discuss a Rascals opening in Stamford. She studies the menu and I watch her closely, figuring she's doing competitive research.

"I can't stand the menus in these places," she says, putting it down. "Everything is so fattening." She unfolds her napkin. "I can't find one thing I can eat without feeling guilty." I'm surprised. Vicky is thin, but curvy and perfectly proportioned. "What are you having?" she asks, as if it's vital that she knows.

"The chicken stir-fry. They said it's low-fat."

She smiles. "We know that's a lie. It's probably delicious, but loaded with grease and I shouldn't." She shrugs. "What the hell." She takes out her Day-Timer, makes a few marks, then closes the book. "I never had a weight problem," she tells me, "but now that I'm approaching forty, I find it hard to look at myself in the mirror. So I've started a diet." She talks to me as if I'm a confidante instead of her assistant.

"You have a great figure," I tell her. "Really, you're perfect."

"Hardly. I've let myself go, so now it's time to pay the piper."

Our food comes and I watch Vicky eat. She cuts chicken, vegetables, and noodles into bite-sized pieces as if she's dissecting something. Just like Shelly. Pick up a string bean, inspect it, chop it up, let it sit. In the glare of the white sunlight, I can see where Vicky's face is lined around her eyes and where her lipstick bleeds. As she hunches over the table, worried about being forty and fat, she looks ferretlike.

I excuse myself and go to the ladies' room. I examine my face in the mirror. I can see where I've lost weight in my face; my cheeks are drawn and my features are prominent, especially my nose. My eyes bulge in my shrunken face and I look pale and unhealthy and ugly. Like a skinny ghost girl. Like a girl who is dead but inhabiting a body. I tremble with rage. "I WILL NOT END UP LIKE YOU!" I say to the mirror. "I am not YOU. I am ME. I will not end up like that. It wasn't luck. YOU HAD A CHOICE. You made the wrong fucking choice."

When I return to the table, I savor my lunch. I enjoy every chunk of chicken, every water chestnut. I eat ravenously and greedily, relishing the sweet soy sauce on my tongue, the hard vegetables I gnash between my teeth. I can't lift the fork to my mouth fast enough; I can't chew, I can't swallow to meet the pace of my hunger and my sudden desire to be filled. When I'm finished, I order dessert. I rub my stomach, aware that I am full. I feel the food inside me. And it feels good.

I walk into the kitchen. "Daddy, I'm home!" I look around. There's a note on the counter:

> Frannie, I'm at the gym for my kayaking lesson. Come meet me and we'll have dinner together. Just you and me. Love, Dad

At the health club, I walk outside to the pool. Five men wearing life preservers and goggles paddle through the pool in bright red kayaks while an instructor calls instructions. A sixth man is in the deep end, practicing what it's like to capsize. Every few seconds I see him come up from the water and then disappear. I feel as though I'm watching a cartoon.

My father waves his paddle. "Just a little while longer, Frannie!" he yells, exhilarated. "We're almost done."

I watch for a few minutes as the men splash around, the noses of their kayaks bouncing off one another. The man in the deep end keeps thrusting himself under and coming up. My dad paddles toward him. The two of them go under and come up in sync like they're performing a weird water ballet. I hear my father sputtering. From this far away, it sounds like he's laughing.

Kayaking lessons aren't the only thing my father's doing. He's also taking ballroom dancing, skeet shooting, wine tasting, and Mediterranean cooking. He's a one-man activity fair. All this has to do with the new woman he's seeing. Her name is Ruthie and they met in group. They go out for dinner and to the theater and dancing and to potlucks. She's been trying to get him to go to a bluegrass festival in Kentucky. She wants to rent a truck, fill it with hay, and sleep in it. He doesn't want to go and I don't blame him. I don't know if he's happy, but he's sure as hell tired all the time.

I wait for him in the lobby while he changes. Occasionally my eyes water as I think about Charlie. I pick up a pay phone, dial slowly, and hang up when I hear his voice.

"Where do you want to eat?" my father asks when he finally emerges from the locker room. His hair is slicked back and his whole forehead is exposed. I never realized how big his forehead is; it's smooth and rounded like an eggshell. "Why don't you dry your hair?" I ask him. "I can wait."

"It's not wet. It's gelled."

"Excuse me. I didn't know you were suddenly Vidal Sassoon."

"Ruthie says it makes me look younger." He squints. "What do you think?"

"I think it looks wet."

We decide to eat at Rascals for old times' sake and when we get there, I'm surprised that I don't recognize anyone. When the waitress comes over, it takes me a long time to decide what to order. "What are you having, Daddy?" I gnaw on a breadstick.

"Ribs. With an extra side of barbecue sauce."

"I thought Ruthless had you on a diet."

"Frannie, just order and stop worrying so much about what I'm eating."

I sit with the menu. My father fidgets and the waitress breathes heavily. "Frannie. Our waitress doesn't have all day." He smiles at her.

"I just can't decide." The waitress can't be a day over twenty. She's wearing a name tag that says SYLVANIA. Her pants are too baggy, her shirt is wrinkled, and her tie is stained. "What do you think I should have?" I ask her.

How the hell should I know, you fucking idiot, I bet she's thinking. She shifts her weight from one foot to another. Her behavior annoys me and I'm about to tell her so, when it strikes me that I must have looked the same way. It's only temporary, I tell her silently, bloated with maturity, it gets better. Then I remember I called Charlie a Rat Boy. I can't believe I said that. God, I hate myself.

"I'll have the chef salad with ranch dressing on the side and extra crackers. And please bring an extra plate." The girl flees as if released from a cage.

My father wants to know what the extra plate is for. "Your ribs," I tell him.

I look around for Paulie. When Vicky hired me, I wrapped a bottle of champagne in one of my dirty duck aprons and sent it to him with a note safety-pinned to the bib:

> I'm hanging up my apron, but I'll never forget what you've done for me. Thanks for everything. I'll make you proud. Love, Frannie AKA Wanda.

When he called to thank me, he got all choked up. As I look around the restaurant, I start to cry.

"What's wrong? Mommy said you had a fight with Charlie. You haven't made up?"

"No, we did. I'm crying out of joy."

"Please, Frannie. It's okay if you don't want to talk to me, but don't be obnoxious." He leans forward. "You know … if you talked about …" He trails off.

"I know, Daddy. I just don't feel like talking right now."

"Fine. Just wanted to let you know I'm here." He gets up. "I have to call Ruthie."

"Please don't invite her to dinner. She's like a child who constantly needs the channel changed."

"Tonight's the anniversary of her husband's death. She asked me to check in." He walks away and I sit and sulk.

"Frannie! Don't tell me that you've lost your job and you need some shifts!" Paulie walks over and I stand up to hug him. "We miss you around here," he says. "How's the job?"

"Good. Everything's fine." I smile. "But I want to ask you something and I don't want to be out of line. So if I'm saying something inappropriate, I'm sorry, okay? Anyway, I met a guy … Forget it, you don't need to hear this."

"Am I complaining?"

"I'm just all fucked up. This guy is the best thing that ever happened to me and I completely went off on him. I guess I'm depressed and I know it has to do with Shelly, but I can't figure out how. I know, well, Vicky told me about your son and I thought you might … I just thought you might have some clue as to what's wrong with me."

He stares at me, and for a second, I'm afraid I pissed him off. "Frannie, when someone you love dies, it hits you in weird ways. When Tommy died, Vicky clammed up. And me, well you know me, I hate to talk about anything emotional, but I started blurting it out to everyone." For a second, Paulie is lost in thought. "Tommy died of SIDS. Did Vicky tell you that?" I shake my head. "It wasn't our fault. Neither of us could save him. But we blamed ourselves and in our worst moments, blamed each other. In the end, it cost us our marriage." We both look up to see my father walking toward the table. "All I can tell you, Frannie, is that you have to move beyond your own guilt. You can't dwell on the dead. You have to stay with the living." He squeezes my hand. "And there's no one more alive than you."

"Mom? Can I ask you something?" She walks quickly on the treadmill next to me, pumping her arms. It's a mini Spa Day. We're getting our nails done and she's paying for both of us to have massages, but there won't be any haircuts. According to my mother, Collette met some guy and took off for Lisbon. "I bet the bitch is holed up in a motel in Las Vegas, shooting up heroin," I said. My mother laughed. She hates Collette. The last time she saw her, Collette asked my mother to stop talking about Shelly. "It's bad for the shop," she said. "It brings down morale. Death is so *unnatural*." To which my mother snapped, "How the hell can you say that? You look like the goddamn Grim Reaper." And the honeymoon was over.

My mother has her Walkman on so she can't hear. I shake my hand in front of her face. She slows her treadmill. "Do you want something?"

"I was just wondering … Mom, would you be embarrassed if I never got married?"

"Of course not. It's your life, Frannie honey. If you don't want to get married, don't." She looks at me. "Does this have to do with Charlie?"

I nod. "He hasn't even called me."

"You asked him not to. You could call him, you know." I walk to the mirror. My mother follows and we talk to our reflections. "From everything I've seen and heard about Charlie, I think he's a good guy. I like him a lot. But you have things you need to work out before you commit yourself to someone."

"So you think I'm wrong for him?"

"I didn't say that. I just think you need to sort out who *you* are first."

"Do you think it was stupid to tell him I needed time to myself?" My mother shakes her head. Then she slowly lowers herself to the floor. "But I said something really mean to him. What if he realizes he doesn't want me? Maybe he thinks I don't care about him. What if he forgets about me?"

"I can't tell you what he'll think, Frannie. But I can tell you that if it doesn't work out, it wasn't meant to be." She rises slowly, then lowers herself again.

"Mom, I can't talk to you while you're exercising. Please stop and listen to me."

"I will, Frannie. Right after this set." She mutters something I can't hear.

"What?" I ask

"SYV. Dmitri, my trainer, tells me to say SYV." She lowers her voice. "Squeeze Your Vagina. If you squeeze your vagina and exhale every time you bend, you won't hurt yourself. Oh look, there he is! Dmitri!" She waves. "SYV!"

Dmitri has a well-toned body that glistens with perspiration. When he lifts his arm to wave, I can see that he has shaved off all the hair in his armpit. "SYV, Maaashaa!!" Dmitri yells across the gym. "SYV!"

"Mom!" I screech. "He's disgusting. He *shaves*."

"He's not disgusting. It's a European thing. Now, do some knee-bends with me. Come on, breathe in, squat slowly, come on, Frannie." Reluctantly, I hold the bar and squat. "Don't forget, SYV. And one, and two, and Frannie! You're not breathing!"

Hours later, after taking saunas and showers and getting our nails done, my mother and I lie on her bed. She flips through a magazine with her thumb and forefinger. "Do you think about Shelly a lot, Mom?" I ask absently. I pick off my nail polish with a paper clip.

"Of course. Please, Frannie, not now. I'm not up for a big talk."

"I wasn't going to make a whole big thing, Mom. I was just asking a question."

"Well it's a silly question. Of course I think about her. She is … was … my daughter. I think about her every day." Her face contorts. "Frannie, please. Please go see Marilyn."

"I don't want to talk to her. I want to talk to *you*. You're my mother." She doesn't answer at first. Finally she says, "Frannie, there is so much pain in watching your daughter grow up. I mean, it's wonderful, but it's also so fleeting. One day, she's stumbling through the kitchen, then suddenly, you're sitting next to her as she backs out the driveway, and you realize that she's different from you, in a grown-up way. And it's you, the mother, who has to adjust because she's just going to keep growing. But despite the pain, there's also hope, that your daughter is going to live a better life than you did. When Shelly died, all that was snatched from me. I'd give anything to change places with her, but I still have you and that keeps me going."

I lie on my stomach and she reaches under my T-shirt and tickles my back. Her voice filters into my ear as if from a dream. "She always wanted to be more like you. She said you were fearless and funny; that she was too intense, too serious. But she wasn't too serious. She was just Shelly. Sometimes I imagine that she's alive somewhere with a husband and two kids. And she's happy. All I ever wanted was for you two to be happy. I guess it never came out right." She traces the letters of the alphabet. I feel my own name being spelled.

I love the feel of her hand tickling me. She lulls me to sleep, whispering "Frannie Badannie" like I'm a little girl. I am struck by the thought of my mother dying and I burrow my nose deep in the pillow. A tear dots the case, which I rub with my cheek. Don't leave me yet, Mom, we can help each other through this. As I drift, I don't know if my mother is talking or if I am imagining it. Her voice is a lilt now, a cloud above my head, lifting me. I want to talk more about Shelly, about how we feel, how much we miss her, but I can't find my voice. Softly, as my mother tickles me, I fade away. Her whisper carries me and for just a little while, I rise, I fly.

24

Bryan Thompson, Dr. Demento, calls the next day. "I've been really busy," he says, "but I've been thinking about you."

"You have?" I think about Charlie. He should have called me by now. If he really cared about me, he would have called me. I tell Bryan that I've been thinking about him, too, wondering what he was up to.

We meet for a drink. We get very, very wasted. I tell him about Ruthie. "So listen to this," I slur, hanging on the bar, "Ruthless sleeps over, and in the morning, she makes Hungry Man breakfasts, then hovers over me while I eat. So one time, I say, 'Look, Ruthie, I have a mother, and it wasn't so successful the first time, so back off!'"

Bryan laughs, leans over, and kisses me. "You look so good."

We kiss for a long time. We have a pretty good time, laughing and drinking, and since it's late and we're liking each other, I invite him to sleep over so he can meet Ruthless himself.

We're standing at the bar and I'm right next to him. His hands are inside my pants. "Sounds like a plan," he says, digging deeper.

We stumble out of the door. "I'll drive," I say. "I mean, you're a doctor. If you get caught, you could go to jail, right?"

"Right-o." He pushes me into the backseat. "Let's do it here.

Oh God, I want to be inside you right now. I can't wait." And then we fuck right there, not because I like him, not because I want to, just because.

"Hungry?" I ask Bryan through the film in my mouth. I nudge him. "Bryan, get up." Wobbly and sick to my stomach, I pull on my nightgown and pitch him my bathrobe. "I'll be back in a second. Get dressed."

In the bathroom, I study my face. I'm a fat whore dried up like a prune. I can't believe Bryan is in my bed. What was I thinking?

When I walk back into my room, he's standing. "Please don't make me go downstairs, Frannie." He tries to nuzzle my neck, but I push him away. He reaches underneath my nightgown, but tugs too hard and the seams split.

"Stop it, Bryan. Jesus, come on!" I put on my JUST DO IT sweatshirt. "You said last night that you wanted to meet Ruthless, so let's go."

There was no message from Charlie last night. This makes five days in a row that he hasn't called. I decide that Charlie is an asshole and a liar. I hold my rage in my head like a prisoner, even though I know I should release it now, before the depression comes. Because it will.

Ruthless sees Bryan before my father does. Obviously, they know he spent the night and they must have spoken about it because she's not her usual effusive, dopey self. "Hello," she says coolly. "I'm Ruth Brown. I'm a friend of Mr. Hunter."

"Bryan Thompson. Nice to meet you." He stands reluctantly in the doorway and tugs on my bathrobe, which is way too small for him.

"Sit down," I tell him. "You want coffee?"

He looks at Ruthie. "It's okay," she says. "You can come in. Can I make you some eggs?"

"Eggs are good," I interrupt. "Where's my dad?"

"Outside getting the paper."

Bryan sits at the table. When my father walks in, I can tell he's startled to see him, but he doesn't say anything. He just sits and slurps his coffee, making even more noise than usual.

"David," Ruthie says slowly, "this is Bryan. He's a friend of Frannie's."

My father grunts at Bryan without looking up. I bring a box of Pop Tarts to the table. Ruthie sets a plate in front of Bryan and I tear into the Pop-Tart box. "Want one?" I hold up a pastry to my father, but he ignores me. He licks his thumb and turns a page. "I'll take the metro section," I tell him sweetly.

"I'm reading that section."

"Then I'll take the magazine."

"I'm reading that, too."

"Fine. Be that way."

Ruthie puts toast in front of me. I cut the crusts off and slather on guava jelly. I lick the spoon and stick it in the jar. Ruthless takes the jar to the sink and rinses off the spoon. Then she closes the jelly and puts it in the refrigerator. I give her a fuck-you eye roll. "Bryan's a shrink," I say. "And he's even more screwed up than we are."

Bryan glares at me, but doesn't say anything.

"That's wonderful," my father mutters. "I'm so glad you've brought him home with you."

"Well, we were going to tell you in a more formal way, you know, like with a party and everything, but ... well, Bryan and I are getting married." There's dead silence. My father looks at me, then returns to the paper. Ruthie is speechless. "God," I mutter, "can't *anyone* take a joke?"

Brian gets up quickly. "Well, Fran, thanks for breakfast and all, but I really gotta go." He walks out the back door, toward the garage. "Bryan!" I screech, "you're in my bathrobe."

"Oh yeah. Well, I guess I'll go. I have a friend who lives out here. I'll call him to come get me." He stands by the stairs, as if waiting for me to offer to drive him home. "Sounds like a plan," I say. "Use the phone upstairs." I gaze at him, thinking, *You can fucking walk home for all I care.* He must see the disgust in my face because he backs away and runs up the stairs, two at a time.

"Thanks a lot, Frannie," my father says. "I really appreciate this."

"Oh, but it's okay for you to have someone sleep over?"

"It's *my* house."

"So now you want me to move out?"

"If you're going to bring home strange men, you're damn right I do."

"Bryan's perfectly normal." I'm sweating underneath the sweatshirt. I feel like such an asshole. "Daddy, I'm—"

"You're what? You're sorry? You're always so sorry after the fact." He spits flecks of toast as he hisses at me. "Maybe you should think about someone other than yourself once in a while."

"David, please. Don't yell." Ruthless puts her hand on my father's arm. "Frannie's right. I should have asked if she minded."

"Fuck that." My eyes widen. I've never heard him say "fuck" before. "I don't have to ask her permission. This is my fucking house and I'll do whatever I want in it. Frannie, find your own fucking apartment and get on with your life." He storms out of the kitchen. Ruthie and I look at each other, but neither one of us has anything to say.

During the night, I dream that I am dead. I know I am dead but I am also conscious, watching. I'm in something like a tube and it's hard to get air. Shelly is with me for a second, then she's gone. I know in my dream that Charlie still hasn't called. "Get up," Shelly says. "All it takes is one step. Just one." I rap on the tube, but no one comes. There's a hiss and a bang and I'm in a group therapy circle. I realize that I am Shelly or rather Shelly is me, but then she's outside me, nuzzling my neck like Bryan. I turn over to get away from her and wake up in a heap of blankets, on the floor of my room.

"I'm going to a psychic," I tell Abby the next morning on the phone. The door of my office-ette is closed, and I'm sitting with my feet on my desk. "Sue gave me the number of a good one."

"Don't waste the money. I'll be your psychic. Today you're going to be really depressed about a dark, handsome man." She says this with an edge to her voice.

"I'm going to look at an apartment this afternoon."

"I said I'd go with you on Saturday," she snaps at me.

"I want to go *today*, Satan, not Saturday."

"Fine, I'll meet you at the broker this afternoon, but I don't have hours to spend looking at apartments. I *am* a lawyer, you know." Randy must have done something to piss her off because she's completely possessed. But I'm not in the mood to talk about it. "Charlie still hasn't called me, Abby. It's been six days."

"You told him not to," she says firmly. "You say, 'Please don't call me for a while.'"

"I know, but it's not like I meant it. Do you think he still thinks about me? What if I write him a letter? But then he'll know I'm dying to talk to him."

"You are."

"But I don't want him to think that, Abby. You *know* he should call me."

"Frannie, you called him a Rat Boy."

"He told me I had fat legs."

"You forced him to." She sighs. "Frannie, yes, I believe he should call you, but he hasn't. So can we change the Charlie chant? I have a life, too, believe it or not. And Randy is going to a dinner party tonight and I'm not invited."

"Do you want to go?"

"No, but that's not the point. I'm his girlfriend. I should be invited to everything. God, this makes me so mad. He's going to some celebration dinner for some guy he knew at St. John's. I know there's gonna be strippers there, I know that's why I wasn't invited. I just know it."

"Abby, why do you think Charlie hasn't called me?"

"Maybe you really hurt his feelings, maybe he's busy. Or, I don't know, maybe he met someone else. Frannie, I—" But she doesn't get a chance to finish because I slam the phone down so hard, it cracks.

"I was only kidding," Abby says later at the real estate office. "You didn't have to hang up on me." I ignore her. "I'm sorry. Jesus, lighten up, Frances."

"Stop telling me what to do. If it were you, you'd be carrying on for days."

"I would not! Look, I said I was sorry. Can we please just see this apartment and go home? We have to be back at my place by eight. Randy's coming over."

"I thought *I* was sleeping over."

"You are, but Randy called and wants me to go to this dinner. You can come with us."

"Why would I want to go to a party with you and your stupid boyfriend? Abby, you could have said something to me earlier, you know. Jesus, you are so selfish."

"I am NOT selfish. I said you can come if you want. What the hell is bugging you? Fuck it, just call Charlie if this is how you're gonna be."

"Girls!" We're interrupted by Mrs. Diamond, the broker. "Are you ready?"

Fuming, I walk ahead of Abby and follow her out to the street. We walk to another building a few blocks away and take the elevator to the third floor.

"It's small, but reasonable for New York." Mrs. Diamond opens the blinds. Sunlight washes through the room. The apartment is a little bigger than my bedroom, but there's an exposed brick wall, a big window, a kitchenette, and a bathroom. I could put my bed in the corner, a chair maybe and a television. It's small, but it's right by the park. And four blocks from Charlie.

"It's a little smaller than what I'd planned," I say slowly. "I don't know. Maybe."

"Small?" Abby exclaims. "This place is *tiny*!! And it's filthy."

I look at Mrs. Diamond. "How much is it?"

"Nine-fifty. We ask for first month's rent, last month's rent, and a month's security up front. And of course, our fee." She touches her perfect chignon.

"That's too much," Abby interrupts. "Frannie, you can't pay nine-fifty for this place."

"I'm working now, Abby. I can afford it."

"I know you can afford it. It's just not worth $950!! Besides, this place is way too far west!"

But maybe, I think, maybe I'll run into Charlie and his new girlfriend. I bet she has a heart-shaped ass and skinny legs. *This is*

Tiffany, he'll say, *she's an astrophysicist.* "I like the West Side, Abby. And I'm the one who'll be living here, not you."

"Frannie, you can't be serious. You only want to live here because it's close to Charlie." She turns to Mrs. Diamond. "What's the lease arrangement?"

"One year upon approval. We do a credit check and—"

"I'm sorry," I interrupt. "She doesn't mean to ask so many questions. I love this place. I just have to think about it." I lie down on the floor in my suit.

"Frannie!" Abby yelps. "Get up. What are you doing?"

"I want to see what it will look like when I'm lying in bed."

"Frannie, you can't be serious. This place is a dump."

"Abby, stop being so damn rude." I get up and walk to the window. Two little boys are playing baseball in the street. I think about Charlie singing the National Anthem.

Abby looks sheepishly at Mrs. Diamond. "I don't mean it's a dump. It's just for that kind of money, she can get something nicer. What else do you have that we can see?"

"Abby, stop talking about me like I'm not here," I spit. "I am HERE. I EXIST and I can make my OWN decisions!"

"Well la-dee-da. Just forget it, Frannie. Find your own damn apartment." She walks out without looking back.

"You didn't even want to come!" I scream. "You just want to go home and wait for RANDY!" My yell comes out like a belch. Trembling, I turn to Mrs. Diamond. "So do you have some other things?" She nods and starts to say something, but I cut her off. "Look, I'm sorry. I've changed my mind. Can I call you next week and set up another time? I promise I'll come alone." I motion toward the door. "I hope she didn't offend you."

Mrs. Diamond waves her hand. "No problem. I know how sisters are."

"Sister? She's not my sister."

"Well you girls sure act like sisters." She shakes her keys. "Are you coming?"

I am surrounded by long shadows that look like bars. I can hear the boys laughing but their laughter slowly fades and I'm not sure if I heard it inside my head or out. There's a buzzing in my ear that starts out slowly and I try not to listen, but it keeps coming, it breaks up in my head like heat; fuzzy and warm but full like a balloon and I feel myself sweating. The buzzing becomes a hum and soon it's my brain, the sound of me thinking and maybe it's still connected, but I'm not sure maybe something snapped and maybe I'll always hear this fragmented heat and it's hot, it's hot, it's so hot. I keep seeing images of Shelly. She's writhing on a bed and my mother is on top of her, giving her mouth-to-mouth, kissing her, *the kiss of death.* I found her, I was the one—it was me. Why did I go into her room? Her white angel body glowed in the moonlight, beckoning me, but she'd already risen, she was already gone.

Something smells like rotted garbage and I focus on the smell that lives in my head, something noxious and evil that I birth through my nose and mouth as I breathe out. She's alive, I think. She's inside me now. I lower my head and try to blink away the hum but I'm carried off again and I can't come back, this time it's different, this time, it's the real thing: the snapping and the heat and my head is splintering and I breathe in, but I feel like I am blacking out and blacking out and Jesus, someone help me ...

"Are you all right?" Mrs. Diamond is next to me now, very close, but she sounds like she's at the opposite end of a tube. *All right all right all right* echoes like a bad connection.

"I don't have a sister." Was that out loud? I'm not quite sure where I am. I feel myself falling. "My sister's dead." I hold out my arms, but before I can steady myself, the ground rushes up to meet me.

"I'm sorry," Abby says on Saturday as she gets into the Subaru. "I didn't mean to be such a bitch the other day."

"I'm sorry too."

Abby reaches into the backseat to kiss my grandfather hello. "Cool hat, Max." He's wearing a baseball cap that says I LOVE BAY-WATCH. "Do you like *Baywatch*?"

"What a show," he says. "Boom boom boom. What a pair of knockers!!"

"Grandpa! I'd expect that from Freddie, not you."

"Ah, Freddie talks too much. I love *Baywatch*. That's why Charlie got me the hat. Did you see my hat?" I think about Charlie for a second, then make myself stop. It's been over two weeks and we still haven't spoken.

"I thought he was blind," Abby hisses.

"I think it's *selective* blindness. He can only see when what's her name—Pamela whatever—is on. Actually, I did catch him watching it once with his face squashed against the TV screen. It was really disturbing."

"Don't worry," Abby says, dismissing me. "Randy does the same thing."

My grandfather asks where I'm taking him. "We're just going for a drive, Grandpa. Sit tight." Abby looks at me questioningly. "I have something I need to do," I tell her. "Just chill and enjoy the scenery."

We drive for about a half-hour through the suburbs. Summer's almost over. I crack my window and breathe in the cool air. "Look at the trees," I tell Abby, pointing. "Look at the colors. Aren't they beautiful?"

"Lovely, Frannie. Absolutely fabuloso. Since when did you give a shit about nature?"

I shrug. "They remind me of registering for school in the fall, of new notebooks, you know, the feeling of starting over."

"Are you gonna burst into song now?" Abby asks. "Jesus, rain-drops on roses, Julie."

My grandfather leans forward and asks what kind of car we're in.

"It's a Cadillac," I tell him.

"I've never been in a Caddy this small. But boy, Caddies are nice cars. Nice, smooth ride. And they hug the curbs. And get very good gas mileage."

"This is the latest model, Grandpa, that's why it's small, and I think you watch way too much TV."

After a while, my grandfather dozes off. We drive for another fifteen minutes until I pull into the cemetery where Shelly is buried. It's a small cemetery, miles behind Lindsey, close to the point where the land juts into the ocean. This point, or peninsula really, is about five miles long and is the place that gave Lindsey Point its name. Very few people know it's here.

Lindsey Point was Shelly's favorite place when she was a kid. She'd ride her bike here and sit on the rocks by the water for hours. The cemetery was closed a long time ago, but my parents asked the county officials if they could bury Shelly here. They said yes and my sister is the first person to be buried at Lindsey Point in the past fifty years.

As we stop in front of the gates, Abby asks me what I'm doing.

"I need to pay my respects, okay? And I wanted you to be here." I turn to my grandfather who is sound asleep, cradling his *Baywatch* hat. I think about waking him, but decide against it.

"Abby," I say, "please get out of the car."

"You sure you want to do this?"

I nod. Slowly, she gets out and stands next to me. We walk into the cemetery. All the older plots have headstones that are broken or crumbling from old age and decay. In the back, as close to the water as possible, is Shelly's. My parents got her a traditional, gray marble headstone, but they lopped off a corner to make it look like the others. Shelly would have liked that, they said. The inscription is simple: her name, the year of her birth, the year of her death, and her favorite quote: *Hitch your wagon to a star.*

I stand in front of Shelly's grave. I can hear the waves lapping the shore and the sound of the gulls overhead. I feel like I'm in the middle of something sacred; something vast and profound and much larger than myself. It's a shame, I think, as I unfold a piece of paper, that I never shared this place—or this feeling—with my sister.

With this in my head, I begin to read. "Shelly, Mommy asked me to say a few words at your service, but I wasn't ready back then. But now I am, so here goes." I pause. Then I take Abby's hand.

"The funny thing about having you as a sister is that you were always *there*. When we were kids, you were a pain in my ass. But now that you're not here, I realized that a sister is a gift that can't be replicated. A sister can make you cry with one look and shame you with one remark, but no one can make you laugh as hard; no one can keep you as honest; and no one can make you feel, with just a phone call, that you belong. You can hate your sister ferociously, but you will never stop loving her. Or needing her. Your sister is your history; she is your memory. Shelly, you protected me in ways I never realized. And what is so sad to me is that I never realized how safe I was now that I no longer am.

"Our relationship flipped a lot. You were the younger daughter, but many times I looked up to you like you were my older sister. I relied on you because you were smarter than me and more capable. Maybe that wasn't right, maybe it was too much pressure for you, but I couldn't help myself. I don't think that Mommy or Daddy could, either. I think all of us wanted you to be everything we couldn't. And that was probably unfair, but it was only because we believed in you. And in how special you were.

"I know that you wanted to be a lot of things. And I know you didn't change legal history, or discover the roots of anorexia, but Shelly, you did change me. You gave me something to shoot for. You could recite Shakespeare and understand Freud, and not be embarrassed to dance in your nightgown with a couple of girls in a mental hospital. People love you, Shelly, perhaps no one more than me, and you deserved that love.

"We went through some long stretches where we weren't close, but Shelly, for all the times I didn't listen to you or didn't love you enough or pay attention or was jealous and spiteful and just plain mean, I'm sorry. It was a Sister Thing, and I hope that you forgive me. I wish I could have said all this before, but I didn't know so much. I've been learning about you, Shelly, and it may be a long time before I have all the answers, but one day maybe I will.

"Things are different now. Mommy is still Mommy and I realize now that she made you as crazy as she made me, but it's not so terrible to be crazy like us. This guy I met, Charlie, thinks I'm adorable. Go figure. But he talks to me, Shelly. I actually found someone to talk to. Anyway, we're not talking at this *moment*, but if he ever decides to speak to me again, I'm gonna tell him. You were right when you said that all you wanted was someone to talk to. Even at eight years old, you knew. Anyway, Mommy's on her own now and doing okay. And Daddy is emoting these days, which is pretty fucking scary, but I know it's for the best.

"I miss you, Shelly, and I will continue to miss you every day for as long as I live. You inspired me, you inspired all of us to be better people. I keep feeling around, trying to find you. But I know you're here, I just have to keep listening. 'Frannie,' you said once, 'I just want us to be friends—like real sisters.' Well we are, Shelly. You're my real friend. You're my *sister*. And nothing can ever change that. You will always be on my mind and in my heart."

When I stop, I don't feel like crying. I smell the trees and the grass and the wild flowers around my feet. I suck in the sweet, salty air, hold my breath, and wait. What I feel is a freedom I've never felt before, it's something I think is called deliverance.

I turn to Abby. She's crying. "Abby, it meant a lot to me for you to be here." She nods, unable to speak. "I feel all these things for Shelly and I wanted to tell her." I hug her, hug her hard, and then I say softly, "But I also feel them for you."

"I called him." I twist a tissue. "Did I do the right thing? We're having drinks later." I pause. "I don't know what I'm going to say. That's why I came to see you—to help me find the right words."

"There are no right words, Frannie. But maybe I can help you figure out how you feel. What to say will just follow naturally." Chubby rises to hand me another tissue. As she settles back down, I marvel at how much weight she's lost. "You look really good, Marilyn. Oh, can I say that kind of thing?"

She laughs. "You can say anything you want. Thank you. So why did you and Charlie have a fight?"

"It was my fault. I've been depressed and I took it out on him. I can't sleep, or I couldn't for a few weeks. Bad dreams." I count the pictures on the wall. I've been doing it more than usual, counting.

"And these dreams? What are they about?"

I roll my eyes. I knew this would happen. "Mostly about people dying. Do you think I should stop seeing him? I mean, he didn't call me for almost two weeks."

"You told him not to. So who's dying in these dreams?"

"I don't know." Now I'm annoyed. "But I needed time to think. I still wanted him to call me. We were ... are ... in a relationship."

"But you asked him not to call you so you obviously meant it. You're a smart girl, Frannie. You did it for a reason. Is Charlie in these dreams?"

I shake my head. "My mother told me to wait. But I couldn't. I had to talk to him."

"Why?"

"Because I miss him." Tears fill my eyes and I focus on the paintings. One looks like Europe. I really should go there someday.

"Is Shelly in these dreams?" I nod and she scratches something on her pad. "Do you miss Shelly?" she asks softly. I nod. "Are you angry she's gone?"

"Of course. I've been doing what you said, going backwards, trying to understand, but everyone I talk to has a different opinion on the subject."

"What do you think?"

I shrug. Suddenly warm, I take off my jacket. "Do you think Charlie wants to break up with me? Well maybe he won't break up with me, but I'm sure he'll tell me to get my act together." I look at Chubby. "It's hard to date someone who's crazy."

"Is Charlie crazy?"

"No, I was talking about myself. *I'm* crazy."

Chubby shifts in her seat. It's hard to call her Chubby now, but that's who she is. I tell myself I mean it in an endearing way. "I don't think you're crazy, Frannie. In fact, I'd say you were very sane. Do you want to be crazy?"

"No. But I obsess a lot. I count things in my head. Isn't that crazy?"

"No, maybe it's just your way of finding patterns, of putting your thoughts in order."

"But I don't count things that matter." I pause. "You don't think I'm crazy?"

She shakes her head. "In light of your family's history, I think that you have dealt with things quite sanely."

"Do you think I should break up with Charlie?"

She shrugs. "I can't give you an answer. Frannie, you're an intelligent woman. Trust your instincts. Listen to yourself."

"Then why do I feel like I always make the *wrong* decision? Like I'm letting someone down or missing an opportunity?"

"Making decisions is hard for everyone. You can't always control the outcome of your decisions, so you focus on their details to prepare for what will happen. But you can't prepare, not like that. If you never choose, all you have is what may be. But sitting on decisions is very uncomfortable. The power of what may be is only illusory. There's an expression: life happens while we decide how to live it. Real power comes when you make a decision and deal with its consequences. And that has to do with identity and self-esteem."

"I've learned a lot about Shelly," I tell her. "Mostly things that were painful. I always thought she had this totally secure identity, like she was sure of everything, but maybe she wasn't. Maybe she didn't feel comfortable relying on herself. I think she was afraid to grow up."

"What else did you learn?"

"I learned that I use men the way Shelly used food. To deny myself. I've fucked a lot of guys, but none that I liked. They all thought I liked them, even *I* thought I liked them, but I didn't. Not really. In retrospect, they weren't very likable people. But I didn't think enough of myself, I guess. I gave up my power to speak. Anyway, instead of saying no, I would shut down, hate myself, and obsess, and it would somehow get flipped around, and *I'd* feel rejected when I didn't even want the guy to begin with. Like how Shelly wouldn't eat. You know, the denial of the self thing, I don't know. Shelly talked about it once, but I didn't understand. Now I do." I pause. Then I tell her about Rat Boy. "It was like I totally lost myself. I gave him so much power. He treated me like shit and I went back for more. I know I wasn't a victim. I know I had a choice. I could have said no. I want to be clear about that. But I don't understand why I didn't."

"I think that for you, not saying no was about protecting the guys' feelings rather than asserting your own. Both you and Shelly were raised to take care of other people, even at your own expense. In theory, the people you take care of will take care of you, but it doesn't always work that way. So you have to learn to be generous with men *after* you know they are worthy of your kindness and *after* they've earned your respect, not before."

"That could take forever."

She smiles. "Not always. Not if you *believe* you are worthy. But society doesn't make it easy for women. Girls are taught to be good, to be nice. They aren't always taught to be honest and to assert them-selves, especially with men. And I agree with you. Shutting down while you're having sex is a way to disconnect from your emotions. And it is like anorexia or bulimia because you're doing something that's emotionally and physically self-destructive. Unfortunately, it can assume a life all its own and it's so hard to break the cycle once you're in it. I must tell you, Frannie, you have very good insight when you let yourself."

"Yeah, I'm fucking Freud." Chubby smiles. "The problem is," I tell her, "I don't think I can have sex with Charlie. I want to be with him, but I don't want to lose myself. I want to be present, you know? I don't think I've ever been present before."

"It takes time to believe in yourself, Frannie, and to learn to trust someone enough so that you don't shut down when you're with them. But you *can* have a relationship and still retain yourself."

I shrug. "It's not that I don't believe you, Marilyn, it's just that I don't believe you."

She smiles. "So tell me about your depression."

"I think about Shelly. I cry. I wish I had paid more attention when she was alive, gotten to know her better. Sometimes I under-stand why she wanted to die. Sometimes it's so painful." I wave. "It's just depression. It's not like I'm going to kill myself."

"What?" Chubby says. "What did you just say?"

"I said, 'It's not like I'm going to kill myself.'" Then I stop.

"What, Frannie? What are you thinking?"

"I don't know. Maybe the depression isn't about why Shelly killed herself." I pause. "Maybe it's about why I didn't."

"And? Why didn't you?"

I struggle to think about it. "I can't, Marilyn, I can't."

"Why? What do you feel?"

"Guilt, mostly. And anger. I try to talk to my parents about Shelly, but it's too painful for them. I don't have anyone to talk to about her."

"You switched subjects. Instead of talking about you, you're talking about Shelly."

"It's difficult for me to talk about myself this way." I study the paintings again. Finally I say, "I know Shelly's dead, but I can't say she's gone or—I know this is going to sound weird—but I can't say she doesn't know things. I feel guilty that I have a boyfriend and a new job and a best friend. I feel guilty that I'm moving on and she can't."

"Frannie, you're entitled to a life. Wanting to move on is healthy. Wanting to want things is healthy." She pauses. "I can't take away all your pain, Frannie, but over time I can help you to reconstruct your history to understand the way your family operated and how you evolved within it. Maybe that will help you to stop feeling guilty about things over which you had no control, and to value yourself enough to believe you're worth thinking about and being cared for." She smiles. "And maybe I can help you feel like you're not losing yourself when you're with Charlie.

"I marvel at how you've coped," she continues. "You've made decisions for yourself, good decisions. You're making your *own* destiny; a destiny to which you're entitled. It's not luck; it's not chance. Your destiny is a *choice*." Chubby's eyes water. "You and Shelly had a lot to contend with. You're both sensitive, intelligent women with strong emotions; emotions that sometimes act like whirlpools threatening to suck you under." She smiles sadly. I feel like her sadness is for Shelly, but maybe it's for me, too. "You're a brave woman. And you need to trust yourself and believe that you deserve to want and—" *Don't dwell on the dead, Paulie said. Stay among the living.*

I cut her off. "And I deserve to live. Maybe that's why I can't think about myself. Sometimes I feel that I'm not important; that I'm not even worth thinking about. But I want to live, Marilyn, I do. I want to get married and raise a daughter who can sit in group and tell everyone I fucked her up. I *want* these things. I know the struggle is hard, but I'm not going to give up." I sit back, feeling very powerful. "I *am* brave," I say. "And I always thought I was such a coward."

Marilyn smiles like she has a secret. "Why, Frannie? Why are you brave?"

"I'm here," I say softly. "I survived."

25

I wake up to a beam of sunlight. I kick the covers off my naked body and let it warm me. The clock says nine-thirty. I nestle my nose in the pillow. I wish I could stay here all day.

It's too early to call Abby so I sit up and survey the room. Trophies line the walls, along with model airplanes, G.I. Joes, part of a chemistry set, and an old model train. There's a poster of Farrah Fawcett wearing a red Lycra bathing suit. "Charlie's Angel?" I whispered to Charlie last night when he set my bag on his bed.

It's Grandma Gert's eighty-fifth birthday and Charlie asked me to come out to Los Angeles to celebrate it with his family. "For our six-month anniversary," he said.

"Five and a half," I corrected him. "You can't count the two weeks we spent apart."

He grinned. "If you hadn't come crawling back, we wouldn't be together at all." I nodded wisely. The old Frannie would never have let that go, but with Chubby's help, I've come to understand that Charlie is painfully insecure and needs constant reassurance.

Truth is, I didn't want to come. Sleeping in strange beds makes me tense, which sounds funny coming from a girl who almost made a career of strange beds, and I've gotten used to sleeping in my own bed in my own $950-a-month apartment ($31.67 a night). But because of the reassurance thing, when Charlie kept saying how happy it would make his mother, I gave in. Besides, I love airplane food.

"Frannie, wake up." Charlie taps on the door and climbs into bed. His hands touch my hair, tickle my neck. "We have to go down," he says, kissing me. "Breakfast."

"You go down. I'll catch up."

"If you're not down in five minutes, I'm coming back." He glances at my Snoopy nightshirt on the floor. "Please don't come down in a nightgown. It's one of my mother's things." I turn over. "Two minutes," Charlie says and shuts the door behind him.

I pull the sheets up and notice the dried come, evidence that he snuck into my bed and ripped off my nightgown at four-thirty this morning. After months of long, intimate talks, Charlie and I finally made love. And now we can't keep our hands off each other.

We arrived last night and rented a car. I wanted to see the Viper Room and Keanu Reeves's house, but Charlie wanted to get home. When we pulled into the driveway, it was weird. The way Charlie described his parents' house, I thought I'd be spending the weekend at the Kennedy compound. Instead, it looked like a regular ranch-style house, circa 1975.

"So THIS is Frannie." Charlie's mother, Agnes, ushered me in. I expected a big woman with fat fingers, but Agnes was petite with a silver bob and red lips that matched her nails.

I politely shook her hand. "It's nice to meet you. I've heard so much about you."

"And we've heard so much about YOU! You are such a pretty girl. Usually Charlie goes for these skinny little nothings, but you, you're so healthy!"

I clenched Charlie's upper arm. "She means you have a nice body," he whispered. "She doesn't mean you're fat." He turned to his mother. "Where's Grandma Gert?"

"She went to bed hours ago. She tried to stay up but you came too late. Weren't you supposed to be here at nine?" She looked at her watch. "That was hours ago. But it's okay. We watched the

Tonight Show." She turned to me. "It's on late so we never see it. But tonight was special, meeting you. It's perfectly all right you were late."

I wondered what Charlie had told her about me. He probably told her I'm dying to marry him and steal all her money, which is only partially true. Ever since I've been seeing Chubby, I put the marriage thing on hold. Right now, it's one of those things that, like step aerobics, seem much better in theory. Agnes's money, however, is another discussion.

"You hungry?" Dr. Hirsch, Charlie's dad, pulled my bag from me. His voice was overbearing as if to say, of course you're hungry, you foolish girl. He led me into the kitchen where Agnes had spread out lox and bagels, whitefish, herring, tuna, chicken salad, and three kinds of cream cheese. There's no way, I thought, that I am eating this shit at midnight. But the next thing I knew, I was huddled over the table, shoveling food into my mouth like I was being executed at dawn.

Agnes is at my door. I can tell by her nail tap. "Frannie, darling. We're eating."

"Coming, Mrs. Hirsch." I put on my nightshirt and go to the bathroom.

After brushing my teeth, I open the medicine cabinet and spy a pill vial with no label. Inside there's a few assorted pills. Nothing I recognize. I peer underneath the sink. Metamucil, an enema box. Nothing I need. "I'll be right down," I call over the banister. Then I go into Charlie's room and pick up the phone. I let it ring a few times, but Abby doesn't pick up. Afraid they'll think I'm a spoiled princess, I rush downstairs to view the savages in their natural habitat.

"Good morning," I say brightly. Charlie and his father nod. Grandma Gert stares out the window. Agnes is standing in front of the refrigerator, her back to me. "Good morning, dear." She turns around. "Do you want ... uh ..." I lift a hand to my face. What? Toothpaste? She regains her composure. "Would you like coffee?"

I nod. "Please." I slip into an empty seat. Grandma Gert watches a teenage boy mow the lawn. Her lips move as if she is speaking, but no sound comes out of her mouth.

"Good morning, Dr. Hirsch." He peers at me over the top of the paper. "Morning, Frannie. Did you sleep all right?" Charlie kicks me under the table and grins devilishly. He thinks I came twice this morning. It was really only once, but I was feeling generous knowing how tense he gets around his father. "Great, thanks." I turn to Grandma Gert. "Sorry we missed you last night. We got in late."

Grandma Gert smiles at me in sudden recognition. Her lips part and I can see her thick gray teeth. "Bonnie!" she says triumphantly. "You've got so much hair now."

"Grandma," Charlie says patiently. "This is Frannie Hunter. My girlfriend."

She peers at me. "Where's Bonnie?" Bonnie was Charlie's high school girlfriend whom he hasn't spoken to in fourteen years.

Charlie shrugs. "Grandma, I think she's at her own house."

"I'm sorry, dear." Grandma Gert pats my hand. "Meantime, you seem nice."

I thank Agnes for the coffee. She stares at me, raises her eyebrow, then looks away. What? What did I do? "Frannie," Charlie hisses. "You didn't change!"

"Oh God, I forgot." I catch myself as I lean over and notice that Snoopy's left eye is a quarter-inch higher than his right. I cross my arms. "I rushed down here," I explain to everyone. "I didn't want you to have to wait."

"That's fine." Agnes sniffs at a bagel then puts it down. "It's not like we've never seen a girl in her pajamas at the breakfast table before. We'll live through it."

But will I? I turn to Grandma Gert. "Happy birthday. Is today your birthday?"

"I don't know," she says sincerely. "Is it?"

"Of course it is, Mom," Dr. Hirsch says. "Today you're eighty-five. We're having a party."

Grandma Gert looks at Charlie. "So why isn't Bonnie here?"

"I don't know." Charlie's voice rises. "I haven't seen her in a long time."

I try to eat with my arms at my sides. I think about going upstairs and changing but that would only call more attention to myself. Agnes flits around the table, setting tomatoes and onions on the table, as well as Swiss cheese, butter, cream cheese, and lox.

She hovers over Charlie like a bat. "Have another bagel." She points at the bread basket. Gleeful, Charlie gorges himself. He looks at me and squeezes cream cheese through his teeth with his tongue. Agnes lifts a knife and fork to cut his lox. And *Charlie lets her!!* (Exhibit A–reason for Charlie's insecurity.)

Grandma Gert picks her teeth with a fork. "Mom, don't do that!" Agnes snaps. "Would you like another piece of bagel? I'll put cream cheese on it for you."

Grandma Gert scrunches her nose. "Cream cheese gives me gas. So how's Yale?" she asks Charlie.

"Princeton was fine, Grandma," he tells her. "I finished nine years ago. I also finished law school."

"You're a lawyer? I thought you wanted to be a doctor."

"So did I," Dr. Hirsch grunts, then laughs like it's a running joke. But I know it's not. (Exhibit B–reason for Charlie's lack of self-esteem.)

I cut in. "So, Mrs. Hirsch, what time are Eric and Anita coming?"

"Three or so." She casts a glance at Charlie. "They'll be on time, I'm sure."

"Yeah, when they ply Anita away from the bar," Charlie mutters, helping himself to a third bagel. Charlie mentioned that his sister-in-law is a recovering alcoholic. He also said that everyone refuses to talk about it. (Exhibit C–family in constant denial of addictive behavior–Jeez, I'm getting good at this.)

"So when's Bonnie coming?" Grandma Gert breaks off a piece of bagel. Her hands shake and I am reminded of my grandfather. I spent a few days with him before I came out here and God, what I wouldn't give to be back there right now.

"Bonnie's not coming," Charlie says firmly.

"Why not? She always comes."

Charlie looks at me and mouths "Sorry." "I called her, Grandma. She can't make it."

"That's too bad. She's a nice girl. You should meet a nice girl."

"I met a nice girl. This is Frannie. She's here to wish you a happy birthday."

"Well, hello. Why didn't you say hello before?" She squints.

"You look like Bonnie. You have more hair." She turns away. "Meantime, *she* didn't wear her underwear all day."

I gulp my juice. Dr. Hirsch finally puts down the paper. "So Frannie, I'm told you hail from Lindsey Point."

I nod. "I grew up there. I just moved into Manhattan, though. To be closer to work."

Charlie puffs out his chest. "And to me." He reaches for another bagel. I can't stop staring. Jesus, Charlie, that's your fourth. A train stops, you know.

"Huh. Agnes and I hate New York. We both grew up there. It's a nice place to visit, of course, but I can't imagine why anyone would want to live there." Charlie's father is thoughtful. "What's the altitude in Lindsey?" he asks.

"Excuse me?"

"The altitude. What's the altitude in Lindsey?"

"I'm not sure, Dr. Hirsch, but I guess it's the same as out here. Not too high, not too low." I squeeze Charlie's hand under the table.

"What kind of question is that, Dad?" Charlie barks. "Do you know the altitude in L.A.?"

"Yes I do, son, in fact. It's 11,000 feet above sea level at its highest point, if you must know. Los Angeles is a flat basin surrounded by mountain ranges on the east and the Pacific Ocean to the west. And I'm not trying to give Frannie a hard time. It's just a question." He looks at me. "You don't mind, do you? I just thought you would know since you lived there all your life." He whips around to address Charlie. "You know, Charles, it wouldn't kill you to give a damn about where you came from!"

Dr. Hirsch lifts the paper to hide his face. Charlie slumps in his seat. Agnes butters a muffin and quietly slips it onto his plate. Grandma Gert picks this particular moment to ask again when Bonnie is coming.

"She's not coming," Charlie says tightly. "Grandma, Bonnie is dead."

At noon, Agnes decides that she and I should take Grandma Gert for a ride. "We'll go to the mall." She picks a thread off my sweater with her perfect red nails. "How does that sound?"

"Great. Love it. Charlie?"

Charlie looks through the mail. "No, you guys go. I'll hang around here."

I lower my voice. "You sure? Charlie?"

He glances up. "Yeah, I'm sure. You go. Have a good time."

Agnes helps Grandma Gert into the car. "You can sit in the front with me," she says gaily. I put her Louis Vuitton purse, the real thing, I'm sure, in my lap.

"So Charlie tells me you're in marketing." Agnes adjusts then readjusts her rearview mirror. I marvel for a second at her perfect skin. Although Charlie denies it, I bet she's had major facial renovation. No woman her age can look that good. I wonder what my mother's doing. I suddenly long for her boxer-short hat and fake Gucci bag. Agnes looks at me and I try to smile. "What exactly *is* marketing, Frannie?" she asks.

I smile. "I don't have the faintest idea. I fake it. I think that's the secret of being successful in business."

She laughs. "The same thing's true about marriage." Agnes adjusts the rearview mirror again. She lowers her voice. Call me madcap, but I smell alcohol. "Being married is hard work, especially when you live with your mother-in-law. There were times when I thought Geoffrey and I—"

"STOP!"

I whip my head around. Grandma Gert clutches her pocketbook, her face pressed against the window. "Are you all right?" I ask. Grandma nods then says, "SLIPPERY WHEN WET."

"What is she doing?" I ask Agnes.

"She reads the street signs."

"I see." Car sick, I hit the window button and down it goes.

As we move toward the mall, Grandma Gert picks up the pace. "LIVE BAIT." (*Live Bait?*) "NAKED GIRLS ... CAUTION, OVERPASS ... SPEED LIMIT 55. SPEED LIMIT 55. SPEED LIMIT 55." By the third time, Agnes takes her foot off the accelerator.

"Well," I note, "she seems to get every one."

"Every one." Agnes eyes Grandma Gert in her rearview mirror. Her hands grip the steering wheel, her knuckles white. "She doesn't miss a trick."

*   *   *

"So how was it?" Charlie asks when we get home. "Did you buy anything?" He glances at the floor. At my feet are four shopping bags from Neiman's, Saks, and Lord & Taylor. I shake my head. "No, but you did."

"Oh? What did I buy?"

"Two dresses, two pairs of shoes, a new pocketbook." I smile wryly. "And a hat."

"A hat? Since when do you wear hats?"

"Grandma Gert thought I should buy a hat. Bonnie always wore hats. Funny, you never mentioned that."

"The only hat Bonnie ever wore was a baseball cap at camp."

"Well, this one cost you $75, so you'll learn to love it."

Charlie puts his arms around me. "I appreciate you being here," he says sweetly.

"I know." I pick up my packages. "Anytime." I look around. "Where's Eric? It's three-thirty."

"He'll be here any minute."

"I have to go to the bathroom," I tell him. "I'll be right down."

Charlie smirks. "Tell Abby I say hello."

Upstairs, I huddle on Charlie's bed. "Abby, pick up," I hiss. "It's me."

"Where the fuck have you been? I gotta talk to you!"

"I'm at Charlie's parents," I whisper. "Remember? Gidget Meets Mr. and Mrs. Moondoggie? I can't just pick up the phone whenever I want. It's not like I'm at work."

"So how's it going?"

"Did you ever see the movie where some guy wakes up and realizes that everyone else in the world is an alien? Well, I'm that guy. Get this. Mrs. Charlie took me shopping with Dr. Charlie's mother whose boat set sail ten years ago, but she was left on shore. We go to the newsstand and Mrs. Charlie buys $100 worth of Lotto tickets. She's got this system where every number she picks corresponds to a specific event in her life. Today it was 1976, the year she found a tumor in her breast. And she tells me this. Like, 'Hello, Agnes, that's a little more information than I need, thank you.'" I pause. "So then we go shopping and Grandma Gertie calls out all the names of the stores, one after the other. She gets stuck on Yves St. Laurent and we stand there for ten minutes till she can pronounce it. Then in the dressing room at Saks, she has some sort of breakdown and starts crying."

"Grandma Gertie?"

"No, the mother. She was babbling about this and that, about Charlie never calling her and her husband never fucking her. I don't know. Maybe it was the wine."

"You guys went out drinking? Did you do shots?"

"We stopped at this little cafe. I ordered a glass of wine, Jesus, I needed it intravenous. Mrs. Charlie ordered a glass of wine, too, and we got to talking so she ordered another and then I guess another. I lost count. But Grandma Gert didn't. No sirree. She counted every single one."

"Jesus. Where is she now?"

"Lying down. Told Dr. Charlie that she had a headache."

"Seems he's been saying the same thing to her, I mean, if he's not fucking her or anything." Abby stops. "Do you think people their age still have sex?"

"I don't know, Abby. Jesus, I'm stuck in the Twilight Zone with no medication and you want to talk philosophy?"

"Calm down. It's only a weekend, for Christ's sake."

"But if I marry Charlie, these people will be my FAMILY!"

"You hardly grew up with the Waltons. Anyway, I have to ask you something."

"Make it quick." I feel as though someone is watching me. "Come on, Abby. I think they're assembling for a seance downstairs."

"Randy said something to me the other day and I want to know what you think about it. Check this out. He wants to go back to Bermuda."

"So what?"

"Fraaaaannie," she clucks, "what if he asks me to *marry* him? Bermuda is for people who are getting engaged or on their honeymoon. Don't you think it means something? I told him I'd go. Do you think that was stupid?" She pauses. "I don't know if I want to marry him. He's okay, but maybe he's not the *one*, you know. What if—"

"Abby, I really gotta go. Let's talk about this when I get home."

"But he already bought the tickets."

"And you already said you'd go. You don't have to marry him. If he asks, just say you need more time."

She's quiet a second. "Well, it is a free trip and I do need a vacation. Did I tell you I was lead counsel on—"

"Save it. I'll call you later. Go to Bermuda. Have a good time. But don't get engaged unless you call me first." Jesus, I say to myself, hanging up. How does she function when I'm not around?

"What did you do to my mother?" Charlie asks as we wait for Anita and Eric.

"I didn't do anything. She just had some wine. What's the big deal?"

"She's plastered. I can't believe you."

I look around. Grandma Gert is snoring in a recliner with her head back, her glasses on her head like a second pair of eyes, and Dr. Hirsch is holding a golf club, putting balls into a little plastic cup. "Did you ever think she might need it?"

"We're here!!" Eric and Anita burst through the door, carrying their son, Barry, who is wrapped in blankets. Eric has a thick beard and a short-cropped Afro, and Anita is a heavyset woman wearing a pair of slacks and a huge cape. For some reason, I thought Anita would be tall and thin with golden-blond hair, prancing around in a thong. But she's not; she's just regular.

Eric shakes my hand. "Hi, Frannie. Charlie didn't tell me you were so pretty."

"Back off. You already have a wife." Charlie kisses Anita and takes Barry from her. He walks over to the stairs and sits on the bottom step, cradling his nephew. Watching him stroke the baby's head makes me want to tell him that I love him. Because maybe I do.

Charlie's father looks at his older son. "Nice to see you, Dr. Hirsch." He leans forward to hug Eric, but Eric pulls back. "Good to see you, too, Dad. Where's Mom?"

"Resting," Charlie and Dr. Hirsch say in unison. Charlie casts a mean glance at me and I shrug.

"So you got the couch?" Eric asks Charlie, who nods. Eric and

Anita recently moved from New York to L.A. and gave Charlie their extra couch. "How did they get it through the door?"

"I don't know. I guess they stood it on its side."

"But the elevator isn't that tall," Dr. Hirsch interjects. "Did they take the top off?"

"Maybe they used the stairs," Charlie says. "I was at work. The super let them in."

Eric is thoughtful. "There's no way they can take the top off the elevator. Are you sure that elevator is too short?"

"When I came home, the couch was in my apartment. They got it in somehow."

The conversation goes on for another five minutes and I listen to all the intricate ways the movers could have gotten Charlie's new couch into his apartment. I feel the faint stirrings of anxiety, but I breathe deeply and the moment passes.

"I'm going to talk to Anita." I stand up. "Does anyone want anything?"

To a chorus of no's, I make my way into the kitchen. Anita is sitting with Barry.

I touch Barry's head. "He's a beautiful baby."

"Thanks." She kisses him and plays with his finger. "He wasn't always this cute. A few weeks after he was born, we were in the park and an old man stuck his head in Barry's carriage. When he pulled his head out, he told me I had a lovely carriage."

I laugh. "Well he is certainly cute now."

Anita looks around. "So Agnes is upstairs?"

"Yeah, she and I went shopping. We had some wine." I stop before giving more graphic details, remembering Anita's alcoholism.

"That's nothing new," she says dryly. "So you've been dating Charlie how long?"

"Five months, give or take. I really like him. He's a great guy."

"Yeah, he's a sweetheart. Hopefully, he escaped the Hirsch curse."

"The what?"

Charlie walks into the kitchen. "Hi, Anita. I didn't tell you how nice you look."

"Come here, handsome, give me a kiss." Charlie leans down

and she kisses him on the lips. She lingers. Horrified she's gonna slip him some tongue, I cough loudly.

"So you've met Frannie?" He puts his hand on my shoulder.

"She's pretty." Anita hovers over Barry. "But I thought I was the love of your life."

"Will you excuse me?" I ask. "I'm gonna go upstairs and change for the big fiesta."

"I'll come with you." As we climb the stairs, I hear Dr. Hirsch and Eric arguing if Reconstruction began in 1866 or 1867.

When we get up to his room, Charlie immediately starts kissing me. "Charlie," I whisper, "your mother's next door."

"She can't hear us. Come on, you got me so horny!"

"I did? I thought it was Anita?"

"What? Oh, the kiss. She always does that. She's been trying to get me to fuck her since the day she got pregnant. I guess Eric won't. Did you smell her? She's been boozing!"

I stare at him. How can someone who appears so normal come from such a ridiculous family? We have two hours until everyone else gets here. I wonder if Charlie would be mad if I went home. "You don't have to drive me to the airport," I'll tell him. "I'll just take a cab."

I lie back against the pillows, a little concerned about the Hirsch curse. "By the way, Charlie, about your parents. What's the Hirsch—"

He cuts me off. "They're great, aren't they?" He beams. "A little quirky, but whose parents aren't? And they really like you. I can tell."

I wonder how they'd act if they didn't. "Your grandmother wishes I was Bonnie."

"My grandmother thinks you *are* Bonnie." He pulls out a photo album and points to a small girl with a Dorothy Hamill haircut. In the picture, a younger, more vulnerable-looking Charlie has his arm around her. They're laughing. A sign above their heads says CAMP LAKEVIEW. "This is Bonnie." I stare at her. She does look like me.

Somewhere I have a picture of Shelly and me when I visited her at Camp Galaxy. In it, we have our arms around each other and we're standing in front of Shelly's bunk. In my memory of the picture, we're just girls, not too fat, not too skinny, just girls. I have to find that picture, save it for my kids, maybe show it to my daughter Rochelle when she asks who she's named for. But I won't tell her it's a fat farm. I'll save things like that for when she's older. Out of context, they seem horrible and they're not the whole truth anyway. Like Chubby says, they're just pieces of a larger puzzle. Now, when I think back, those moments seem minor in light of everything else, or perhaps in light of everything else, they finally make sense.

I touch Bonnie through the plastic. "She's cute," I tell him. "She's really cute."

"She's sixteen. This is the last time my grandmother ever saw her."

"She's still cute," I say, smiling. "And you look happy."

"I didn't know how to be unhappy. But I know I'm happy now. With you. Frannie, you make me happy."

I kiss him, a long lingering kiss. "Me too, Charlie. I'm happy, too. I'm gonna take a nap, okay?" He nods. Before he walks out of the room, he reminds me that after dinner, the whole family likes to play Trivial Pursuit. "Does your dad play?" I ask fearfully.

"Of course. He takes it very seriously. We have to calm him down sometimes, remind him it's only a game." Charlie grins. "It's really fun."

I lie in Charlie's bed and pick up the phone. "Mom?" I say. "It's me, Frannie."

"Is everything all right? Are you being nice?"

"Of course I'm being nice! I called to tell you something." I pause. "Remember all those times when I said you and Daddy were crazy?"

"Where are you going with this, Frannie?"

"Nowhere. I just want to tell you I've met your match. Meeting Charlie's parents makes me feel like you and Daddy are Mike and Carol Brady."

"Thanks, Frannie. I appreciate that, I guess."

"Hey, Mom, I gotta go. But I love you. And Daddy, too," I add, thinking of Shelly. "And Grandpa. I love all of you."

"Frannie, honey." She laughs. "Let's not go too far here, okay?" But before she hangs up, she whispers like a child, "I love you, too, Frannie. You're my girl."

I hear a door open downstairs. The rest of the Hirsch clan are arriving. What a freak show this should be. They really need some therapy around here. In fact, I bet they could get a group rate.

I lie on my back and count the cracks in Charlie's ceiling. What if I'm becoming too therapy-friendly, like too self-righteous? Am I a fanatic? Do I sound like a fanatic? Oh God, I'm like New Age. Soon I'll be channeling with Shirley MacLaine. I *must* discuss this with Chubby. I can't get in too deep. Before you know it, I'll be buying crystals and having my charts done. Relaxed against the pillows, I breathe deeply and begin to fade. There's no way I'm giving up meat. No way. The rushing ebbs. The waves recede. I allow myself to drift. And soon, because I can, I let go.